KT-437-979

THE CORPORAL'S WIFE

GERALD SEYMOUR

THE CORPORAL'S WIFE

HODDER &
STOUGHTON

First published in Great Britain in 2013 by Hodder & Stoughton
An Hachette UK company

1

A CIP catalogue record for this title is available from the British Library

Hardback ISBN 978 1 444 75855 9
Trade Paperback ISBN 978 1 444 75856 6

Typeset in Plantin Light by Hewer Text UK Ltd, Edinburgh
Printed and bound by Clays Ltd, St Ives plc

Hodder & Stoughton policy is to use papers that are natural, renewable and recyclable products and made from wood grown in sustainable forests. The logging and manufacturing processes are expected to conform to the environmental regulations of the country of origin.

Hodder & Stoughton Ltd
338 Euston Road
London NW1 3BH

www.hodder.co.uk

For
Gillian
and
Jacqui and Becky
and
Harriet and Georgia

PROLOGUE

He was already awake.

He heard the footsteps in the corridor, the clanging of the doors as the bolts were pulled back, the whimpering cry of one man, then the shout, anguished, of a second.

He had not slept. In the last hours, segments of his life had slipped by in his mind – picked up, discarded, lost – and those were the good times, with his parents up in the villa on the north side of the city, and when he had roamed in the foothills above his home with his brother and cousins . . . And there had been the times when his behaviour had hurt those he cared for. There were fleeting thoughts of where they were now, whether they knew what would be done to him that morning, whether they prayed or wept or sat silent, numbed, and held hands, or were in ignorance and still asleep. He had thought of them, and his friends. In the hours before they came, he had squatted in the corner of the bright-lit cell, facing the door, his back against the angle of two walls, and thought of her.

He was Johnny. It wasn't the name given him at birth, and didn't come from his society or its culture. Before he had dropped out of the university, second year, bored and chafing at its restraints, some had said he resembled the actor Johnny Depp, and it had stuck. He was Johnny now to all who knew him – even the people who brought his food, who had interrogated him and tortured him with beatings and pliers. He was Johnny to her. He had taken comfort during the night from thinking of her. He had not spoken her name in all the weeks since his arrest: if he had, he would have condemned her.

He had a photograph. He held it as the footsteps came closer.

He doubted he would look at it again but took a moment to gaze down at it now and hoped it would stay in his memory to the last.

He held it in his palm and saw the tremor, not a shake, which pleased him, and the scarred fingertips from which the nails had been pulled. The photograph was from a booth that supplied passport-sized pictures. The black *chador* covered her shoulders and hair; a veil hid her nose and mouth. Johnny had done international literature at the university. He knew of a Dr Samuel Johnson and also of that man's remark: 'When a man knows he is to be hanged in a fortnight, it concentrates his mind wonderfully'. He could see her eyes, the small brown mole at the extremity of the right one; he recognised the defiance that blazed in them – and the mischief. It was to protect her that he had insisted the photograph should show her in 'good *hijab*', so that she would be unrecognisable to investigators. Her eyes were a soft blue.

He had guarded the photograph from the time of his arrest, through several cell moves, courts and interrogation rooms . . . and when they had brought him to the wing housing those awaiting execution. It had been rolled tight or crumpled close, a scrap in the pocket of the jeans he wore now and that he had worn when he was taken. He had created the fun, and the light, in her eyes, which had been captured by the booth's lens. When she had met him, it had been months, years, since she had laughed or giggled . . . Once, the photograph had been seized by a 'trusty' prisoner, who had come to escort him from one block to another. The man had glanced at it, then thrown it down as valueless.

He smoothed it, drank in the strength of the eyes – wondered where she was, what she was doing, whether her husband was in bed beside her or away. Those who knew Johnny, and recognised him as an agitator, a coke-taker, addicted to alcohol, an activist, would have found it difficult to believe that a married woman, living close to the bazaar and from a background he would hardly have known, could captivate him. He pushed himself up and faced the door.

He screwed up the photograph, made a tiny ball of it. It was in his left hand, his fist clenched round it.

The bolt scraped. The noises – fear and shock – of the two men to be executed with him were louder.

The guards came around him. His arms were pulled behind his back and thongs were wrapped tightly round his wrists, then fastened. It hurt, but pain was of little importance to him now. He walked, didn't allow them to push or drag him, through the door. He looked into the faces of the other two men. He didn't know whether they were political opponents of the regime or drug-traffickers, rapists or murderers. He saw slack mouths, glazed eyes, sunken chins, shaking shoulders. He heard their muted terror.

Softly, Johnny said, 'Don't let them see your fear or they'll have won.'

He took his place at the front. There was a nudge at his elbow, and he started for the end of the corridor. He could feel, against the softer skin in the palm of his left hand, the screwed-up paper that was her picture, little bigger than an orange pip. They went briskly, and he set the pace.

At the end of the corridor there was a grille of wrought-iron bars. It was opened noisily. Three times, since Johnny had been transferred to the block, he had heard others taken out at dawn. Some had been brave; others had screamed and struggled; a few had been in a state of collapse and were dragged. He walked briskly.

The gate closed behind them.

In the lobby beyond, his interrogator waited. He was a stout man, with a seemingly permanent cold sore beside his mouth and breath that stank of chillies. He had always looked away when Johnny was whipped with the cables and when the pliers wrenched off his fingernails. Johnny had wondered whether the interrogator – after a hard day inflicting pain in the name of the regime – went home and played with his children, then made love to his wife, or if he sat alone in his living room as the darkness closed round him, hearing screams and seeing blood. He tilted his head, looked the man in the face and sneered. The interrogator didn't know about the woman Johnny had, briefly, loved. That was a triumph.

There were no other interrogators in the lobby, which told him that the other two men were classified as criminals: they had not been convicted of *mohareb* – making war against God and His Prophet – the offence of which Johnny had been found guilty. His interrogator caught his glance, would have expected him to look away, but he did not. It was the interrogator who broke the contact. Good. Johnny walked on. He knew the route.

They went out into the faint first stirrings of dawn. He could see the shape of the mountains in front of him, and from the east part of the sun was visible. Against it were the gallows, the nooses and shadows that fell from them.

He held her picture and remembered her. There had been a riot: he and thousands had protested the theft of their votes; an idiot had been re-elected by fraud, and the paramilitary *basij* had come to break up the crowds shouting and chanting for the end of the regime. The *basij* had fired gas and charged with batons. She had come round a corner and been too confused to run. The *basij* had caught her and beaten her, then had been driven back by volleys of stones. He had found her as she cowered on the pavement. He had seen her beauty and swept her up in his arms.

The garage had been close by, and he had taken her there. After the shock and terror, he had discovered mischief in her eyes, and loathing. He had a room over the workshop, where two old men repaired motorcycles and scooters. Their love had lasted just over a month before he had been taken. She was married, and wore a ring, thin gold: they ignored it. Neither of them mentioned her husband: not his name, his place of work, or why she was betraying her marriage vows. Twice during that month he had had a day off work. On one they had spent longer in the room above the garage, and on the other they had had time to ride out of the city on his scooter – the day the photograph had been taken in the booth at a petrol station. Precious hours.

He heard the other men's teeth chattering, and forced himself not to shiver in the early-morning cold: 'Be brave,' he muttered from the side of his mouth.

They were hurried forward now and hands gripped his arms. There were three nooses, and three metal-framed chairs with plastic seats, perhaps from the guards' canteen.

He remembered how it had been with her when they had made love – some afternoons the scratches on his back were deep and bled.

If he shivered they would think he was frightened and would have won. He would give them nothing.

He carried her face in his mind. The second time he had met her Johnny had taken her clothes off gently, eased them away. At first she had been nervous, then hesitant – then she had defied her upbringing.

After arrest some talked of attempting to negotiate with an interrogator. Give him something in exchange for mercy. Johnny hadn't. If he had given names, there would have been more boys alongside him, guilty of disputing barricades with the *basij* and countering the gas with petrol bombs and stones. If he had broken, the woman's name might have slipped from him. He would have gone through fire to save her, and would dangle at the end of a rope to ensure her safety.

He could feel the tiny paper ball of her picture, clenched in his fist. They let him choose: he went to the centre chair, feeling the chilly wind on his cheeks. Beside each there were men who wore dull olive uniforms and black balaclavas to mask their faces. Why did it matter if those who were moments from death should see the features of their killers? He considered it a sign of cowardice.

Men crowded around him and he saw confusion in their expressions. He realised they didn't understand why he was smiling. It was the dry smile he shared with others of his age who lived on the north side of the city, in the foothills, and demonstrated his contempt for them. Hands clutched at him, but Johnny made a sharp movement, and their grip loosened. They would have lifted him but he stepped up on to the chair. The noose was level with his face. They allowed for no drop so he would die by choking. He didn't know if his name was on an Amnesty list, if telegrams requesting mercy had been sent from abroad to the Supreme Leader, or if anyone cared.

The photograph was a squashed pellet in his hand but her image lived with him. The others were at either side of him now, and a hooded man used a short stepladder to climb behind each one and put the noose in place. Johnny could feel the rope against his chin.

He clenched his hand, saw her, felt her and heard her laughter.

The stepladder had gone.

The sun was a little higher and lit him, as it had lit her through the windows of the room above the garage . . . He felt a hand on the chair back.

Johnny said clearly to those at either side of him, 'Fuck them, guys – fuck them.'

The chair was pulled away. He kicked in the air and pain billowed in his throat. His breath came harder and his fists loosened. Johnny saw her face and, with the last of his strength, he tried to tighten his left hand. He saw and heard her . . . Would she remember him?

He didn't know. He was losing the fight to live. His fist slackened and the paper pellet fell to the ground. Her picture would be among the rivers of urine that always gathered under the gallows on a hanging morning. A trusty would swill it towards the drain, with the photograph, and the sun would dry the ground. His last words, audible only to himself: 'Fuck them.'

He felt himself slowly circling, and death was close.

I

He was sitting on the bed and the girl, in front of him, knelt on the floor. His head was down and he did not look into her face.

The image on the screen in front of a woman in a locked room a floor below was monochrome, and the audio effects were good: she could hear him panting. The watcher and the occupants of the other room were quite different in origin and background but the sex trade had brought them together on that autumn evening. The madam of the brothel, which was above a small hotel on a poorly lit street, set back from the prime property overlooking the Gulf shore, was a Lebanese Christian from the port city of Jounieh. On her screen, fiddling with the man's shoelaces, was a girl from the west of Ukraine; the low-wattage bulbs beside the bed hid the blemishes on her face and the dark roots of her dyed-blonde hair. The man was Iranian, which ensured that he had been allocated the room with the best camera and microphone.

The woman seldom commented on the punters who visited her eight-room establishment. It had a waiting area with a pretence at a cocktail bar, where temporarily unemployed girls waited, and a bathroom with two showers. There was a small curtained-off area, where the maid waited to change sheets, if necessary, and there was the room with the screens. The woman, large, her face caked with makeup, kept her eyes on the screen. She had already sized him up: he was pathetic.

The girl from Ukraine, a veteran of Paris, Berlin, Naples and Beirut – where she and the madam had met – was the best. In that light, any healthy male, the woman thought, would have been fighting to set his hands on her. He wasn't. He sat slumped, head down, breathing fast. His shoes and socks were off, and now she removed his trousers. His hands rested on his belly.

Two Arabs had brought him to her premises. They had been with the Romanian girls, had paid, and left after the madam had told them their colleague required a 'longer service'. The client with the Ukrainian girl was to be kept in the cubicle: the images and sounds were being recorded. The madam was not political, but the money she was paid each week came in dollar bills, and was substantial. She had been waiting for an Iranian, as had those who paid her each Thursday afternoon.

The girl folded the trousers and laid them on the chair against the wall where his jacket hung. The picture above the chair was of a couple copulating but the man seemed not to have looked at it.

Now the girl edged his legs aside and wriggled between them. She took his arms, prised open his fists, laid his fingers on her shoulders and began to undo his shirt. He was shaking and the his eyes were closed, as if he was unwilling to look at her breasts. The madam thought that if the Ukrainian couldn't arouse the man, no one could. The shirt came off, was folded and laid on top of the trousers. The vest was next.

A bell rang. Annoyed at the interruption, the madam licked her lips, slipped out of her office, locked the door and went into the waiting area. Two Norwegian sailors, officers: they'd have taken a tender ashore and were here before they hit the hotel bars. A quick exchange of money, and two of her girls were chosen at random. She went back, locked the door, peered at the screen and turned up the sound.

The sex act held little interest for her. When she went on holiday – the Seychelles or the Maldives – she would buy the services of a teenage boy. It confused and amazed her that men paid so well for a woman. She already had this one's money, but he was still sitting motionless on the bed.

The girl turned her head, eyebrows raised, towards the corner of the room where the lens was hidden. Then she went on with her job.

Her robe slid from her shoulders. She edged a little to her left and shifted her knees, exposing her breasts and crotch to the camera. Her hair hung down, hiding much of the man's face as she kissed him. He didn't hold her tightly; neither did he push her away. It was as if he endured it and didn't know how to end it. He would not have wanted to opt out in front of the men who had brought him and be seen as a prude. They would have come to her brothel because her rates were competitive. She gave her cards to the bankers who occupied the high-rises near the harbour.

Iranians of interest came to the city to check bank accounts and work out how to counter financial sanctions, authorise transfers and make covert foreign investments. He had followed that route and those who had brought him had been pleasured at a discount. She chuckled. This man had paid the full price.

The Ukrainian girl had his pants off and, although the night was warm, he shivered, as if he were naked in the snow of the mountains above Beirut – the madam had known them as a child.

The girl was the best. She did what she could. She rubbed her nipples against his mouth, nose and cheeks. She did all that could have been expected of her, and failed.

She eased off him. The camera showed he was flaccid.

The Iranian had his head in his hands and sobbed. The girl stood, then went to the chair, reached into an inside jacket pocket and found the client's wallet. She opened it and held it up. There was money in it, and a picture behind plastic showed the ayatollah who had led the revolution; a pocket contained an identification card. She held the wallet closer to the camera, exposing the card.

The photograph was of the man who held his hands over his face and shook with sobs. The madam could read Farsi. She had a good knowledge of the languages her clients spoke.

The bell rang again. She cursed. The girl was replacing the wallet in the jacket.

It was what the madam was paid for. That was why the tall Englishman had come five months earlier and put to her a proposition. He had spoken of a trap set and sprung, of confidentiality and considerable funding for her business, her holidays and what she referred to as her pension. Now she dialled the number she had been told to ring if a particular scenario was played out. On the client's identification card she had read his name, 'al-Qods (Jerusalem) Division' and 'Iran Revolutionary Guard Corps (Pasdaran-e Inqilab)'. She felt a frisson of excitement: she had played a part in a game that was almost beyond her reach.

The bell rang again.

The madam did not expect to speak to the Englishman himself. When the first payment had been made a young woman had been with him: she would be the contact. She glanced again at the screen. The Ukrainian played her part well, but the man beneath her was still sobbing. The call was answered. She told her contact who she had in the seventh cubicle. The young woman squealed in excitement, said she would be there and cut the call.

It was not exceptional for a man to come to her premises, pay and freeze, but it was unusual. She left her room and went to greet the new clients, apologising for the delay and smiling. She imagined a car with diplomatic plates speeding across the city.

There was a folk duo in one corner of the bar, and a widescreen TV showed a football game in the other.

The pub was Petroc Kenning's sanctuary. Because of his height he stood at the bar in a place where he could see both attractions and know his scalp was safe between two ceiling beams. Part of the building was four hundred years old, and it stood beside one of the old coaching routes to the West Country from London: travellers to Gloucester or Bristol would have stayed there overnight. He was PK in the Service, Pet to Polly, his wife, and Petroc to her parents – the reason he was in the Black Lion, and had been every evening of the five days he had been on home leave. He knew that Polly had already told them that her husband, little Archie's dad, wouldn't share with them any detail of his work as station chief, Dubai. They were awkward around him so he came to the pub. In two more days he would go from Didcot station to Vauxhall Cross for staff assessments and budget reviews, leaving early and returning late, and in nine days' time, he, Polly and Archie would be heading back to Dubai. It was a good posting, among the best for any foot-soldier of the new generation. It put him firmly on a fault line of conflict. The folk duo's anthem had ended and his phone buzzed: the double note of an incoming message.

The fault line offered what he craved. He read the text. He wanted accolades, authority and advancement. He wasn't happy to coast: he pushed himself and looked for his efforts to be rewarded.

'A wasp in the jam jar'. He understood, he felt cheated. It had been his idea, his baby. He had used his considerable debating skills to force it through the committees that reviewed such a scale of expenditure – and it had bloody happened off his watch. She would be there, and likely have with her a couple of ex-marines from the station who did security for them. He started to elbow his way towards the door.

A man said, 'You all right, mate?'

'Never better.'

He was outside, in the darkness, and started to run. He had been an athlete at university; now he worked out in Dubai gyms and on the pavements at dawn before the killing heat came up.

He snapped into his mobile: 'Me, Polly . . . Yes, I'm running . . . Pack me a bag – don't forget my passport. I'm going into town, VBX, then I'll be away . . . Yeah, it's important – about as important as it gets. Please, just pack and be ready to take me to Didcot . . . Bigger than anything that's happened to me before.'

He ran on through the darkness. His mind lurched between images of Celeste, the Lebanese woman who ran a good-quality, clean and disease-free whorehouse, and Katie, who would be there on the ground, trying to create control, but he couldn't see the man who was their target. He thought, as he ran, that he was teetering on the edge of triumph.

Short and not athletic, Katie was rated for her attention to detail and analytical skills. The ex-marines stood behind her. The man would have needed a sledgehammer to get past them.

She was happiest when scrolling through newspapers from

Tehran and specialist documents, looking for names and discovering who ran which office and held what responsibility.

Now she confronted him. He was dressed. He wore polished shoes, trousers with a crease, a clean shirt and an old but cared-for jacket. She had no office diplomats with her, ready with advice. Her boss was in the UK, and by now would be on his way into Central London. She had not been able to raise the head of Iran Desk, and the dogsbody was waiting for a train and hadn't a secure link with him. So far she had spoken only to a duty officer: 'Sorry and all that. 'Fraid I've never been where you are. We're trying to put together some sort of task-force. Best I can do is suggest you dominate him. Pretty obvious. Keep him unsettled and off balance, and wait for the cavalry to get there. Apologies for being so inadequate, but good luck.'

She sensed the Iranian was broken. His eyes were red, his fingers worked continuously and his breathing was erratic. He had been in the cubicle with the Slav woman when they'd arrived. He'd sat on the bed, with her on a chair, smoking. One of the marines had taken the man's wallet from his pocket and passed it to Katie. He was Mehrak, al-Qods, a corporal. He was thirty-four a driver. He was stationed in Tehran and his card gave him access to a barracks in the centre of the city. He was . . . What? A *corporal*? She remembered her grandfather exploding when he was fishing on a Lancashire river. A fly had been taken and a rod arched. Not a salmon or a sea trout, just a 'bloody vermin pike'! He'd calmed down, taken the fly from its jaws, slipped the fish back into the current, swigged from his hip flask and remarked that it had made his day.

How to make hers?

'Dominate him.' She stood in front of him. She wore jeans and a loose blouse. Her arms and head were bare, and back in her apartment her dinner was cooling on the table beside the beer she had looked forward to for most of a dull day. She had come out too fast and wasn't dressed to confront an Iranian zealot, with God and hell-fire spilling out of him. Now he would be frightened.

She took hold of his chin and jerked it up. *Dominate.* 'Why couldn't you screw the hooker, Mehrak?'

She saw the misery in his face, the shame, and the gold ring on his finger. She spoke good Farsi, colloquial and vulgar.

'Adultery. Cheating on your wife. How would the Qods view that? Here on duty, are you? Spending your time in a whorehouse!'

She thought him barely worthy of her time or the expense of the honey trap so carefully fashioned by the station chief. But the Qods was top of the heap . . . His ID said he was a corporal, a driver . . . and he was in Dubai. 'Who do you drive, Mehrak?'

Those who knew Katie from home, university or the Buenos Aires station, her initial posting, or from the canteen at VBX wouldn't have recognised her: she oozed authority. She had no boyfriend in either Dubai or London, and had minimal knowledge of brothels or the men who patronised them.

She said, 'Well, Mehrak, if you're going to play dumb I'll play rough. There's a film, with soundtrack, and I promise it'll be on the Internet by morning. We'll make sure the site doesn't go down with the number of hits it'll take. You'll be the biggest laugh from Cairo to Sana'a and Khartoum to Istanbul. Couldn't get it up. Do you want to get on the plane and face the music at home? Your people will be thrilled with your behaviour, but I doubt your wife will be very forgiving. Now, did you hear my question?'

He looked up.

'Who do you drive, or are you in the pool?'

She was told. Katie could have punched the air. She knew the name. There was a restricted file. She nodded.

They pulled him to his feet, hustled him through the door, down a flight of stairs and into the car. He was on the back seat, squashed between the guys, and she drove along the coast road towards the embassy.

She was a small, hunched figure. She came off the bus and walked fast along the pavement, the stalled traffic in the road belching fumes. Little of her was visible, certainly not her ankles or wrists; she would have been held up as an example to others by the modesty police. Men worshipped her beauty, they said. Farideh had hidden her face with a veil, which kept her warm and acted as a filter against the smog that hung over Tehran in the winter. She wore cotton gloves and the handles of her shopping bag, heavy with vegetables, cut into her fingers.

She hadn't met the boy that evening. Married for seven years, unfaithful to her husband for four, she was never reckless in her liaisons. She didn't know when her husband would return from his journey. Now, she would walk to the four-storey building that was their home, climb the stairs, unlock the door and enter the loveless apartment.

Love was outside Farideh's front door. The boy would have walked on hot coals to be with her, but she had refused him that evening.

She was twenty-five, had been married a week after her eighteenth birthday, and the boy wanted to be her third lover in the last four years.

Her eyes, high cheekbones and full lips were hidden under the headscarf and veil. If she was careless, she might be arrested, taken with her lover to a gaol and hanged. When she thought of hanging, her hands trembled and she had to clasp them so tightly that her wedding ring gouged into her finger. She wanted to be loved, but not loved by *him*.

She hated her husband, despised him. He was abroad. Farideh had not been told when he would return, whether it would be late that evening or the following day; neither did she know what he did for the brigadier, or the duties assigned to him by al-Qods. She knew nothing because he had told her nothing before he left for the commercial flight to Dubai out of Imam Khomeini International. She knew nothing because she had asked him nothing.

On the stairs she met a neighbour from the floor above. He was a bus driver, but his son worked at the university and gave him money so he could afford an apartment in this block. The man ducked his head and didn't look into her covered face. It was a nervous reaction, shared by the others on the staircase, because her husband was in the Revolutionary Guard Corps, and drove a man who had significant authority. Sometimes a big polished Mercedes saloon was parked on the kerb. The man flattened himself against the wall, where the paint needed renewal, and didn't speak.

If she was careless, any of her neighbours on the staircase would revel in the chance to denounce her, the wife of a corporal in a prestigious unit.

She climbed the final flight, rummaged in her bag for her key and went inside.

The heating was turned down, a sensible economy. She stripped off her coat, headscarf and veil, looked around and saw that his bag was not dumped by the bedroom door and the washing-machine in the kitchen wasn't on. She went into the bedroom and saw that he was not lying on their bed. They did not make love, but they slept there, back to back. Often she placed a bolster between them so that he couldn't touch her. He didn't know that she had taken two lovers in the last four years. He would have killed her if he had found out. Her husband, Mehrak, whose advances she had refused for many months, had punched her and closed her eye. She had gone to work the next day, at the insurance company, and in the office, where she was on Reception, she had offered no explanation. He had not been violent since. She would hang by the neck if she were careless.

She switched on the television, clicked though the channels: a documentary on Zionist brutality in the Gaza Strip, a programme on abject poverty in the land of the Great Satan, and a mullah discussing public morality as written in the Holy Book. She left it on. Her husband would never divorce her. It was said she was beautiful, a judgement passed by men and women, and he would be humiliated to accept – in public – that he had failed to hold on to her. Could *she* divorce *him*? It was impossible. And there could be no life with any of her other men. She began to unpack her shopping.

Farideh barely acknowledged her parents and elder brother, who worked at her father's stall on the edge of the bazaar, selling good-quality linen, and rarely saw them. She was polite when her husband's mother and the remainder of his family visited on a festival or birthday, and she appeared dutiful. The family that mattered to her was small and tight-knit: two elderly men, skilled mechanics, who wore oil-stained overalls and could repair any engine – car, motorbike or scooter – and had a room over their yard. She was tied to her new, hidden relations, not by blood but by dependence and survival. Their safety rested on her being always careful. She had been with them tonight and had drunk their juice but had not welcomed the man who yearned to be her newest lover.

Her supper, alone, would be bread, goat's cheese and a tomato. She didn't know when her husband would return, or where he was.

She didn't care.

It had not been a good year for the opium farmers of Nimroz province. There had been a plague in the poppy fields so that much of the cultivation had failed and many of the laboratories for the refinement to raw heroin had been idle. The origin of the plague was greed. In past years many farmers had rotated their crops, planting wheat one year and vegetables another, sometimes going for barley or maize, then ploughing and sowing poppies. Without rotation, the crop had withered. The cause of the greed was the reward that opium and refined heroin provided. They were hard times for the farmers of Nimroz, but the suffering was relative. The insurgents were reasonable and took a cut in trafficking fees on the crops' movement by lorry to the hidden refineries where the chemicals waited, brought in from mainland China. Poppies needed fertile agricultural land and well-irrigated fields. The water-filled ditches were of good quality in Nimroz, and provided the best growing conditions; American taxpayers had funded their construction through USAID in the 1950s. For all the difficulties, the refining of opium into heroin continued.

At one refinery two men, working with cleaned oil drums and a portable generator, had completed the process of refining fifty kilos, then had divided the brown resin into two-kilo slabs. Each was wrapped in waterproof paper, and bound with heavy tape, then packed in a cardboard box.

The farmers made a bigger profit from poppies than from any other crop, and in the refinery the self-taught chemists received higher rewards than if they had prepared drugs for the Charsad Bestar hospital in Kabul, Afghanistan's best. But they, the traffickers, lorry drivers and camel herdsmen would earn a fraction of the sum the consignment would be worth, once it had been transhipped across the border with Iran, then Turkey, over the strait and into Western Europe. The huge sums involved meant that many sought to work in the trade.

The first leg, from a hut with wooden walls and a corrugated-iron roof, was on rough tracks, requiring a four-wheel-drive vehicle, and the men escorting it were heavily armed, prepared to shoot and kill to ensure that their consignment reached the next stage in the long chain. In the darkness, using only sidelights, a Nissan drove towards the west where, hours before, the sun had sunk.

Tadeuz Fendon was first into the VBX building, the yellow and green monster squatting beside the bridge that spanned the Thames. There was always a whiff of expectancy when big men strode through the security gates, flashing their entry cards. He didn't stop to pass the time of day with the uniformed guards, but made for the lifts. Sara Rogers was a couple of minutes behind him.

They seemed to have arrived from separate starting points, as they had intended. Inter-office relationships, for senior staff, were frowned on. She was his 'squeeze', and his gatekeeper. She took a lift to the fifth, south-east wing.

Tadeuz Fenton ruled Iran Desk: he knew what he wanted, where to climb, and it was difficult, almost impossible, to find his footprint on a contentious matter. He understood what his superiors wanted and what resonated with the more junior in the outer work area. Principal on the wish list was an 'enemy'. He could have said that it was not for the Service to sit on its backside and churn out analysis: that was left to the hacks of *The Times*, the *Washington Post* and *The Economist*; the Foreign and Commonwealth office was stuffed with classics graduates capable of the same output. He believed that the new breed of young people in the Service wanted something worthwhile to *do* and something rotten to change for the better. He liked to say to the new breed that the 'ethics crap' FCO spouted put a ball and chain on the ankles of Service officers, that they were not hired to be ordinary. Could the men and women of VBX survive without an enemy? Hardly. He had elevated Iran to the status once enjoyed by the old Soviet Union in Cold War days. There had been the fallow years, with the Irish, organised crime, and the supposed weapons threat of the Iraqi buffoon. Even al-Qaeda had proved a dream opponent. Thank God for an 'enemy'. May the Lord bless Iran.

Dunc Whitcombe was there by the time the coffee had been made, and Mandy Ross. The girl in the UAE was coming through on the secure link, and Petroc Kenning was in a taxi from Paddington. He sat down, stuck his feet on his desk, spoke his thoughts – Mandy took notes – and Sara was on the phone, with the scrambler. He would have called it a 'high-octane time . . . what we're here for, and what we do best'. God, after all these years of being bereft, Fortune had blessed them with an 'enemy of value'.

The reinvented Soviet Union, with or without short-range missiles based in Kaliningrad and capable of striking any NATO capital, would never have the same clout as the original, and personnel had been driven to drink by studying the drones' aerial views of mud-walled compounds in north Waziristan. Important to him: success in Iran would distance the Service from the shambles of the dossier and Iraq. He had spread the word, galvanised the young people, flattered and cajoled his elders, and had wrung resources from them. Because he now stood face to face with the respected opponents in the Ministry of Intelligence and Security (Vezarat-e Ettela'at va Amniyat-e Keshvar or VEVAK) and had on his wall the satellite photograph of its buildings in the parkland complex to the south of the Shahid Hemmat Highway, north

Tehran, he had carved for himself a place of importance in the building, and was envied for it.

His door opened, no knock. Petroc Kenning might have run from his taxi and used a staircase rather than wait for a lift – it was always so exciting when the building came to life after hours, personnel were recalled, and an atmosphere of crisis management flourished.

'Well done, PK. Good to have you here, where you ought to be. Your push, and there's a nasty little creature in the jam jar. First class – you deserve it. It won't go unrecognised. Dunc'll bring you up to speed.'

Dunc Whitcombe briefed. There were the cutbacks, and the Secret Intelligence Service was no more secure against financial stringencies than Work and Pensions, Education or Transport; the heating was off and wouldn't come on till dawn so they all had on their coats and scarves, and Mandy Ross was wearing a shapeless woollen hat.

Tadeuz Fenton waved for Dunc to wrap, then he held court. 'Don't get ensnared with his rank. He drives Brigadier Reza Joyberi of the Qods division. That's a high rank in the Qods, as you know better than I do, PK. The Qods has brigadiers you can count on the fingers of one hand. They're important players. You don't make brigadier if your job description is OC latrines and cookhouse. Take this perspective: and our leader, bless him. Go up to the clouds with our own supreme leader'

He waved expansively at the ceiling. Two floors above, at the extreme western corner of the building, was the office suite of the director general.

'Who knows him best? Not me, not his deputy or any of the branch heads, and certainly not the politicians who appointed him and wouldn't have the bottle to fire him. I'd say, without fear of contradiction, that Benny does. Benny knows him better than anyone, probably better than his wife, certainly better than Henrietta the bull terrier in the outer office. Benny has a Browning in the glove box. There's no security with them. The director talks. Benny would never acknowledge that he's listening, and would never comment unless invited to. Benny would be his sounding board, would keep an unwritten diary in his head. They go everywhere together. Benny's there when the sun's coming up and he's still there at the end of the day. He sees everything, learns everything and is totally trusted. What I'm saying, PK, is that the brigadier's driver is probably as good as it gets. We'll get him out of there fast. Shift him to where we can do the work. I expect a treasure chest of good material. We've started making arrangements for his flight.'

'You going to bring him here?' Kenning asked.

Mandy, alternating between the phone and her keyboard, raised her eyebrows. Sara looked up from the pad she was scribbling on and shook her head decisively. Dunc frowned.

'Not here – at arms' length. We're going to Vienna. Best place. Fewest questions asked, and we get a free run at him, no interference. I mean, he's not going to turn into a best friend, is he? We milk him – or bleed him – then cut him loose and he can set up a kebab stall in Munich or drive a taxi in Warsaw – Christ, I don't know. We'll have a file on the man he chauffeurs and who whispers in his ear. He'll know where all the skeletons are buried. I'd say, with what would happen to him, a loyal driver who can't keep his dick in his trousers thereby disgracing his unit and his boss, he should be grateful to us. You've done well, PK.'

The meeting broke up.

Sara Rogers asked him quietly, 'Austria – Vienna? You're sure about that?'

'It's totally right. We've a good history there – and he'll be at arms' length.'

'Not dangerous for us?'

'Not at all. I feel good about this. It'll be straightforward, no complications, believe me. And I can only sit at the top table if I have something to play with and something significant to barter.'

'Why are we doing that, skip?' A navigator's question to his captain.

'Ours not to reason why – that sort of stuff.' A captain's answer to a reasonable question, concerning the diversion of a C17 Alpha Globemaster, prize product of the Boeing Corporation and in the dark camouflage colours of RAF Transport Command, from its normal flight path out of Bastion in Helmand, north of Kandahar.

'I'm not inside that loop. The touch-down, I'm told, will be of minimal duration, like fifteen minutes for the take-on of two passengers. One will be assessed as a potential security risk and watched by the loadmaster. They'll sit in the cargo section, away from the personnel, en route to Akrotiri.'

There was a grin. 'Spook stuff?'

And a gentle put-down: 'I wouldn't know and wouldn't care to ask.'

'I didn't think we were still up for that sort of thing.'

'Please, just the route – Bastion to Al Dhafra, UAE, then out of Al Dhafra for Cyprus . . .'

'On the priority scale, must be something high up the ladder. Agreed, skip?'

'Maybe they're bringing a box of dates – or a sack of camel dung for the Brize rosebeds.'

The diversion would be plotted, with the extra fuel it would necessitate. Take-off was in fifteen: the first of the personnel for rotation were streaming off the buses towards the steps, and an Afghanistan deployment would be over – thank Christ and good riddance to the fucking place, as most would say . . . The cockpit and cabin crew would be wide-eyed when a passenger with a security issue and an escort came on board at the first touch-down, the captain could guarantee it.

It was long past midnight, and Mandy Ross had the home number of the head of the section that handled 'increments'. The cutbacks had not only chilled the building at night, but had reduced to free-lance and short-term contracts those who did jobs for which full-time employment was no longer considered justifiable: the increments.

She was told, 'Bloody hell, Mandy, they don't grow on trees. We've hardly done that sort of thing since the Cold War. Had a bit of a spike at the Libya time . . . Anyway, this is the best I can do. Full names first, then home phones. You want three, right? . . . Here's five names, and good luck. From the top, what they like to be called . . .'

'It's not a kids' party we're organising. Do they want paper hats as well?'

'Funny crowd, the babysitters. They like to be called Auntie, Father William, Nobby and—'

She interrupted, 'Who do we have in Vienna?'

'Just a man who stayed on after retirement – well, redundancy, actually. He was a bottle-washer to Hector Kenning – remember him? Uncle of Petroc and—'

'And when he has to be tucked up, what name does he prefer?' Mandy Ross tried for sarcasm and thought she came over as peevish. She was given another number and told that if she called it she would reach Sidney.

She hung up, allowing the man to go back to bed. She didn't know the world of the so-called 'babysitters', and knew equally little about defectors, if that was what the wasp in the jam jar proved to be – volunteer or compromised. She drank some cold coffee, lifted the phone and punched the number for 'Auntie'. It would be a learning curve, about as steep as it could get.

He sat in a corner of the secure room. Katie had solid shoulders and fancied she might need them: the responsibility for the business going forward rested on them. He had lifted his head and stared at her.

The senior man in Abu Dhabi, eighty miles and ninety minutes up the coast road, was in a Qatar-based conference hosted by the Agency, and the Bahrain station people were there. The Service couldn't get their hands on a charter for another six hours, and by then the diverted flight would be on approach over the Gulf.

His confidence was the precious commodity. He was a wild animal in a cage, she reckoned, stunned by the suddenness of the trap closing, therefore hunkered in that corner, baleful, watching and uncertain. Katie had not the experience to begin a debrief, or the rank to offer deals. He gazed at her. She wondered how she compared with the Ukrainian tart on the video, whom she had met briefly in the brothel: a pleasant-enough woman, with a sweet smile, generous with her cigarettes; she looked raddled under the brightness from the cubicle's centre light. Katie, in comparison, might have seemed flat-chested and wide-hipped; her hair – cut short – wasn't coloured. The corporal-driver would never have come across a woman like Katie, a junior officer in the Service, carrying a burden that practically bent her double.

She assumed his confidence would grow. She and the ex-marines would not be able to frogmarch him up the steps and onto the aircraft if he chose to resist. He would be an idiot, she thought, to go voluntarily.

He had refused food and coffee.

Disorientation was what she hoped for, and confusion, the inability to think clearly – his mind should be addled with doubt.

Each minute that passed on the big wall clock by the door closed the window of opportunity – a phrase much used by lecturers of the probationers coming into the Service: a 'window' and an 'opportunity' were never to be ignored. Katie knew that the damage done to the station's funds exceeded sixty-five thousand pounds. The money had sweetened the madam, was an inducement to the girls, who would scrap to get their hands on an Iranian. It had paid for the webcam, the microphone in the smoke alarm, and the recording kit in the inner office. Funny, but the man had not seemed concerned about the papers stuffed into an inner pocket of his jacket. Everything from the jacket was now in a plastic bag, with his wallet and his open-return air ticket. A bag, with overnight clothes, stood at the feet of an ex-marine but it contained nothing that interested her.

Katie was not authorised to offer inducements, to mention an annual stipend or cash payment. She couldn't question him because she had no knowledge of the areas that the interrogators would choose to work over. She could not add to the threats and insults that had been acceptable currency at the start. How to *dominate*?

She strode backwards and forwards in front of him. She had

taken a call on her secure mobile from PK, the boss, telling her of the diverted flight. When it had rung a second time, she had gone out into the corridor, leaving him with the ex-marines, and had been told what she could say – no more.

She was a woman who showed him no respect and no fear. She confirmed prejudices and stereotypes. She prayed for the hands of the clock to speed up.

She had a half-blue from Oxford in lacrosse, another in netball. She showed him no kindness. Nothing in her actions betrayed a vestige of sympathy for him. He was a commodity, and the sooner he was shipped on, the better. He would know of the British intelligence apparatus, perhaps have more respect for it than he had for the Agency. Since childhood, he would have learned of the perfidy of the British Service, the tentacles it had spread, and he would know of the evil, duplicitous men employed at the Old Fox's Den in Tehran – the embassy complex on Ferdowsi Avenue, now closed. He'd regard her as a devil.

It was not her job to be liked, loved, admired.

She paced. The ex-marines stood stock still, one before the door, the other beside it. The clock's hands edged across its face. He spoke. She would have said then, if challenged, that she was engaged in 'dirty business'. Had her tutor, who was fulsome in praise of her academic success, known where she was and what she was doing with her first-class honours degree in ancient history, he would probably have cringed. Her mother had oozed pride on the cocktail-party circuit in rural Cheshire because her daughter had passed through the arduous civil-service recruitment process. Katie was of that generation, new to the Service, who believed it a waste of energy to play intelligence games without an end result; to compete without trying to win was alien to her. A 'dirty business', but she had signed up for it.

Fearful, a mutter she hardly heard. The question was repeated. 'What will happen to me?'

Mehrak watched her. He could see the tightness at the thighs and crotch of her jeans as she eased round to face him. The movement tightened her blouse, pulled at the buttons. He could see her arms below the short sleeves, her neck, throat, mouth and hair.

She seemed to consider his question and weigh the options of a reply.

He knew that he smelt of sweat. It was damp on his back and his vest had absorbed it. When he drove the brigadier, Mehrak was always careful to spray the inside of the Mercedes with air-freshener, and to use a roll-on antiperspirant at his armpits and groin. Now he could smell his socks – and the scent from the whore's body. He had a picture in his mind of the shame and retribution facing him. He had been in a brothel. He had paid for it with cash supplied to him for his travel needs. He would have brought moral disgrace on himself and on the Qods. He had betrayed the trust placed in him by Brigadier Reza Joyberi. He would have lost his marriage – faltering, but so important to him – to Farideh. He could see her face, the expressions flitting across it as the Internet showed pictures of a man from the Qods, in a Dubai brothel with a prostitute older than himself. He had shamed her.

He asked again. 'What will happen to me?'

He was told. He seemed to see a newspaper in the clattering confusion of a print shop, a TV announcer on a dawn news programme and a coastguard cutter quartering the harbour beyond a section of sea wall. He was told and he slumped. He didn't know who would mourn him.

He closed his eyes. He prayed to his God that there might be a tear on Farideh's cheek. The woman spoke brusquely and didn't seem to want his opinion on what was planned.

He asked one more question: 'Why am I important to you?'

The woman continued to pace, reached the wall, spun round and retraced her step. She didn't answer.

His alarm went and Zach woke. He hadn't drawn the bedroom curtains and the orange glow from a streetlight fell on him. He yawned.

He was alone in his bed.

As the son of the boss, he was a misfit on the site. Zachariah

Joshua Becket was twenty-seven. His father was a builder, employing a dozen men, while his mother did the books and kept the VAT records in a wooden shed at the bottom of the garden. Zach no longer lived there. His home was a back room in a house owned by a widow. He had no photographs of his parents, George and Bethany, or his sister, Lizzie, who was in her last year at sixth-form college. There were no posters from the walls of his room at home, or any of the pictures, and few of his clothes.

He crawled out of bed, then pushed himself upright. He didn't turn on the radio – not from consideration of those still sleeping in the house but because it was too early. He shouldn't have had to get up before the first bird chirped.

It had not been intended that Zach would work for his father. He should have finished at the school in London, and found some niche for his languages, but he had dropped out. He had packed in the course a few days before the end of finals, had chucked what he had brought south into a bag and walked out into an early summer morning to take the first train back to the Midlands. Zach Becket had been the first of his family to win a place at a university and had quit when he was about to get the honours degree he had worked hard for. What was he going to do now?

The following Monday he had been dumped at a site where his father had a contract to build a four-house terrace and passed to the foreman, who had been told that the boss's son was to be given no privileges.

A letter had arrived a week after the exams had finished: he had been awarded first class honours on the strength of 'exemplary' course and module work. He'd shredded it. The guys at work would have understood better than his mother and father, and they hadn't a certificate between them. On ending an affair: 'Best not to mess around – ditch her, tell her she's history and you've found someone else. She'll get the message and disappear. Life moves on'. It had been a love affair and it had died. His love of the historic Persian culture and its poetic language had seeped away. His tutor had badgered him with calls, then texts – *outstanding student, great linguistic talent, don't waste it* – then abandoned him.

He groped his way in the dark to the bathroom, had a shower, then dried himself. He didn't need to shave because he was a labourer.

He wore tattered jeans, stained with plaster, paint and bitumen, and a thick tartan shirt with a fleece; his boots were steel-capped and caked with mud. He also had a beanie, a waterproof top and a fluorescent jacket. His helmet was on the floor with the bag that held his sandwiches and flask. He pulled the duvet over the sheet and his night shorts. There had been a girl there three weeks ago – he'd liked her, perhaps too much, and had left her to sleep on after he'd gone. He hadn't called her again.

He was the boss's son and therefore had to be on site with the first of the shift. Among the brickies, the sparks and the others there was confusion as to why a guy with the brains to go to university was now working on the site. He knew he was treading water – but not for ever. There would come a day when he'd shrug and move on to something that tested him . . . just not today. The trouble was, each day that passed made it harder for him to 'get a grip' and 'stir himself' . . .

Outside, the bag on his shoulder, his helmet on his head, he stepped into his boots, lit a rollie and waited. When the van came, he was finishing the smoke. The stubble was thick on his cheeks and chin, and his face was tanned. He looked to be a can-do man, which he was, but also one without ambition.

He stepped into the back and grunted his thanks at the back of the driver's neck.

2

They were in flight, cruising high. He had never been in an aircraft that huge. When Mehrak flew with the brigadier to locations distant from Tehran he travelled in a twin-engine, propeller-driven plane, or in one of the few C-130 American-built transporters that used – because of the sanctions invoked against his country – parts cannibalised from other aircraft. Flying out of Tehran, civilian or military, men prayed silently and clasped images of their loved ones: disasters were frequent. But this aircraft's engines ran smoothly.

He had been driven to the air-force camp in the back of a van, squatting on the floor, the woman beside him. Sweat had soaked their clothing. He had heard the plane land and the roar of engines slammed into reverse thrust to slow and stop it. The van had moved again. She had told him to hurry when he climbed the steps, and at the door he should follow the men who would take him to his seat.

They had been at the top. One man wore a side-arm in a webbing holster, and another had a short-length baton hanging from his belt. They had taken his arms and led him inside the main cabin – a great cavern – where a third had held up a serge blanket. He was hustled forward and the woman was on his heels. A curtain was tugged back, and he saw that they had prepared a cocoon for them. They were now two hours into the flight. He was strapped into a harness.

He thought the woman was pretending to doze. She had said nothing of substance to him since they had been in the room to which he had first been taken. The plane seats were small, narrow, and her bare arm touched his elbow. She had made no concessions to modesty. Why should she? Had she not pulled him out of a whorehouse? He thought she despised him. She was a courier and would deliver him: he didn't know where, or when, or why they had gone to so much trouble for him, a driver. She had told him, with a cold smile, what would be happening on the ground and on the water in Dubai.

During the night, a radio station had announced that a man had been seen to go into the sea to the north of Dubai Creek, beyond the fish market. Friends who had been with him had said he was drunk when he had run away from them across the beach and waded out.

Also that night, a small item appeared on the front page of the on-line late edition of the *Khaleej Times*: friends, unnamed, had reported that an Iranian, in the Emirates on business, had gone into the water. A search had been launched.

Eventually, enough sources had reported a man in the sea for a United Arab Emirates coastguard cutter to join the search for him. The Dubai police were said to be looking for a washed-up body on the empty sands.

The woman had smiled when she told him of a pack of lies, and he had understood that time had been bought, a few hours, maybe days, less than a week. She had looked pleased with herself, and then her features had resumed their chill.

The curtain had been pulled aside and a pair of plastic trays passed through the gap. Both contained a bottle of juice, a cellophane-wrapped sandwich, and an apple. He'd thought himself clever, and abruptly switched his for hers. He had feared he would be drugged or, poisoned. Her face had remained expressionless.

At first, when the aircraft had lifted off, there had been a ripple of talk – in English but with differing dialects. The others on the flight must have been curious about the detour and the two new passengers. But their interest had died as the flight had gone on. He wanted to pee. How should he tell her?

He pointed to his groin, and nudged her elbow. She said nothing, unfastened his harness and waved him through. The two men took him forward, one in front, the other behind; a door was opened and a toilet revealed. He went in and tried to close the door after him but was blocked. Mehrak unzipped and peed. His penis was as shrivelled as it had been when he was in the whore's room. He convulsed with shame, shook, and the urine went on the metal floor. He pulled paper from the box, wiped up the mess, dropped its into the pan and pressed the button. The hands had hold of him again.

It was half a dozen paces from the toilet to the curtain that hid the two seats. The woman stood there, arms folded. A wave of laughter hit him. He saw now the rows of seats, the heads and shoulders. The hands pushed him forward and he was through the flap.

She told him to put himself back into his pants, then do up the zip.

'Fuck you, woman,' he hissed.

She stared at him, through him.

The man with the gun and the other with the baton were at the curtain but she waved them away. Those who had laughed at him, young men and women wearing the camouflage of desert troops, had enjoyed the spectacle he'd made. He had seen the same uniforms in Iraq, in the south, when he had been on the ground with his brigadier. They had worn civilian dress – often a long *dishdasha* – and had been unarmed, with bogus identification. They had checked out routes for the supply of munitions and weapons. They had seen the British military at checkpoints, riding in their armoured vehicles and sometimes patrolling irrigated fields or on the streets of al-Amarah. Then they had not laughed at him. In the eyes of some he had seen naked fear as they studied the sides of the road, where rubbish was dumped, and searched for the bombs that could kill them.

He was slumped in the seat. The woman did not bother with her own harness, or to remind him that his was not fastened.

Who could he curse? Mehrak, the brigadier's driver, could have targeted his wife – whom he yearned for and who did not allow him to touch her. He could have sworn again at the woman beside him, her hip against his, her arm against his elbow. He could have channelled the hate against the two young men at the bank who had been assigned to 'look after' him when he had delivered, to a senior manager, the sealed envelope from his officer and received another, which held updated details of four accounts. He hadn't argued with them when they talked of 'time to kill' and 'time that should not be wasted' and of 'the best girls'. He could see the paste on the whore's face, the drooping breasts. There were many he could blame . . .

But the blame lay with him. The engine pitch changed; the seat below him seemed to judder. Tears of self-pity rolled down his cheeks.

He didn't know why they had chosen him.

In family lore, Uncle Hector was on a pedestal, thanks to his prowess in the Secret Intelligence Service during the glory days of the Cold War.

Petroc Kenning called and woke him. He made few decisions on intelligence-gathering without his uncle's advice. The phone rang for an age, then was picked up. There was a pause while Hector lit the first cigarette of the day, then a cough. Petroc said why he had phoned.

Another cough, then the reply. 'Where's the little beggar from?'

'Tehran, the Qods division. It was my plan. I pushed it through, and I'm comfortable with it.'

There was a splutter, then a chortle. 'Good man. Proud of you, chip off the old block. Where are you taking him?'

'Tadeuz reckons Vienna.'

Another pause. Then another cough and a clatter. Petroc assumed his uncle had grappled for cigarettes and lighter and succeeded only in dropping them.

'He was with me there. On my last posting to Vienna, I had Tadeuz Fenton before he went up in the world. He was a sponge, absorbed what he was told. Yes, Vienna's excellent. A moment of history. I think I've said it before to you but history is always at the core. Forget it at your peril and—'

'You *have* said it before, Uncle. History and its value. Many times.'

'Vienna's better than anywhere else. Austria was a "failed state" twice: after the collapse of the Austro-Hungarian empire in 1918, and again after the Allies carved it up in 1945. That sort of record weighs heavily on the national psyche. They adopted neutrality and wanted to be everybody's friend. They love the Americans and quite love us. They have excellent relations with Moscow and sell heavily to Iran. Everyone's welcome. Same goes for intelligence-gathering and espionage. The city used to be awash with agents. You couldn't walk round the Ring without meeting old friends and old enemies, all supposedly covert . . . Look, if you go to Switzerland, you'll have tedious bureaucracy crawling all over you, and the Swedes will be wetting their pants and delaying co-operation. The Austrians don't do this ethics rubbish – they leave that sort of thing to the theologians. And, of course, you'll have Sidney, first class.'

The laughter came again, then a burst of coughing. Petroc assumed his uncle had retrieved the packet and lit up again.

'I understand we have Sidney's name, but others are making the contacts. More important, Uncle, we're thin on the ground with people of experience in the defection business. Who do I talk to?'

'Was Rollo Hawkins before your time?'

'Saw him in the corridors a few times. Only know of him.'

'I'll get his number. Hold.'

Petroc's uncle lived in a little terraced house, with two bedrooms, close to the river in Worcester – easy for professional cricket and for walking his dogs. He wondered if the old boy had put on his slippers before he'd gone off in search of his contacts book, and how much of the cigarette he would have smoked before he found it. Petroc would not have been in SIS had it not been for the excitement his uncle had generated, and probably his uncle's string-pulling. He waited, and was rewarded for his patience. The number was dictated and he repeated it.

'A good defector is heavy currency, Petroc. Might make your

name, but you'll know that. But if you don't know what you're doing it might explode in your face. You'll find no one better than Rollo Hawkins.'

He cut a good figure. He was not tall – many of the men around him dominated his slight build – and not heavy in the chest and hips. He had no jowls, and his hands were small, the fingers narrow, almost delicate. His eyes roved continuously. He did not appear to be a man who inspired nervousness in those around him. None of the junior officers who walked with Brigadier Reza Joyberi would have contradicted him: none would have told him to his face that he was wrong in any assessment he made; none, behind his back, would have been foolish enough to criticise a decision he had confirmed. A man who had risen to the most senior ranks of the al-Qods division had arrived there neither by luck nor accident.

He dressed differently from those who escorted and briefed him. If he was visiting a missile battery, ground-to-ground or air defence, those with him would be in military uniform and he would wear civilian dress – slacks, polished slip-on shoes, a collarless shirt and a lightweight grey jacket. Should he be with civilians, inspecting a laboratory or an area of the University of Technology where nuclear or chemical research took place, those with him would be in civilian clothing and he would have chosen the fatigues of the Guard Corps. It was his style to ask few questions, to listen keenly to what he was told, then to pick the best from the bones. He would write a paper, then send it as an edict to those he had seen. It would have been unwise for any of them, officer, scientist or engineer, to gainsay his final decision. Any who ignored an instruction given in the name of Brigadier Joyberi, al-Qods division of the Guard Corps, faced a dismal future, their influence curtailed, with the possibility of arrest or detention.

His duties were many and increasing.

The sun came from behind him, throwing grotesque shadows over the concrete platform and the rocks below it. He watched as a giant oil tanker negotiated the shrunken shipping lane from the

Gulf into the Arabian Sea. It was the Strait of Hormuz, a choke-point through which a fifth of the world's oil supplies passed. Dislocation of those lanes, or the threat, through missile strikes, the sowing of mines or the use of fast patrol boats, was a primary weapon in his country's arsenal. He had responsibility for the protection of the batteries, the reinforced bunkers where the mines were stored and the harbour where the patrol boats were moored.

He listened. He was told the likely success of the defence system round the missile sites, and queried the readiness for dispersal of the patrol boats. The previous week he had been to the uranium mine at Yazd: he had found its protection inadequate. Ten days before he had been to Esfahan: orders to deepen caves, air-raid shelters, had been issued but not carried out. The threats of sabotage grew and Zionist menaces were ever more shrill. Responsibility burdened him.

Other matters queued for his attention. Among them were the bank accounts, which could be accessed via offices in Dubai, what they held and where investments should be made during the recession that gripped the global market. Another matter was the scale of imports – widescreen TVs and Apple-brand computers, pads, phones and MacBooks: a rightful 'benefit' for those prominent in the service of the state. Then there was his wife's health and . . . He had heard brave predictions of how an enemy could be stalled by the defences of the missile and gun battery and how an enemy's fleet could be countered by the skilful use of acoustic or magnetic mines. Brave predictions. He had seen the American war machine. The brigadier had been in Iraq to organise the training of the foot-soldiers who would lay the explosive-force projectiles that could blow out the interior of an Abrams main battle tank. He had been on the ground in the rocky outcrops and steep-sided valleys of south Lebanon, advising Hezbollah field commanders when the Zionists had come with their armour, artillery and airstrikes. He understood modern warfare, so he was burdened with responsibilities.

Now a new one was loaded onto him.

One of his talents was to make those who met him feel he had their attention, that they alone – if their work was satisfactory – were at the top of his list of priorities. If Iran was attacked by the Great Satan and the Zionists, there would be retaliation abroad against American assets, their allies and Israel. He carried a crushing workload. A lesser man might have crumpled under it.

He looked into the eyes of each man who spoke to him, sought out weakness, indecision, exaggeration. His beard was neatly trimmed, not the cut of a poseur but of a tidy-minded man, and his silver hair was short. His clothing might have come from any good tailor in a bazaar, and was not beyond the financial reach of those around him. They would have regarded him as a credit to the principles of the revolution. His voice was quiet but direct, and men hunched forward to hear him better. He had control. None would have known that his driver collected statements from a bank in Dubai, and that associates organised the importation, without Customs hindrance, of valued electronic equipment.

Later he would go to Bandar Abbas. He would tour more facilities with his staff of liaison officers, then take the train to Tehran: fifteen hundred kilometres, nineteen hours, and a chance to brainstorm with them. The laptops would be battered as the papers were written. On arrival the next day in the capital, he would be met by his driver and his workload would again be stacked in front of him.

His opinion: it would go hard for them if the United States attacked – and the great tanker, maybe ferrying a hundred thousand tons of crude, slipped from sight.

He showed no sign of it, but would be glad to return to familiar ground, and have his driver's familiar face close to him. A good man, reliable.

Her home should have been better furnished. Her husband was in the Qods, a lowly corporal, but he earned nearly four hundred American dollars a month. Farideh, on the reception desk of an insurance company, was paid two hundred. No family on their staircase had such a large combined income, yet they were on the edge of poverty and struggled.

As did so many.

She knew of the poverty on the different floors. Her staircase, going up four flights, covered the front doors of fifteen other apartments. No one ever complained in her hearing. She was from the Qods and was not trusted. Her neighbours smiled thinly at her and hurried past. She endured the loneliness because of the room above the garage and the adoration of the aged mechanics.

She had finished dressing and would be warm against the cold – she had seen from the window that snow was in the air. She went through the apartment, clearing and wiping surfaces – she had no affection for her husband but she had standards. Her family were respectable, God-fearing, supported the revolution, and they, too, suffered a new poverty: the linen shop on the north edge of the bazaar had fewer customers, and the ones who came bought cheaper cloth. She and her husband had less cash because Mehrak paid his brother's bills. The brother had been a computer engineer but had been sacked and had found no other work. The rent had to be paid, his family had to eat, and Farideh's husband kept them.

There were flowers on the table. Mehrak had left them. She didn't know where he was and hadn't asked where he was travelling to. She didn't know what business he was on. She was indifferent to where he was and what he did. He brought flowers home and would put them on the table. She didn't thank him – and certainly didn't kiss him, not even on his cheek. She would leave them on the table until they wilted, then put them into the bin.

She let herself out and locked the door behind her. There was more thieving in the capital this year. Her husband, a loyal supporter of the regime, would not have admitted that the government's tax hikes and lower subsidies led to increased crime. She heard footsteps on the staircase above. They stopped. Whoever – the hospital orderly, the post-office official, the carpenter – had heard her door opening, closing, then being locked didn't want to pass the time of day with her.

It was a cold morning, and on the street, hurrying to the bus stop, the chill wind hit her. The cold crawled through her *chador* to penetrate her jeans and sweater. She shivered. She had never shivered in the room over the garage. Farideh took a bus to work. At that time, it was always crowded and women were relegated to the back, clinging to straps or the backs of seats. Every morning, she stood on the left side of the bus and could see out through the grimy windows. It was a better view in the afternoon when she returned home with her shopping and stood on the right.

The route took her along the Vali Asr Avenue, then right onto Enghelab Avenue, when she would be on the left. At the time she went to work, traffic clogged the wide thoroughfare and the bus crawled. She could guarantee she'd see the place.

She waited at the bus stop.

There was, Farideh knew, a problem of heroin addiction in the Islamic Republic. The men at the garage said it was caused by the strict laws against alcohol, that people should be able to escape from the dreariness of life with weak beer but instead they resorted to the needle. She was addicted to looking from the bus window at the north side of Enghelab.

The addiction had taken hold four years ago. The previous evening, there had been nothing on the television or radio. Mehrak had said there were small disturbances in the city centre, a few terrorists paid by the Americans, and that the president had been re-elected, which was good for the future. Without a second thought, she had voted for him. That afternoon she had walked with her shopping to the bus stop on Enghelab. She had been deep in thought, considering the price of the bread she had bought, and worrying about whether the yoghurt was too old because it had been marked down. There was to be a film on TV that night, with Norman Wisdom, her favourite, and . . . She had come round a corner to find the street filled with the black uniforms of the *basij*. They were masked, carrying clubs and wearing motorcycle helmets. Her first reaction: there would be no trouble because the *basij* were there.

The gas was fired. Stones pelted around her, skidding away from her towards the paramilitaries. She had turned and seen the young people, whom she would have called 'terrorist enemies'. More gas was fired and some of the canisters were hurled back. The *basij* had charged and laid about them now with clubs. She had frozen – she couldn't move from the middle of the pavement. She was on *their* side, a loyal and unquestioning supporter of *their* leader. She had voted for *their* president. She had been felled by a swipe from a *basij* who rode pillion and hit her with a pickaxe handle. She had been sprawled on the pavement and two on foot had come, running, and beaten her with their weapons, a truncheon and a length of metal piping. She was choking on the gas and sobbing.

The *basij* had gone forward another hundred metres, then had been among the narrow streets. Stones and bricks, from a building renovation, had rained on them and they had been driven back. Anyone in their way, on the ground or reeling out of control from the gas, they hit. They were close to her.

She had flinched back, and her bag was beyond her reach. The yoghurt had burst open and the bread was flattened. She had prepared to be hit again – but then he had come. She had not seen him until his hands had clasped her and the hem of her *chador* had ridden up. His arms were under her thighs and round her back. He had bent to pick up her bag and had carried her into an alleyway. Her headscarf had loosened and her hair was on his bare arm, his face inches from hers. Her *chador* was torn at the throat but he ran fast with her. There was a square. A metal gate was ajar, and he had carried her through it.

She was Farideh, the wife of an al-Qods corporal, and he was Johnny, who came from the old rich of the days before the Imam's return from Paris and lived high on the hill above the city. She had gazed into his eyes – and might as well have taken heroin. Each day, going to work and coming back, she would look for the side street on Enghelab, the corner she had come round with her bag of shopping, and would glimpse, down that street, the dark slit of the alley. That was where he had taken her and where her life had changed. That evening she would be there.

A bus came, and she pushed onto it. Whether she lived or died from a tightening noose depended on her being careful, never reckless.

'I wouldn't want there to be any misunderstanding, Miss Ross – and, I appreciate this is not a secure line – but a property such as the one you want, and in the time span available for arrangements to be made, doesn't come cheap. I don't want to sound vulgar, Miss Ross, but it's pricy . . . No problem?'

His wife, Anneliese – head cook at the Canadian Residence – put a steaming mug beside his notepad. Before dawn the suburb outside the inner city, between Favoritenstrasse and Prinz-Eugen-Strasse, was still dark. Sidney clasped the phone and scribbled with his free hand.

'Of course, Miss Ross, you'll need me as local liaison, and my wife as cook-housekeeper. There's cleaning to be done, you'll have me to drive, and Anneliese to cook. We'll buy ourselves out of our present commitments. I'm sorry to introduce this element, Miss Ross, but there will have to be generous recompense. I appreciate you won't be shopping around, and that you want to nail it.'

Christmas coming early. Call the Canadians on the mobile. You're sick. Indefinite.

'A pleasure still to be wanted at the cutting edge, Miss Ross – and, of course, there's transport. Vehicles for hiring. Yes, soon as I'm off this call, I'll get matters in hand.'

He rang off and took a deep breath. He was sixty-nine, and had been dumped when old Hector Kenning had gone home, vacating the Station Desk. He was a fixer, made things happen. He lived in a world of discounts, favours and obligations, and earned money from the embassy where his wife worked, from the Americans and the Belgians. Sometimes policemen and criminologists from Europe or South America, with jobs at the United Nations Office for Drugs and Crime across the Donaukanal, needed a contact who couldn't be traced and he'd do the cut-out. Sidney could be everybody's friend. He imagined that the local crowd, at the British embassy, were outside the loop, probably happy to stay there but resented an invasion of their territory. He sipped his drink, and heard her cough into her phone as she told a night-duty clerk at the Canadian embassy she had flu.

'I don't know what it is, my love, but it sounds a cracker, and the budget seems open. Happy times.'

He kissed her. She hugged him. The book of contact numbers was in a floor safe. He extracted it. Hardly a car moved on the street below his apartment window, barely a pedestrian on the pavement. It was a good address, and reflected his ability as a facilitator. It would be a big one and would bring back the old days, the best, most triumphant times. What he loved about 'a big one' was that you never knew where it would end. It was as unpredictable as the roulette wheel in the casino on Kärntner Strasse.

First he arranged the 'safe house', remote and discreet.

Tilting his chair, he enjoyed a matchless, privileged view. Tadeuz Fenton, leader and manipulator, with the enviable record of almost never backing a losing cause, would have considered it his right to look out over the river, and the barges or pleasure boats far below. In the distance, mist-shrouded, stood Parliament, where his nominal bosses sat. He told them, as a rule, only what they needed to know and extracted authorisations with sometimes jaundiced presentation of facts. In his world he was supreme, and the director general, burdened by demands from 'customers' – the new-speak jargon of the ministries across the Thames – for insights and intelligence on the intentions of the Islamic Republic, allowed him a loose rein. From the door, Mandy Ross told him what she had agreed with the fixer, Sidney, and remarked on the prices quoted, which were close to exorbitant.

'Cheap at the price for what's coming our way. A snip.'

He smoothed his hair, which was important to his persona: it was sleek and silver, the parting ramrod straight. He always wore a tie, but would loosen his shirt's top button on arriving at work. When Sara hung his jacket in the cupboard, the knot would come down an inch, no more, and would stay central. He was half Polish and half English, but he had been reared in the arms of the Secret Intelligence Service.

Tadeuz Denya, a former Polish Army officer, a refugee from successive regimes of Nazism and communism, lucky to find work in a basement as a translator, had made pregnant an archive section manager, Lilibet Fenton, of a good family. Neither abortion nor marriage was considered. The Pole had been transferred to GCHQ, Cheltenham, and had – it was rumoured – prospered there. The archivist had borne the child, gone back to work as soon as she could and fronted up the scandal. As a young man, Tadeuz had joined straight from a red-brick campus. The lesson of his birth was wariness. He did not support failure, or take the arm of the isolated. He had heard it said of him that his touch 'turned base metals to gold'.

He was brought, by Dunc Whitcombe, a thin file titled 'Reza Joyberi (Brig), al-Qods, IRGC'. He demanded paper, said there was value in a sheet in the hand that added provenance. A single photograph was included that showed a young man in filthy combat gear, clutching an assault rifle in a marsh wilderness. It was dated 1984, close to three decades old.

'Dunc, a man who takes care not to be pictured over thirty years is a man climbing fast. Anonymity is survival. He has the rank of brigadier, considerable importance, but doesn't draw attention to himself. He's a high-value target. The ones who parade themselves are the cardboard cut-outs and don't concern me. I like what I see.'

He had the pages across his desk and read briskly, making marks with a sharpened pencil on the text's margins.

Sara Rogers had pushed open the door and was half out of her coat. She said she'd waved off PK and his babysitter team from Heathrow – 'An odd bunch but they're what we have' – and that 'the corporal, if that's what he is', was on Akrotiri, waiting for the lift with the escort to the drop-off. She kicked off her shoes and headed for the coffee machine.

He laughed. 'Maybe we should treat ourselves to a plate of biscuits. It's first class. I want to say, not that it'll ever be minuted, how well you and Mandy have done in getting all this up and flying. The favours pulled in have been of the best quality. To get those lifts from the air force – blood from a stone – was superb. We have someone very close to a man of huge power and influence in that unpleasant regime – that threatening regime. We're getting an open door for very little expenditure, and it comes with minimal danger to our own interests. It has the stamp of something good. Petroc and his people will flush the stuff out of our little man and we can sit back to enjoy the view. There'll be much riding on it, including the prestige of the Service, and we'll not be found wanting. No blow-back, high value and – I repeat – minimal danger to us. The sun's shining.'

Rain ran down the plate-glass windows and blurred the buildings across the river, but Tadeuz Fenton beamed.

The cell was the last one down the corridor of the detention block. As a concession, the door was left open and he'd been brought a hot meal and a soft drink, neither of which he had touched. Two RAF policemen stood guard, one at the door and one at the block's entrance: immaculate, armed, silent, intimidating. Katie had been offered time in the mess, and had refused it. She sat on a hard chair and could see into the cell past the hip of the guard. She had a beaker of tea – had wanted nothing else. The aircraft that would fly them on was an HS-125 CC3 executive jet, with a crew of three and room at the back for six passengers. Usually, she was told, it was at the disposal of an air vice marshal. It would take her and him, with two more of the RAF police detachment, the thirteen hundred miles – about three hours in the air – before she dropped him, then started her return journey to the Gulf.

Little impressed her, but this did. First, a diverted transport, and now luxury to the end-point. She knew he was regarded as 'useful' but such treatment was usually reserved for a 'top of the range' captive.

He sat on the bed. It was not her job to befriend him or offer comfort. She saw her role as keeping him wrong-footed, off-balance psychologically.

His face was in profile to her. His mouth twitched and he licked his lips. His breathing came in spurts broken by sighs. She couldn't see his eyes because his hands masked them. She wondered what, now, governed him – the aftershock of the tart and his inability to 'do the business', or the disorientation of the flight out, not knowing what awaited him? Her opinion: the sooner they had him in the company of those waiting for him, and PK, the better. Couldn't happen soon enough.

His feet and hands were still now and his thighs were no longer trembling. There were no more tears. She reckoned he'd toughened up. He'd be hard work, as he slowly regained his control.

A radio crackled, was answered. There was the thud of boots in the corridor. They went out into the fresh sunlight to a car and were driven to the small jet. He seemed to hesitate and there was a moment of defiance in his face but he would have known she would go for his eyes with her fingers and his balls with her knee, that the uniforms would club him into submission. He went up the steps.

She followed. He was like a man recovering from an anaesthetic – PK's problem, not hers. She hoped to be back in Dubai in the early hours of tomorrow. An Australian girl, a first secretary, was hosting dinner in the evening. Her job would be done and forgotten.

'What a pleasure to meet you, Mr Kenning. I'm Sidney. I was very fond of your uncle – he's keeping well, I hope?'

'Very well, thank you.'

Petroc Kenning had come through the arrival gates and the man, light on his feet, had skipped forward and put down the marker. Might as well have said, 'You can trust me, and it would be wise to listen to me because I was with your uncle when he ran this station.'

The background brief had said Sidney was an able smoother of paths. The smile was confidential, an insider's. A wave of tiredness engulfed Petroc, and a yearning to sleep. He had failed to get any answer either in Vauxhall Cross or at the airport to his calls to

Spain. He knew less about defectors and how to treat them than could be written on a half-sheet of foolscap: no other section on the third or fourth floors had seemed to offer that expertise, and Tadeuz Fenton had waved away his anxieties with 'Pretty straightforward. Follow your nose and it'll all be spilling out in your lap.'

Sidney limped and pain creased his face. 'Don't worry, Mr Kenning – it's arthritis. The pills take care of it.'

'Good to hear it.'

'I've fixed the house.' The old accent, east London, had lasted well after half a lifetime abroad.

'Excellent. I look forward to getting there.'

Petroc knew he could have been warmer to his uncle's old retainer. His voice had been clipped, poor behaviour in a team leader, but he didn't care. He turned. The babysitters followed him. The Service employed eccentrics and seemed to find niches for them. First, there was Auntie – he was at least fifty, smelt of talc and sounded like an Ulsterman. Behind him was Father William, in his mid-forties, with a shock of white hair and a west Middlesex whine. Last through was Nobby, red-haired and quietly spoken.

Petroc did brief introductions. His phone rang. He veered to the side, looking for an oasis of quiet.

He heard a distant voice: 'I think you called me. I'm Rollo. Your message said you were short of tactics. I'm happy to help. Shoot.'

'Dross or precious stuff. Never get excited until you know the answer to that, and ask the questions with rigour – first priority. I have to warn you that the signal where I am isn't great, but the battery's charged and I'm happy to help, Petroc. I'm rather flattered that Hector spoke well of me.'

He had a quality telescope on a tripod, and useful binoculars hung at his neck. Rollo Hawkins sat on the low wall of the viewing platform and his wife, Stephie, was crouched on a collapsible three-legged stool behind him, with a rucksack at her feet that held hot chocolate in a Thermos and sandwiches. Both were well wrapped against the cold of the coming night. If they hadn't spotted them by then it was unlikely they'd be successful, but there were still young enthusiasts around them, with similar gear, whose eyesight would be keener. Barely an evening passed, last light, when Rollo and Stephie were not at the platform, on a hill and dwarfed by the mountains, in the hope of seeing bears. It was their obsession. Their target was the European brown bear, and there were estimated to be some thirty living in the area. Rollo and Stephie knew most of them by sight, had their own names for each one, and thought themselves blessed. He had been the foremost SIS expert in the handling of defectors.

His teeth chattered, and he gulped a mouthful of chocolate. 'Photographs and videos from the drones and audio eavesdropping all have a place, but nothing beats the HumInt factor. Human intelligence rules. I always tell the Yankees that their technology seldom equals the results provided by a man who's on the ground or has just been there. Any defector – let's call him Joe – with trusted access to the heart of the enemy's secrets, is to be taken seriously, but first the question must be answered. Is he overrated because he originates from a covert source? Could the material he brings have been taken from magazines, from what is already in the public domain? Is the "trusted access" indeed special? And the question cannot be sidetracked. Could he be, in our vernacular, a *plant*, or might he be judged a *dangle*, in Agency talk? Was he introduced by your opponents to provide disinformation that will deflect correct analysis? Is he infiltrating to find out what you know, what you wish to know? The question must be answered: is he unimportant and talking only good talk, or is he sophisticated, committed and a fraud? Assume you can answer my question. He's the genuine article. Most who came to us or to the Americans – they used me frequently and still do – from the Soviet Union were drunks or womanisers and greedy. Always worth going back to MICE. Money's straightforward; Ideology is rare, but valuable; Ego is tedious but leads to massive resentment from the Joe – but you tell me, Petroc, that you're in the realms of Compromise. You have a man who is *shitting* himself – is frightened of you. He is disoriented, confused, and at first is prepared to bend to the duress you've put him under. For how long will he be more terrified of you than of whatever world is behind him? You must use that time well, Petroc. You flatter him. Respect him. The Joe is Iranian, you say. You promise wealth, a new life. And, believe me, you'll suck out what you need in the first hours and days. You go to it all the hours that God gives. Petroc, call me again any time. You'll have heard all this before, a high-flyer like yourself, but sometimes it's worth having core points reiterated. A pleasure to help . . . We're not favoured tonight but I hope Stephie and I'll be rewarded tomorrow. The bears are eating well and putting on fat for the winter hibernation. Good luck.'

They were at the gate. The barrier was down and a sentry stood behind it, with an automatic weapon, a Steyr 5.56mm assault rifle, slung across his chest. A light rain was falling. All of those outside the Chrysler Grand Voyager heard the roar of the aircraft on approach.

Petroc peered up at the charcoal grey cloud over him, Auntie and Nobby behind him. Father William had stayed inside the vehicle with Sidney, who had driven them and negotiated with the guardhouse to park on the verge. Sidney had said they were at Fliegerhorst Brumowski, close to the town of Tulln, eighteen miles north of central Vienna. It had been a *Luftwaffe* base, then the Russians had used it until they'd pulled out, and the USAF had based a transport squadron there. It was now Austrian military property. Protocol dictated that they did not come through, and that no Austrian personnel had contact with them.

The aircraft broke the cloud, and banked sharply for touchdown. Its lights flashed against the fragile early-evening light. Petroc's mind was blank. One thing to set it up for a creature to creep into the jam jar, another to see it happen. Lights blazed at the porthole windows. He might have caught a glimpse of a face. He felt a frisson of fear.

'Interesting days ahead, guys. I think we can be certain of that.'

She was first out and had the front passenger seat. The driver had leaned across her to unfasten the lock. She carried the sick bag retrieved from the aircraft cabin. A military policeman slid open the side door of the transport, then offered a hand to Mehrak – the corporal – but he ignored it. The second policeman followed him. Both had left their pistols on board with the crew. She walked towards the barrier, set a good pace, and saw Petroc Kenning waiting there. The overhead lights showed the strain on his face. The barrier went up and she stepped to the side. She folded down the top of the sick bag, then tossed it away, as if it held nothing of importance. It was caught by a man with red hair, who lunged forward from the right of her boss. There was a line, white-painted, under the barrier, which she would not cross.

Mehrak, the corporal, kept walking. There was a moment when he was alone and another when PK had gripped his hand, not with enthusiasm. Two others had hovered away from the light and now closed on him. He didn't look back. Katie made a farewell gesture with her fingers, and was rewarded with a curt nod. A typical PK gesture, but she understood the excitement her boss would be feeling – and it might mean promotion. She watched the people-carrier drive away, its headlights bright on the road, then walked to the transport and swung herself in beside the driver. Her job was done.

She murmured, 'They also serve who only stand and stare . . .'

'Beg pardon, ma'am?'

'Someone has to walk behind the Lord Mayor's carriage with a bucket and shovel, do the humble stuff.'

'If you're finished on this one, ma'am, you might just be well out of it. No offence.'

'None taken.' They were driven through the almost deserted base and back towards the apron. A fuelling tanker stood beside the aircraft. She said, '"Well out of it". I wouldn't argue with that.'

Without shining a torch into his face, Petroc Kenning couldn't see the man's face. His head had been down at the barrier and the Chrysler's lights were subdued so only the outline of the man's features was visible. He tried to remember everything he had been told by an old man stuck up a hill in northern Spain, likely with vultures high above him. He had to remember everything and make it his Bible. He yawned.

He had crumpled the sick bag and slid it into his jacket pocket, but had stolen a glance at its contents: bank envelopes, with a crest, and a laminated ID card from the Qods crowd.

He turned once just as an oncoming lorry's lights spilled into their car and illuminated the man's face. A chance to read him? The eyes stared ahead, dull. Everyone at the Cross had said it would be a straightforward business, that a good outcome was inevitable. No one had spoken to Rollo Hawkins.

There was a no-smoking sign in front of him, but he took a packet from his pocket, with a throwaway lighter, and passed them to the babysitters. They each took one, and so did the man. Petroc was thanked, first in Farsi then English, and there were the flashes of flame as the cigarettes were lit. He understood why he'd been thanked. Katie, clever girl, had not offered their man one – not in Dubai, on the aircraft, or at Akrotiri. She had made Petroc the guardian angel who dispensed the fags. When he twisted back to retrieve the packet and the lighter, a bus's lights showed him that the face and eyes were dull again and that the gratitude was past.

They headed in silence for the safe house and tension ratcheted in the vehicle.

The van pulled up.

His hand had been on the door lever as soon as the driver had turned into his street. He had barely stopped, but Zach had the door open.

'Hey, mate – you sure?'

'Sure, thanks,' Zach answered.

The driver wheedled, 'But it's Shane's birthday.'

'Sorry – my apologies to him for the no-show. I'll see him tomorrow.'

'We'll all be there except you.' The driver tried a last throw. 'There'll be a kitty, won't hardly cost you.'

'I doubt I'll be missed.'

The driver reversed out into the street, cleared the parked cars and accelerated. He didn't wave. Shane was a bricklayer, one of the best Zach's father employed. Zach hadn't forgotten a present, and a gift-wrapped carton of Marlboro Lite had gone into Shane's bag at lunchtime, but he'd evaded the question when he was asked if he was coming to the Adelaide that evening.

He went up the path, slipped off his boots, shook the mud off them, opened the door and went in. He was tired, cold and dirty. It had been a pig of a day because of the rain. It was difficult for the chippies because they did carpentry in the open, and bad for the brickies when a squall hit the barrowloads of mortar with which Zach kept them supplied, and the sparks bitched when they were wiring close to unglazed windows. In ninety minutes they were all due at the Adelaide, and he wouldn't be there. He went upstairs.

He wasn't one of them. Doing barrows, driving the dumper and shifting pallets of bricks or concrete blocks beside them five days a week and sometimes on a Saturday didn't make him one of them. He was the 'boss's kid', and sometimes, thinking he was out of earshot, they referred to him scathingly as 'The Scholar' and sometimes 'The Toff'. He tended to sit apart at mealbreaks, so he didn't hear about their girls and kids, and what they'd managed with their betting slips. It was as he thought it should be.

He unlocked the door, and the room facing him was barren of any trace of Zach Becket, as he had intended. He put his boots on a newspaper, unread, by the door and heeled it shut.

It wasn't their fault that he was the old square peg. There had been a job in the winter, on a site, that had taken the van past the mainline station. Men and women, in their suits with their laptop bags, had been hurrying for the fast trains into London and Birmingham. They were into 'professional' careers, where he should have been – and might still be one day. Or he would take over the business and employ the men he now worked with. It could't last, the drift. Was he miserable? Not particularly. Stifled by self-pity? Not that anyone would notice. Was it somebody's fault? May be his own – there were few other candidates to share the blame. He had fallen out of love with his studies, and the option available, his tutor had texted, was translating at the Cheltenham intelligence base, GCHQ, or hacking through newspapers and listening to broadcasts from Iran for the BBC's World Service.

Now he wasn't challenged. A teacher had once said that Zachariah Becket needed challenges, a conveyor-belt of them; that he reacted well to the stress of competition. There were no challenges in front of him and none that he knew of hovering over the horizon.

Later, after he'd showered, Zach might go and get a takeaway, then read in the quiet of his room. By the time the party at the Adelaide was in full swing, he'd be alone, with the poetry of that country's history. It had been in the last two months, since the evenings had closed in, that he had gone back to the small pile of books he had brought back from London. The poetry had captured him long ago, but his life was hollow now, so even that could't fill it.

3

He lay on the bed. The ash from the cigarette was about to fall on his throat beside the rest.

Without shifting his shoulders, Mehrak could reach for the packet on the bedside table, the lighter and the ashtray. They had left him his watch so he knew he had woken just before five – he had adjusted his watch to the new time, on the woman's instructions, when they were on the aircraft, beginning the turbulent descent. It was now past eight. Mehrak had neither been drunk, nor had taken heroin. He had been exhausted from the stress of the kidnap, as he thought of it, and in bed by ten, asleep soon after. In the three hours on the bed, with the cigarettes, he remembered everything that had been said, and all that had happened around him.

He knew they had travelled along the bank of a great river into a small town, with tidy streets, then along a narrow road, little more than a track, to a house set away from others. They had parked beside an old tractor and he had been shepherded fast through a back door, which had been opened by an overweight woman whose clothes bulged. She'd said, 'Welcome, sir,' and stepped aside.

In a lobby, the one who had met him at the air-force base had said, 'Right. Apologies for the lack of talk in the vehicle, Mehrak, but we don't want misunderstandings and confusion. I repeat, my name is PK, and my colleagues here are Auntie, Father William and Nobby. Our driver is Sidney. We're going to make you comfortable and, above all, we're going to do the right thing by you, given that your circumstances are unfortunate. I'm told you speak some English, which is excellent, but for business we'll use whichever language you prefer, maybe Farsi and maybe not. For household matters it's English.'

He had been taken down a corridor, then up a flight of stairs. A door in front of him had a key in the lock. The woman opened it, switched on a ceiling light and bobbed her head as if it were her privilege to show him his room. The driver, Sidney, had said he should sit down and rest. Later PK would want to eat and talk.

He could hear movement in the room next to his and on the stairs. Twice, footsteps had stopped outside his door. It had been locked from the outside when he'd gone to bed, but there was a small shower cubicle with a toilet in an alcove with a curtain. The ash broke – he felt it fall on his skin. He stubbed out the cigarette, half smoked, alongside the other butts, and swung his feet off the bed. He urinated, then washed himself. There was a new toothbrush in a mug, with a tube of toothpaste. He had been told there were clothes for him in the wardrobe. He found jeans and a shirt, a pullover, underpants, a vest and socks. They all fitted well. There were trainers on the wardrobe floor, his size.

The bed had been comfortable; the curtains were of good material. A painting of a ruined castle hung on a wall, with photographs of a smiling family around the tractor at the back of the house. He had been brought to a home.

Mehrak was thirty-four. He had been born in the year of the Imam's return to Iran from Paris, when the revolution had chased away the corrupt family of the Shah. He had had little education, and his sole ambition as a child had been to follow his father into the al-Qods division of the Islamic Revolutionary Guard Corps. His father had been principal escort and personal guard to a colonel.

Mehrak was a good driver, a better than average shot with a handgun, and was said to have a 'dogged enthusiasm for learning and betterment'. He had practised and trained and, at only twenty-one, had been assigned to Reza Joyberi. Other aides had come and gone, but Mehrak had lasted: he drove the Mercedes, walked a pace behind his man, had a PPK Walther in a leather waist holster – and he had married.

He knotted the trainers' laces, stretched his back and stood at the window to look through the gap in the curtains. He saw her as clearly as if she was framed in the window. The then Colonel Joyberi and Mehrak's father had found the girl. She was from a good family, and was said to be pious, dutiful and obedient.

The night before, as he was given a meal of soup, bread, cheese, tomatoes and fruit, he had not known whether he had been lied to or told the truth.

PK had said, 'You will find with me, Mehrak, complete honesty. You can believe what I tell you. Get this into your head. We've done you a massive favour. I don't know which of your friends took you to that whorehouse, and I don't want to know why you agreed to go there. It's the sort of place where the girls make sure the client is filmed and recorded. The result goes on the Internet and to employers or families. In-focus pictures taken on state-of-the-art surveillance cameras would have picked up every wart on your skin. You're a married man, Mehrak, and a member of an élite force, the al-Qods division. You were on an important assignment for your country, travelling abroad and paid for by the state. You spent the state's money in a whorehouse. You're about to bring disgrace on your family and shame on your military unit. A man who pays for sex throws away the trust of his wife and commander. The Internet pictures would have destroyed you. Your illegal use of state funds is enough to have you dangling at the end of a rope. Luckily, we heard of your situation and would like to think a deal can be done. You talk, we'll help. Have you seen many hangings, Mehrak? I doubt they're quick and painless.'

And PK had put some cheese into his mouth.

Then, he'd added, 'In my business Mehrak, we talk about "false-flag penetration". In your case, it implies that you may be a decoy, given to us to confuse us and tell us lies. I don't believe that's true of you, but should we learn that we've been deceived, it would go badly for you.'

Only PK had eaten with him. The others had sat against a wall and watched.

He had pushed away his plate when PK had said, 'We start

work tomorrow, but we're making this effort to save your skin in a good cause.'

A notebook had come from an inner pocket, and a silver propelling pencil. He gave his full name, his father's and his wife's. He confirmed the address of the barracks where the Mercedes was garaged. Sometimes he was in English and sometimes in Farsi. Why had he gone to the bank in Dubai and received a statement to a numbered account? He had hesitated, stumbled on an answer in English, then reverted to his own language. The pencil had jabbed his lower arm and he had been told to speak up.

He had said it was Brigadier Reza Joyberi's account, then took the path of treachery and gave the addresses. He had memorised the account details of two more banks. Then he reconstructed the diary for the week before he had flown out, the last month, and the last quarter, and said where he had driven the brigadier. As if it hardly mattered to him, PK had written brief notes.

His door was unlocked quietly. He thought he might as well have been manacled with a chain fastened to a wall. He was a traitor, and in the Evin gaol, such men were hanged by the neck until they were dead.

It was her fault. She was to blame. She had done it to him. He didn't drop his head into his hands or weep but bit his lips and drew blood. Auntie was there, smiling at him, and Nobby was behind him. It was because of her that he had done it.

Had Petroc Kenning taken holidays, what he saw from the front door might have given him ideas. But he didn't: no one did on the Iran Desk, fronted by Tadeuz Fenton. The Islamic Republic was too volatile to abandon at any time so Petroc lived and breathed Iran. The best he could say to Sidney was that the 'safe house' ticked all the boxes.

The previous evening after their arrival, it had rained, but then the skies had cleared and near dawn a frost had formed. Petroc stood on a patio and smoked. The foreground was taken up with neat lines of cultivated vines. Already this morning small tractors had drawn trailers into position and women were hacking off the bunches of grapes and dropping them into big plastic buckets. He liked what he saw. There would be good wine again for him to drink tonight after the corporal had been put to bed and he was analysing the day's notes, which Auntie would help him to type. Later, every man, woman and teenager would be on the slopes, picking frantically. Who would notice strangers in a house rented at short notice? It was likely that he and the babysitters had moved into the village at the best possible time.

The vines were in front of him, to the sides and behind the house. If it went well, he would be there long enough to sample most of the better labels that came from this village, Spitz. The community, with the exception of the farmers who owned the vineyards, lived along a tight series of roads running between the old houses, and a fine church, with a tall, angular steeple, dominated the centre. To his left was the main road between Krems and Schallenbach – Sidney had said that the summer brought the tourist hordes, with a regular flow of passenger craft along the river, but they were gone. The river was high and, beyond a ruined castle, it turned sharply. A tug boat came upstream, dragging a fleet of barges against the current.

He was unlikely ever to quit intelligence-gathering in favour of private industry. Wealth would escape him. The probability was that he would retire to live on a government pension. It would be a frugal existence, and Polly's parents would have to dig deep if Archie were to have the education his mother wanted for him. They seemed in good health so an inheritance wasn't imminent.

A million pounds, banked wherever the client wanted it, seemed a waste of resources to Petroc Kenning: he didn't think Hector would have talked in such terms – more likely he'd have got to work on the toenails. PK could offer a million, which seemed to him far in excess of what might be owed to a corporal. And the man was a turncoat: he could never be respected.

There had been men in the Service when PK had been a fresh-faced recruit, who had known Harold Adrian Russell Philby and felt his treachery keenly. He had been told that on 11 May each year, since 1988, veterans of the Russia Desk drank vintage champagne from paper cups on the anniversary of the spy's death.

His uncle had already been part of the post-war Vienna legend in the days of Maclean and Burgess, and had talked about the atom traitors.

PK wanted a career that marked him out as a competent professional, who had justified the faith in him of his mentor, his uncle – but the way to justify it was, apparently, to thrust a million pounds at the corporal. If the man coughed, networks would be wound up, arrests made along the Gulf, targets evaluated, locations confirmed, and they would be inside the minds of the leadership, under their skin and flaying it.

PK called inside, 'Let's go to work.'

He flushed.

'. . . that's what we'll do for you. A million in sterling, which is about one point five million American dollars.'

His heart pounded.

'We'll help you set up a new life. You'll live where *they* can't find you. Maybe start a little business. It's generous.'

He blinked, could barely see the man across the table. He reached for the cigarettes.

'That's what you'll get, Mehrak, for complete co-operation. It's how we show our gratitude. In return, you give us every installation you visited, every checkpoint, every air-defence battery that you went to inspect with the brigadier, every scientist you met and every engineer . . . Everything.'

His fingers trembled. He couldn't take a cigarette from the packet and tore the flap.

'There's no going back, believe me. You know what'll happen to you. Do they do most hangings off chairs or tables? I think I read somewhere they've started bringing tables from the staff room at Evin into the yard where the gallows are – the tables have wheels so they're easy to drag away. There's no going back, Mehrak, so you have to believe us. Start walking forward and don't stop or look back.'

He had a cigarette out, but each time he flicked the lighter, his breath extinguished the flame.

'It's not my place to pass judgement on why you were in a whorehouse, Mehrak, and failing to get anywhere with a Ukrainian tart, but I reckon that as you were there, you won't find it a big deal to leave your family – your wife's called Farideh, yes? When we've done the work, you'll be able to meet any number of attractive young women.'

He had the cigarette in his mouth, gripped the lighter in both fists, lit the tip, and spluttered on the smoke. A million and a half American dollars was . . . A sheet of paper lay in front of him and there was a pen in his hand. He signed his name, and the paper was gone.

'A five-minute break, Mehrak. You have much to live up to if you're to earn your money.'

Petroc watched as Father William and Nobby took the corporal towards the kitchen where fresh tea would be served in a glass. A smart woman, Sidney's wife. She must have been on the Internet to learn how they liked it in Iran. Auntie held the camera, pulled a face, then flicked to play-back.

Petroc saw the screen and the man signing the contract. He said, 'Nails him to the floorboards. We can do the deductions later – board and lodging, tax, security expenses – still be a good amount. We're going to squeeze him till the pips squeak. It'll be satisfying. At the end of the day he'll give us insight on the bowel movements of the regime, the pecking order of the hierarchy, and all its military postures, attack and defence. All invaluable, should we go to war with them. He's only a corporal, but one with unqualified access. Can't be bad.'

The drivers and those tasked with guarding the packages of refined heroin had stopped to brew tea. There were four vehicles in the convoy and each carried in excess of a hundred kilos, so – among the ammunition boxes, belts of bullets, projectiles for the launchers, sleeping bags and bread – each Nissan pick-up had cargo already valued at half a million American dollars. It did not concern the men that behind them, in the provincial centres, idealistic foreigners tried to lure the farmers away from the opium crop.

They talked quietly, as they squatted with the cups in their hands. A small but significant proportion of the drug's value would go into their purses.

The agronomists from Britain, the United States and Germany said that the land should be used for growing wheat, vegetables, tomatoes and fodder for dairy cattle. If a farmer grew potatoes he'd be lucky to earn one American dollar for two kilos. Each time the heroin was moved, its value increased, as did the need for vigilance on the part of the drivers and guards.

They talked and sipped tea, and a little spiral of smoke eddied upwards from the fire. There were brothers, cousins and men related by marriage; they lived well thanks to the trade. They were favoured. The rewards for the drivers and guards outweighed concerns for their safety.

One had not joined the group: he was sulking because the marriage of his second eldest daughter – a good match, one likely to forge a strong alliance with a clan leader – would not take place. He stayed in the cab of his pick-up and chewed a strip of dried goat meat. He was not a trained fighter – neither were the others: all in this group were familiar with the weapons they carried, but they didn't do combat with the forces occupying their province. They didn't understand the fire power of their enemy – it came so fast.

This driver, alone, reacted. He turned on the ignition, stamped on the pedals and won traction. The others didn't hear the helicopter until it had climbed over the ridge some five hundred metres behind them. The driver didn't know the detail in the manufacture of a Hughes M230 Chain Gun firing a 30mm cartridge at high velocity, but he recognised the silhouette of the Apache. In a low gear, he surged for a network of gorges a kilometre ahead. He had judged, correctly, that the killers in the sky would be more interested in destroying a dozen men and three vehicles than in chasing him and losing the big group. He left behind two of his cousins and his brother's wife's brother.

He drove at the highest speed the Nissan could manage and threw up a trail of dust. He hoped to save his life and protect his cargo. When he reached the gorge, he pulled up in the lee of a sheer wall, and in shadow. Behind him he saw merged columns of smoke. The helicopter circled the target area, then veered away towards the sun.

He didn't go back to see what the machine-gun had done. It would have been God's will that some were taken and others were not. He drove west, towards the frontier.

Later he realised that there were three shell holes in the pick-up's floor and one of the sacks was punctured. Several bags had split and the resin was oozing out. He threw away the damaged sack and its contents. Further on, under an overhang, he parked and wrapped a blanket round his body. He would sleep in the shade of the rock. He had the evidence of the shall holes to explain why half of his load was lost. God's will.

The two aides travelling with him had been met by a driver and gone in the jeep sent for them. They had been reluctant to abandon him but Brigadier Reza Joyberi was adamant. He'd thanked them for their work on the visit to Bandar Abbas and other locations on the Gulf, asked for the typed-up papers they'd discussed on the train to be couriered to him that evening at his garrison office, and waved them off. He'd said his driver was no doubt temporarily delayed in the traffic.

He had not rung the corporal's mobile phone immediately, but had paced on the wide steps of the station entrance. The building towered behind him: an architectural monument to the old regime with a marble façade. Now, a portrait of the Imam hung as a banner, ten times life-size, from the wall to his left. He looked out onto Rah-Ahan Square and tried to spot the Mercedes in the columns of vehicles skirting the trees and fountains in front of him. The visit to the coast was planned, the schedule agreed. The corporal had been told the arrival time of the train. The Mercedes should have been parked at the bottom of the steps in front of the area allocated to waiting taxis; when he had appeared at the top of the steps the corporal should have jumped out of the driver's seat and smartly opened a rear door for him.

Outwardly, he did not show frustration or anger. He stood erect, holding his briefcase, his jacket sufficiently full across the chest to hide his shoulder holster. A few minutes had passed since the aides had left him. Annoyance nagged. Principals of the al-Qods had been killed in bomb attacks or by shooting in most quarters of the country. He was a prime target of the Americans and the Israelis; he had a professional respect for the Jews' intelligence apparatus, the Mossad, and professional envy for the resources available to the Americans' Agency.

He stood on the steps and couldn't see his car. He felt vulnerable: an assassin could have walked to his shoulder unnoticed, could smile at him and produce – a sharp, clean movement – a short-barrelled pistol, fire it, and be gone before his knees buckled. Women would be screaming and men would be backing off, but the killer would be gone. The thought gripped him.

He took his phone from his pocket and snapped through the list of names. He called his driver. His corporal's phone was switched off, he was told, and the message urged him to 'try later'.

The last time his driver had been late to collect him, eleven months ago, there had been a blow-out of a rear tyre. Two calls had warned him of the delay, and he had been held up for only nine minutes. Other than that, he could not recall being left to stand on a pavement or step. The man should have been back from the Gulf trip the previous evening – at the very least he should have been warned. He made another call, to his driver's home: it was not answered. The pretty little wife would be at work. He had been at the corporal's wedding but, when asked, his driver would give no reason as to why there were no children. He swore softly.

He walked down the steps and away from the station to join the taxi queue. He gave the name of the garrison camp in the heart of the city. Yes, a pretty girl, and her husband had failed him.

* * *

The agent of the Ministry of Security and Intelligence followed Farideh. Each time she moved or sat, so did he. He was Kourosh – his parents had named him after the first king of Persia, dead now for two and a half millennia. He worked in the teams dedicated to the discovery of spies sent by the Agency or the Mossad into Iran, and he was besotted with her.

She thought he was a mistake.

She had been in the room above the garage, which she kept almost as a shrine to Johnny, whom they had hanged. She had not made love with Kourosh: probably, one day, she would, but not yet. No one in her office would have believed that Farideh, wife of a corporal in the al-Qods division, toyed with a counter-intelligence officer. She was sitting. He was on the far side of the table. She allowed her opened hand to rest on the polished wood. He laid his on it. Her *chador* hung on a hook behind the door and she wore tight jeans with a blouse. He had been permitted to open two buttons, but not a third. She stood. So did he. She went to the sideboard, where the kettle was. He held the glasses; she poured the tea. He stirred in the sugar, and she went back to the table with her glass. He brought his and they sat down. He gazed into her face, mesmerised. He was like a puppy, she thought, wanting to please, clumsy, and devoted. An MOIS investigation had identified Johnny as a 'provocateur', an 'enemy of the state'. It had provided the prosecution with evidence that had been sufficient to hang him.

It almost amused her that she could bring the agent here, where she had been with Johnny and make a fool of him. She had met him through Mehrak.

After a meeting, the brigadier's driver had been asked to take two MOIS officials back to their headquarters; he would return later for his own officer. There had been talk in the Mercedes of a light-fitting, which was sparking, in an official's home. Her husband – always one to 'brown nose', as Johnny would have said with contempt – had said he knew a man who could do the work: she had his phone number at home. They were not far away so he had diverted there. Mehrak had stood on the pavement and shouted for her – it had been high summer, three months ago, and the windows were open. She had just washed her hair when she came to the window – no scarf or veil – and it had hung across her face. Mehrak had told her to bring his book of phone numbers from inside their front door, and to cover herself. She had come to the pavement, with a towel over her head, and given him the book. He had relayed the number to the officer, who had written it down, and she had taken the book back upstairs. She had exchanged little more than a glance with Kourosh of the ministry.

She sipped the tea, so did he. She licked her lips and saw his eyes flicker. She would sleep with him, one day.

Some of Johnny's books – novels and from the university course he had abandoned, were on a shelf. The clothes he kept for when he needed to alter his appearance were in the chest-of-drawers, and there were documents, too, forged or stolen. Records stood in a rack, American jazz – he had played them on the old turntable, not loudly, the sound muffled by the repair work below. There was a photograph of him, young, with his family, and a picture of a woman, who wore a veil below a single slit that showed only her eyes. There was a third photograph: a young man, his hair flopping on his forehead, stubbled cheeks, a tribesman's clothes – he carried an assault rifle. She had loved him as she had loved Johnny and he had been, to her, the Captain, and was dead.

Kourosh was in the division of counter-espionage that specialised in surveillance.

She came to the repair yard two or three times a week, squeezing inside the gates. The agent must have devoted three days, minimum, to following her. He must have watched her leave home in the morning, take the bus, go to the office that employed her, visit the market, and see her father at his linen stall, then go to the garage. He must have waited for her . . . and done it again and again, so that he had established a pattern in her life and in her husband's. She had come one evening three months ago and her friends, the old men, had been quiet and had watched her nervously. One had pointed to the stairs, then shrugged.

They were, to her, Excellency and Highness. Long ago, they

had driven and maintained the vehicles used by the extended family of the Peacock Throne. They had slid away from view when the *bazaaris* had turned against the royal family – holed up in useless luxury in the Niavaran Palace – and had paid discreet cash for the yard and made a new life. Johnny had used them to keep his 125cc bike, a Norton, on the road when the spares it required had dried up. Johnny was their hero. He had not betrayed them, or her, when facing torture and when execution was close. Johnny was their first love. They had bowed and scraped to excellencies and highnesses, and now they kept old motorbikes and scooters on the road. They had the room above the yard and it had been Johnny's place. She had been there with Johnny, and later with the Captain, and one day she might allow the agent to lie beside her and loosen more buttons. But he had been a mistake.

Farideh yearned for love. She did not know how, in that city of fourteen million souls, she might find it – never with her husband. It had been love with Johnny and had started to be love with the Captain, in a squad with special duties and on assignment in Afghanistan. It was Excellency who had told her, four months after his arrest, that Johnny had been hanged. It was Highness who had gone each month to the Captain's home, saying he had been asked to look for a reliable scooter at a good price. Twenty months ago, at the door, he had faced an elderly red-eyed woman who had spoken of her son's death in a distant war. Love had eluded Farideh again.

She finished her tea.

She tapped the back of his hand briskly and gave him a brush kiss on each cheek. They always left separately. From the upper window she had a partial view of the gate; she saw him go through it and walk away. Farideh shrugged into her *chador*, knotted her scarf under her chin and buttoned the veil over her face. She gathered up her shopping, switched off the lights, looked a last time at the shadowed pictures of Johnny and the Captain, then went down the stairs. She kissed Excellency and Highness through the veil, her smile hidden. Both men worshipped her and, if she wasn't careful, she might reward their affection by killing them.

She thought her husband would be home, from wherever he had been, and hurried to the bus stop.

'Where does he live?'

Mehrak said that Brigadier Reza Joyberi's home was in Shahrak Shahid Mahallati district, a compound of the regime's élite, and gave the address. The house faced north towards the mountains.

'Does he have guards there?'

Mehrak said there were men, without uniform, in cars in the district but there was no road block and no specific security at the property. He said that the brigadier always carried a holstered handgun.

'His main workplace is where?'

An enlarged map of Tehran lay on the table between Mehrak and PK, and he named the garrison barracks, rather than the headquarters of either the Revolutionary Guard Corps or the al-Qods.

'The main volume of his work now?'

He had responsibility for the security of the nuclear installations at Isfahan and Bushehr, Mehrak said, and for the research divisions at the technology university. There was a committee that reported on the security of the establishments against aerial or ground attack; it was led in rotation by the main personalities. Brigadier Joyberi would take over in three months. His tone was flat, emotionless. There was – Mehrak lit another cigarette – anxiety about the explosions at munitions bases near the capital and the deaths of prominent people; the Zionists were blamed.

'What actions will be taken, Mehrak, to counter infiltration at these places?'

He assumed he was being filmed and recorded because his questioner took only sparse notes, insufficient for a transcript. Each time he scratched in his memory for detail, he seemed to see the brigadier's face. Sometimes it was wreathed in smiles and there would be a joke in the car between them. Sometimes he had laughed with the brigadier until his sides ached. On other occasions his boss's face had been cold, set, his eyes distant, especially when Mehrak took an envelope and an air ticket – it had happened four times – and was told which bank in Dubai to visit. Why him? The brigadier would have thought him too stupid, too loyal, to be concerned about the undeclared accounts held abroad.

Auntie sat behind him, and Nobby was against a side wall. The window was behind him and he could hear the drone of tractors. Inside the house, a vacuum-cleaner was in use, and he smelt food cooking.

As best he could, Mehrak answered the questions put to him.

'Thank you, Tadeuz, very helpful.' The Cousin grimaced.

'Something for us to chew on.' The Friend rarely offered praise. 'A little something, but *something*.'

A routine meeting was winding down. The Friend and the Cousin had come from their respective embassies – Kensington and Mayfair – and were admitted to an area of Vauxhall Cross set aside for liaison sessions. Tadeuz Fenton had brought a sparse meal to the table, and sensed the boredom of the American and the Jew. He imagined that the Agency and the Mossad would have shared a taxi over Westminster Bridge and decided *en route* what the British deserved to be given. On matters Iranian, they were the big players, the stars, and liked to hint at involvement in explosions that wasted military gear and commanders' lives in what was referred to as a zone of crisis. Politeness was maintained, but Tadeuz Fenton had known from the first meetings he had attended, in the fortress block of Grosvenor Square, that sharing was proportionate to what he had to offer. Papers were shuffled, phones checked, briefcases locked. The talk had been vague, of schisms in the upper echelon of politics.

He smiled. 'I don't like to run before I can walk, and wouldn't want to raise premature hopes, but we believe we have an individual under our control who is – or has the potential to be – rather choice.'

The Mossad man, the Friend, reacted, indifference gone. 'Would that be inside or outside Iran?'

'Outside. Picked up on a sting, a honey trap. Sadly our main man in theatre was on home leave and we didn't have the officers in place to do the coercion, pile on the pressure and ship him back. We've brought him out of the Gulf . . . but, as I say, early days.'

Tadeuz Fenton didn't fish, but knew several who did. They tied flies, then floated them down a pool in a remote river, hoping a salmon would bite. He yearned for the moment.

The Cousin beaded his eyes on him. 'What is it, Fenton?'

'There's a brigadier, the al-Qods crowd, Reza Joyberi—'

'You've not gotten hold of him? You surely . . .'

'I wish. Not a man of that stature.' Tadeuz Fenton could smile graciously and deprecate himself, which played well with Americans. The Israeli hadn't responded. They seldom did – but the United States didn't have Iranian missiles aimed at Massachusetts or California and the British weren't facing a rocket programmed to land on Coventry Cathedral. The Mossad man, the Friend, had good reason to be serious. 'We have a Joe who is close, very close, to Joyberi. We have him out of their reach and have today begun a detailed debrief. As soon as we extract worthwhile material, which I hope to start producing in the next few hours, it will, of course, be shipped to both of you.'

The cousin interjected, 'Joyberi's a big cat, and anyone near him is high value.'

The Friend said, 'We'd want access to him, and soon. And, immediately, we wish to be inside the loop. Top of our list would be – if relationships deteriorate to the point of military intervention – where they would strike at our interests.'

'I second that. Sounds good, Fenton. Getting stuff out of that place is near impossible. Congratulations.'

Tadeuz Fenton ushered them to the door. He thought he had justified his place – hanging by his fingernails – at the top table. 'As soon as it's available it'll come your way – and I'll work on the access thing. I'm optimistic of a good result.'

He took them into the wide lobby and saw them out through

security. Had he left hostages to fortune? No. Open and shut, simple stuff. And he had enhanced respect.

Where there had been confusion there was now a nagging, uncomfortable clarity. Iranian investigators worked in Dubai and fed back what they had learned.

A radio station had received a call from the 'Coast Guard' reporting a search initiated off-shore after a man was seen wading into the water. An on-line newspaper had taken an alert from the police concerning a missing person last seen on the beach and starting to wade out; they had initiated a search after a radio station had been told that an unidentified male, believed Iranian, was missing, last noticed on the shoreline. The Coast Guard had been tipped off by an on-line newspaper that a body had been located in the water near to the beach. The source of the messages, and disinformation, could not be identified.

A conclusion? In Brigadier Reza Joyberi's office it was already understood that a combination of circumstances had allowed his driver, the corporal, to disappear and that a security investigation was now to begin – almost forty-eight hours after the last sighting. Two bank employees had sworn that the courier who had brought a communication to the bank and taken from them an answer had left them on the street, and they had gone home. They could help no further.

Who was responsible? What would be the consequences? The brigadier didn't know. His life, he realised, had turned a half-circle, from confidence to hesitation, from sureness to uncertainty.

'At the entry to the Isfahan secure area, which is Zone 3C? What authorisation is needed, and whose signature is required? Go through the procedure, Mehrak.'

Sidney had just come into the room and heard the question. He wore sneakers and moved soundlessly; they seemed hardly to notice him. The corporal was still at the table, but Petroc Kenning circled the room slowly. Sidney had known of Mr Hector's nephew since the kid had first been packed off to boarding-school: the old man had displayed a photo of him, framed, as captain of a junior rugby team. He thought Petroc Kenning was losing his man. Not stupid, Sidney had been *there*, done *that*, seen *it*.

He wouldn't have survived in Vienna, a man whose services were in demand, unless he'd had the nose, the eye and the ear. He wouldn't have had the contacts book that listed the industrialist – on hard times and facing a tax inquiry – who'd take anything, cash in hand, for the rental of the villa on the hill outside Spitz. PK had complimented him on finding the place. He'd answered: 'The owner thinks it's for a porn-movie shoot over the next couple of weeks. Just a joke, my sense of humour.'

And, just a little thing but a trademark, he and Anneliese had looked up Iranian recipes on the web, and she'd do the man proud that evening when a break was called.

He had been retired by the Service on his fifth-fifth birthday but hadn't considered going back to London and grafting for a living there. He had all the contacts in the old espionage capital that anyone needed. He had been mentioned in despatches for fighting off an ambush in Aden, with the REME, and awarded a Military Medal: a hotel had been evacuated in Lisnaskea, Northern Ireland, a primed bomb at the reception desk, and a disabled guest had been left behind; an officer had bellowed that Sidney was not to go back inside but he'd told him to go fuck himself and had brought the guy out.

From slipping in to empty the ashtray and replace the tea glasses Sidney had learned that the Joe was wising up. He didn't answer straight off as he had in the morning and through the early afternoon, but took his time. Tired? Sidney didn't think so. He reckoned the Joe was back-sliding on the good stuff and needed to think about what he was saying. He himself didn't say anything – it wasn't his place.

'At 3C we did not have a pass or a signature. The major who commanded the guard detachment took us through and our ID cards were given to the gate, noted, then handed back to us. I don't know what would have happened if I had not been with the brigadier.'

* * *

'Zach?'

'Yes, Dad.'

His father had come onto the site as the daylight was failing, had joshed with the guys, then stood on the track Zach used for getting concrete, slopping in a wheelbarrow, into the ground floor.

'Is it a good time?'

'You're the boss. Of course it's a good time.'

'Let's walk a bit.'

His father seemed distracted and ill at ease.

'Problems, Dad?'

'Something I'd rather not be doing.'

'Spit it out.'

He sucked in his breath, then sighed. 'I'm letting you go, Zach.'

'*Sorry, what?*'

'You heard – it was clear enough. The job at the school, the Education Committee's cancelled it. The surgery up in Spa Lane's on hold for a year. I'm scraping the bottom of the barrel for work, spinning this one out for another couple of months. I'm sorry.'

'But I'm your *son*.' He hadn't anticipated this.

'Didn't expect you to make it easy – and your mother said you wouldn't. Pete and Danny are going too. The rest of the guys I'll keep as long as I can. Everyone who's staying has kids, a mortgage, and doing what they do is all they know. I owe it them.'

'What about me?'

A finger was jabbed at his chest. 'It's time you looked after yourself. It's been too long since you made your own decisions. You always used to. You insisted on going to London on that course – wouldn't change tack and do something useful. And it was your decision to cop out in the middle of exams so the money went down the drain. Bored with the course, I think you told your mother. I sorted you out, put you on the payroll. Couldn't have it said that my son was work-shy. No one in our family ever has been. What else did you decide? Looking to take over from me and run the business better than I can? Don't think so. Going to be one of the boys? No. Sorry, Zach, but last night clinched it,

Shane's session in the pub. You decided it didn't matter to you. They're my people and they matter to me, so I'll move mountains to find other work for Pete and Danny. That's how it is. What I'm saying, Zach, is that you should get yourself something that stretches you.'

Neither his mother, his father, nor his sister had ever talked straight to him before. There had never been an inquest around the breakfast table. If they had felt his decision to quit his course was rubbish, they had never said so. Now he realised that a dam of pent-up feelings had been breached. For years they had skirted round the subject of his future, where he was going.

'Yes, Dad.'

'You'll get a month's wages and you'll finish on Friday. The men I'm keeping need the money and know nothing except the building trade. You're better than that. Go for something that tests you.'

'Thanks for telling it like it is, Dad.'

They hugged, and he fancied his father's eye might have been damp – for the first time: he was a hard old beggar.

Zach remembered a day when he hadn't crossed the road. It was a winter evening, dark, on a north London street, and a man had been walking along the pavement when some kids had come out of an alley. He'd had on a suit and an overcoat, and was carrying a briefcase. The kids had hit him hard and fast, kneed his groin, then run off with the briefcase after a snatch search for a wallet. The man had struggled to his feet and stumbled away. It had happened two years ago. Zach had gone on twenty paces, then told himself he must play the Samaritan, but the victim was gone and the street was empty. Too late. Zach hadn't been to a police station and made a statement, had let it lie. He was ashamed, and the chance to redeem himself had never arisen. He held close to his father.

'Another thing – you'll never attract a decent woman, like your mother, if you don't find something worthwhile. For God's sake, you're better than this.'

4

The smoke seeped from Mehrak's lips and nostrils.

'The enrichment plant at Qom, when were you last there?'

'Two months ago.'

The room was fogged. Condensation ran in streams down the windows. Did the brigadier have responsibility at that location? He did not: he was there to advise. Had they gone inside? They had entered the underground facility. Deep underground? They had not entered the enrichment area. He could see, from the smoke hovering over the table that PK's eyes were watering, He kept rubbing them, aggravating the irritation. They didn't tell Mehrak not to smoke.

Undisguised exasperation. 'You didn't go far underground, but you went a little way. Correct?'

'That is right.' A photograph was pushed across the table. He could see the prominence of the hills, the buildings alongside the road and the great pit in the ground, with the track winding on the outside and descending. He remembered when he had driven there that he had been careful to watch for fallen rocks. It had seemed a half-finished construction site. Laden lorries inching down ahead of him and others stacked up behind. In the photograph, he spotted the place where he had been directed to park the Mercedes. He had been in uniform that day, wearing a sidearm, the brigadier's escort, so he was entitled to join the group of men welcoming the visitor. They had gone into the access tunnel. He had thought it like an ants' nest, filled with scrambling activity. There was the noise from the ventilation ducts, the air-conditioning and the generators. It was a labyrinth, and he had been inside.

'How many entrances, Mehrak?'

'I only saw one.'

'Did you come out the same way as you went in?'

He dragged at the last of the cigarette. It was still early in the morning, breakfast hardly digested and the ashtray nearly full. The question was repeated, a snatch of annoyance in the tone.

'It's simple enough, Mehrak. Did you leave by the same route?'

A finger pointed to the photograph, and he saw the small shadowy shapes, monochrome images, of the lorries and the few cars allowed into the restricted parking zone. He knew about the power of bombs. In his mind he saw the detonation of the ground-penetration monster that the Americans possessed that caused rock-falls and landslides, and imagined the gaping mouth of that tunnel sealed. He thought of many men and women, alive when he had been there, entombed. He imagined that the lighting and the power would fail and that the air would grow fetid . . .

'The same way in and out? Yes, Mehrak, or no?'

He had slept poorly. He couldn't have said that the bed was too hard or too soft or that the room was too warm or too cold. He had tossed, turned and examined each step of the road he had taken: how else he could have responded. He had done the business in the bank, and two men, who had said their job was to 'look after you, like a brother,' had bought him a meal that had cost what to him was a fortune. They had drunk alcohol, he had not, and he had heard the suggestion that he was a man of the world. He had thought of his humiliation at lying against Farideh's cold back, saw the multi-coloured bruise at her eye, and remembered how she had gone to work where her office could see what he had done to her. He could have refused the men's offer, could have taken a taxi to the airport and presented his ticket at a desk. He had not. Instead he had shrugged – he hadn't wanted to seem frightened of 'entertainment', had thought it would 'punish' his wife – and had gone. He could have walked into the brothel, allowed the two Arabs to go off with their girls than have made an excuse and taken a taxi. He had not. Would Farideh have cared if she'd known? He could no longer read his wife's mind.

'Mehrak, is there a problem?' He heard an edge in the voice. 'Yes or no – entry and exit.'

He stuttered, 'The same way.'

'Thank you, Mehrak. Remember, you agreed to co-operate. Please consider your side of the obligations. Do the principal staff live underground or do they come out at the end of their working day? Are they housed above ground?'

He saw the woman. He didn't know her name. He saw each movement of her fingers as she had slipped off the robe she had worn in the outer area. He hadn't chosen her, but she had taken his hand and led him through the drawn curtain into the corridor. He could have pulled away, but he had not. He had thought of Farideh, of how she would walk past him, naked, from the bathroom to the bedroom and seem not to see him. She had been in his mind when he had sat on that bed.

The British woman had come into the cubicle, had threatened him with exposure – adultery, disgrace, misuse of public funds – had talked of video and audio tapes. He had imagined the images of himself, crumpled, pitiful, mocked. The brigadier had enemies, as all prominent men did. Those enemies had circled, snatched the brigadier's driver and used him to hurt a target. Could he have dressed, walked past the woman and her escort to a taxi and faced the consequences? He might have been able to, but had not. And at the aircraft steps, he could have refused to go further, but he had not. He had signed, but he could have torn the paper to shreds. At many moments, he could have resisted and rejected them, but he had not.

'Mehrak, the scientists and engineers, do they live above ground or below?'

'They live in compounds at Fordo, go by bus each day to the tunnel.'

'Thank you, Mehrak. Were the materials brought by lorry checked for sabotage at the tunnel entrance or before they descended to that point?'

He fixed his gaze on PK's face. He dragged on the cigarette, than stubbed it out and let the smoke blow between them. 'What is my future?'

'We'll talk about that over lunch, perhaps this evening. Now, we're working.'

'How do I live, when you have finished with me?'

'We'll discuss that later, when I'm ready. When are the lorries checked?'

He subsided. He was alone. He took another cigarette. Any man who had seen Farideh spoke of her beauty. She had been his. He had brought her home. He had failed to interest or control her. He had failed to satisfy any part of her.

'The lorries go into a sealed area at the top of the descent and are searched there. They are not searched again at the tunnel. The cargo then goes by forklift to where it is wanted.'

He had been told, in conversation with a secretary when he had waited in an outer office, that the main enrichment area was eighty-five metres below ground, protected by rock. It would be their tomb.

'Mehrak, I understand, believe me, that this is difficult for you. You should understand what we're offering you – financial security, a new life and identity, not just as a driver and corporal but as a man who is respected and trusted by his new friends. Do you believe there are other tunnels for entry and exit, and do you know of the ventilation holes?'

He thought of his wife and silence hung around him. The smoke had thickened, and the sun was low. It glowered over the frosted grass and spilled onto the table. He thought of what he had done to her, and took the blame for it. He couldn't blame her.

Farideh had been told to sit. She was in the kitchen and the chair was hard. She should have been at work an hour ago. Kourosh was with them.

They had brought no woman to question her. Kourosh – who had once said he wanted nothing more than to sleep with her – didn't speak. He had not been first through the door but had hung back when she had opened it and they'd barged in, flattening her against the wall. She was shown a card of the Ministry of Intelligence and Security. She had been in her blouse and jeans. A man had told her to go to the bedroom and put on appropriate clothing. Her anger had been genuine.

What was their business? What right had they to come into her home? Did they not know her husband was an official of the al-Qods?

When they had started to search the apartment, to open drawers and tip out the contents, go through pockets in the wardrobe and and sift papers, what were they searching for?

No one answered her. It would have been the same when the men from MOIS had gone to Johnny's mother's home and rifled though his possessions, finding sufficient evidence to pass a sentence of death. She could see, through the open door, that Kourosh was in her bedroom, the bed unmade, and would have seen the indent at the side, where she had lain, naked except for the fine cotton nightdress that had been a present from Mehrak's mother. He was on the far side of the bed from hers, going through her husband's pockets, shelves and drawers, sifting among his clothing. She didn't know if he had betrayed her. A false move, and she could kill him; a mistake from him would kill her. Neither showed recognition of the other.

Later, the questions.

'Where is your husband?' She didn't know.

'Don't lie. You know where he is.' She snarled back that she hadn't lied, she didn't know: they should ask the brigadier where her husband was.

'Has he run away?' That was ridiculous, she said, but the idea shook her.

'When was your last call from him?' She said he hadn't called her since he had left their home four days ago.

'He didn't ring you from the airport, or Dubai?' She hadn't known he'd gone abroad. What was he doing in Dubai? They didn't tell her.

'When were you expecting him back?' She snapped that she didn't question her husband on work matters.

'Where's your phone?' She pointed to it on the low table by the door and tried to assume an air of innocence. The man in front of her slapped her face. She had been – until the first of the *basij* had beaten her – a loyal, unquestioning supporter of the regime. She had assumed – until Johnny was taken to the gallows – that only the guilty and enemies of the Islamic Republic were targets of MOIS agents. Her face stung. Beyond the man, Kourosh looked at the ceiling. Would he give his life, as Johnny had, to protect her? Would she give her life to— Her handbag was emptied over the table. Her purse, cosmetics, hairbrush, ID, smart card to get into the office and the notebook in which she wrote her shopping lists cascaded out.

They opened her phone, removed the SIM card, dropped it back on the table.

'Where's my husband?'

It was four years and a few weeks since the *basij* had beaten her, and since she had let him made love to her. She pictured him – sallow, a little overweight, jowls, pockmarks and uneven teeth. There was a scar on his forehead that she knew was from the shrapnel of an Israeli bomb, and blisters on his ears from the desert heat of eastern Iraq.

'We think he has fled Iran and gone to a foreign power. We think he's betrayed us. We have an arm that will reach to wherever he is. If you had knowledge of this and failed to denounce him, if you thought that soon you would leave Iran to join him, then you were deluded. There is no mercy for those who wage war against God, for traitors.'

Another asked, 'Do you have a passport? We haven't found one.'

The laugh was brittle and laced with contempt. 'I'm the wife of a corporal, I work on a reception desk. Why would I need passport? Where would I go? Paris, Rome?'

She was hit again. The other cheek. This blow was harder: her lip split and she was flung to the floor.

Kourosh was the last to leave. He hadn't looked at her.

'I want my wife.'

The man, PK, seemed not to hear. The question was put again: 'What time would the principals arrive at the tunnel entrance?'

'I want to be with my wife.'

'What time in the morning do the buses drop the principals, and what time in the evening are they picked up?'

'If I cannot have my wife, I will go back.'

'Are you tired? You're talking shit. We're all tired – "I will go back,"' he mimicked Mehrak's slow English. He seemed to freeze, cold face and cold eyes. Mehrak, for fuck's sake, you were in a whorehouse. Can we move on?'

'I want to be with my wife.'

'You've said that. What time?' The man, PK, had in front of him a large pad and his questions were scrawled across the pages, then ticked when Mehrak answered them.

'They arrive at seven in the morning and leave at six in the evening. I want my wife. If I am with my wife I will tell you where on the road they are best ambushed, where mines could be put, what is the car that is used by the director and by the director's deputy. I will tell you the list of the targets that al-Qods has drawn up if the Zionists attack our facilities, where, abroad, we will strike. I will tell you what I know of the responses if an attack is made, air or ground troops, as I have heard them in the car . . . There has been talk in the car of reports from agents who are in Berlin and Washington, and in Tel Aviv, and where they have access and what they learn . . . I want my wife.'

A pen was thrown down, and the notepad pushed away. He thought the man, PK, tried for self-control, then abandoned it.

'Mehrak. Listen. Not many men who love their wife go to whorehouses. The two, on a set of scales, don't balance.'

'The oil installations at Dhahran, in the Kingdom, will be bombed. The Israeli embassy in Mexico City, the British military installations in Gibraltar, the Sixth Fleet that is in southern Italy and where the reprisal would come by submarine and frogmen . . . You want more, PK? I want my wife.'

Were they listening to him? Yes. The session broke.

'I don't know what he's done, the fool.'

What Farideh, the corporal's wife, knew of surveillance she had learned from Johnny. She had learned more from the Captain. She took two bus rides, each time boarding and stepping off late, then walked through a defile in the bazaar, near her father's linen stall, and went where a vehicle couldn't follow. She had been on a wide street, doing windows and reflections. In central Tehran, the cold hung in the air with the risk of sleet in the evening. She had been to work.

There she had faced clients of the insurance company. Her colleagues and superiors, the motorists coming for cover, would have seen the marks on her face, where the skin had reddened, and the small cut on her lower lip that was oozing. She had made no attempt to hide the marks or to explain them. They might have thought her husband had hit her again. No one would have believed that the wife of a junior official in the al-Qods unit had been hit by men from the Ministry of Intelligence and Security – and no one would have believed that the young woman, an example of loyalty, duty and humility, had been accused of complicity in the flight of her husband to the agencies of a hostile power. It had been suggested she might go home. Was she tired? They were curious, she could see, and nervous, but none wished involvement. She had said she would go home, had left by the back entrance and started the anti-surveillance procedures that two lovers had shown her.

'He's a creature of the regime but they say he has run to an enemy. It's impossible.' She was in the garage. She told Excellency and Highness what little she knew and what had been done to her. 'He drives a car, is stupid, a thug. What could he know that an enemy would want to hear?'

They kept at their work, never looked at her. A carburettor had been stripped and spread across a bench, and a Vespa scooter had been cannibalised so that another could survive. They neither stopped nor interrupted her. They had never said that it would have been better if she had never come, if Johnny had never seen her. It was four years since Johnny, whom they had known since he was a child, had brought her here for the first time. She had been bleeding, bruised, in shock, and he had taken her up the narrow stairs into the room over the workshop. The bruises had barely gone before it was over, and she had waited each day – as they had – for the agents of the MOIS to come for them. Johnny was dead.

Two years had passed when she had drunk tea with them and gone back to the marriage that shackled her. Then she had brought the Captain here: handsome, carefree, fearing nothing. The old men had never criticised her for bringing him to the yard and exposing them. Johnny had lasted four weeks and the Captain had been with her for five, then had gone. He had died in faraway Afghanistan, working as an expert in ordnance. He had been mentoring on the laying of bombs. An officer who had been with him, working in uneasy alliance with Taliban fighters, had said he had not been himself on that mission. He had been 'distracted and his mind was elsewhere'. A Canadian sniper had killed him at 1100 metres: he had allowed himself to be fully visible and hadn't first scanned the ridge on the far side of the riverbed.

His mother had told Excellency what had happened when he had gone to her with the story of having a scooter for her son to buy. She had confided to him that a photograph had been returned with her son's personal possessions – a woman's head, all but her eyes hidden. Farideh believed the Captain's infatuation with her had killed him: they had made love in the room above the workshop – it had been noisier, faster and more brutal than it had been with Johnny.

They started to reassemble the carburettor.

'He's a fool – it can't be true.'

Highness said, 'But he has ears and is close to the seat of power, as we both were. He'd be a great catch for the Americans, the Jews or the British – to any of the revolution's enemies. Don't dismiss him.'

Excellency said, 'We must be vigilant. Take great care.'

She left them, didn't know where to turn – and headed for her home.

'"Everything you want, or nothing." Is that a direct quote?'

'That was exactly what he said. I asked how he would show his gratitude.'

'What did you get?'

'He talked about the accounts and scams of two other brigadiers, one from al-Qods and one from the general IRGC. Our boy was driving and Joyberi had an investigator, corruption business, in the back with him. It's drugs. The conversation was four months ago and our boy may not be the sharpest knife in the box but has a good memory. He spilled values, bulk of shipments and the dates they went through. He's revelling in it, thinks we're on the back foot.'

'Are we?'

'We are – because it's a hell of an ask. But if we turn him down, what'll he do? Go back? It'd be a gamble. He'd have to rely on friends in high places. He's a fighting man.'

'I'm listening.'

'He's been in Afghanistan, south Lebanon and Iraq. Two fire fights. We caught him at a moment of maximum personal crisis, but he's starting to manage the difficulty. Stubborn enough? Probably. Oh, and he says . . .'

'Yes, Petroc?'

'Yesterday afternoon he should have been at Tehran Central railway station to pick up his man. The brigadier would have been left high and dry, not best pleased. Very soon, if not already, the security apparatus will come up with the right answer and put a ball and chain on her ankle, know what I mean?'

'Yes indeed.'

'Tadeuz, I'm passing you the parcel. You have to make fast decisions and—'

'Don't state the obvious, Petroc. I'll be back.'

In the secure room at the embassy, Petroc Kenning cut the link. He had used the facility to transmit in 'burst' form the principal sections of the audio. The analysts needed it, evaluation would follow, something for them to worry at in terrier mode. The Vienna station chief had sat outside the room, with its lead-lined walls and no window: his world was to do with meetings at the International Atomic Energy Authority and shadowing Tehran's people, looking for weakness, sexual, financial or ideological, and interpret the language of Iran's prime negotiator. Petroc didn't know him but had begged use of the facility. He was sweating when he came out, and didn't dare to hope. He thanked the station chief and was led out and up the stairs. Sidney was parked behind the closed gates in the backyard of the embassy compound.

They'd done the tour on the way in from the village on the Danube. Sidney had seemed disappointed that Petroc – Mr Hector's nephew – had shown little interest in the sights of the city. One stone fountain was much like another, as were statuettes of eighteenth-century generals on prancing chargers. A statue of Mozart and another of a woman draped in a sheet and holding a spear seemed sufficient. He'd perked up at the Russian war memorial, with a double-lifesize Red Army soldier perched on a high plinth, a gold-leaf helmet and an AK assault rifle. Polly would have liked the city, would have wanted an opera evening.

He came out into the fading light, with more rain about to fall. The car door was opened for and closed after him. Sidney started the engine, eased out through the embassy's gates onto the road, then stopped.

'Is the kibosh on it, Petroc?'

He did not enjoy the familiarity, but Sidney had been Hector's sidekick.

'It'll get "careful thought".'

'Not knocked down?'

'Not yet. Are we staying here or going?'

Sidney ignored his question. 'Have you seen her picture? It was in his wallet.'

'I have.'

'Great-looking woman. He can't walk away from her. Can I tell you what I think, Petroc?'

'Do you need permission, Sidney?' He'd tried irony, but knew it would go unrecognised.

'We all think, Petroc, that we understand women, but we're pissing in the wind. Closed book and all that. He loves her but I don't think she gives a toss about him and it's driving him mad.

Given the opportunity, he sloped off to Cock Alley because he's not getting it at home. Are we going to fetch her?'

Were they? Tadeuz Fenton was already in a hole and was likely to dig deeper. He'd let the word drop to Friends and Cousins that an interesting fish had been reeled in so the pressure on him was building and would inevitably get heavier. Would he take the chance, call the corporal's bluff and leave the door open for him? Or would he go the extra mile? And the rest.

'This would have been perfect for Mr Hector, right up his street.'

'And times have changed, Sidney.' He paused. 'It would be a hell of a show, though, what legends are made of.'

'Right now you're covered in crap, Petroc. Pull this off, bring her out – the Yanks'll be wetting themselves – and you could walk on water. You'd be right up there with your uncle – a star.'

The car moved off but didn't turn back towards the Rennweg. Instead of heading for the ring road it went on down Jauresgasse, did a couple of blocks and Petroc saw enough of the flag to recognise the lateral stripes of green, white and red. Sidney braked, flicked open his door and stepped out. Petroc watched. Sidney's business was at the side of the building that housed the mission of the Islamic Republic of Iran and involved the quick use of a sharp penknife. There was a little garden, with a wrought-iron fence and shrubs poking through it. A rose in full bloom was weighed down by rain water. One slash, and Sidney had the flower. There might have been a camera on him, or not. He walked back, eased into his seat, wrapped the stem in a tissue and passed it to Petroc.

'I'm sure you know your Robbie Burns – Hector did.'

The question rang in Petroc's ears: 'Are we going to fetch her?'

They drove fast back to the safe house. He knew Tadeuz Fenton well enough to picture him and his postures. 'Are we up for it? Why not?' Petroc thought it was the stuff that reputations were made of, a career tipping point. His uncle Hector was a colossus. Failure to answer that question, 'Are we going to fetch her?' made officers into journeymen. Why not fetch her?

* * *

'Don't even think about counting us in.' He had a pleasant voice and rarely raised it. Barrie was the liaison officer at Vauxhall Cross for the Special Boat Service, and was covering that afternoon for Angus, Special Air Service, who was at a veteran's funeral in Hereford. 'It's a categoric "no". I don't want to hear any more. I'm sorry, Mr Fenton, but you'll have to look elsewhere. Frankly, my advice is to bin it because whoever you get will have a bad experience. The proposition isn't viable. It'll end in tears. It's not for us.'

'Thank you for your frankness, Tadeuz, and for explaining your thoughts, but I'm going to decline the invitation.' Since he had become CEO of an internationally recognised supplier of private military contractors who had experience in guarding British diplomats and agents of the Service, Marcus had never before turned down an offer without seeing a full brief. Offices down the corridor and on lower floors of the Mayfair headquarters were stuffed with former Special Forces men and those who had taken early leave of the intelligence family across the Thames. He spoke softly into the phone and realised he had damaged his link with a valued source of income. 'Forgive me, but the only men you'll get for a job like that are the sort of cowboys we try very hard to keep off our books. Cowboys are the kiss of death. They foul up and spread collateral. The proposition reeks of desperation and I doubt it's been thought through. You face a setback so you bite the bullet. It's mad. You won't find anyone worthwhile prepared to contemplate it.'

The sign on the waiting-room door stated that smoking was prohibited. It was ignored.

Ralph Cotton, the youngest, arrived last – he'd had furthest to come. 'I'm a bit late, but it's been a bugger of a journey. Do you know what it's all about?'

The eldest, Michael Wilson, had only had to cross Central London to get to Contego Security offices in Ealing's high street. 'Only that the brown stuff's in the fan, and it's panic stations, spook business.'

Walter Davies lit the cigarettes. 'Are we likely to be first choice, or have we come off the bench?'

There was quiet, mirthless laughter in the waiting room. The main companies used smart West End addresses that had 'class' written all over them. Not too much of that in the far west of the capital. They waited, which private military contractors did well. Anyway, all three of them would be glad of some work – any work, within reason. They heard phones going in the inner offices and stressed-out voices, but no one had told them what to expect, only that *it* was being put together. They weren't men who did war stories or talked themselves up, and within fifteen minutes of Ralph Cotton's arrival they were slumped and asleep.

'What am I looking for? The best – what else? The best linguist with the biggest balls.'

Persian Studies were taught at the School. Sara Rogers had walked over the bridge, taken a tube ride across London and slipped into the building behind the Senate House of London University. She knew the lecturer, tentacles spread wide from Vauxhall Cross into the world of academics. Behind her was a developing madhouse. Whether or not she approved of the route taken by her superior, her mid-week lover, was immaterial. Loyalty ran deep in her. She knew the lecturer and trusted him. Sara Rogers had come from the ranks in the Secret Intelligence Service, had been a copy-typist when she joined and now was gatekeeper to one of the powers in the monstrous building. The lecturer she had cultivated assiduously over the years was a director of the School's Persian language (Farsi) and literature course. Her trust had its foundations in the death of the lecturer's grandfather – an army officer put before a firing squad on the roof of a building in central Tehran during the second week after the return of the Imam. It had been strengthened by the death of his father, from kidney failure, after a security police beating following arrest on his return to Iran to visit elderly female relatives. His hatred of the regime was nurtured quietly, so he was unlikely to be compromised, in Sara Rogers's judgement: a vociferous critic might have been turned, phone calls reaching the activist and telling him, or her, of what *might* happen to members of an extended family still resident in the Islamic Republic.

She was at the back of the building in a small office on the fourth floor and the majority of the kids were in the union near the main entrance. The corridor was quiet.

She was brusque: 'I'm hitting brick walls. I don't want an Iranian boy – no offence, and I'd trust you with my life – because I don't have time for background checks or for getting into his head. My office can't throw anyone up. Neither can the flower people in the big place. I need help so I've come to you.'

The 'big place' was Whitehall and the 'flower people' were the diplomats of the Foreign and Commonwealth office. A woman on one of the Gulf desks had done an insertion job a few years back and been commended, had laughed when she'd heard what was proposed, then pleaded inadequate Farsi. Anyway, her hair was almost golden. Tadeuz had authorised Sara to go outside. And there were enough potential SIS, FCO and MoD young people coming through the School to ensure its good co-operation.

She could be specific. 'I want a good kid, one who can play native if the examination isn't too rigorous. Language has to be excellent – and they have to have balls.'

The lecturer paused, considered, then reached down to a drawer in his desk, unlocked it and produced a bottle of dry sherry and paper cups. He poured two good measures and talked. The school had the best reputation in the country, was superior to Cambridge, in immersing students in Iranian culture. The aims of the three-year course were to enable the student to read, write, speak and listen, and to understand the beauty of the poetry of the last several centuries. Serious students boosted their language skills with audio tapes, satellite TV, Iranian films, and stayed close to the BBC Persian Service and its broadcasts to Iran. They went through stages of being confident in the language, then functional and, if bright, would be operational. If a student was 'outstanding' his language skill would be extensive – *fluency*, as good as it gets. The drawback: there were no longer exchange visits to Iran, too much political baggage, and any who did get there were on a two-week tourist visa and might backpack a bit but wouldn't have enrolled in an Iranian university. He sipped his sherry.

'How many do I get to choose between?'

A wry, smile. There was just one. In a world of box-ticking, one *might* be considered suitable for approach. There had been a boy who had proved an exceptional and unlikely linguist, the best in a decade, and he had missed all the stereotypical profiles. He came from the south Midlands. His fingers flew over the keyboard and the screen jerked to life. The first of his family to win a university place, he had chosen the school and Persian. He had been way ahead of his peers, but had fallen out of love with the course.

'Maybe we're getting there. How far out of love?'

Most students, the lecturer said, were tolerant of the excesses of the regime. They countered stories of stonings, beatings, political arrests and public executions with references to 'rendition', Guantánamo and Abu Ghraib. They did not like the proliferation of nuclear weapons, but did not condemn Iran for wanting them and pointed to threats from Israel, America, Britain and France to justify the Iranian programme. And there had been the election four years back. It was clear that the regime had stolen the votes, but as the kids had seen it, the true blame lay with those at the heart of the conspiracy to destroy Iran. Goldman Sachs, the CIA, J. P. Morgan. One had not bought into the generality. They had started their final exams. The lecturer had believed this student would sweep the board bare of awards, but he'd walked out, gone home. He'd bought a postcard at Euston station, had addressed it to him and written: 'I accept you cannot parachute in democracy but I have no further interest in studying a nation and its leaders and peoples where fraud and corruption are so dense. I apologise for wasting your time and thank you sincerely for many kindnesses. Best, Zach.' He put the card in the letterbox at the station, no stamp, and had left the School's radar. The lecturer had never heard of him again, but had lobbied hard enough at the School for him to be awarded his first-class degree, then had phoned, written and texted with employment suggestions. He had received no reply. The student was 'outstanding', 'the best', and to have quit in the middle of his exams on a point of principle – his revulsion at the larceny of the regime and its violence – showed he had balls.

They laughed. The screen was tilted towards Sara Rogers.

He said, 'He's highly intelligent, determined and has character. Why else would I have worked so hard to try to bring him back to the fold? He's one of those kids that sort of lose their way in education and miss out on fulfilling their promise. That doesn't mean he's a waste of space. Anyway, He's all I have for you. Good luck.'

She saw the address, a home phone number and the names of the parents. She put the details of Zachariah Joshua Becket in her phone. 'And he's a good guy? Can you recommend him? Is he capable and . . . ?'

Capable? The lecturer shrugged. It might depend on what he was asked to do. They shook hands.

Walking from the building, threading through the students who milled in the hallway outside their union, Sara Rogers thought this might be as good as it would get. Life was about the art of the possible or some such. Outside, on the steps, with a cold wind whipping her, she rang in.

He watched Mehrak, the little corporal. One of them was always with him.

They used the interview room with the view over the vines, and women swung big plastic buckets of grapes onto the trailers. The rose was in a small glass vase in the centre of the table. Auntie had been told, but Mehrak had not. Auntie understood the significance, also that decisions with seismic consequences had been made behind the door of the secure room and in London. He'd said it to himself: *For real* . . . He had asked himself: *Does he justify the hassle?* Sidney – too full of himself, shouldn't have been on the inside of the team – had explained the significance of the rose and where it had been taken from. Auntie, too, knew his Burns, could have recited several of the Scot's better known verses and had seen the picture.

He had the previous day's English paper in front of him and

worried at the crossword. For Auntie, all of those dealing with the Iranian were walking in a minefield, and he couldn't judge what small-talk to make. Petroc Kenning had been in three times since his return from Vienna and had put probing questions about detail, each preceded by 'We're looking at this very seriously, but we have to know what we're going to get' and 'It's a huge step, not to be undertaken lightly' and 'I have to persuade people that you're worth the effort.' Thc corporal told him the locations of storage bunkers for warheads, conventional, and the logistics of munitions shipments to the Hezbollah forces, directed by the 1800 Unit, in south Lebanon. The final time, Petroc had quizzed him on personalities at the Natanz enrichment centre and the new leadership there. Then he had hurried out, his pad covered with pencilled notes.

Would he have done the deal? Or would he, instead, have left the front door open and enough euros on the hall table for Mehrak to buy a bus ticket, then one for the train to Vienna and a taxi to the embassy? Would Auntie have believed Mehrak?

My love is like a red red rose
That's newly sprung in June . . .

Her picture was on the wall in the secure room and was blown to twice life-size. The pixels showed up the imperfections of focus and blurred the outlines of her cheeks, but couldn't destroy her prettiness.

My love is like the melody
That's sweetly played in tune . . .

Sidney had said the love between them was one-sided. Could be – she was awesomely pretty and he had been hauled out of a brothel. It made no sense. The man came alive when questioned and seemed to sense his importance, but slumped each time Petroc left him. Auntie, aged fifty-three, understood little of man's attraction to woman, except that extreme danger so often followed the linkage.

As fair art thou, my bonnie lass,
So deep in love am I . . .

He could smell the talc he had sprinkled on his body, but the scent of the rose won through. He lived with his sister, Maureen, in Cloghy on the Ards peninsula of the Province, and their spaniel. Over the years he had been in the pay of the Royal Ulster Constabulary, A Branch of MI5, then the SIS, and stayed in London in a one-bedroom Battersea studio. He regarded himself as near to Heaven when he was with the dog, braced against the winds, and walked along the coast of the Irish Sea. He had experience with defectors, had handled 'touts', who had been compromised or turned from the Provisional Wing of the Irish Republican Army and become informants. He realised the value of men who betrayed their friends, community or country. He didn't have to like the traitors, but he would be formally polite. He thought it appropriate that the red rose was on the table.

And I will love thee still, my dear,
Till a' the seas gang dry.

He appreciated the man's loneliness, and the doubts that ate into him . . . and he thought that the game Petroc Kenning was playing now stank of risk. Too sour for Auntie to stomach? Irrelevant: his opinion would not be sought. The light was failing and he couldn't concentrate on the crossword. The silence was a wall between them.

At the entrance to the site, Dunc Whitcombe introduced himself with a bogus name, smiling as he always did when he lied. He'd brought with him an interpreter that FCO used in tandem with the Service, a national, who was elderly and a long-time refugee from the regime. There was serious mud in front of them and Dunc murmured that it would be better if he waited close to the gate, then repeated, as he had many times in the car, what was expected. He went forward, found a sort of bridge over the slime, single planks end to end. It challenged him but he made progress. He wore a trilby, always did to go to work, and would have been the only man on the site not hard-hatted.

He heard a grinding squeal, then a shout. 'Do you mind getting off this?' The man behind him had a wheelbarrow of wet cement and needed the planks.

He said affably, 'I was looking for Zach Becket.'

'Looking in the right place. You've found him – but not till this lot's delivered.'

Dunc Whitcomb stepped off the plank, stood to the side and the mud came over his shoes. The barrow's wheel squealed again and the load went past. He heard chortles, and thought he might have been the cause. He had a handkerchief, put out that morning with his clean shirt, underwear and socks. He regained the plank and tried to use the handkerchief to wipe off the mud. If it went pear-shaped now, he wasn't sure that another option existed. The mud clung to his feet. The barrow wheel squeaked closer.

'I'm Zach, what can I do for you?'

In front of the Friend and the Cousin, there were single memory sticks, pushed across the table to them by Tadeuz Fenton. The Israeli and the American sensed the crisis and didn't hurry him.

'I've told you what we have and this is a taster of what we're getting. We value it but we've hit a wall. We're dealing with a man on the edge and he's closed down on us. The evaluation is that he's not a waterboard or fingernail-removal case. Something marginally more subtle is required. I'm going out on a limb. Gentlemen, I need help from each of you.'

He was a minor player, and accepted it. They had had a bare ten minutes with the sticks but would have been able to use their phones to fast-track into a sense of the material on offer. Another view: he wanted to kick the ball round the park with the Agency and the Mossad. The Agency would nod each time the Stuxnet virus, which had eaten into the software of the enemy's nuclear computers, was mentioned, and the Mossad would offer a raised eyebrow when a nuclear scientist or engineer in downtown Tehran flicked his car ignition and went on a fast ride to Paradise. The MOIS big players would regard Tadeuz Fenton – if they knew of his existence and had bothered to prepare a dossier on him – and his efforts as having little more than nuisance value.

He told them the time scale and what he wanted. The Cousin whistled and the Friend gulped, then drummed his fingers on the table. He was humiliated that he had had to grovel but didn't doubt that both could deliver on his requests, if they cared to.

She finished her presentation. 'That's about it, as background and the mission statement. If you don't want a part in it, please, close the door after you. Otherwise sign on the line.'

There were three sheets of paper on the table, printouts. Mandy Ross pointed to the place, took a pen from her handbag and waited to see who would use it first. She thought that Contego Security would have produced those most likely to join up: a small firm, off the smart circuit's radar, offering a little more of a family than the bigger companies. She wondered how troubled a man would have to be to accept the offer, and how out of love with life. She had been given their files by the chief executive officer, had skimmed them in his office and knew who each man was, and who would lead. Only a brief hesitation. Wilson first, the veteran, then Cotton, the youngest, who looked as though he had once had money but was now familiar with hardship. Davies was last and signed with a flourish.

She took back the pen, bagged the papers and grimaced. 'Excellent. Thank you. I'm sure it'll be a good show.'

Among the three, hardly a word had been said, but now Wilson spoke up: 'Hope you're right, ma'am. Special Forces would have been the natural first call and they're not here – they turned it down. Companies like Control Risks, Aegis, Erinys and Olive would have been next in the pecking order. So, it's us, which means a fuck-up, excuse me, is rated as probable by the best and the brightest, and a fuck-up where we're going is bad news. But, ma'am, you'll get a best effort from us. When do we get to meet the golden boy?'

He might have had a beer too many. He had the back seat of the car to himself and was sprawled across it so he could lapse into and out of sleep. Dunc drove and the Iranian, no name given, was in the front passenger seat.

They had gone to the pub. Before that, though, the man waiting by the car had started to talk to him in good street-quality Farsi, no explanation. Why the hell did a guy in a suit come onto a building site in the south Midlands, ask for him, then trek him off to talk Farsi? No explanation. They'd talked about newspapers in the capital, the price of tomatoes in the bazaar, the best films that were likely to come onto the circuit of the capital's cinemas, the looming election, the jobs crisis, the traffic and the city's smog. They had talked for nearly three-quarters of an hour.

Then Dunc had touched the man's arm and he'd stepped back two paces. Dunc must have asked him something because the man had given a vigorous nod – as if Zach had passed a test with flying colours. Then Dunc had sent the man to the car outside the site gate, and had made the proposition.

Zach hadn't argued, hadn't haggled about the money on offer, equal to a couple of months of what his father had paid him. He thought he had been treated as an adult. Dunc had been blunt and to the point. *What* was required, *when* and *why*. He wasn't given a week to make up his mind, or told he could sleep on it. The light had been slipping and they were still talking when the shift ended and the team were piling off the site. He'd called to them: if they wanted a pint off him they should be at the Adelaide in an hour. He'd had an offer of work and was taking it. Then Zach had put a newspaper on the back seat of the car, because his clothes were filthy, and had directed the driver, Dunc, to his lodging.

He'd a shower, put his jeans, waterproofs and fleece into a bin bag, then sluiced the mud off his boots and wiped them half dry with kitchen roll. He left the food and milk from his fridge in a box outside a neighbour's door and put the rest of what he owned into another bag. A note for his landlady on the table, his thanks, and a month's rent, supplied by Dunc. Outside, he'd put his key through the letterbox and they'd gone to the pub. He thought it was to humour him that Dunc, from London, hadn't demurred about the pub, but the man's eyes had stayed on him, judging him.

The boys were there. Where was he going? Down south. How long for? Open-ended. What was he going to do? A bit of this and a bit of that. They'd lost interest and drunk the beer. There had been satellite football and a band that was auditioning for a Saturday-night slot. The place had a mellow feel and the music was sentimental, its message about loneliness, home and a girl. Dunc had asked if he needed to phone his parents and Zach had said he didn't – the site manager, Terry, would tell them in the morning. Was there a girl he wanted to speak to? No. One minute he'd been in the pub, and the next he was gone. His exit would have been masked by the band's anthem and the goal scored in the match. He would have been in the car park, maybe inside the car and turning onto the road, before any of them had realised he'd left.

The immediate destination? He didn't ask.

The people who'd be escorting him? He'd find that out.

The woman to whom the proposition would be put? Time for that later.

Zach Becket dozed. He couldn't have given a sensible answer if someone had asked why he'd accepted a ride with a stranger towards a country that was paranoid about spies and infiltrators, and inflicted punishments that fitted crimes. He didn't know why he'd agreed to travel, but he did know a little of the poetry he'd learned years before. *The Book of Kings*: Ferdowsi, writing fifty years before William's archer had put an arrow into Harold's eye –

I am deathless,
I am the eternal Lord
For I have spread the seed of the Word . . .

The car took him to the airport.

And Zach didn't know whether he heard the man say, into his hands-free phone, or had dreamed it, 'He's been very good . . . A clear road, and we're making good time . . . Say again . . . Will he stand strong? Maybe. Look at it another way. He has to. We're all up the creek if he doesn't . . . What do I think? With him, we have a chance. You know, funny thing, he never blinked. As if he'd been waiting for me, hoping I'd call by, was doing him a favour. He's a bright enough lad, and seems to have some fibre to him. Can't say more . . . I'll see you there . . . That's my bottom line, a chance. Can't say more.' Might have dreamed it, might not. What had he done? Well, he'd crossed the road. But that was only a start.

5

The huge aircraft had lifted, tilted to a sharp angle, and they were up.

Goodbye to Ramstein, near to Kaiserslautern, Germany, and the 521st Air Mobile Operations Wing. Hello, some time ahead, to İncirlik in Turkey, and another American oasis, the 39th Air Base Wing, far from home. A flight had brought them from Northolt to the USAF base, and there had been an hour in a lounge, sequestered from any facilities, with a guard at the door. They had been called forward and had gone by bus to a distant apron, where Zach had gulped at the sight of the transport that would take them south, east, and beyond the far edge of the Mediterranean.

They were the only passengers. The cabin was filled with pallets on which crates were covered with netting and strapped down with floor stays. They had been given an emergency-procedure drill during taxi and Zach had listened hard. He fancied the woman had too, but the man in the suit hadn't, and neither had the 'guys'. The American sergeant had sounded bored with what he had to say – but he'd seemed to imply that if anything went wrong then the hope of getting out was marginal.

They climbed and the four engines moaned. The air inside the cabin seemed to sing, and when they levelled out the same sergeant brought plastic beakers of coffee and candy, a thick, toffee-like substance. Music started up on the speakers, country-and-western.

This leg of the journey was 1,500 miles, the American had said, and would take a bit more than four hours, if they weren't troubled by head winds, or speeded up by gales behind them. Zach had never been in an aircraft remotely similar.

It wasn't the only thing new in his life. He had heard them out, Dunc and Mandy. Mandy was beside him, and Dunc had a canvas seat on the other side of the guys. Dunc still wore the suit in which he had come to the building site. His shoes had been worked on during the wait at Northolt, a machine in Ramstein had done a fine job and now they shone dully. He had met Mandy at Northolt, with the guys. She was alert and aloof, and he thought she wanted to erase any sign of her femininity. She wore a pair of black trousers, with a matching jacket and a white blouse. Her hair was cut short. Dunc's talk had taken place in the half-light on the site, and she had reinforced the message in a corner of the waiting area at Northolt.

He had said: 'It's a matter that we in the Service regard as exceptionally important, and we're bending over backwards to make it work, but I would be derelict in my duty if I didn't emphasise that the risks involved are very real. You're entitled to turn round, finish your shift . . .'

She had said, 'You have to be up for it. We're providing you with the protection we hope is adequate. We've asked you because it's not appropriate, in our current political climate, to put in those who work for government. Same reason as the shooters aren't from Hereford or Poole but the private sector. Take a deep breath, Zach, and either go through the gate when the flight's called or make for the exit. You won't get another chance to choose.'

Neither Dunc nor Mandy had asked why he hadn't walked. Maybe they weren't interested. He couldn't have said why he was there. Justification would come later, he was confident.

The aircraft had long levelled out. There were blinds down over the portholes. It was black-painted, a big beast, and there was a sweet, even rhythm to the engines. The cabin lights were dimmed and the music was soothing. He didn't sleep, and neither did Mandy, but the shooters did.

They hadn't welcomed him, but neither had they been hostile. He'd sensed they had eyed, weighed and evaluated him – not unlike when he had first come onto the site, the boss's boy, and the rule had been run over him. They were his escort and the introductions had been cool: they were Ralph, Wally and Mikey. He thought Mikey, the eldest, ran the team.

The bags had been delivered to the aircraft at Northolt when they were in their seats. They had been carried into the cabin by two Military Police and dumped in a forward stowage area. They had not been opened until they were at Ramstein, with time to kill. The items had been ticked off against a handwritten list on a single sheet, and the shooters handled the stuff with care. Mikey had done the ticking, Wally the sharing out, and Ralph had bagged the items so that each man would have what he needed. For each, 1 SIG Sauer P226 pistol and three magazines, empty, plus 100 rounds. And for each, 1H&K G36K assault rifle and three magazines, empty, plus 200 rounds of ammunition in sealed cardboard boxes. And, also, for each, six smoke grenades, and six 'flash-and-bang' grenades. There was a personal medical kit for each, including Zach. He had been shown a tourniquet and bandages, antibiotics and paracetamol, and had stuffed them into his rucksack with his socks, one half-decent shirt, his best jeans, underwear, T-shirts and a thick sweater. A 'trauma bag' went to Wally, and the satphone was left with Mikey. None of the weapons was armed and the American, who called himself a 'loadmaster', had them all up forward and isolated from them. They had all been given maps, and there was the photograph. Zach had that. It was in a cellophane sleeve.

She looked straight out at him. The eyes in the picture were unwavering and lanced his. She was Farideh, which meant 'unique', 'precious' or 'delightful'. Her eyes had challenged him. He couldn't imagine that, having seen her face, he would turn his back on her. The image was head and shoulders, shot in a street, and was blurred. She had made no attempt to pose. Mandy had told him it had come from the wallet of a defector, who would fail to deliver unless he was reunited with his wife. There was magnetism in the eyes, and he had thought it the more powerful because she had made no effort to please the man behind the viewfinder.

They had given him a map with a red cross on a building, and a satellite photograph of a street, with parked cars, people on the pavements, buses and vans, shop fronts and a doorway circled in the same red ink. Dunc had said, 'We asked him where his home was, where his wife would be, and he told us the district in the centre of Tehran, the street, number and floor, which side of the staircase, and we thought, Oh, that's easy. Aren't we lucky she's not living under the Supreme Leader's bed or in al-Qods country, but somewhere nice and easy for extraction like a street in the middle of Tehran?'

He had studied the map and tried to recall where he had been on his one visit, two weeks, and a kaleidoscope's images had competed.

He hadn't asked about their firepower, why they thought it was needed. He didn't know the route in or the route out. The transport churned through the skies, and he realised that Mandy was asleep, her head on his shoulder. He would have liked to root in his rucksack for the picture of Farideh, but that would have woken the intelligence officer and embarrassed her. Zach sat still. He was bewildered by his lack of reaction. He thought he should have been trembling, with surging adrenalin, or wanting to piss himself, and demand answers to a dozen questions, but there was none of that. He was calm and noted that the guys didn't fidget or lick their lips. They took it in their stride and he copied them.

He realised he didn't need the picture in his hand because it was sharp in his mind. He had no sense of time or distance, only that the journey had started and that its end was obscure. Her eyes questioned him.

Short of a hundred metres from the window on the first floor of the block, to the right and easy to see from her viewpoint, Jamali sold hardware, every gauge of screw, bolt and washer. A little more than fifty metres to the left, by the street-light, Ali was famed in the neighbourhood for his ability to get failed refrigerators, cookers and washing-machines working again. Farideh was at the window. She couldn't sleep.

The street was almost empty, and the pavements too.

The men were in shadow, but they smoked and their cigarettes glowed when they dragged on them. There was a back entrance into the block, between a warehouse where a store in the next street kept furniture before shifting it to the showroom, and a prefabricated building in which a businessman stored paint. She assumed that if men were watching, from two sides, at the front of the block, there were more at the back.

She had draped a blanket over her shoulders and held it tight around her. The men outside Jamali's and Ali's doors might have glimpsed her skin or her nightdress. Farideh had nowhere to run to, no passport and no money.

She had been told that her husband had fled and was believed to have betrayed his country. It made no sense to her. At no time, in her hearing, had Mehrak uttered even mild criticism of the regime: he had never complained of Iran's economic difficulties, the unemployment that stopped his brother working, or the foreign sanctions that punished his government. He hadn't mocked the corruption of the élite. He had been in Iraq and south Lebanon, war zones, for his country, had worked day and night in the service of Brigadier Reza Joyberi. He had never complained or criticised.

She smiled, hidden, and shivered because the window was poorly fitted and let in the cold. She was not complicit in anything her husband had done. She didn't know where he had gone or on what business. She would have run away if Johnny or the Captain had wanted it. She watched the pricks of light from their cigarettes, wondering if one had binoculars focused on her and could see her hair, her throat, the shape of her body. She understood nothing. Her brother-in-law had come with his mother early that evening to accuse her – but she didn't know what crime she had committed. The men from the MOIS had been to their home, too, and had interrogated them. Her brother-in-law had the marks of a fist on his cheek, and a bruised eye. They blamed her. No neighbour had offered sympathy or comfort, and all would have been questioned that day. Her father had telephoned, and there had been a crackle on the line, which was usually of good quality. She had sensed his fear.

Mehrak's family supported the regime, didn't question its actions. Not one family on Farideh's staircase would have voted against the Supreme Leader's candidate for the presidency. Her own father and mother were unquestioning in support of the regime. All, in differing ways, would have felt disgraced by the arrival of the MOIS on their doorstep.

Easy for Farideh to be brave when she had been in the room with Johnny above the repair yard where Highness and Excellency toiled, and when they had made love, seeming to know somehow that their time together would be brutally short. Easy for Farideh to be puffed with courage when she had worn the *chador* and the veil, and rode pillion on the Captain's scooter, her wedding ring visible, him in uniform, with medal ribbons. No little bastard of the chastity squad would have tried to stop a hero of the military driving his wife out of the city. Easy to be brave. Kourosh had given her nothing and was a mistake.

She stayed at the window far into the night, the lights switched off. They kept their vigil, and so did she. Fear gnawed at her, and she didn't know what she could do, or where her future lay.

He couldn't have said whether Rollo Hawkins welcomed the call or not. It was past midnight in the Cantabrians and he'd spent a hard day in his garden, then hours on the viewing hill – rewarded with an adult female and an immature male in good view.

Petroc explained the development, of earthquake proportions, and asked for his thoughts. He had his feet on the sofa, a whisky in his hand, and the house was quiet. He listened to the dry, unemotional voice, sometimes broken by fierce coughing.

'So many times a woman is at the heart of it, pushes a man over the edge – am I allowed vulgarity? Your uncle liked it – a life turned upside down because of an itch on the foreskin. They might be intelligent men, who have risen high, or cattle drovers, but the urge rules them. We had Oleg Lyalin, in the Soviet times. He had a mistress, a colleague's wife, and would lose her if he was shipped home. Vitaly Yurchenko was a big catch for the Agency when he defected, but he was infatuated with the wife of a fellow diplomat at the Soviet embassy in Ottawa. She turned him down. It was the end of his imagined romance with her and with the Agency. He walked out on them, went home. Yuri Nosenko came to the Agency because while he was a senior KGB officer he'd run up too big a bill on prostitutes and couldn't fiddle his expenses enough to clear his account. He was another disaster who couldn't keep his hands off bar maids. Or we could get contemporary – Thank you, dear, so kind.'

Petroc imagined that his small, elderly wife, cocooned in a dressing-gown, had brought him a mug of tea.

'Wonderful. Where was I? Contemporary. The Russians recently slapped a twenty-five-year sentence on a Colonel Potayev, a senior intelligence officer, hard labour and all the trimmings, except it was *in absentia*. He's now living in Virginia with his wife. He didn't slip away until he knew she and their two kids were safely there. For him, it all ended happily, but it doesn't for everyone. Let's talk about an Iranian. Am I boring you?'

'Keep going, Rollo.'

'You'll know the story, but it's worth repeating. The case of Shahram Amiri who defected from his job in health and safety, Iranian nuclear. He toured classified installations giving advice on the dangers of the materials, access everywhere. He was important enough for the Agency to flip him out of a pilgrimage in Saudi, then offer him five million dollars and a new life. Very good – what could go wrong? Pretty much everything – the wife and the small boy. The wife was supposed to be brought out of Iran by the Agency, with the child. Maybe they left the detail of it too long, maybe they thought they could set him up with a blonde. He couldn't live without his wife and kid, and the pressure on him would have built. Back at home, the regime hassled her, searched her, called her in for rough interrogation. No way she was getting on a plane for the USA and a share of the millions. She was stuck at home, suffering, as was her extended family. He was responsible. He didn't, of course, ring her direct. Might have tried a cousin on the other side of Tehran, and the cousin called another cousin. Word came back that she was in serious trouble, might be going to gaol or worse. What price then the five million bucks? He turned his back on his new friends and went home. He was pictured in Tehran with a bouquet of flowers, his wife was beaming and he was holding his child high. The spinners did a cock-and-bull story about him being drugged by the Americans on his *hajj* and kidnapped. A few dumb people down in the bazaar might have bought that, but not the people who mattered. He was reportedly hospitalised after the early interrogations, reportedly tried in a closed court when he could stand up again. Reportedly he'll hang, may already be dead. Petroc, the story of Shahram Amiri shows what happens if a family isn't moved fast. There's one difference between your case and his. Ready?'

'Yes, Rollo.'

'Why would the Agency care in the Amiri case? They'd had him for the best part of two years, had probably extracted all there was to squeeze out. Your man, Petroc, still has much to tell you. You need him to co-operate. You have to get the woman quickly before the net goes over her, before they've reacted to your man's disappearance. Move fast and with commitment.'

'The team's in the air.'

'A bizarre attribute, of many men in the trade: they believe they're tough, hardened by the world in which they work, when in fact they're as soft as maidenhair fern. Your initial reaction might have been to ship him down to the Gürtel district of Vienna, shove him through the door for half an hour and get him back to work, but, as I remember, he made a mess of that down in the Gulf. To open him up, Petroc, you'll have done the right thing . . . but it's a high-risk gamble.'

'A career-defining gamble.'

'Of course, in old Hector's time it would have been *de rigueur*.'

'Hector would probably have driven down Enghelab Avenue in the turret of a Churchill tank and picked her up. I'm grateful for your time, Rollo. Now go back to bed.'

'Not sleeping well because one of our males hasn't been seen for too long.'

'Let's hope he shows up.' He cut the call, and wondered where they were, how far into their journey – and why they had taken his shilling.

'Look this way – that's it. A smile would help.'

He had been drinking a last glass of juice before bed, and had learned a card game from Auntie. Before that he had been working on the diary they'd asked for, where he had been with the brigadier, whom they had met and when. He had enjoyed the cards and the juice. The red-haired one, Nobby, was taking the picture and the flash went. He hadn't registered the camera, but had managed the smile.

'Thanks. One for my souvenir gallery.'

Nobby nodded at him, then was gone. They were all correct, but there was no friendship from PK, no warmth from Auntie or Father William. Nobby was the only one who smiled with him.

Auntie said it was time for bed.

They had told him that the process had begun. That evening, he had believed it. He sorted the deck of cards and slipped them back into the pack. He finished his juice. He hadn't been outside today. He had stood at the windows and looked out at the vineyards that climbed the hill and slipped away below the house, the men and women who cut and stacked the grapes. There was a church, and a great river beyond the houses further down the valley. He had seen cargo being pulled up the river on barges, and the afternoon had been bright with crisp sunshine. The light had fallen on the ruined walls of a castle. Once, emboldened, he had gone through the kitchen to the back door, passing the woman who cooked and cleaned for them, but the door had been locked and there was no key.

Once, he had stood, almost defiant, at the front door and waited: he tried to test them, make them fashion an excuse. They hadn't bothered. For five minutes more he had stared at the inside of the door, then Auntie had come for him, taken his arm and brought him back to the table. There had been two holsters, empty, on the back of the kitchen door. Nobby wasn't armed, nor Auntie, but Sidney carried a weapon in his belt, tucked against his hip, and Father William wore a lightweight windcheater and the right pocket sagged.

Auntie led him and Father William followed. The woman and Sidney were clearing the last of the kitchen surfaces. They went up the stairs. The door was open. His bedroom was at the far end of the corridor. He could see through the door and PK was hunched at a table. The photograph that had just been taken was on the laptop screen in front of him. He thought he looked relaxed, calm, and there was almost a smile at the corner of his mouth. PK turned the screen away.

Farideh was on the wall behind the laptop. It was the picture from his wallet, huge. Would she come? Or would she refuse, turn her back on them? He didn't know. There were maps to either side of her picture, and aerial views of that corner of central Tehran.

PK called, 'Big day tomorrow, Mehrak. You'll need a clear head. Sleep well.' His toe nudged the door. Sight of the laptop was lost and his wife's picture.

A little push from behind him, and Father William spoke: 'As the boss said, a big day, Mehrak, so get some sleep.'

He went through the door, which was closed after him. His bed was made, neat lines, and the pillows plumped. The key turned in the lock. He didn't know if he could believe them.

They were out of İncirlik.

Dunc and Mandy had gone. Dunc had hugged him, almost clung to him. Mandy had shaken his hand. The farewell had been in a transit area, a murmur of 'Good luck.' There had been Americans in the room where he and the guys had waited. It seemed they were civilians – in jeans, sweatshirts and anoraks; some had ponytails and others' heads were shaven. They were louder than the air-force people at Ramstein. When they had headed for the stand, Zach had seen rows of transport aircraft and clusters of floodlit fighter bombers.

Mikey had sidled near to him. 'Don't gawp – they're Agency, reckon they're top shit. Don't ever bend your fucking knee to them.'

The aircraft was two-engine, propeller. When they were up the American pilot had said his name was Dwight, and that the aircraft was a Cessna 406 Caravan; they would be at an altitude of 24,000 feet and have a cruising speed of 230 miles per hour. The route was over Turkish territory for as long as possible, then a fast run over the northern mountains of Iraq, across its air space and down at Sulaymaniyah, which was Kurdish. The pilot had said that, if they bust a gut with the old bird, he hoped to be down before first light.

There was a thunderstorm but the pilot didn't divert to go round it: he went straight through the middle and Zach didn't know how life could be worse. At that moment his destination took second place to the turbulence.

The price was bouncing higher as the wheels of the lead truck rolled over the rough track. The convoy's speed was governed by the cumbersome progress of the first vehicle in the column. The pick-ups behind had gathered at a water-hole, where caravans, camel traders and narcotics transporters waited for the armoured truck to lead them across the frontier. Two of the twenty-five remaining packets of that load would be given as currency to the warlord who had invested in the sheets of tempered steel welded into place. They covered most of the bodywork and most of the windscreen of the vehicle charged with battering a path through concrete walls, or coils of barbed wire, and bridging the ditches scooped out by earth-moving plants and fighting off the Iranian Army or Iranian border patrols. There could be heavy fighting and two machine-guns were mounted on that vehicle – once a long-wheel-base Land Rover of a British unit, abandoned in a sand drift seven years earlier and lovingly restored, with 178,000 miles on the clock, and going well.

It needed to go well. The convoy leader, the nephew of the warlord who had taken the two packages from that one pick-up and had an armful of similar parcels, had chosen a section of the frontier where the Iranian authorities had erected the wall and wire but had not dug a ditch. A heavy iron triangle was attached to the bonnet, with the blunt, scarred point facing ahead. The spike would break through the concrete blocks, then snag the wire. If a patrol was watching that sector and had the firepower to stall the Land Rover, blood would flow. And blood would flow, too, if an Iranian force intervened and found itself outgunned.

The frontier was a merciless place, and the hike in price of each two-kilo package guaranteed that charity was banished there. And men died because a package now valued at five thousand American dollars would increase hugely once the frontier was breached. The same package, out of Afghanistan and into Iran, had a marked-up price on it of eight thousand American dollars.

Far away, in offices staffed by personnel of the United Nations Office on Drugs and Crime, the border of desert dirt between Afghanistan and Iran was called the 'entrance gate' for the outside world's heroin. A hundred tonnes of the drug, uncut and undiluted, came across the sand each year. Casualties among Iranian troops and police were the highest of any nation in the fight against narco-trafficking. But statistics carried little weight at an hour before midnight when the spike hit the wall. Tumbler wires triggered klaxons and sirens, an automatic weapon started up, flares were launched. A rocket-propelled grenade, surplus stock left behind by the Red Army, silenced the guard's machine gun, and an American-surplus Browning belt-fed weapon, issued to the Afghan National Army and sold on, quietened rifle fire from a dune's ridge.

They went through intact and and would drive another dozen kilometres to the rendezvous. There, more vehicles waited. Heroin went into Iran and was replaced with electrical goods, television sets, laptops, cigarettes and anything else on which the Afghan administration would charge duty if it travelled along a road policed by Customs or was airfreighted into Kabul.

Within an hour, the heroin was moving deep into south Khorasan and towards Birjand, and the armoured Land Rover was heading for another clash on the way back to the Nimroz area.

The early duty was Father William's. He was in the secure room, with the phones, the boss's laptop, the poster-sized picture of the woman, the maps and the TV set that had the relay wired in.

The image on the screen was pin-sharp. The curtains were not tightly drawn in the Iranian's room and the dawn lit his face. The cigarette in his mouth threw a shadow on his chin. They talked, he, Nobby and Auntie. Sidney included himself when he could. They discussed the man they called the corporal. *Not settled* and *Not responding* and *Unwilling to make the final break* and *The matter of the wife: a last throw and a hell of a dangerous one.* Father William believed it a good way to prise open a man's mind; he watched the screen, saw the regular pulling on the cigarette and seemed to read defiance in the face. Worse, the man seemed to regard himself as a prisoner.

He was Father William in his family, on the street where he lived in the south-west suburb of London and at Vauxhall Cross. He was Father William because of the white hair that jutted off his scalp. His daughters had given him the name:

'You are old Father William,' the young man said,
'And your hair has become very white;
And yet you incessantly stand on your head –
Do you think at your age it is right?'

He had been white-haired as a young man when he had started with SIS, in the Century House days, as a pool driver, then occasional security escort and courier of confidential documents. He had no academic qualifications but was better read than most around and above him. He had understood the 'red, red rose' Sidney had brought from the Iranian embassy's garden and was irritated that the older man, who bordered on a spiv, had known his poetry.

His wife was a legal executive in a Twickenham office and his daughters worked in a Central London shop; Father William might reflect that none of them had noticed his absence. When did they need him? They took an old-fashioned family holiday each year in the north-west of Scotland where they viewed sea otters, occasional whales or dolphins, and read books in front of log fires. He did the driving. He was pleased to have come to Austria. A long-gone uncle had been here – perhaps he'd have a chance to go to the town called Judenberg where the young squaddie had been sixty-eight years before. Most recently Father William had watched over two Libyan air-force officers, pilots of fast jets, who had defected to Malta, then been shipped to a rented house in Wiltshire. They had been easy. He thought he had been chosen for this assignment for no better reason than that he was available.

A cigarette was stubbed out. Another was lit.

Father William knew his Burns, and more than the favoured first verse of the 'red, red rose', and recited then, to himself, the second:

As fair art thou, my bonnie lass,
So deep in love am I;
And I will love thee still, my dear,
Till a' the seas gang dry.

It made no sense. He imagined an arranged marriage, a match made by those in influence and the elders of families. A chauffeur-cum-security guard of low rank was handed a girl of uncommon prettiness, yet went to a whorehouse.

The picture had gone. The close-up photograph of the corporal had been sent on its way. It would now be in the hands of the messenger. He thought of the speed with which they had reacted to the situation, and the panicked pace of events.

Putting men across that frontier: was it an act of folly? Perhaps. And was it Father William's job to speak up about it? Perhaps not.

He watched the man, thought no good could come of him.

* * *

There were Americans at Sulaymaniyah, on a crisp bright early morning, who drove them by Humvee from the airport, where the formalities were ignored. Zach would have said, if asked, that he believed the Americans were out of Iraq; but they were still in Kurdish Iraq, in the extreme north-east, and Sulaymaniyah. An American passed an envelope to Mikey, who tore open the flap, glanced inside and handed it to Zach. He had the picture of the woman, and now the photograph of her husband. He was embedded in a world he didn't know.

He didn't know about the officers of the Central Intelligence Agency, two men and a woman, who had squashed them with their bags into the Humvee and driven at speed from the airport, past the buses and cars of civilian traffic, then through the military block beyond the terminal buildings. There had been a curt wave from the driver to the guards, as if this was a piece of territory the American had bought. They went out onto a highway and left the tall buildings of the city behind. Mikey had asked how long. The woman had said an hour. Mikey had poked Zach's rib, had his attention.

Mikey had said, 'Haven't talked before because I don't rate drip-feeding information. Listen and concentrate. I don't do it twice. One lesson is paramount: we all have a job to do and we all rely on that job being done. You rely on our professionalism, and we rely on yours – except we don't know whether you have the necessary skills. Don't ever forget that we're a team and we'll behave like one. We're as good as the weakest among us. Don't let that be you.'

Mikey had talked, filling the hour.

They had gone past fields and farmers' compounds, had seen cattle in sheds and old tractors on the roads, herds of goats and sheep. Thick smoke climbed from chimneys and kids were at the side of the road, waving as the Humvee sped past. While Mikey talked, Zach gazed past the driver's shoulder. The ground climbed and there was snow on the summits of hills. He heard what was expected of him: language and urban driving, the approach and the talk. He was told their territory: security, tactics, safety. They wouldn't second-guess him, and he wouldn't question their decisions. At the end of the briefing he had asked one question.

'Have any of your guys been inside Iran before?'

'No. Have you?'

Zach had said he had been in Iran for two weeks, five years before, on a student visa. He had heard the woman snort in the passenger seat and had seen a little shake in the driver's shoulders, as if he chuckled. The American in the jump seat, who had the rifle across his knees, had turned his head sharply.

'Well, we'll live with it,' Mikey had said, with a wintry smile.

'"In the land of the blind, the one-eyed is king,"' Zach responded.

He wondered why they had sent with him guys who'd do security, tactics and safety yet had never been on the ground and couldn't order a glass of tea at a roadside. The road was desolate and high, traces of snow were on the yellowed grass. The occasional trees were stunted and bent. He saw a woman burdened with firewood. She would have had to search hard for it.

They climbed and the road surface deteriorated. They came to a small quarry and the driver swung into it. Mikey said it was a good time to put the boots on so they all crouched to fiddle with laces and hooks. The shoes went into Zach's sack, which had space for them. They were parked beside a heap of burned-out vehicles – some were peppered with bullet holes, crisp little marks on the fraying rust. The Americans were quiet now and their radio was turned off. The woman had a cell phone on her lap and watched it, waiting for it to ring or vibrate. Zach remembered the snort, the chuckle and the turned head.

'And you go across most nights, do you? You're regulars? You all speak the language well?' Zach used Farsi, challenging – and won. They looked blankly at him, the woman and the two men. Zach said, in English, 'I was wondering if you go across regularly, and speak the language.'

'We don't,' the woman said. 'And we don't have more than basic Farsi. But we settle the bills and keep the show on the road. I hope that sounds adequate . . . We have friends, and when the friends call we'll walk you to them. Do I like all of the world in which I live? I don't, and learn to exist alongside it. I don't go in, none of us does, and I don't lie awake at night and shed tears. I don't want to read about you in the *New York Times* or in the Kurdish local rag. If I don't see your picture or hear about you I'll be thankful. We don't have a church here, but there are some good Mid-West Americans who run a school on Christian principles in the city and sometimes we have a little prayer meeting. I value that when it happens. Next time I go, I'll think of you.'

Her phone warbled. She read a message.

The one in the jump seat leaned forward and was shown the screen. He said to Mikey, 'We'll walk you forward, like we said, and pass you on. Let's get it done.'

The woman passed him a sheet from a notepad. He read the handwriting and raised an eyebrow, then returned it. The paper, screwed up, went into her pocket. She said, 'We're told the way's clear. Good luck, stay safe.'

They were out and the crisp air wafted on Zach's face. Mikey, Ralph and Wally had their weapons bags, and Wally had the trauma kit. Zach hitched his rucksack onto his back.

A track led out of the quarry and went up between rocks, skirting a small torrent. The driver was pointing at it. The woman waved. They were not twenty metres out of the quarry, on an exposed slope, without cover, before the Humvee had done a three-pointer, grit flying from under the big tyres. They were not fifty metres up the hill, with a ridge far above them, before the Humvee was at a bend and accelerating, and not a hundred metres before the Humvee was gone, no more than a fading memory.

'Fuck them,' Ralph said.

'Ditto,' Wally said.

'Easy, boys,' Mikey said. 'Stay with me, Zach, right up close.'

They pushed on. Ralph led, Mikey following, Zach hard to him, and Wally had the rear. An eagle flew high above them, circling wide, and Zach wondered if there were rabbits or a fox for it to swoop on. The light caught the beauty of its wings and he tripped. He'd been gazing up, paying no attention to his next footfall. A hand caught him from behind and Mikey looked daggers at him. He could have kicked himself. Each time his boot landed on the ground it left behind little specks of dried mud from a building site a dozen miles from the city of Coventry. He noted that the guys in front and Wally didn't dislodge stones or kick up grit.

He didn't think of home, the men he had worked with, or the guys around him. He didn't think of the woman who was in an apartment on a side-street in central Tehran. He thought only of where his boots landed. The eagle called, reedy and thin, but he didn't lift his head.

He cannoned into Mikey, who had stopped. The path, near the top of the ridge, curved at a thorn bush. A man sat there. He wore the long shirt of a peasant and baggy trousers that were pulled in at the ankle. His feet were bare but for heavy leather sandals. He had on an old jacket that would have been expensive a quarter of a century ago when it was new. He was unshaven but not bearded, had sallow skin and wore an old beanie.

Good English, educated: 'You Brits are always late. Be late for your own funerals. Which of you is the star?'

Mikey gestured at Zach.

The man said, Farsi now, 'If I could just do my little check, the one I always do for visitors from Mary Ellen, fine girl. The mullah says to the street sweeper who cleans, each day, the pavement outside the mullah's villa, "Ali, why are you so fat?" How does the street sweeper reply?'

Zach answered, 'The street sweeper says to the mullah: "I'm fat, Excellency, because each time I screw your wife she gives me a biscuit. Then I go and screw your daughter and she gives me a biscuit too. I eat too many biscuits, which is why I'm fat." The old ones are the best.'

The man came forward and kissed Zach's cheeks. 'Very good. From now we'll speak Farsi. What's your name?'

They were at the ridge and stepped over it. The track went on down.

'I'm Zach, and—'

'You're one metre inside Iran and already you've made a mistake. I tricked you. Your name is no business of mine. I can be Moshe or Ali, David or Mahmoud. I have a name for wherever I sleep. For me, for your friends, be wary. Come.'

The man led and they went fast. Far below there was a rusty old lorry, and the sun glinted on its load of a few old cookers and fridges. Zach felt chastised for his error. He wondered why he had stepped forward on the building site. The border was behind him, receding fast. When the fear came his legs weakened and his stomach seemed loose, but there was no stopping and no turning back and the eagle called again but Zach did not look for it.

They had taken the flight up to Van, where they were met. He was young, introduced himself as from the embassy in Ankara, passed them a bulky envelope and led them to the car-hire desk. He completed the forms with them, translated and scarpered. He could have been in the Service, first posting abroad, or perhaps had been press-ganged from Consular or Trade by the station chief. He'd wanted less than nothing to do with them. Mandy had driven – inappropriate, probably, in these parts, but she'd swung a headscarf over her hair and had settled behind the wheel. He had navigated. An awful road skirted the lake, and there was a worse one after Agri, playing chicken with lorries driving from the border, frustrated by a lengthy Customs hold-up.

They'd arrived in Doğubeyazıt and felt shredded. They'd bought bread, cheese, tea bags, unrecognisable coffee, milk, and old, bruised fruit from a petrol station. Dunc had started a list for the morning. The property rented for them was marked boldly on one of the maps provided by the embassy, and they'd found it. They hadn't taken in their surroundings, which were a confused wilderness. The key was in the door. They'd stumbled inside and switched on every light and every heater.

Dunc Whitcomb looked at his watch, cradled the mug of tea. 'Where should they be?'

Her eyes were closed, as if the strain had caught up with her.

'Should be across, if the Israelis have done their bit. Makes you shiver, the thought of an Israeli on the ground there. Beyond any call of duty that I'd know.'

'And our boy . . . God, should I have dragged him into this?'

'Bit bloody late to go soft, Dunc.'

The Cousin said, 'I hear, Tadeuz, that we handed them over in good shape, sent them on their way. There'll be a big pay-back. You owe us.'

The Friend said, 'We did the pick-up, and we're ferrying your team, Tadeuz. But when they're dropped off they're on their own. The extraction we've suggested is a commercial arrangement, not linked to us. You owe us, too.'

Out of the corner of his eye, Tadeuz Fenton saw that Sara Rogers was seething. He said, 'You helped because of the quality of the intelligence we've already provided, so can we skip the shit and behave like civilised intelligence-gatherers?'

The Agency, Tadeuz knew, would not have provided the transport unless their analysts had recognised the worth of the material already submitted by Petroc Kenning. The Mossad, notorious for their secrecy, independence and usual refusal to hold hands with another Service, would have summoned one of their stars only if what they had already heard had taken their knowledge beyond old boundaries. The corporal was a jewel, and belonged to Tadeuz. He said, 'But we're grateful for your help. When this is over, we'll deserve a drink or three.'

There was a map on the table. The Cousin reached forward and gestured at a point on the red frontier line that was due west of Sulaymaniyah. The Friend eased him aside and traced a route along a winding Iranian road that ended in Tehran. Sara Rogers leaned across and indicated a range of high mountains, the border separating Iran from Turkey, where they would come out, Zach, the team and the wife.

Tadeuz Fenton was no longer a good Catholic, but he crossed himself.

* * *

'What do you know?' They had come with the dawn.

She had had warning – she had been at the window from before the first light had spread from the east, where the great deserts were. She had seen their cars. She hadn't dressed. The vehicles had stopped level with the doorway from which the men had watched the entrance to her block through the night. She had lain sleepless on the wide bed, but had gone often to the window, with a blanket round her shoulders. She had seen the brigadier get out of his car, the Mercedes that was Mehrak's pride and joy. It blocked the street.

'I promise you, Farideh, that it may go badly for you. The judge may consider it impossible that a man can defect to the enemy of the Iranian people without the knowledge of his wife. He might feel that the duty of a wife is first to the state, and second to her husband. He would expect her to know of his intended flight and go to the authorities to denounce him.'

She had heard heavy feet on the stairs, then fists beating at the door. She had opened it. They had pushed past her. She knew so much about the brigadier – her husband spoke of him often. She hadn't seen him since her wedding. Now his eyes flickered. She wondered if he felt awkward to be close to her when she was wrapped only in a blanket. He would have seen her hair, throat, wrists and legs below the knee, the curve of the blanket at her breasts and hips. She stared at him. He had chosen her. Her parents had thought it an honour that their daughter should marry a man in the al-Qods division. They hadn't realised that the limit of his ambition was to serve his officer. The brigadier stood in front of her, his eyes glazed. He had lost the dynamism his rank gave him. His hand snaked out and grasped her chin.

'They're difficult times and we face great dangers. The threats to the state are many. In such times, for the crime of waging war against God – which you would face – there would be no mercy. I couldn't help you, Farideh. What did you know?'

Her hands had held the blanket. Now she used them to pull his hand off her face. It was a gesture of defiance. He didn't slap or punch her, which surprised her, but the blanket slid off her shoulders.

'I knew nothing,' she told him. 'I was second in his life. You came first. He spent more time in your company than he did with me. He ignored me. In fact, although I said I came *second*, I was actually third, after the al-Qods division of the Islamic Revolutionary Guard Corps. Most nights when he came home I was already asleep and his supper was on the table. Most mornings when he left, before it was light, I was asleep. Where has he been? I don't know. Why did he go? I don't know. Ask yourself, Brigadier. Where did you send him and why?'

Farideh was trembling. She thought she saw a trace of a smile on his face. There was also a trace of sadness and regret. There were five other men in the room. None of them had called her 'whore', or rushed to retrieve the blanket for her. She thought he was lost, unsure.

She said quietly, 'I am only his wife. I know nothing. He didn't tell me anything.'

'If you have lied to me . . .'

'I have not.'

He was – Mehrak had told her this much – one of the few men in the state with unlimited power. She thought he believed her, and that he was confused. He was no fool, but now he didn't know which way to turn. She picked up the blanket and put it loosely around herself.

He left, and the men followed him.

From the door she was told, 'If you've lied, there will come a time when you will beg to die.'

The door closed.

From the window she saw the big Mercedes and the other cars leave, but the watchers stayed in the doorways.

He had used minor roads after leaving the track, then metalled surfaces either side of Sanandaj. They had taken a ring road round Hamadan and gone north. The capital city was a subdued glow of light.

He was coming home.

He would not be acknowledged, and neither would the young

man beside him. The men in the escort were, after a fashion, professional and he thought they would have appreciated that deniability was essential on such missions. They were hidden, with their kit, behind the cab. The bolt behind his seat had to be unscrewed and removed to reveal the hatch leading to the compartment that was built in with a false bulkhead. It had space for three men and their kit.

When he had worked on the hits, the assassin had used a motorcycle to take down a scientist, an engineer or a high-ranking military strategist, then drive to an underpass under a trunk road into the city and torch it. He had sat in his lorry, complete with its load of unwanted fridges, cookers and washing-machines, waiting to take the assassin and his driver to the rendezvous and know that they were free and heading for home. A night later or two they would be in Haifa or Tel Aviv, but he would be in his temporary home and nursing the stress.

No deal would be done to save him. A thousand men and women of Hamas and Hezbollah had been worth the freedom of one soldier in the IDF, Gilad Schalit. If he were captured, he would die. No bank held the amount of bullion it would cost to free him if he were picked up. The man beside him was either an innocent or a fool to be so relaxed. Eli Cohen, hanged in Semiramis Square in Damascus, beyond the reach of help, was a hero of Israel. He himself was the fixer, the linkman, the facilitator for guns and get-away people. He was a fool. He lived on the edge, hugged shadows. He assumed he had been offered by the Institute for Espionage and Special Tasks because of the imperative need for HumInt sources. The British had a chauffeur and now needed the chauffeur's wife. Human intelligence, war clouds gathering, was the priority. He drove.

Rare for him to pass judgement, but he had liked the guy beside him and his Farsi had improved with each hour before he'd fallen asleep. The fixer had to be able to read men. This one had the fingernails of a casual labourer, but that would have been a temporary occupation. He was intelligent and maybe had kept it hidden – he'd listened intently to the details of the pick-up for the run out.

The fixer had emphasised that the window would be open briefly and that the rendezvous must be kept. The lights of Tehran intensified, but he turned off at a junction and pulled up behind a deserted fuel station. A vehicle was parked there, out of view. It seemed a shame to wake the guy.

6

'It's bigger than London, square miles and population density, and choking under the smog. It's third world to look at, and in the standard of living where we are now, but in the north, where we're not going, there's a sophistication that's Rome or Paris. Technically, in spite of the regime, they can do almost anything we can.' It helped Zach to talk as he drove.

They had their own vehicle. It had been tough at first for Zach to be behind the wheel. He'd taken the track behind the ruin, negotiated a slip road and come onto the highway. The tallest buildings of the city pierced the skyline ahead, and to his left was the great range of the Alborz; the snow gave lustre to the upper ridges. Mikey did the map work and the satnav – they'd turned the woman's voice off. Mikey had said that they were sure to take a wrong turn down the road and end up facing a wall, but there was to be no shouting. They were all going to be doing their best, he had said, and there was no room for criticism.

Zach had taken that to be directed at himself. He was in the central lane of three. His foot, on the brake or the accelerator, balanced the car's speed with that of the vehicles around him. He used the horn when he had to.

They had a full tank.

They'd had the big conversation after the Israeli had left them. They'd come out of the hidden compartment in the lorry with the gear, and there'd been no great farewell. He'd punched Zach on the chest, over the heart, nodded to the guys, then climbed back into his cab and pulled away. He hadn't waved or wished them well. The big conversation had been about the weapons.

Off the highway, heading for the centre, and the area a few

blocks to the north of Enghelab, they were past the airport turn. Zach dug deep in his memory for where he had been during his student visit: two and a half day's in a hostel in Tehran five years ago, 2007 on the infidel calendar. He'd done mosques, the bazaar, galleries of antiquities, and had spent nearly half of a day at the railway station to buy a ticket to the south. He hadn't driven anywhere. It had been out of the question to hire a car, way beyond his budget. Anyway, the buses were cheap, the metro was new and there were the shared orange taxis, always the locally made Paykan. He thought he remembered stretches of road, the outside of a building, or a square.

The big question. There were three guys with him. They had enough firepower between them, he could reflect gloomily, to start a minor war. The big question's tag-on was: *what were the weapons for?* And: *when are they used?* They hadn't got into the vehicle until they'd discussed it: no raised voices, no misunderstandings.

The traffic had thickened and slowed. Drivers and passengers alongside them had more time to glance at them. On the big question, Zach had said, 'Don't we call it Rules of Engagement? I should have thrashed this out hours ago, certainly at the base in Germany. I didn't know when I signed up that we were taking that stuff. How can there be any innocent explanation? If a traffic cop stops us because an indicator light isn't working, what happens?'

Now eyes raked them, not hostile or suspicious, just curious. They knew it was a mistake to stand out from the crowd. On the big question, Ralph had said, 'We're not bullet-catchers, we don't do glory-boy stuff, but we do protect you. We aim to prevent circumstances in which any of us is taken. Simple.'

He had come off Enghelab, left the university's central library behind, had wormed through a mob of students and was near the main campus of the technology university. He was on Valiasr Avenue, and nothing was familiar. A teenager on a bicycle had wobbled close enough to catch the end of his handlebars on the offside mirror. He had lurched but hadn't come off. From the time he had taken the wheel, Zach had dreaded a traffic fracas, a crowd and a policeman pushing his way forward. He swore.

There had been an Iranian, an exile with a rare wit, at the School, and he'd liked to indulge in vulgar or obscene talk with a new lecturer. Zach had learned gutter-speak from him. It flowed back. He hadn't used or heard it in more than five years, but it came in a torrent. He left the kid in the road, near cowering, and a couple of drivers hooted applause at him. He thought he'd passed a test when Mikey had laid a hand on his thigh and squeezed.

Wally had said, 'We have to put you there, alongside her. You do the talk and – miracle of miracles – she'll come with us. You're talking about what happens if one arsehole puts his hand up. Might be a hundred thousand police in the city, armed, and another hundred thousand paramilitaries, but they don't know who we are or where we're going. A hand goes up. What happens? He's blown away. The last option will always be open. We don't end up sitting on the floor of a cell and wishing we'd reached for the hardware. If nobody told you, I'm sorry, sunshine, but that's how it is.'

He passed the City Theatre and the park, and went on to Shirzad. He knew where she lived and where she worked. He didn't know, if she wore 'good *hijab*', how he would identify her. He had said that if they were lucky they'd likely be on her street before she went to work. He didn't know how they would make the approach. A committee would decide and then he'd be launched. On the big question, Mikey had said, 'We shot them up in Iraq, and we zap them in Afghanistan. If they hadn't envisaged a fight, they'd have sent Boy Scouts with you. Leave this to us.'

He'd read that tension 'crackled'. Now it enveloped them. In front there was a junction, with a turn to the right. He couldn't read that street's name, but it matched the map. A man using a stick crossed the road and Zach braked.

Her street gaped ahead of him. She was the reason that a man in a suit had come to a building site in the south Midlands, why they had been dumped on aircraft. The voice in his ear murmured, 'Go for it, Zach, if you've nothing better to do.'

* * *

'Shit.' A man crossing the road, a young mother pushing a pram, a war veteran who'd lost an arm, and many who hurried to get a bus or taxi would have seen the vehicle that had stalled in the middle of the road at the turning to Rafah Street. It was a van, and a ladder was roped to the roof. Another ladder protruded from the back where the tail flap was roped up. They would have seen into the storage area – cement sacks, a wheelbarrow, tool bags, a stack of concrete blocks and paint pots. It was the debris and kit of a small commercial builder who did jobs round a neighbourhood. Typical.

Those who saw it would not have realised that four men were inside it. They would have seen only the two in the front: the passenger had well-cut hair but a dirty face, and his mouth and nose were covered with a filter for protection against air pollution – not an unusual sight in Tehran. The van was blue, but the sides and doors were dusty, the windscreen too. The driver would not have attracted attention – except when he had sworn at the kid who had nearly scratched the door, gutter language that had raised laughter: a vehicle in that condition, and a driver angry at the possibility of another scratch or scrape. Scores had seen the van, had passed it, eased out of its path and given way to it at junctions. They had seen the driver and the man beside him with the mask, and none had noticed anything about them that was remarkable.

There were many attacks on Iran's territorial integrity that day – agents were loose, secrets probed for, computers stretched in their capabilities to extract covert detail; the public was warned in broadcasts and newspapers of the dangers posed by foreign spies. None of the men and women close to the builders' van had seen the deception it posed. Now it was in the middle of the road, blocking two vehicles. The man crossing had stopped.

The van moved. The traffic edged past it on Shirzad, and the brief hold-up was forgotten. The van went into Rafah Street, named after that part of the Gaza Strip where many martyrs of the Palestinian cause, fighting against the Zionists, had died.

From his counter, near the door of his hardware business,

opening early as he always did so that 'trade' could buy what they needed for the day, Jamali saw the van. He saw it past the backs, shoulders and heads of the men who waited in his doorway and had left a heap of cigarette ends there. He would have to clear it himself later.

The van moved slowly forward. From behind Zach came a murmur, 'Too fucking much. That is just the pits. It is shit.'

The street was the beginning of the journey – or the end.

Mikey had told them what he'd seen, and they'd done what squaddies did: they'd sworn. They were no longer in the world of Catterick, Warminster, Aldershot or Colchester pubs with a regiment in Iraq or Helmand, but they behaved as if the clock had been turned back. It was their way of dealing with the blow.

Mikey had seen a knot of men in the doorway of a hardware store: their eyes were fixed on the doorway to a block four storeys high. Mikey had the aerial photograph on his knee, and the map of the streets off Shirzad and bordering Enghelab Avenue.

Wally said, 'We're too late.'

Down Rafah Street, on the same side as the hardware store, there was another business: outside, a man moved old cookers and fridges onto his pavement space; a group of men allowed him to manoeuvre around their legs. They didn't back off or help, just looked up Rafah Street, their eye on the same place, the doorway to the apartment building.

Ralph tried humour: 'I got here as soon as I could, ref. Honest.'

'Fucking well wrap it,' Mikey said. 'Too late and too early. Too late because there's goons here. Too early because she's still inside. She's there, our Foxtrot.'

'And our sunshine boy can't walk up the stairs, ring the fucking bell and—' Wally was interrupted.

'Don't need the obvious. Keep moving.'

Zach did as he was told. Men of the Ministry of Intelligence and Security or VEVAK, or whatever they called themselves this week, were 'goons'. He was 'sunshine' or 'sunshine boy'. The wife of the chauffeur, Farideh, was Foxtrot, and her husband, Mehrak, was Mother. He thought that was part of their old life and doubted they'd ever be free of it. He did as he was told, because Mikey was the boss, and drove slowly down the street. He saw a café and a launderette, a kiosk where newspapers and cigarettes were sold, and a store in which there were tins on shelves and bread on the counters.

He dawdled in low gear and reckoned that if he was any slower he'd attract attention. If he brought the eyes of two sets of goons onto him then maybe the shooters would come out. In the mirror he could see the goons at the hardware store, middle-aged men. They had jobs, wages and status, just as they'd had when he was here for his two weeks and when he was at the School where the kids had refused to accept what goons did on the street. If he looked out through the windscreen he could see a scooter idling ahead and then the other goons. He couldn't park outside the building's entrance. He couldn't do circuits of the block – he might not be spotted the first time but would attract them the second. All this bloody way, all this fucking effort . . . He was swearing in his mind because the guys did and it was contagious. It was their language and that of the men on the site, but not usually his. He had neither military experience nor the discipline of the man and woman who had flown out with them. Nothing in his life, he realised, could have prepared him adequately for where he was and what was now expected of him. He could see inside the building to a darkened lobby. He ducked his head and saw the windows. He thought a dark shadow crossed one.

'What to do?'

'Don't rightly know, sunshine. Giving it a think,' Mikey said.

He couldn't go any slower. He was on Rafah Street in central Tehran and the operation was screwed. It was madness. How did men, like Dunc, and women, like Mandy or the American in the Humvee, get themselves signed up to such lunacy? It was about the stakes. He was level with the men at the shop that sold second-hand electricals, and now past the kiosk and the café. The scooter had stopped at the junction in front to wait for a traffic break. When it came, Zach would have to follow and Rafah Street would be out of sight. He thought Mikey's mind was churning. It was one thing to make a plan with photographs, maps and aerial pictures, another to be on the ground, eyeballing goons. The stakes were high so lunacy was permissible.

He heard Ralph's voice. He said, laconic, 'She's out, Foxtrot is.'

'You sure?' Mikey twisted in his seat.

'Ask the goons. They'll tell you it's her.'

She came out. There was a fine drizzle in the air. She had met two of her neighbours on the stairs and they had cut her. It was as if she was marked with a curse. It would have been known throughout the building that her husband had disappeared, had made trouble, and that investigators had been at the apartment, again, and that a man of importance had come in his Mercedes, which had filled Rafah Street.

She wore a *chador*, with a veil that hung below her eyes to cover her face. That day she had put on a pair of leather boots, black with a red inlay. Two years ago she had lied that she had saved for them and bought them herself. The boots had been a gift from the Captain. She had been out of the city with him, on his scooter; they had gone high into the Alborz and beyond the tea houses. He had brought a blanket and they had made love on the ground, almost naked and noisily. They had come down on a rough path to the scooter and she had stumbled. The heel from her shoe, cheaply made and from China, had snapped off. He had taken her to a shop in the north of the city, near to where he lived. She had never before owned an item of clothing or footwear that had cost as much as she earned in a month. She had told the lie that night when Mehrak came in from work. Today she was wearing black woollen gloves and was carrying a shopping bag. Behind her, the apartment was darkened. A van, its rear door flapping, was about to turn out of her street.

After they had left she had gone back to bed, lain down and closed her eyes. She hadn't slept. She had started to wash and dress an hour after they had left, and their threats had seared her mind.

The van seemed to loiter on the far side of the street, and she saw a face in the cab. She thought the fine rain might turn to sleet. A sharp wind funnelled down the street. The headpiece of the *chador*, over her hair, was damp.

They reacted. Farideh could not have said whether they were the same men who had been in the doorways. They dropped their cigarettes. She turned left out of the building, and they followed her. A half-turn, and she saw that a car, a black Paykan with privacy side windows, had come off Shirzad, filled her street and idled. She understood. She would be followed on foot as she walked, and by car when she took the bus. She looked ahead. She thought the word was out along the length of the street. The man in the kiosk with the newspapers ignored her, although she knew him well and often bought Mehrak's cigarettes from him. At the store where she bought bread, the man was putting out the sign on which he'd chalked his best offers. He looked away. She walked with her shoulders back. The men in Ali's doorway had also discarded their cigarettes. They were waiting for her.

The escort followed her to the bus stop. Several women stood there, all in 'good *hijab*'. Before Johnny had picked her up off the pavement, she would have thought, as her mother did, that such dress was appropriate. She was among the crows who would ride in the back of the bus. Some of the men had piled into the car that had followed her down Farah Street, and others were at the bus stop, close to her.

'How do we know her? Which one is she?' Wally asked.

'Look for the shoes,' Mikey said. 'Black with the red slash.'

'Which stop?' Ralph asked.

'When it comes, get up close, sunshine. Look for the shoes, boots. Watch them on and watch them off. Can you do that?'

Zach almost laughed. He was in central Tehran, a capital city that believed itself at war, that had political law and order problems and was policed against dissent, revolution and the breaching of morality codes. What to do? Get to a bus stop, then bend down and check for footwear with a red line on black leather. He said, 'She's going to work – her office is on the map. That's where she'll go.'

'If she doesn't?'

He gritted his teeth. 'She'll go to work.'

'On your head be it, sunshine . . . On all our heads.'

The bus came. There was almost warfare as the women struggled for a place in the rear section. The tail car was close behind the bus, and a scooter was alongside. At least three of the men had boarded at the front. Zach was tucked in behind. He had seen only her eyes. The bus swayed into the traffic and was hard to follow. Did he have any reputation with the shooters? If he did, struggling through dense traffic, it was on the line.

The recorder's spools turned.

Questions put: 'The last time they did an air-defence exercise at Natanz, what was the estimated success rate? Aircraft downed?'

Answers given: 'They claimed one hundred per cent success. That was what they said in the command bunker.'

'Your man, what did he say?'

'He said it was shit. He said the figure was unreal. He also said that the warheads for the ground-to-air would need three hours' warning because they must be taken from the storage and engineers fit them to the missiles. He said they wouldn't have three hours, and the engineers needed to arm the warheads didn't live in the silos but had to come by bus.'

Tiny cups of strong coffee, made in the kitchen by Sidney's wife. More cigarettes.

'What can they do abroad, if they're attacked?'

'He talked of this. Maybe a hundred days ago there was a briefing in the Ramadhan barracks, with many people from embassies abroad, all al-Qods, attached to security and labelled as diplomats, with cover. They hold explosives and detonators, and they have targets. I have given you some principal targets. But the explosives are there and the targets will be American first, Israeli second. I think the British are after the Germans as priority. Each embassy has its own list – Rome, Berlin, Paris, Vienna, Madrid.'

'How would it be done?'

'It is expected there would be two days, maybe three, of tension and build-up to an attack. In that time the bomb equipment will be moved from the embassies to covert positions.'

'This is excellent, Mehrak.'

An answer without a question prompting it: 'I do my best. I thank you for what you do for my wife.'

The bus stopped.

A dozen women spilled from the rear door, half of them in black with their hair covered, men around them. There was another van, larger, between them and the stationary bus. The bus started again and fumes belched from the exhaust. Which was she?

Zach said, 'I think this is where her office is.'

The bus pulled away. They scanned the pavement for her. Zach and Mikey had the best view, with Ralph and Wally squashed behind them. Mikey saw the motorbike first. Then a car arrived. Zach thought it was the one that had been in Rafah Street. Three men jumped out.

She was in the middle of the road on a traffic island. There was a gap, momentary, and Ralph pointed. The woman with her head covered was wearing boots with a red flash on them. She was being tailed, men following her. She had to wait for a gap in the traffic before she crossed to the far side of the road, but the goons didn't bother: they had ID in their hands, raised it and the drivers paused to let them through. She went into a building. Zach said the sign over the glass door was for an insurance company. They were double-parked now and being hooted at. The woman was followed by a tail, who loitered outside the door. Hope slid away.

Wally needed to pee. Ralph said that the Israeli had left a bucket with the builders' tools. He hadn't supplied any food or water.

A man was at the window. He was affable, overweight, everybody's friend. He spoke through the glass to Mikey, and Zach took over. The man needed him to move the van so he could get his car out. Zach backed, the car drove out and the man waved.

Zach put the van into the space. She would be at work for the day. What should they do? he asked Mikey.

'We watch, wait, think, and hope for some luck.'

'I'm very sorry.'

Farideh was at Reception, had straightened her pencils and notepad, cleaned her telephone and the computer screen, and changed the date on the calendar. The Human Resources man had bustled forward and said what he had to say. He had mumbled an empty explanation, repeated it, and she hadn't moved. Anger blazed in her.

'You're sorry? For what?'

He stumbled. 'I'm sorry I must ask you to leave.'

'Why do you ask me to leave?'

She didn't have a university degree, as many who worked for the company did, but she was a hard and reliable worker.

The reason for her dismissal was clear. 'We have to protect the good name of the company.'

The man from Human Resources had his back to the door and the street. She could see past him. Her watchers had already lit their cigarettes. She didn't know whether they were the same men who had been in the doorway of Jamali's or Ali's business, but they had a kind of uniform: grey slacks, black shoes, a jacket under a black-leather coat or anorak; their hair was cut in the same way, short but not shaven; they had stubble on their cheeks and they smoked. They were a little aside from the door. Every adult living in Tehran knew the dress of the men from Intelligence and Security. Anyone approaching the door, needing a fire and theft policy, or one against breakdown or accident, would know that a worker in the company was under close surveillance.

'It's not the fault of any colleague here that you've attracted the attention of those people. During the night, the executive officer received a call from a responsible person asking for details of your behaviour. We require you to leave.'

'What severance pay do I get? What notice of termination am I being given?' She already knew the answers: no severance sum, and she must go after she'd cleared the drawer in which she kept her few possessions: a bottle of water, a packet of sanitary towels, and some throat sweets. They would know that her husband worked in the al-Qods division of IRGC and that he drove a man of status: Mehrak had dropped her at the door occasionally from the Mercedes. If a woman within the 'family' of the al-Qods was under close surveillance, it was a serious matter.

His voice dropped so that he was barely audible. 'There's nothing I can do. I'm just the messenger. I wish you well, Farideh.'

He probably did wish her well. Until now she had always been able to manipulate him. She had taken afternoons off to meet Johnny, and whole days when the Captain had driven her out of the city. She had allowed him to give her chocolates. She had always been correct with him but never distant. Maybe he was wetting himself because of his perceived closeness to a woman who had attracted the interest of Intelligence and Security.

She was handed a sheet of paper. She didn't bother to read the close-printed terms of her dismissal, just scrawled her name on a dotted line. Then she opened the drawer and dumped the contents into her shopping bag. She didn't acknowledge anyone at the desks behind Reception. She adjusted her veil and walked to the glass door. She went out into the street. The drizzle had indeed turned to sleet and the wind blustered across the pavement. The cigarettes were thrown down.

Johnny had taught her, the Captain had added to what she had learned, and Kourosh had refined it. On the street, she felt true fear. She didn't notice the fumes kick from the exhaust of a builder's van on the far side of the road, or an artisan slip out of a flapping rear door. She saw a man swing his leg astride the pillion of a motorbike and others hurrying towards the open doors of a Paykan.

She would use what she had learned from Johnny, the Captain and Kourosh, and go to the one place that might be a haven, and the only two men she could trust.

* * *

Her face was projected on the screen. Kourosh, alone, knew the image did her no justice. A small room on the fourth floor was filled with men. The day's duties were handed to the teams by a briefing officer. They were star performers, the best, and they considered themselves at the cutting edge of the war against covert infiltration of the state. They reckoned they could sniff out the agents of the Zionists and the Great Satan. Each time a bomb exploded in the capital, and a chemist or physicist died in the wreckage of his car, it was a personal insult to such men. All but one had worked as a team leader in either south Lebanon, Damascus, or Baghdad and Basra. That evening they would arrest her.

Authorisation was needed and was guaranteed, the briefer had said, but because of certain elements connected to the investigation – and the seniority of a person close to it – a signature must be obtained. All would be in place by the evening. And for that day? There was the ongoing watch on the man who had a hire-car business in the Gholak district in north-east Tehran, and some would spend time there. There was a travel agent on a street south of the central bazaar: he often – too often? – travelled abroad to tourist fairs specialising in Russian, Ukrainian, Bulgarian and Romanian resorts; his phones were monitored and so were his computers. He was watched. At the end of the day, they would take the stairs to the first-floor apartment on Rafah Street.

Kourosh's gut twisted. He was married, his wife was seven months pregnant, and he was in danger. He shuddered. There would be no interference from a senior official. Whoever might have an interest in the investigations would not be tolerated. It would be a long day until the time for her arrest . . . she might name him.

He was in his office, had been there since leaving Rafah Street. The Mercedes had been driven by one of the team accompanying him. Brigadier Reza Joyberi had seen two of them smirk when the blanket had slipped off her shoulders. He might have flushed. He thought word would have spread among the men that she hadn't cringed from him. He was vulnerable.

He had gone to his office in the barracks. In a rare moment of weakness, he had walked past the glass-fronted annexe, where the guards waited for their officers, and peered into the corner where his corporal should have been. Another man had been there, a colonel's driver. He had gone to his office. He had not been brought the day's newspapers or a piece of cake. He realised he didn't know where cigarettes were sold in the barracks. He hadn't needed to know. He felt in his pocket, took out a packet, opened it and counted how many were left.

Surprises confronted Brigadier Reza Joyberi.

His telephone crackled in his ear. Twice he shouted at a man to speak more slowly and clearly.

His desk-top computer refused to link him into the secure site where he worked. An engineer had flicked the keyboard and been evasive as to a solution. A colleague was in a meeting that was not to be interrupted. An inspection that afternoon of security procedures at an arsenal fifteen kilometres from the capital – arrangements made three months before – was postponed. He was not told who had given the order or supplied with a new date.

He recognised what he was experiencing. In his career, he had seen men who were 'isolated'. Each 'success' gained allies but every 'failure' lost them. Sinking men had tried to call him and he had either not replied, not called back or forgotten them.

It was hard to believe that his chauffeur had been targeted by the Zionists or the Americans. A rumour had seeped back from across the Gulf that investigators there had identified a brothel, now closed. More rumours spread about deception of the Coast Guard, the police, the newspaper and the broadcasting station. That his chauffeur was considered worth an effort on such a scale could at first be dismissed as ridiculous. Then his mind cleared. Conversations with the military or IRGC local commanders in the back of the Mercedes as it purred along major roads, and a driver whose eyes seemed never to leave the road. Evenings in the traffic jams of Tehran, at the end of a long day, when he had vented his frustrations at the neatly cut hair on the back of the head in front of him. A morning when he had put a sealed envelope into the hand of the corporal with a flight ticket, a wad of cash, a number and a password. He had never before doubted Mehrak's loyalty.

Petroc Kenning had told them that the material gathered that morning had been of real value. A reward was on offer.

Nobby thought of it as a banana thrown to a chimpanzee. The boss, PK, would be transmitting material to London. Sidney was shopping in the village, and Father William was on his bed because he'd be taking the night shift. The banana was a brief walk: Nobby and Auntie would take the corporal up the hill for a breath of fresh air, as recompense for good work. It would give Anneliese a chance to push the vacuum-cleaner round the ground-floor rooms and open the windows to get rid of the smell of stale smoke.

There was another reason to take him out.

The fog had lifted off the river. The village was laid out below them. Nobby would have mutinied at the thought of carrying a firearm. Auntie didn't mind: he had a pistol in his belt, while Nobby pocketed, reluctantly, a telescopic police baton. He'd done the course.

They wrapped him up well in a heavy coat, a beanie, gloves and boots.

The other reason involved an internal dispute.

Nobby, with the baton, walked a pace ahead. Auntie was a little behind. They sandwiched him. There was a faint rumble of traffic on the road below, a bypass cutting off the village, and the drone of a couple of tractors. A little of the year's harvest remained to be cut. Nobby knew a bit about wine, but not as much as most of the Service's officers: many regarded it as a badge of honour to be informed on years, crops, labels and the merits of different vineyards. On the river, which was a surly grey, a tug dragged a snake of barges upstream. There were no tourist boats. The bell in the church tower struck.

The dispute had centred on the corporal.

Trusted or not? Coughing up the real stuff or holding back? What was his idea of a life after his wife had joined him and he'd been squeezed dry? Was he truthful? Nobby's view: he didn't know. The boss thought it was manna from heaven, that they were getting the best and the brothel trap was as good as it gets. Auntie and Father William tended towards the boss. Sidney, no pedigree with them but known to an aged relative of PK, wouldn't vouch for him. The wind came through the gorge, whipping their faces and clothing.

Auntie said, from behind, 'It'll be good, Mehrak, when your wife comes, and you've a good chance of a new life, a secure one. A start.'

Nobby led, hearing the scrape of feet coming after him.

'You're in the hands of generous people. The mistakes you made are in the past.'

They approached an arch built of old stone. In the house there were books on the village – the product of a fledgling tourist agency, Nobby thought. Four hundred years ago, the books said, this had been one of seven gates into the village of Spitz, already an important place for wine; it had been the focal point of an attack by the Swedish Army – the defenders had been massacred. So, this was the Rotes Tor, the Red Gate, from which the Swedes had gone down the hill into the village and done their pillaging and raping on a grand scale.

Nobby had a degree in modern languages: he could read the German guidebook; he spoke Spanish and Italian too.

He'd married while he was at Warwick University, but they'd gone their separate ways within a couple of years and divorced fourteen years ago. He was forty now and would be Nobby for the rest of his life. There was no new wife but he had a girlfriend, Kathy, in FCO, now posted in Kazakhstan, the embassy at Astana. She sent him emails about being on the steppes, horse-riding with a commercial attaché. Nobby lived in her flat but she charged him rent – had put it up a couple of months ago. He knew he was regarded as pleasant, clubbable and unambitious. He did his job, stayed below the radar, and shunned responsibility. Put simply, Nobby didn't know whether the corporal was intelligent enough to use them as a means of moving on. He had done Irish turncoats and a Libyan interrogator. Each was different. He found the psyche of the defector unfathomable – 'I mean, what a totally dumb thing to do.' There was a bench by the old gate and a misty view.

'Set yourself up in a business. Keep to the quiet life, no waves. You've a good future.' He sat down, but the corporal did not. Neither did Auntie. Auntie stayed behind him. Trust did not exist. Did Nobby like the man? Not at all. Was he ever going to like the man? Improbable. He thought the place beautiful, and that he was privileged to be there, high above the Danube and the gorge, but it was wasted on him. And on the man they guarded. 'I expect you're tired. That's natural. It was a tough session, going back so far into your memory. Just concentrate on the future – your wife with you. Any idea what sort of business you might get into? We have people who can help with that.'

All of them lived with the photograph of her. Nobby did, and Auntie and Father William, and PK had pressured for the extraction to happen, and Sidney had had the cheek to stop the car by their embassy and 'nick' the red rose bloom growing off their diplomatic territory.

Auntie said, 'What about your wife, Mehrak? What do you think she'd like to do?'

The man was crying silently, his hands clamped on the back of the bench. His knuckles were white, Nobby saw, and his shoulders were shaking. It was halfway through the first day that the boys had spent over the frontier – poor beggars – and in two and a half more the call would come through of the pick-up, or the phone in Petroc Kenning's pocket would stay silent. The next two and a half days would be tough. The man cried and made no effort to get a handkerchief from his pocket. Nobby did not intervene but watched the tractor and its trailer below them, and the women lopping the grapes. They'd be tough days, hard to weather. Maybe only the corporal understood quite how tough.

They were back from shopping in Doğubeyazıt where there was a SPAR. Dunc had pushed the trolley and Mandy had filled it.

Dunc used to do it with his wife on a Saturday morning, but he'd been divorced now for the last eleven months and separated a year before that. It was what Mandy did with her husband early on Sunday mornings. She'd paid too, and put the receipt into her purse. They'd driven back to the accommodation and parked.

The sun was up and the wind was cold.

She said, 'I've written what you'd put on a postcard, about the place. "Dear Tad, Dog is a dump. As many sheep as locals in the main boulevard. It stinks, is seriously short of regeneration and is Mafia-land, Mandy xxx". Too long, but bollocks to that.'

'I reckon you're selling it short. I've put, "Dear Sara, Have settled in and we have excellent views, not only of the corporation rubbish tip. Not mugged yet, but are optimistic our turn will come, Dunc." Let's have a cup of tea.'

God alone knew how the Ankara people had come up with this address. They were clear of the town of Doğubeyazıt, whole population was ethnic Kurdish, and had a garrison of mechanised paratroops who were ethnic Turks. The road from the town ran towards the Iranian border, fifteen miles or less, but there was a track to the left of the road that ducked behind an escarpment where the house was tucked away. From Mandy's bedroom, it was indeed possible to see the rubbish tip, but the views were excellent. The peak of Ararat was clear from both bedrooms and the living area. It was ten miles away and the cliché-mongers would have said it was 'iconic.' He said it was 'fantastic' and she thought it 'awesome'. There was the main mountain, a Little Ararat and more peaks to the east, where the road ran.

She unpacked the plastic bags and he was on his knees at the fire. The town was a 'dump'. It was shabby and dirty, a proportion of the building work had been abandoned, the cold was brutal, most of the shops were half empty, the cars were ancient and poverty had settled there. The comforts of Europe seemed an age away. The jeeps with the well-wrapped troops of an occupying force cruised past the deprivation.

They'd talked about it the night before, after their picnic meal in the kitchen, and had swapped what they knew of the tensions between a Kurdish population and a Turkish government in this area: ambushes, killings, arrests, gaol, torture, guerrilla bands, army patrols and road checks. They'd talked about the economy of the town – smuggling, corruption, organised crime. The town was a 'dump', but the property in which they were housed was spacious, comfortable, well furnished, clean, and had cost money. It was stone-built. It had double glazing and decent rugs on tiled floors. The crockery, utensils and cutlery in the kitchen were new and the fridge worked. So did the cooker. The fire took.

There were glass doors onto a patio. The aspect showed Ararat, where Noah *might* have been and where his Ark *might* have beached. Smoke from damp wood belched in the grate. Ararat, snow-capped, the winter probing lower now on its slopes, was the backdrop. He assimilated what was close. Beyond the patio there was rough ground, with a mix of goats and sturdy, short-legged sheep grazing on yellowed grass. There was a rough post-and-rail fence, which enclosed a compound of worn, churned earth where the vegetation had long been trampled out. A cluster of horses gathered around a broken hay bale. Dunc thought them fine-looking, and they had a ruggedness that suited the bleakness of the landscape. Strange that the horses hadn't been there when they'd reached the house, or in the closed field when they had gone into the town to shop. Dunc thought them bred to work. He knew nothing about horses, but now he felt a part of something timeless. Mandy was behind him, and he hadn't heard her come in. 'Timeless' meant biblical.

'It beats Bognor,' she said.

He struggled for words. 'The vista sort of puts things into proportion. Take out the corporation rubbish tip, and what's changed in the last few millennia? It's extraordinary.'

She passed him his mug. He gazed at the horses and should have understood but did not. He should have realised what had funded such a fine building.

The thought came to him, a shock. The face of Zach filled his mind. His hand shook, slopping the tea, and he heard her disapproving tut. Beyond the horses was the road. Far up the road, where the heavy trucks ran, was the junction, and past the junction were the hills and the frontier. He could see a little of the line and over it, but the young man he had bearded on the building site was invisible. He thought God might damn him for the plausibility of what he had said to him. It didn't matter that Zach Becket had seemed to welcome him and his proposition. That was why he had spilled his tea. God might damn him.

He was given orders and obeyed them.

She led.

'Slippery as an eel,' Mikey murmured.

'No idea where, but she's learned it.'

The goons couldn't match her counter-surveillance skills.

Had it not been for Mikey's commentary, Zach would have grasped only half of what she was doing. Ralph made the calls, his head wedged between Zach and Mikey's shoulders, although Mikey had first shout on speed. She was causing havoc with the goons. Twice their car had gone too fast and picked on the wrong black *chador*. It had tucked into the slow lane and idled behind a woman, discovered the error, had to brake – and she had lost them. More than once the motorcycle had turned in the traffic, chancing a limb on the respect given to an ID card. The goons on foot had run, stood on pavements and traffic islands, then pirouetted, their phones to their ears and sprinted to catch up with the wheels.

She did cut-outs. She did double-backs. She did shop doorways. In through one entrance of a supermarket and out of a side door. They'd have lost her themselves but for Ralph's eye. They had forgotten they were thirsty. Mikey said it wasn't that the goons were piss-poor but that she was quality.

They ignored their tiredness.

North of Enghelab and west of Belavar, Ralph rapped an order and Zach braked. Ralph was out of the van and walking after her. Zach didn't have to be told – it was easier for him to follow Ralph's head bobbing among the men on the pavement.

He had lost the woman. And *they* had, too. Mikey confirmed it.

Zach couldn't remember the last time he had carried out instructions to the letter without arguing. It was apparent to him that a pattern was in place. Mikey was their leader, Ralph was expert in surveillance, and he didn't yet know Wally's talent but expected to learn it.

A time would come when Ralph would lead them to where she had gone and they would confront her. Zach would talk. He wouldn't have Mikey on his back or suggestions in English from Ralph or Wally. His turn in the spotlight would come.

He swung off the avenue into a narrow street. There were small businesses on either side, and he could smell food cooking. Sheets hung from upper windows and dripped damp, music played, and he was drawn back to when he had last been in the city, its sounds, tastes, scents. He slowed to a crawl.

Mikey's hand was on his arm, squeezed, and he stopped. A woman pushed a pram past him. He could hear a man and a woman shouting at each other on a floor above. Kids kicked a ball in the road, one wearing a Real Madrid shirt, the other Inter Milan.

'She was good,' Mikey said. 'Too good for the goons. But Ralph instructs on the courses.' He chuckled.

Wally's hands were on Zach's shoulders, pressing down for encouragement.

Ralph stood by a set of half-open gates into a yard. He pushed them wider and backoned. Zach saw Mikey ease a pistol from his belt, check the magazine and the ammunition in the breach. His finger was tight on the trigger guard.

'You good, kid?' Mikey asked him.

Zach nudged the van through the gates and into the yard. Ralph closed them behind him. They all had a job to do, and now it was his turn. He swung his legs out of the cab, stretched and cleared his throat, then walked towards a door. He thought he was alone.

They heard the gate scrape open and Highness went to deal with the customer.

'What shall I do?' She was sitting on the rug, facing the long couch where she had lain with Johnny and the Captain. She cradled the glass of tea that Excellency had brought to her. She had told them what had happened, and Excellency had squeezed his eyes shut and shaken his head. Highness had clucked as he always did when his nerves were stretched. They didn't have to tell her that they were in danger now because of her.

A voice at the door, speaking Farsi: 'My name is Zach. Farideh, I came to find you.'

7

All eyes were on him. There were two older men – late seventies or even eighties – and one had reached to his belt. Zach assumed a pistol had once hung there. The expression flitting across their faces was of fear.

'I've come to bring you out.'

Perhaps someone in one of the great agencies of the state had written a procedure for moments like this – what to say, and how to say it. He had been unable to rehearse – the guy on the doorstep selling encyclopedias when he was a kid would have made a better job of it – but he had good Farsi.

'Bring you out and take you to your husband.'

The men, dressed in mechanics' overalls, seemed hardly to hear him. Their eyes were locked on the guys behind him: all three had come with him through the workshop and up the stairs. There had been the soft voices to guide them and they had come light-footed across a landing and paused by the door. Mikey had laid a hand on his shoulder, propelled him into the room – and he had seen her.

Who did he represent, Zach wondered? In his mind he saw Dunc, who had the charisma of a building-regulations inspector but had effortlessly hooked him. And there was Mandy, with the brisk efficiency of a manager at any wholesaler's supplying breeze blocks. He realised now that the seniors had kept their distance. Zach might have appeared on a screen for scrutiny, but then the lesser stars had been called out, Dunc and Mandy. Mikey, Wally and Ralph were not from the pedigree Special Forces . . . He was *expendable*. The word clattered in his skull. They all were. He should have found out where their loyalties lay and where he stood on their priority list. He had not analysed their job. She looked at him from the floor.

'Your husband's in Europe, in a place of safety.'

He had no idea what she was thinking, whether she believed a word he'd said – did she understand what he'd said?

Briefly he was back at the School, in a group of second and third years. The lecturer was Iranian-born and so were the other five students. They spoke Farsi at home and couldn't understand his love of their language. He knew he spoke it well, but *they* had said he was 'remarkable'. They had played games at the table, – a shopping expedition in the bazaar, or an argument over a newspaper column at a bus stop. Sometimes they wheedled and at others they argued. He had survived alongside them, had never been the passenger: she had understood everything he'd said.

'. . . and we've come to take you out and reunite you with him. This morning we saw you were followed and we understand the danger facing you.'

The old men looked past him and would have seen the pistols Mikey and Wally were holding. Ralph had brought a bigger weapon. They didn't speak. Neither did she.

'Your husband gave himself up to the British mission in Dubai, and is safe. He wasn't kidnapped or coerced. He volunteered to leave the region and the responsible British agencies are tasked to protect him. We're here to take you out so that you can join him.'

The photograph he had seen did her justice. She wasn't film-star beautiful, but something about her captivated him.

What was it? Her simplicity, for a start – and vulnerability. Her skin was clear and she wore a touch of lipstick, but that was all. There was, as he read it, innocence in her gaze. The gate to the yard creaked.

Because she didn't answer him, he ploughed on. He pulled the photograph out of his pocket and held it close to her face. 'That's all I have to say. We're here in secret, of course. Your husband is well taken care of. He wants you beside him. A new life, a new start. The offer is just for you, not your family. It's clear that you're already under surveillance and your arrest is probably imminent. We need to go.'

The old men were close to her. He couldn't gauge the relationship, only their love for her. He looked away and took in the room. Below, they'd walked through a workshop where mechanics fixed motorbikes amid engine oil, grease and dirt. This room presented a sharp contrast. She was sitting on a clean rug from a craftsman's stall in the bazaar. In front of her, against a wall, there was a small double bed, silk cushions at the head. He assumed it was her bolthole. Why did Farideh, wife of the corporal, need it? The answer shouted itself at him. There was a table to the side with two photographs on it, both in silver-plate frames. He heard Mikey's fingers snap with impatience.

'We were sent to bring you out. My colleagues say you used good techniques to lose the surveillance, but we haven't much time. So that you know, we'll be going north-west, via Qazvin and Zanjan, Mianeh and Tabriz. We'll meet men who will take us over the mountains and into Turkey. For now you've lost the tail, but that just increases the danger you're in. They'll be searching hard. We have to go – now.'

One photograph showed a young man smiling, with a confidence that bordered on arrogance. Zach recognised a lover. In the other frame, the second man wore combat fatigues and a *fedayeen* scarf, a holster was slung against his thigh, the handle of a pistol protruding from it. There were tribesmen in a clutch behind him, like the ones Zach saw on the television news. Afghanistan. Another lover.

'No goodbyes. We have to go – now.'

No response. If she was thinking about what he'd said, she gave no sign of it. Time to reflect on his own motivation. He'd been set a challenge, trusted to go where only idiots went. At the School they had tried to talk about the post-election riots and on the television news there had been video images of the *basij* rampaging. It had shown the brutal suppression of the demonstrations – and the newsreaders had reported on the trials and hangings. Few in the School had accepted the wrongness of a stolen election . . .

'I say it again, *please*, you have to come with us or we'll turn our backs on you, leaving you to hope the surveillance never catches up with you.'

She gave Zach a small smile, and frowned. Now she would answer.

'I loathe him.'

She said it clearly. She might have slapped his face: he had looked at the photographs of Johnny, hanged in Evin, and the Captain, killed by a sniper. He had looked at the bed. She had a little English, which might have carried her into a university course, but she had married. He translated for those behind him – his protection. Rain pattered on the window panes.

She said, 'I detest him.'

Excellency whispered in Highness's ear.

'I have done nothing. I am innocent of any crime.'

The wind blustered against the gates into the yard.

'I hate him. Why would I go with you?'

He heard an oath and imagined their faces falling. His mind churned. 'Did I hear you right? No problem. We'll just catch a bus home, and tell our boss she didn't like her old man and was happy where she was. Win some, lose some. A wasted trip. Laugh or cry?' Zach had nothing to say.

The wet was in his face. The counter-intelligence officer, Kourosh, had lurched into the main street and was clear of the alleyway that led from the repair yard. He was shaken and confused. He should never have been there. It had been, he had thought, his last chance.

He had come through the gates – had needed to push them only slightly to get through. The lights had been bright in the workshop. A scooter lay on its side with the engine parts on the bench. He had heard the voice at the top of the stairs and the door into the room was ajar.

He and his colleagnes were the cream. They were feared, they had access, they received all the small envelopes they could handle. Traders who knew where they worked seldom charged them for any item without first adjusting the price to include the expected discount. In his home he had flat-screen TVs, a desk-top computer and a quality phone for his wife. His and her parents received the best, and he could walk along his street with a swagger. He had all he needed for a life of relative comfort – except the wife of the brigadier's driver.

It was a pursuit that could have destroyed him. The corporal's wife was a dream. When the fools who would be put across the border into Afghanistan were gathered together, their eyes glowed with excitement at trying on the waistcoat into which the explosive sticks, the clusters of nails and the detonators were sewn, and they heard of virgins who awaited the *shahid* after he had blown apart his body. They were a tool, the more accurate equivalent of artillery shells. He had seen those eyes, and the light in them, and had sensed the longing for martyrdom. He was no different from the men he despised. She dangled him and could destroy him.

He had heard in the command centre that she was to be arrested that evening and that she had thrown off her tail. Kourosh had known where she would be. He had gone to warn her that her arrest was imminent, to give her a chance to flee the city or to stay hidden in the workshop's upper room. He had never been able, fully, to undress her. He thought that in reward for his warning she would allow him to unfasten all of her buttons and zips. He would be watched by the man who had been hanged in the Evin and the man who had been shot in Afghanistan, which would heighten his excitement. He had heard.

At the top of the stairs, barely daring to breathe, he had seen the side of a man's body – anorak, jeans, a roughened hand with an old ring on it and a pistol he recognised as a SIG Sauer P226.

He knew the route they would use and that they would go that day.

As a counter-intelligence officer, Kourosh could analyse accents and this one, with its pure Farsi, intrigued him. He knew Kurdish speech textures from investigations of the usual ethnic allies employed by the Mossad, and the Azeri intonation from the Arab south-west of Iran where the American Agency infiltrated.

The Pakistanis had links with Baluch people across Iran and in its far-eastern border area. He hadn't seen the man who had spoken and couldn't fault his speech, but recognised him as a foreigner. There had been an increase in British-originated signals from Dubai in the hours after the driver's disappearance, and it had been reported from a military base to the north that a British transport aircraft had landed during the night. He assumed the speaker's nationality.

He had thought that Farideh would be grateful for his warning. She would have sent away the old men who tinkered with out-of-date machines, and would have demonstrated her gratitude on her back. He was out of the alley and in the street. He was a product of the revolution and hunted its enemies.

In the road, horns exploded around him. He heard the scream of tyres, abuse directed at him and fingers raised in insult. For a moment he was rooted to the spot . Then he began to walk.

He crossed the street decisively.

Beyond Enghelab and the park was the office from which he worked. He had seen past the SIG Sauer P226 to the bed, smooth and not creased. He should have been welcomed onto it. He could have screamed. His wallet bounced in an inner pocket of the anorak. Her picture was inside it, hidden.

Kourosh returned to his office.

She was in a huddle with the two men. They were whispering. He heard nothing clearly.

Time gone could not be reclaimed, and time lost was risk heightened. The old men had their arms round her shoulders, made a wall and gave her the illusion of safety. She didn't argue with them, and he couldn't see her face. Once, he had turned to Mikey and grimaced, but Mikey's hand had stayed on his arm and the grip had tightened: she needed a moment to clear her head.

But she *loathed* her husband. And she was *innocent* of any crime.

He thought he had made the pitch well. But he would be blamed for failure, not the guys. Nobody had said her marriage was a sham. Nobody had said either that she had a shag nest above a garage, with pictures on display of the men who had mattered to her. He was angry, and knew it was because he was frightened. Nobody had told him anything.

They would quit. Soon he'd be revving the engine, Ralph or Wally would be dragging back the gates and he'd reverse out. He'd do the first leg of the drive, and the space allocated to her would be empty. He wondered, as he waited for an answer, what the boys on the site had said about him. They'd remember the beers in the pub, that the man who had paid had worn a suit. Rumour would have run wild. He'd drive the first leg and get clear of the streets.

On the open road, Ralph would take over. They'd pull in at a lay-by that had cover and Mikey would set up the satphone. There were two call options. If she wasn't with them, it would be 'Foxtrot gone to ground,' no explanation.

He'd be blamed. Who else? Not the guys. He didn't see the two who had come as far as İncirlik holding up their hands, admitting inadequate briefing – least of all her. It hurt to wait, but Mikey made him, and gave them time.

'So, what's a nice girl like you doing in . . . ?'

She didn't reply. She was not a girl and Mandy Ross was rarely described as nice.

The house was outside Doğubeyazıt but close enough to catch a signal for her laptop. She sat near the fire, and shivered. Dunc was on a chair nearer to the window, his mobile cradled in his hands. Nothing to do but wait.

She would have regarded 'nice girl' as an insult. She ran agents. In the world in which she stalked, looking for recruitment opportunities, there was little call for the proprieties. The men and women she searched for were usually damaged, always without adequate defences, and her art was to persuade them that *they* needed *her* more than the reverse. Four years ago, at the behest of Mandy Ross, a twenty-three-year-old Iranian, his family in exile in northern England, had gone back to his country of birth 'to renew ties with his family'. He had trembled with fear at the thought of it, but had acquired the visa and climbed on to the plane. It had been hoped that he would initiate a courier chain into the military establishment. After contact had been lost it was eventually reported that he had died under interrogation. Two years ago, a Peruvian trainee accountant with a love of backpacking had been paid to take a hiking holiday close to the uranium mines at Saghand and Yazd. He had a camera and . . . How close should he have been to the mines? Close enough to be shot dead by a sentry at a perimeter fence – tidier than capture. She embraced 'tidiness'. She could have read a book or the morning's London newspapers on her laptop, could even have done her expenses, but she gazed into the fire, watching the smoke surge up the chimney. Several times she heard Dunc clear his throat, and waited.

She was thirty-seven, had one son and the same husband she had hitched up with in her second year at university. He taught mathematics in a select-entry day school in Surrey; her son went to the same school and her husband ran their home. Theirs might have been called a 'semi-detached' marriage, except that they holidayed together. Her love was for Vauxhall Cross. Now she covered the southern Caucasus and Iran from the north to the Gulf. She rejoiced in the creed of Tadeuz Fenton: an enemy, at last, had been produced, a worthwhile target. Often, late at night, she would dream of knotting her fingers in a mullah's beard and tugging hard enough to drag it out at the roots. On weekdays she left home punctually at six forty-five a.m. and returned after nine thirty p.m. Her son and husband would be watching television or sharing a textbook. Her work took first place.

The signing up of the shooters had been down to her. The best on offer. Contego Security was a likely dustbin for men who would go the extra miles to find danger and not want a king's ransom for their efforts. She didn't dress to flatter herself, or to enhance her career. That day, in the extreme corner of Turkey, she wore identical clothing to what was appropriate when she strode along the Albert Embankment to work: blouse, trouser suit and low-heeled shoes.

Dunc was fidgeting with his phone. The silence was broken only by the spitting of logs on the fire. The view was constant:

fields, foothills, the great Mount Ararat and the lesser peaks. The sole movement came from the horses, grazing scattered fodder.

There had been twenty-three, and now there were twenty. Three more packages of refined heroin had been creamed off.

It was not an ambush but an arrangement.

Safe passage cost three packages. At the turning for Kashmar, the vehicles had left the main road, which linked Birjand to Mashhad. The rendezvous had been in a quarry where stone for the road's repairs had been excavated. There was privacy for the men who had brought the packages with the armoured convoy, and for the officers of the Revolutionary Guard Corps who had the power to guarantee the onward passage of the heroin, towards the Turkish border. They would not be interrupted by police, Customs or the counter-narcotics squads. The team from the IRGC would satisfy themselves on the quality of the product, then remove it, and the resin would be resold for the domestic market at a good profit for the paramilitary force. There were ironies that would have been lost on the men tasked to make the deal. In the last several years, Iran had spent seven hundred million American dollars in the war against drugs, erected fences and barriers, sewn minefields along the 900-kilometre border with Afghanistan; three hundred troops, police and Customs men were killed each year in skirmishes with the smugglers, and almost five hundred traffickers inside Iran were hanged after arrest and conviction. But the scale of addiction among Iranians was so great that there was money to be made in feeding it.

A portable stove heated the water for tea.

The city, further down the road, was celebrated for the production of fine raisins and good rugs. It marketed excellent saffron – and high-grade heroin for distribution to those who could pay. The representatives of the IRGC dealt with many commodities and contracts – televisions and computers, the contract to widen the highway, the construction of a new sewage works or the sale of narcotics.

There was much to talk of as the tea was sipped and the three packages lay at the feet of a major. The rumour, travelling at runaway speed, spoke of a defection. A brigadier was involved. His driver was gone. The brigadier was of the al-Qods, the élite. The al-Qods were all-powerful, had no friends, possessed powerful steel-gloved fists. Would a driver know anything about trafficking? They speculated. There was an assumption among them that a driver, however humble, would be trusted. He could hold more detailed knowledge than a colonel, a major or a captain.

Hands were slapped after the tea had been drained. The traffickers could – had it suited their needs – have pumped a magazine of bullets into the officers of the Revolutionary Guard Corps. If there had not been three packages on offer and an arrangement that was profitable and regular, the officers could have organised the execution of these criminals in the gaol at Kashmar or in view of a yelling mob. The arrangement suited.

There was a last round of brush-kisses. The two groups went on their way.

The remaining twenty packages would be linked with others, some with protection and some not, and the common goal would be the high passes of the border with Turkey. There the protection would end and the cover of darkness would be needed.

He had helped and was praised.

A hard session was over and PK had congratulated him. Sidney had brought in sweet biscuits, and the coffee the woman had made was as sharp as he would have drunk at home. He had talked about the brigadier and a conference he had hosted eleven months ago when al-Qods officers, attached to embassies in Europe, had met at the Hamadan barracks. Who were the targets? Who did best at turning exiles? What tactic imposed the greatest pressure on an exile who had family in Iran?

The men at the conference had worn small badges on their lapels. He had identified some and could quote what had been said. There had been a tour of the city on the last afternoon and they had walked in the parks. It had been warm and the men were relaxed. Mehrak had escorted his brigadier. With formality gone, the men had spoken their minds. Berlin and Rome needed more funds. Madrid had too few staff. There were better opportunities to move in the north of England without attracting Special Branch and Security Service surveillance. He had talked and been praised – and had realised that he might as well have been a bear dancing to a whistle in Turkey, lumbering and humiliated.

PK had gone. The coffee and biscuits had replaced him.

The images swam in his mind. The brigadier had laughed with him when he'd told jokes.

He had betrayed him, turned his back on his senior officer. He could see the face, hear the laughter – and the silence of his wife.

He weighed them. He had to choose between two roads: one led to a prisoner's freedom, the other to a noose. Brigadier Reza Joyberi had laughed when Mehrak joked. His wife, Farideh, had not cried out when he had slapped her face. She had slept with her back to him.

To choose . . .

Auntie pushed the plate of biscuits closer. 'You all right, Mehrak? You've gone a bit pale. Anyway, that was a good session and PK's well pleased. We're going to have a break now, maybe half an hour.'

He remembered how it had been at their wedding, that she hadn't cried out on the first night when he had lain on her. He tried to remember the nights before he had hit her.

'You sure you're all right, Mehrak?'

He chose his wife above the friendship of the brigadier.

Time was up.

Mikey let go of Zach's arm.

They were still huddled in front of him, whispering. He sensed they were arguing with her and she was rejecting their advice. The rain ran in rivers on the window and a leaden cloud hung over the rooftops. Mikey had the look, didn't need to say that he should hit and hard.

He asked sharply now, 'Do you have a passport?'

She faced him. 'I do not.'

'Do you have an airline ticket?'

'No.'

'If you have a passport, which you don't, and if you had an airline ticket, which, again, you don't, do you imagine you could walk into the terminal and board an international flight?'

'I would be stopped and arrested.'

'And you have no way out over the mountains?'

'How would I pay the criminals who take people?'

'So you'll stay.'

'I live a separate life from my husband, a divorce but not legal. He will not go to the court because he fears ridicule. I haven't defected. I'm innocent of any crime.'

'These men are your friends?'

'Yes.'

'They have your love and trust?'

'They do.'

Now he went for the throat. He gestured at the two photographs. 'You slept with those men.'

She flushed. 'I did.'

'Committed with them the sin of adultery, punishable here by whipping, hanging or stoning. Don't answer. Listen. They will take you and torture you. At the end of the first day you'll have forgotten you're innocent. You'll confess to anything – and you'll tell them about your lovers – alive or dead?'

'One killed by them, the other dead in Afghanistan.'

'And you'll tell them of these two old men, who gave you the bed to have the sex that is a crime. They will follow you to the gaol. I've come to take you out.'

He sensed her resistance slacken. 'And then?'

'We'll take you over the border, beyond their reach.'

'Then?'

'We're paid to cross the border with you. Then we hand you over. Afterwards? Not our problem. You get a new life.'

Somewhere a clock ticked, and the rain fell harder.

* * *

Highness told her to go. Excellency wheezed in her ear that she should accept the offer.

What about her parents and sister?

Highness said that family was always put at risk by flight. Excellency coughed, then spluttered that her arrest would do her parents as much harm as her escape.

Would they remember her?

Always, to the end of their lives.

And Kourosh?

Highness sighed, as if the name pained him, then dismissed the difficulty; they'd face it when they had to. Excellency gave a little wave – a small matter that would be taken care of.

Could Kourosh not kill them?

Highness grimaced and Excellency blinked: it would be in God's hands.

Kourosh blundered past the sentry. The man knew everyone who worked in surveillance but he did his job: he asked for Kourosh's ID. If his sergeant had been watching, and had seen an officer allowed through without producing an ID card, the sentry would have been verbally whipped, then punished. Everyone knew it: even the most senior men paused, rummaged and showed their card. The request was ignored. Kourosh went past.

The sentry charged after him, was entitled at that moment to shoot, or swing the butt of his rifle against the back of Kourosh's neck. He had seen the officer's glazed eyes and didn't know whether the wet on his cheeks was rain or tears. He grasped the collar of the anorak and Kourosh's arm swung back fiercely. The sentry staggered. There was no shot and no blow.

Kourosh walked on. He went up the steps and into the building, turned left and passed another picture of the Imam, and one of the Supreme Leader. A colleague called a greeting to him. He pushed through a door. Three women, *chadors* and scarves, one veiled, talking about the price of tomatoes.

The corridor stretched ahead. At the far end, to the left, was his commander's office. The man's reputation was fearsome: he was built like a toad, was incapable of mercy, intolerant of weakness, and his mind was governed by the need to preserve the revolution. Also at the end of the corridor, but to the right, was the large open-plan area where Kourosh and his colleagues worked, the walls plastered with the surveillance photographs of those believed to be enemies of the state.

A man came out of another doorway carrying a tray of empty tea glasses. Kourosh cannoned into him and the tray flipped, but he didn't stop.

There were photographs on the corridor walls that showed men who had been martyred in the service of the revolution, killed in clashes with Azeri traitors and Baluchi rebels, or in Iraq and south Lebanon at the hands of the Zionists, or in Syria. Kourosh knew that armed men had come to take her out of the country. He knew, too, the route they would take. He knew that her husband was in a safe house, with enemies, in Europe, and she was to be brought to him.

He reached the end of the corridor and his legs weakened. The commander's door was open and he saw the man at his desk, using his keyboard, a cigarette burning in an ashtray. The door to his work area was also open and he saw colleagues at their computers. He stopped. He didn't turn right or left, just faced the end wall, panting.

PK came in. Mehrak thought he looked drawn. PK put his file on the table, and sat down.

'You ready to hack on, Mehrak?'

'I am ready.'

'Not tired?'

'I am good.'

PK shuffled papers, chewed a pencil, and frowned. He was dressed that day in black football shorts, long socks, trainers, a T-shirt and a white sweater that had a badge on the chest and red-and-blue stripes round the V-neck. He was smoking a cigarette. Sometimes he offered his to Mehrak. At others Mehrak helped himself from the packet on the table. Mehrak had learned something about his interrogator. There was a wife and a child; the brothel had been his idea and Mehrak the first 'fly in the honey'. He was the sworn enemy of Iran and lived for his work. He had been to Oxford University and had studied history. But PK knew everything about Mehrak, had torn open his life, stripped it down.

'Where is my wife?'

PK looked up sharply, underlined a note, grimaced. 'I don't know.'

'I have the right to be told where she is.'

'My friend, when I know where your wife is I'll tell you. For now, Mehrak, that will have to satisfy you.'

PK was back at his paper, scribbled again, flicked ash from his cigarette. Mehrak gazed out of the window. He saw a tractor, women well wrapped against the cold, with buckets for the grapes, and the church tower, and the great river that disappeared beyond a bend. He saw winter clouds, and his isolation bit at him. He had adequate English but no German, Arabic, French or Spanish. He didn't know where he would live or how he would fill his days. He had not been told the detail of a cash settlement or how he would be supported. PK pushed aside the papers and would have flicked the switch built into the base of the table to start the recorder. He smiled, framing his first question no doubt.

Mehrak interrupted. 'How much money? How do I live? What do I do?'

'All in good time. We'll put together a package. When I have something to tell you, you'll be told.'

'And you have nothing to tell me?'

He saw PK's anger.

'We're going to talk more about al-Qods in the embassies, about the meeting in the garrison camp at Hamadan. When I hear from Tehran about your wife, I'll tell you. I want to know who spoke the most at the meeting, which men from which embassies. Let's begin.'

Mehrak snorted. 'The man from Vienna, he was a leader. You should meet him. Down the road in an hour? Go and meet him. Ask *him* what he said.'

'Don't be silly, Mehrak. I'll put it simply, so you understand. It's fine, Nobby.' The hand with the cigarette waved away the red-haired minder, whose fists were clenched. 'Understand, Mehrak, you have no reason to feel sorry for yourself. You're out of that fucking place and lucky to be. If it hadn't been for my colleague, the girl in Dubai, a brothel-owner would have sold pictures of you to an Internet source, and you'd be plastered across a million screens with a limp dick. Maybe your pretty wife would be watching you. You should understand, and be grateful, that we're busting our bollocks to get her clear of Iranian territory. So fucking co-operate. Who led at Hamadan?'

It was said, and not denied, that the dishes on the high ground at Dhekelia, the military camp on Cyprus, could absorb some two million calls from Middle Eastern sources in an hour. In addition, they could monitor radio traffic across the region. Technicians pored over screens, consoles and keyboards as the computers gobbled traffic. A select few had been given the number of a satphone that would be operated, it was hoped, in central Tehran. The same few were also tasked to report any spike in emergency communications involving the security units of the Iranian Revolutionary Guard Corps, specifically the al-Qods division. The technicians, junior boffins from a Signals regiment or GCHQ., would have appreciated such a specific request – more interesting than the usual wallow in a sludge of messaging. They would understand that the priority was high.

For Zach it was almost the end of his usefulness.

Almost, not quite.

He was still needed to translate Mikey's instructions. She could make no calls, not to her parents or friends. She would go from the yard in the clothing she stood in and there was no question of a bag being collected from Rafah Street. She would not question what she was told to do. He translated, and she nodded.

It was a quick gesture. Ralph's hand snaked out, then Wally's. Their fingers gripped and Mikey's palm was on top. They held it for three or four seconds, then broke. His hand was not required. It was their show now.

He had done the translation and they had her acceptance. All he had left to do was to drive them clear of the city. Then he would be yesterday's fish-and-chips wrapper. None of them had squeezed his fist in congratulation, and he was still shaking from the aggression he had shown her. He had done his job.

She clung to the older men. She called one Excellency and the other Highness. He assumed they were throwbacks from the old regime, hidden away, providing a refuge. She had gone to a chest and pulled open the drawers but they had intervened.

Mikey was at the door. He said, 'What you translated for her, it's for you as well. You do as you're told. Don't try to contribute unless you're asked to. You're both passengers.'

The rain beat on the roof. There was an upper window on the small landing that looked down on the yard where the van was and the puddles around it.

Mikey opened the door – Wally behind him, then her and Zach, the old men and Ralph at the back – and froze.

There was thin vinyl flooring between the steps and the door. It bore wet footprints. There was more damp on the steps, staining the wood. At the bottom of the stairs they saw more marks: a man had come through the doors and paced around, then come up to the first-floor room. Zach understood: someone had entered the yard, heard the voices, come up, listened and slipped away. His stomach knotted.

He had told her the route, and anyone in the yard would have seen the van and its plates. Who was 'anyone'? He put the question quietly, trying to mask his fear. Highness and Excellency wouldn't meet his eye.

She answered: 'It might have been Kourosh. He's infatuated with me.'

'If he heard what we said would he denounce you?' He spoke first in Farsi, then translated each question and each reply.

'He's a surveillance agent in the Ministry of Intelligence and Security.'

The old men shuffled. Wally swore and Ralph punched the door jamb.

She said, 'He can't say anything. He can't explain how he knew. Would he tell them I have a mole on my right buttock? Or that his ambition is to sleep with the wife of a colleague? And he's married, a father. What can he say?'

Zach grabbed her arm and pulled her forward. They followed Mikey, and he heard the clatter of weapons being armed. He took the driving seat and saw in the mirror that she was thrown into the back. The engine kicked into life, the old men opened the gates and rain splashed the windscreen. He had the wipers going at full speed and didn't know whether the first shot would be aimed at him or the engine. He drove out fast, and in the narrow alley, water splashed from under the tyres drenching a passerby. He heard Mikey tap the keys on the phone. Zach glanced at the screen; 'Foxtrot on the run.' He powered towards the wider street ahead, hit the horn and swerved clear of the alley.

8

The traffic was solid.

Murphy's law, Zach thought. If it could go wrong, it would. The turn he had made, based on the map, had led him into a jam caused by roadworks. Maybe five minutes stationary, in a cascade of horns and shouts, and five more crawling. No one walked if they could ride.

She was Foxtrot. She was in the back of the van with Wally, Ralph and the guns. Last thing before she'd got in, she'd shrugged on the *chador* and fixed the veil.

There'd been a shunt. A scooter had clipped the wing of a black car, government type, and a bawling match filled two lanes. Might have been amusing if she hadn't been in the back. Police were running forward. If a motorbike had nicked the wing of a town-hall vehicle, and an argument had raged on the ring road in Coventry, then Zach and his mates on the site would have enjoyed it. But she was on board, and Mikey was beside him.

The traffic moved.

Two taxis were in front of him now, shared ones, packed seats. The protests were at a crescendo, arms snaking out of windows, demands for action from the police. Two police turned away from the accident and strode towards the source of the insults. Dangerous . . . One of the police was at the further taxi, the other at the nearest. A taxi driver might be apprehensive of men from the *basij*, would certainly be wary of conflict with any IRGC guy, but probably wouldn't give a shite about a policeman.

He wondered what else Murphy had ready for him.

Mikey had pale skin: many Iranians did. Mikey had dark hair:

most Iranians did. Did he look as if he'd come off the streets of south Tehran and was entitled to sit in a builders' van? Were his clothes right for his job? Would his eyes betray him, or would he look away and play dumb, if he was ordered to wind down the window? The policeman nearest had a truncheon out and silenced the taxi driver by belting the vehicle bonnet, indicating that the next blow would shatter the windscreen. Now he came forward and Zach saw a man seeking confrontation. He murmured for Mikey to turn away, not to make eye contact. He sensed the movement beside him and realised that Mikey had pulled his beanie further over his head. The guys had no language and no papers – because the Americans at Incirlik or Sulaymaniyah hadn't had time to produce good fakes. Anyway, what was the use of a bogus ID to a man who couldn't argue in defence of the identity given him? They had the weapons. Mikey's pistol, short-barrelled and dark-coloured, was squashed under his inner thigh. Mikey had turned his face, closed his eyes and started a rhythmic snore. The rain poured down and the wipers struggled to clear it.

The weapons were useless while they were stationary.

The policeman came level with them, then kicked the tyre of the taxi. He was drenched. Water ran from his peaked cap and off his shoulders; the truncheon glistened. Zach was next in line. The eyes beaded on him. He wound down the window.

He spoke easily, knew the words: 'What an arsehole, Officer. Doesn't deserve your help. Thank you for your efforts.'

He was rewarded with a short smile and a nod, and the policeman went on by.

There was movement. They edged forward, then cleared the black car with the dent in the near wing and the man who had tried to start his scooter and failed. And, always, the miracle. Murphy had taken a back seat. Two more sets of lights, and the flow speeded. He was onto Enghelab, had passed the Saman Bank and taken the turning off the roundabout that put him on Azadi. The signs were for the Jenah road and Route 2. Soon – if Murphy stayed in his box – he'd be making for Karaj and Qazvin.

Mikey punched his arm, jolting his hold on the wheel and they swerved. Laughter broke out between them, and there were murmurs behind him. He thought he'd done well, that he'd started the process of being accepted by the guys as something approaching an equal.

Another hand, slighter, rested for a moment on his shoulder. There was gentle pressure, and then it was gone. She said nothing. He thought she would captivate a man and . . . A new sign indicated the slip road that would take them onto Route 2. He pointed to the fuel gauge and muttered that they might have three hundred kilometres more in the tank. Mikey nodded. Tiredness, hunger and thirst gripped Zach. She had touched him. They called her Foxtrot. Zach knew her as Farideh. He felt a greater fear now than at any time before – worse than when the policeman had walked in the rain towards them with fury on his face.

Why was Zach there? He supposed it was the same with mountains: men and women climbed them for the challenge. They were in traffic, locked in tight among vans, fast-travelling cars and lorries with trailers. The Israelis had a useful mechanic: the van's exterior was battered and rusty, right for small-time builders, but the engine was well tuned and they cruised comfortably at eighty klicks an hour. He judged that to be the right speed – wouldn't draw attention to them. He stayed in the middle lane and did not overtake. He held the wheel tightly, his knuckles showing white. That way, he had control of the tremor.

He asked, 'When the cop came, if he'd made trouble, what would you have done? Would you have used the guns?'

An easy smile. 'Doesn't matter what I *might* have done. It didn't happen.'

He was bolder. 'We've made a good start, yes?'

'It hasn't started, good or bad. It's all in front of us. Keep your eyes on the road, please.'

He thought he'd been put down when he should have been praised. The men with the guns excluded him; the circle of their relationship was closed to him. Something to resent, maybe, on another day – but he'd no friends among the men he'd worked alongside on the site either, seldom ate with them, rarely drank with them and didn't share their laughter. He was apart from the guns, and it didn't hurt. He could still feel where her fingers had touched his shoulder.

More material was handed to them, a full copy of the transcripts. Some regarded Tadeuz Fenton's delight in moving sheets of paper as eccentric, others as showboating. The Friend and the Cousin, or Gideon and Gunther, as Sara called them, collected the documents, handed in their thoughts and any remarks that had been fed back to them from Tel Aviv and Langley. He liked the personal touch in paperwork being offered, accepted and slid into briefcases, and was rewarded with a moment of gratitude from both men. How long would the warmth last? Maybe as far as the steps outside Vauxhall Cross, or as far as the Underground station.

He was a poor relation. He escorted them to the security gate. His phone warbled.

He murmured an excuse, turned away and answered it. Sara told him the text of the transmitted message. Strange – an oversight by Human Resources: he'd never served a full attachment overseas. He had her repeat it, not that there was much for her to say. He'd done short-notice reliefs as cover for illness, mental collapse and scandal, but never a four-year posting. He snapped off the phone and scurried after them. He caught them by the gates. 'They have her. They're on their way.'

They chorused: 'The wife?'

'They're on their way. Nothing more. Instructions were to keep call-time to a minimum.'

'Are alarms ringing?' the American asked.

'Not that we've heard.' He hadn't expected interrogation – more to have his hand gripped and be congratulated.

It was easier to draw blood from a stone than a smile from the Israeli. A grim response: 'You'll hear and they'll ring.'

He smarted. 'Not necessarily. They may come through without bangs, bleeps and chaos.'

The American said, 'The best-laid plans are just as likely to end in terror.'

'For a man-hunt to be launched a mistake has to trigger it. Plain sailing otherwise.'

The Israeli said, 'It's not a model boat, Tad, floating on the Serpentine. There are always mistakes. Always . . . Keep the stuff coming. I'm getting interest.'

'Yes,' said the American. 'A good response from our people so far. It's always a seat-of-your-pants job, getting people out. You'll see, Tad.'

He waved stiffly, then headed for a lift. When the Soviets and the UK people were in each other's faces, men of his seniority in the Service had known their opponents. There had been files on pretty much any individual who ranked above half-colonel and had a desk in intelligence-gathering. They'd had photographs of them, had known where they went for their summer holiday and what languages they spoke; they'd met them at cocktail bashes thrown by the Indian, Yugoslav or Swiss mission; some were charming, others brutish, and most were worthy opposition. He welcomed and respected the new kid on the block, whether it was the VEVAK people, the men from the Ministry of Intelligence and Security, the shadowy Oghab-2, or the group answerable only to the Supreme Leader. He didn't know the principals. He had seen faces of glowering, malevolent clerics but they weren't alive to him. The targets of espionage were rewarding, but the sense of being under their skin had always evaded him. Now he had his fingernails under the skin of a brigadier general in the al-Qods, which was classified as an able, highly disciplined arm of the enemy. He hoped to create infection there and, by the end, to have flayed it off and caused serious grief.

He was back in his office. Sara said that the director would see him for updates at six.

'Anything from Dunc?'

He brushed against her hip – he often did, and did more than that in the flat high over Chelsea Harbour, but they didn't parade it. He felt confident in the mission and its outcome.

There was nothing from Dunc Whitcombe: he had only a satellite photograph of a desolate house, miles from civilisation, to show him where he and Mandy Ross were. They'd be waiting, as he was.

Dunc Whitcombe went outside. He felt the need to brood. The message had come through on her phone, which meant that she was higher-ranked than himself. Some would have bitched or moaned about the slight.

He stood on the patio outside the living room. The smoke eddied from the chimney and was blasted towards the mountains, where the border was. There were scudding clouds, some pregnant with snow or hail, and islands of blue sky. He didn't look at Ararat, but watched the field where the horses were corralled. A boy came with a bucket.

Zach Becket was in his mind, and the mud of the site where they had met. He saw the pub in which the band had played: the guys had come in from work, with no idea where the boss's son was headed. There had been a car journey south, the snoring of a man tired after a day's work and a drink. Dunc didn't know how Zach would respond when the pressure was bowstring taut. Mandy had told him of the message, 'Foxtrot on the run'. Responsibility weighed heavily on him, with Mandy, too. They would do their damnedest to keep it to themselves.

The horses were cantering from the far corner of the field to meet the boy.

At Vauxhall Cross it was said, and he'd heard it from offices with their doors open, or when he'd turned a corner and surprised colleagues talking about him, that he was called 'Fulcrum'. He had not done Latin at school, and it was the first time he'd needed to sneak to a dictionary. It had come up with 'something that supports or sustains'. Good enough. It was said, whispers carried on the wind, that his contribution to the desk – organisation, analysis, common-sense reasoning – kept it afloat and prominent. He was the marine commando – 'first in and last out' – and it had become second nature to Tadeuz and Sara, Mandy and others to dump work on him.

The horses jostled for space in front of the boy, the better to take from his hand the dried cake or whatever he'd bought.

He was forty-two and his divorce from Alice had been finalised at the end of the previous year. No kids. He lived in a Battersea studio, a ten-minute walk from work. It was still half filled with packing cases of clothes, books, precious odds and ends. Long ago he had taken first-class honours in archaeology at Bristol, and he was good at groping about in mud with a spatula, brush or trowel. He had thought Ararat would be interesting, and any bits of rotten wood, three or four thousand years old, might be fun – if they had time for an Ark hunt. Now it didn't seem important that he had gained little of the craft of gathering intelligence from his academic discipline. He worked Monday through Friday, and usually came in, dressed down, on Saturday. Sundays were for his mother: he pushed her supermarket trolley round the aisles and made a poor job of losing the cares of Iran.

Sunday evenings were his own: unknown to all at Vauxhall Cross, and to his mother, he played clarinet in a trad-jazz sixsome in a back room at the Red Lion off the main drag in Stoke Newington. He had a following, and a few fans – the evenings when he played his solo pieces he was applauded.

The boy had no more cake and fondled the horses' necks.

Was the defector worth the effort? He had to suppose so. He and Mandy would not be told. Anyway, they had no wish for telephone calls, sat-links or mobiles-in-clear, because Doğubeyazıt was a garrison town and would have El-Int people – they, would rely on electronic intelligence in their guerrilla war against the Kurdish separatists – so it wasn't sensible to plaster the airwaves with overseas transmissions. Perhaps the defector was worth the effort, and perhaps he wasn't. Sad if the man turned out to be valueless.

The sun broke through. He saw the movement of a crow's shadow flying fast towards the boy and the horses. Dunc thought the bird might be familiar with them and was hunting for anything that had dropped from the bucket. It was close to the boy now and shrieked loudly. Dunc heard it clearly, and the horses scattered, but the boy didn't move or flinch. He was unaware of the bird until it was past him. Profoundly deaf. The boy's lips moved and he called the horses back to him. They came, but Dunc hadn't heard his voice. Profoundly deaf and dumb. He was a good-looking boy. He wore a pair of faded jeans that were ripped at both knees, a dun-coloured T-shirt with a shirt and a woollen cardigan over it. He had lightweight trainers on his feet, and he couldn't have felt the cold that cut at Dunc Whitcombe. The horses stayed close to him and there was love between animals and boy. Dunc was an interloper. He went back to the windows. He felt the love and trust keenly – he himself was short of them.

Was the defector worth the effort? He couldn't say.

'We're very worried. Other than in the depths of winter, when they're in a hole or a cave, in a state of semi-hibernation, we have sight of all our principals. It's the longest Stephie and I have gone without spotting him. He's such a fine beast, a symbol of all the hard work put in by so many people at the park, but he has enemies – livestock farmers, honey producers . . . Sorry, Petroc – I'm a bit tired, been up since first light. I'm sure your anxieties aren't focused on the absence of a brown bear.'

The voice was quiet and Petroc Kenning needed to press the phone to his ear to distinguish Rollo Hawkins's words. He sensed that he had intruded upon the one-time intelligence officer's private world. Petroc had never seen a bear outside a zoo.

'You tell me that the wife is on the move. We have to sit quietly, perhaps offer something akin to a prayer. You had little time to plan. Difficult . . . If you achieve the extraction – *if* – you stand a chance of the two settling as a couple. A small chance. Very few do. This man, from the background you provided, has a small chance. I would suggest that by now he's suffering from doubt and self-recrimination. He's a little flattered by your attention but it's already diminishing. His self-respect will slide, and cannot be replaced. I'm getting there, Petroc . . . Work him hard. He's not a high-ranking intelligence official from the old Soviet Union or the new Kremlin, a man who can offer insights on policy, give lectures at the Fort, address small, closed meetings.

'Extract what you can from him, then wave him goodbye. He'll be dumped in some European city with his wife on his arm, suitcases at their feet, and will ride in a taxi to a life where regret is piled on the mantelpiece. He won't settle. Who's he going to befriend? He's a driver. Life as a driver is tolerable while he ferries a big man around. Does he want to run a kebab stall?

'Am I rambling, Petroc? Not for me to teach you, dear boy, about egg-sucking, but as valuable as talk about sentry duties on missile silos, and the layout of al-Qods in some grubby town in the Bekaa valley, is the damage you can exploit in their ranks. For Heaven's sake, a brigadier is using his handyman to run messages to a foreign bank where he has an illegal account. That'll play on every radio station in the Gulf, is great propaganda in the psyops world. He's just another zealot on the make when the prices of utilities, petrol, staple food and rents are knocking holes in the roof.

'In Saudi and all down the Gulf the lappet-faced vulture strips a camel carcass to the bone. That's what you'll be able to do with your Brigadier Reza Joyberi. You can reduce him to a hate figure in the bazaar and a laughing-stock in north Tehran. He'll be vilified inside his own circle for turning a spotlight on their activities.

'Excellent. I'm going to have a lie-down now because Stephie and I, and some others, are going back to our viewing-points later for the dusk routine. Milk your man now. Keep him cheerful. Deflect his mind from contemplation of the fact that he's a treacherous little weasel, and only in his predicament because he went into a whorehouse. Good to speak, Petroc, thank you for calling.'

He rang off.

Petroc went back into the sitting room, and sat down opposite Mehrak. The man gazed back at him. Petroc couldn't read him, doubted he ever would.

Briskly: 'Now we're going to talk, Mehrak, about your brigadier's corruption and that of all the other hoods stealing from their people.'

* * *

Short of Qazvin, Zach pulled off the road and took a side trail, which wound away from the highway towards the mountains, not that he could see them.

Fog had come down as the rain had lessened. He'd said, 'Sorry and all that, guys, but I can't go on any longer.' The fog had been as hard to drive through as the rain and he'd had enough. 'Apologies, but I'm half dead.' Mikey had told him to pull off, and that they were ready for the switch-over. None of them had said he'd done well, had earned his corn and might want to pass on the driving. What had sustained him for the last thirty minutes had been the signs on Route 2 that warned of the approach to Qazvin. He had been there, taken a bus five years ago. Every tourist, student and back-packer, with an ounce of self-esteem, made the trip to the town, joined a tour that drove up the hills towards the fortress. He'd climbed the last stretches on foot, stood at the summit and gloried in the view and the clutch of history. The fortress had been built a millennium ago by Hassan Sabah, Grand Master, as a bolt-hole for his sect. Somewhere, in his parents' home, there would be the album of the photographs he had taken that day. The sect of Hassan Sabah was the Assassins, the *hashishiyun*, because the old man had taken the young to beautiful gardens on the slopes below the walls, shown them women in provocative dress, then dosed them on hashish. He had told them the women would wait for them, then sent them out across the region. They killed and were sacrificed. They died believing the women would make a paradise for them.

Each time Zach had read of a suicide bomber – Haifa, Jerusalem, Kandahar, Kabul, Baghdad or Basra – or the anniversary of the London Underground bombing had come round he had been taken back to that fortress, ruined by the last earthquake. It had been captured in the thirteenth century by the Mongol king, Hulegu, and the defenders massacred. During the last part of the drive, the memory of the castle had sustained him.

He had seen nothing. The cloud's ceiling was barely higher than the sides of the lorries that surged past, burying his windscreen under avalanches of water.

He climbed out. He heard coughing behind him, a reminder that others were waiting for him. He couldn't see the high ground, but it took a four-wheel-drive vehicle more than three hours to get to the base of the scramble path that led to the fortress. It was said that the Grand Master had such control of his sect that, to impress a visitor, he had ordered a half-dozen of his men to walk one at a time towards the precipice on the south side of the fortress. They had not demurred and had fallen to their death.

He turned back to the van. Ralph was in the driving seat, Mikey beside him.

It was as if the decks had been cleared and he was of no more use.

The men of his sect were strangers. He didn't know them. He had been told they were a team, that a team was as strong as its weakest link, and that link should not be him. Now he was told to hurry up. He thought he had no more status now than a piece of baggage. Exhaustion swept over him. Zach went to the back door and Wally opened it. He crawled in, found a place between Wally and Farideh, away from the paint pots and the collapsible ladder, and lay on his side. The weapons were armed, the engine purred, and they shook on the rough ground. In low voices Ralph and Mikey talked about the route, and how far they'd go that night.

In the cold Zach felt the warmth of the woman. They hit the road, and the light was dying.

The office stirred. The last coffee dregs were drained, the last of the salad wraps eaten, and men checked their gear around him. It was nearly time.

He had sat in the open area, at his desk, all afternoon and had not spoken to any colleagues. They could have talked work, or of Esteghlal's chances in the next home game against Persepolis, or of a new TV channel for movies. Usually Kourosh made himself part of the groups that formed when the teams waited to get their kit, hear the last briefing and get ready to move out. He liked it best when the talk was of the Zionists' agent they were to lift, when there was a whiff of excitement: nothing better than seeing the door of an apartment cave in under the sledgehammer and drag a man from his meal, his bed or his family, slap his face, fasten the handcuffs and take him, dazed, to the car. Good also when they argued football and tempers exploded. Half of the electrical appliances in the flat he shared with his wife and child had been bought, at shaven prices, from those who knew which warehouse and which backstreet lock-up to visit. Some – not himself – bought alcohol that had come into the country from Turkey or Armenia. Often the room was filled with cigarette smoke and the men played card games – *hokm*, *ghahveh* or *pasur*. All afternoon the room had been alive with talk but Kourosh hadn't contributed.

His desk faced the door into the corridor, which had stayed open.

Across the corridor, between portrait photographs of two more recent martyrs, was the door to the commander's office. He had known when his commander was in a meeting, when the room was empty, when the man was bent over his papers or talking on the telephone.

He could have slipped away from his desk – with the chat around him, no one would have noticed. He could have gone to the door across the corridor and knocked quietly. There would have been a shout for him to enter. He could have gone in and closed the door behind him.

He could have said there was a matter he wished to report. He could have denounced the wife of the corporal in the al-Qods and those with her. He could have finished, 'The British are taking her from Iran. They will go via Qazvin and Zanjan, Mianeh and Tabriz. They will meet a smuggling party near the border with Turkey, beyond Khvoy, and skirt the frontier town of Maku. I don't know how many Britons are involved. Their mission is to reunite her with her husband, a defector and . . .'

The commander's face would have contorted in confusion, suspicion and elation.

He hadn't moved from his seat. He had stayed, smoked, read his screen and ignored the banter around him. He had refused to make a fourth with the cards. Kourosh couldn't argue successfully against his dilemma.

If he denounced *her*, he denounced *himself*. How did he know of the repair yard? How did he know of the woman? How to answer? He didn't know.

A section leader whistled through his teeth. The cards went into one drawer, the electronics brochures into another. Men took down raincoats, cursed the weather, checked firearms, handcuffs and their keys. The radios squawked static. Eight filed out. The commander had come to his door and slapped the leader's arm. They were to take one woman. He opened his wallet. One of them had been in the apartment on Rafah Street that morning, had told the story of the dropped blanket, the brigadier's reaction. The story was entertaining, but Kourosh hadn't laughed.

He gazed at a picture hidden behind his laminated ID card, then pushed it out of sight again. Only the eyes were visible in the picture, which had been taken in a booth at a railway or metro station.

They filed out. He had to go. Kourosh worked as a servant to a society where suspicion killed. He must not arouse it.

A crowd had gathered. Those from other blocks in Rafah Street lined the far pavement. The cars blocked the street, and now a uniformed policeman had arrived at the top junction, diverting traffic. Arguments erupted. The pavement crowd could see inside the first floor because the curtains had not been drawn and there were high street-lights. Jamali, who repaired electrical goods and lived above his business, had perched his thirteen-year-old son on his shoulders. The child gave a commentary that his father relayed.

'Every drawer is taken out. They're angry because they haven't found her. Everything's thrown on the floor, I tell you, *everything* – even intimate clothing. They should have done it this morning. She was there then, and there was a senior man, but they didn't. Now they can't find her. They could have asked me – I'd have told them. They broke the door down. There are pictures, Shia, special, and they're all off the walls and they're stripping the backs off – and they're cutting the cushions open. They don't do this for someone who's taken tomatoes from the bazaar and not paid.

She's in trouble. I never liked them – she's a stuck-up bitch, and he's arrogant because he drives a big man's car. This number of men, and the anger, it's for a hanging.'

No resident of Rafah Street raised a voice in support of the corporal and his wife.

Abruptly, the man who mended electrical appliances was outgunned. A couple lived in isolation on the third floor of the building, because of disability: she had tuberculosis and he had a war wound. Ali had made it his business to take them the bare essentials of food. He had been with them, two floors above, when the security men had swarmed up the stairs. Moments after they had broken down the door he had come down to that landing and hovered. He had not been moved on, so now he could report.

'It must be a charge of treason, or *moharebeh*. So many of them, and they're destroying the place. Everything's broken, the furniture, plates, cooking things, pictures, and they have floorboards up. They keep sending the message back on their radios that they've found nothing, but they're told to look again. She was there this morning, and a big man came. After that she went. It's days since I last saw *him* with the big car. They say she's taken nothing – left money and her outdoor clothes. They say she's fled. I wouldn't help anyone, man or woman, guilty of war against God or treason . . . There was a van this morning that went slowly on Rafah Street. I saw it. It went too slowly, as if a stranger drove it. It was a builders' van, but I didn't recognise the driver or the man beside him. It was the first time I'd seen it in our street.'

Jamali shouted, 'I saw it too! Blue, rusty, string holding the back door shut.'

'Do as I did, brother. Tell them what you saw.'

The crowd, at fever pitch, clapped, and the show played well. On this street, in this district, the votes in the last election for the president hadn't been stolen. Support for the regime was total. No one from Rafah Street or the bazaar district had fought the *basij* in the main squares: many of their sons, cousins or nephews had enlisted. Ali led Jamali into the building and up the stairs, then asked the man at the door if he could speak to a responsible official. It was treason and it was *moharebeh* and the duty of all to help the authorities. The story of the builders' van was told again, and the man who drove it was described.

He didn't have a driver, was dependent on the pool. His neighbours in the complex, homes for the wealthy and well connected, had been collected as usual that morning by their chauffeurs, and some had an additional car tucked behind, ferrying the bodyguards. The brigadier had paced in the cold, waiting. He had called the pool's manager twice to demand a faster reaction. He had been late at Rafah Street and at his desk.

He had known of the planned arrest. A junior officer, from a security section, had come to his room in the late morning. He had been given the co-ordinates of time and location, when the hit would be made on the apartment. He could not have sworn to it, but thought a fleeting smirk had crossed the officer's face: men died in the Evin gaol on accusations that were perceived but could not have been sworn to; men and women were held in the city's prisons when evidence could not be guaranteed. In different circumstances, the junior might have faced a reprimand, demotion or dismissal. The circumstances were not *different*. The word was that his driver had defected. By now, the investigators would be swarming over Mehrak's apartment. He remembered the man's wife.

His own wife was a good woman, dutiful, and had given him a fine son. She looked after him, was cheerful when he wanted to laugh in the privacy of their home, and could be silent when grave matters of state pressed hard on him. She cooked well for him, but her ankles and waist had thickened. Often she was in bed and asleep by the time Mehrak dropped him at the door and slipped away into the night. He undressed quietly. He remembered the driver's wife – remembered her when the blanket had dropped to the floor and he had seen the curves of her body – flaunted shamelessly. He would never forget her – and the defiance with which she had flung back his questions. He felt empty as his sense of catastrophe grew. Now, having worked all morning and afternoon, he was waiting again. He had called the organiser of the car pool three times.

He missed the bastard. He was always waiting at the appointed time, ready with the coffee in the car for the drive to work, the valeting done, and the brigadier's cigarettes in the pocket at the back.

He was nervous.

A bank account existed, privacy guaranteed by a password and a six-figure number, in Dubai. The bank was linked to others that held different denominations of his investments. He had no cigarettes, which fuelled his anger and anxieties. He had bought some yesterday, two packets, and had smoked them. Mehrak had stowed cigarettes in the car where he could reach them, and had kept his lighter filled with gas. He wondered if the Mercedes had already been allocated to someone else. It had been available the night before, had brought him home, but the driver hadn't known the way and had had to be directed.

The junior found him standing beneath the porch over the side door of his office block. In front of him was the wide area where the drivers could bring the vehicles close to the steps so that an important man did not get wet in the rain. No car had arrived. Behind him were the doors and the security desk. The junior came close to him. He might have saluted and stood to attention, and might not.

'Brigadier Joyberi, I have to tell you—'

'What?' he snapped. It was a custom, from birth to the grave, to observe *tarof* – civility, politeness – and begin any conversation with compliments. Neither he nor the junior officer used it now.

'It concerns the situation involving the planned arrest of your driver's wife. Your driver, missing, and assumed to be a defector, while on unexplained business in the Emirates, has a wife, Farideh, and lives in Rafah Street. This afternoon a security team—'

'I know where my driver lives.' He was a brigadier, as high as it was possible to climb inside the al-Qods, one of a group of five. The junior might be a captain, or a lieutenant.

'Of course you know the street, Brigadier. You were there this morning, I understand.'

He was expressionless. A tide had turned. The brigadier

understood little of the sea, but he knew from visits to the Gulf that a tidal flow at Bandar Abbas could rise and fall by up to two metres, and that the movement could not be reversed.

With confidence, the junior said, 'She's gone, Brigadier. She walked out of her office – dismissed as unsuitable – then employed tactics to throw off a surveillance team. They lost her. She didn't return to her home. She's considered a fugitive. It's assumed she'll attempt to join her husband, nominated now as a traitor, and guilty of *moharabeh.* I am instructed to say, Brigadier, that you may be required to help the investigation concerning them. I'm told that your car will come soon, sir.'

The brigadier didn't wait. He walked out into the rain. He went towards the main street running along the side of the barracks. He didn't know which buses went towards the north of the city, his home, but he would ask. The rain soaked him. He remembered his driver, the jokes, and remembered his driver's wife, the fallen blanket. He thought it likely that British agencies had tried to extract her. Would they succeed? He doubted it. He shook his shoulders and the rain fell off them.

Zach woke up. He seemed to be lying on a cushion. He smelt coffee.

Whenever he'd slept deeply, totally crashed out, he didn't know where he was when he woke. He tilted his body and the cushion seemed softer – then, abruptly, harder. Someone gasped.

He mouthed, 'I'm sorry, I didn't know, I—'

She said, 'It's where you slept.'

It was dark. She shifted, and he realised he must have turned over in his sleep, and rested against her, his head on her chest or stomach. He didn't know how to apologise.

He could see the hands on his watch and yawned, then struggled to calculate – he'd been asleep for at least three hours.

The back door of the van was open. He could smell coffee and hexamine – the tablets were between a pile of stones and a metal canteen. He could see the outline of her face: the veil was off and her scarf had been pushed back so that her hair hung loose. He must have made a gesture, which she interpreted. She shook her head. He made sense of the exchange: she had been offered coffee and had declined it. He heard Wally laugh. Ralph came round the back of the van and used his boot to clear the stones. The tablets bounced away and he bent to retrieve the canteen. He wasn't going to be given coffee, and it was beneath his dignity to beg for some. He didn't know them and thought none of them was interested in knowing him. He sat up.

'I'm sorry,' he said, in Farsi, and rubbed his eyes.

'For nothing. You kept me warm.'

'A sin in Iran.'

'A sin to die for.'

Her voice was soft, no more than a murmur, and he couldn't judge if she'd been ironic or serious. He had been sent to bring her out and start a process of reuniting her with her husband – and she had come but had said she *loathed* him. She was to be brought across the border – God willing – and put alongside her husband in the interests of the organisation that employed Dunc and Mandy, that paid Ralph, Wally, Mikey – and himself?

His mind rambled. She was coming out with them. He imagined it: men in suits and women greeting them, her shaking hands and thanking them. A plea from her to be excused. A walk to a bus stop, a ride to the nearest town, and her gone . . . He couldn't see her face but remembered it clearly from the room above the repair yard. He couldn't remember Chrissie's – his last short-stay girl — or the face of the one before Chrissie.

'Thank you for letting me sleep.'

'And for allowing you to snore?'

'Did I? God . . . Sorry. You should have—'

'You slept across me, snored and talked.'

'In violation of modesty. I was in Alamut five years ago. A student. It was possible then to come for two weeks.'

'I was there after the earthquake two years ago.'

'Did you and your husband climb to the top? I did and—'

'I was with my friend, a captain in the army. You saw his

photograph. My husband was away, I don't know where. We went towards the fortress and then to where there were trees. We had brought a picnic and . . . He was killed in Afghanistan. He taught me something of the ways to lose surveillance, and more. He was a true friend.'

Wally ignored them and talked to Mikey, leaning forward into the cab, as if the three of them were alone. The light had gone.

'And the man in the other photograph?'

A calm voice: 'He saved me in the street. The *basij* were beating me, hitting anybody in their way. I was not a part of a demonstration, just there. He saved me. He knew the two old men you saw, and it was his place. From him I learned most of the procedures for avoiding tails – that was what he called them. It was where I went to meet him. With him, I broke my marriage vows and the law of my country. He was arrested a month later. He would have been tortured but he didn't say my name, or give them the place, that room. He was hanged in the Evin. I think it is not a good death.'

'One more.'

'One more, so . . .' She seemed to shrug and spoke without the passion of pain.

'The man who listened at the door?'

'A mistake. I'm not perfect. He followed me there. He could have betrayed me and the old men. I humoured him – I didn't know how to lose him . . . I didn't let him make love to me . . . You slept on me, snored and talked.'

'What did I talk about?'

'Enemies, in Farsi. "Thousands of friends are too few. One enemy is too many." And "The wise enemy is better than the ignorant friend." You said that.'

'I learned them at university, in my first year. What else?'

'You said, "The wise enemy lifts you high. The ignorant friend throws you down."'

He laughed. 'Before I snored or after?'

Old words and recitations surged in his memory. He smiled. He remembered how the language had once excited him . . .

'You snored, you talked, snored again and talked again. Then you did poetry.'

'What poetry?'

'From *The Book of Kings*.'

'The work of Ferdowsi. Was it from "Chapter Six, The March into Mazinderan"?'

'You said it was the speech of Rustem.'

'We did that in the second year. It's not important now, but I walked out on my course. When they stole the votes, the poetry seemed irrelevant. And there was the cruelty. I'm not big on causes, but it seemed wrong to want to learn the language of that culture.'

'They stole the votes and they hanged my friend.'

'I promise I won't talk about poetry again.'

'Are you a fighting man, Zach?'

'No.'

The engine coughed into life. The lights were on, and Wally had squeezed into the back with them. No explanation or schedule was given. They went down the track and away from the mountain peak with the ruined fortress. She was quiet and so was he. They lurched back onto the slip road.

Mikey spoke: 'If there's pursuit, it will have been organised by now. Maximum vigilance. Watch the mirrors and rear-door windows for them following us. Eyes to the front for road blocks.'

Again the weapons were cocked. He shivered, and she was close to him.

He heard Wally ask, 'Any takers for "Where I would rather be"?'

9

Zach heard a bite in Mikey's voice: it wasn't the time for 'Where I would rather be'. They bypassed Qazvin, saw the lights in the distance but stayed on Route 2. At the next major junction they took the right filter. He couldn't see, even when he knelt up and she edged away to give him space, the road, the smaller towns or the side trails to the villages. He didn't recognise anything of the drive in with the Jewish guy . . . Difficult to say how many hours had passed since he'd sat in the quiet with the calm Jew beside him. Just a few – but his life had changed. The men he'd worked with had experienced difficulties, setbacks, money problems, girls dumping them and spells in the Job Centre queue, but their lives hadn't 'changed'. And his part in this operation was over.

It was safe for Zach to assume that if one of these guys had spoken good Farsi he would never have been hauled off the site. He could have said, actually, that it had been 'bad luck' because the evidence pointed now to her having fair English – most kids did in Iran. They studied it through school, and most were computer literate, which was English-based. She understood and absorbed, kept it to herself. She wasn't just 'a pretty little thing'. She'd had relationships, and wasn't the stereotypical corporal's wife from the bazaar district.

The guys talked among themselves. He and she were ignored. The van kept to a steady speed and wouldn't attract attention, but they'd need fuel, maybe near Zanjan or Mianeh. They wouldn't get to Tabriz without filling up, and he felt resentful that they hadn't offered him coffee. They needed food. He assumed he would be called on to use his language when they found a petrol station with an all-night counter for fast food. Or she might hitch her veil, take a wad of notes from Mikey and do the business.

He was, people told him, the least likely person to boast about his intellect, but he had. He could have brushed aside his knowledge of Persian literature, but instead had told her that he had studied it. He knew Ferdowsi, and the Book, but hadn't needed to show it. He was annoyed with himself.

The van purred along the road. Oncoming headlights lit Ralph and Mikey, and Wally wore wraparound shades to protect his eyes.

Zach was there because of his language skill.

His father: 'Why do you want to do that course? What's the point of Persian?'

His mother: 'How are you going to get a job with that? And they hate us there.'

The deputy head (careers) at school: 'I really would counsel you against that one, Zach. Go for something more malleable, something employers look for.

A nice girl at the university's fresher fair: 'What did you say? Persian? Isn't that a total cul-de-sac for language geeks? Weird.'

The lecturer on the school's fourth floor: 'It's not for me to ask why you chose this course. You're here, for better or worse. You'll contribute to a better understanding of a culture rooted in history, which makes you more valuable citizens of society. As for jobs afterwards, well, the best I can say is that they're difficult to come by but not non-existent.'

Why? It was the way he was – difficult, awkward, wouldn't conform. He was stubborn too. It was a trait in Zach that his mother despaired of, his father found tedious, his teachers attempted to circumvent, and girlfriends usually found unfathomable and not worth the effort. If he was told that somewhere was in the wrong direction, he headed for it. Lectured on an error of choice, he committed himself to it. He had walked out. 'You've cut off your nose to spite your face,' his mother had said.

Letters had come to his home after he'd quit, with the School's crest on them, and they had gone straight into the kitchen shredder. Shouldn't he reconsider? his mother had asked. He had refused.

He had deployed the same stubbornness and obstinacy on the building sites: he'd never asked his father for a favour, never sought to advance himself at the expense of the team. One day, he might grow up – might, one day.

He was lulled. She barely moved. They didn't touch, and her body was a few inches from his.

She had found a rug in the van and wrapped it around herself. When headlights lit the cab, speared through the gap, over Wally's shoulders and past him, the brightness caught her eyes, which sparkled. If they were caught, they were condemned. Zach knew it. And she lived with a sentence of death.

Big stuff to have on your plate. He didn't know when the guys would get to play their game, 'Where I would rather be.'

Zach had his own answer. He would rather be nowhere else. Was he sure? Yes.

The guys talked, and he couldn't make out what they were saying. The rain had stopped, and the van ate the miles towards Zanjan. The moon was low in the evening sky, and all seemed well.

She called from the glass door onto the patio. She told him that supper was almost ready, five more minutes.

The moon was climbing, and the ground under his feet had frozen hard enough for him to walk on the mud without it sticking to his shoes. Dunc Whitcombe had no torch. The light from the house didn't reach as far as the fence behind which the horses were kept.

Neither a romantic nor a dreamer, he had only the light from above as evening slipped to night. He could hear only the movement of the horses' hoofs, their snorts. He wondered how often, at home, she cooked supper.

He recalled the nights when he had taken a late train from Waterloo, a half-an-hour journey, and then walked the ten minutes to his home along deserted streets. When he arrived his meal had been either in the oven, dried up, or waiting in the microwave.

The boy – the deaf-mute – had spent an hour with the horses, then left. Dunc Whitcombe knew nothing about animals, had never owned a dog or a cat. He found the horses wonderful – he liked their curiosity and the smell of them, tangy and warm.

Dunc Whitcombe had spent all of his working life at Vauxhall Cross and Century House further down the river. He had believed in the work he had done, and in the value of his own efforts. His marriage was a casualty of his devotion to the cause, and yet . . . He thought it preposterous that men and women like himself and Mandy Ross believed they could change matters, alter the stacking of the bricks. Petroc Kenning would be in the ranks of the true believers, not a doubt in his mind, with Tadeuz Fenton, and the heads of branches. It was predictable that the director – God and his deputy – took it as gospel that the country was safer on their watch.

There was a moon above him and a litany of stars, and Mandy's voice had dissipated into the emptiness. He heard the hoofs crunching on the frosted ground and might have been transported back a century or a millennium. His mind raced. A hundred years before, or a thousand, a man could have stood on this spot, talked to horses and thought he had the talent and the power to change the world around him. He was part of Tadeuz Fenton's army, an expeditionary force, confident in justice and that God marched with them.

On the other side, above the peaks, another army would have mobilised.

He went back to the patio and pushed open the door.

Bloody hell.

A candle was lit on the table. A bottle of beer had been opened and stood beside his place.

Messages crossed frontiers. Business was discussed by telephone, text and email. If the words were spoken, the men talked in code known only to the principals. If the messages were on screens, they used scrambled electronics. The deals rarely aroused disagreement. They were professionals, and relied on old routes of trading. There had been a Silk Road, an Amber Road, many roads. They were still used but not for fine materials, spices or precious stones. Today the merchants bought and sold heroin. It originated in the poppy fields of Afghanistan, and would end up in the bloodstream of addicts in European cities. At each stage of the journey it would rise in value.

There was anxiety among the entrepreneurs of the European cities. It was believed that heroin users were ageing, that young men and women preferred to experiment with synthetics or cocaine and its derivatives. No matter. It was also believed, and printed in the newspapers of the countries where the traders operated, that the global profit from heroin had reached eighty billion American dollars – enough to keep the trafficking vibrant. More than eighty tonnes of the packaged resin came out, each year, from Iranian territory and was fed onto the routes that used Turkey as a bridge. Then it would cross the Dardanelles strait and enter Europe. Cargo moved every day. Fleets of lorries with hidden compartments would arrive across Europe to the great cities where the addicts huddled at railway stations, in squats and office doorways, or loitered in dark alleys to mug and keep alive their habit.

Preliminary agreements were made. It was accepted by the traders that the area of greatest risk to the cargo was at the choke-point border dividing Turkish territory from Iran. There were always 'problems' in that region but the dangers of arrest, trial, and execution did not face the men who that evening – as every other – negotiated.

Calls, messages and confirmations went from Iran to Turkey. They crossed that country from Diyarbakir, Van and Doğubeyazıt and were received in Istanbul. More calls linked Sofia in Bulgaria to Sarajevo in Bosnia-Herzegovina on the Balkans route. Men in Munich, Rotterdam and Rome learned what price had been fixed, and closed agreements. Smaller men ran the trade in Hamburg, London and Manchester, and they made their bids.

It was an industry, and it prospered.

The place was suffocating.

Which of them should he take? Petroc Kenning had to make

the decision: he was gasping for air. The babysitters had their rota but he could have broken it. He might have taken Auntie, Father William or Nobby – even Sidney. He needed someone to drink with, and chose Sidney.

'Often used to have one with your uncle and see him home.'

He didn't bridle at the familiarity – might even have welcomed it. He had 'cabin fever'. It could have been said that Petroc had less to complain about than any of the babysitters: he had been to Vienna while the others had been walked up the hill to the centuries-old gate. The symptoms of cabin fever were clear cut – Hector had told him: irritability; paranoia, a feeling that doom had settled on the enterprise; distrust, of the defector, the babysitters, the bosses, the mission. He experience urges to break the china ornaments in the rented property. He could have argued with anyone, even Anneliese. He needed to get out for a drink.

He walked down the hill towards the village. He set the pace and Sidney panted to keep up. 'I'm telling you, Sidney, Austria was a good call. In France, we'd have had the *mairie* and half of the local gendarmes round by now. In Italy, they'd have sent a company of *carabinieri*. In Germany, it would have been tax inspectors to give us the once-over. It was a good idea to come here. I'm not pissing about, Sidney. Finding this property was a triumph.'

'Thank you, Mr Kenning – or Petroc, if I may.'

'*He*'s no bag of laughs, about as dull as you can find.'

'But he's talking – isn't he?'

They were past the lower vineyards, and there were warehouses now, for the different labels, windows in which the bottles were displayed and pumpkins in doorways. The lane became a road and would soon turn into a street. The church was well lit and he saw men and women going inside. It was the season of harvest festival, the vegetables lifted, the grapes cut, snow imminent. It seemed so peaceful, warm, comfortable and well ordered.

He said, 'You plan a site for a mine, dig a shaft, hit a seam – with me, Sidney? – and hack at it. The seam may last for a decade, a year, a month or a week. Maybe it's the fever, but I'm uncertain as to how long it'll be before the seam is exhausted. You never can tell. An opinion?'

'Don't have one.'

'Can't be sure how much more there is to dig from that seam. It was vague today, no sharp detail. Just have to hope we're not into the scalping, wrong end of the good stuff. And I don't think we've won him over.'

'I suppose you just have to keep chipping away.'

They were at the door of the church, and an orchestra was warming up, testing the instruments. Above the altar there was a finely worked frieze, and a display of fruits and vegetables, celebrating the festival.

'Do you think they know here about our little war?' Petroc asked.

'Look across the square – the memorial. Take a moment.'

Petroc followed him. Beyond the church, a white wall was surmounted by a classic carving of two soldiers, one fallen and the other helping his wounded comrade. Always a purpose. He doubted Sidney did anything without knowing the outcome. There was a street-light and Petroc could read the names of the dead in relief on black-painted metal: there were four Fertls, four Kausls, five named Fuchs and five from the Schultz family. He realised the devastation done to this community.

'They've had their wars, caught a packet and opted out. That's why we're here. They look the other way and can justify it, but we don't seem able to.'

'Thank you, Sidney. Where are we drinking?'

'Down by the waterside, I thought. Can we move on? My great love, Petroc, is medieval castles. Plenty of them here. In Spitz, downstream, there's the Ruine Hinterhaus, amazing preservation. Further down you come to the Burg Aggstein, planted on top of a granite rock. Back towards Vienna – I should have pointed it out – is Schloss Durnstein. Richard the Lion Heart was there. I love them.'

'Which bar? Maybe we can use a guided tour as a bribe, if need be. Personally I'm more in favour of the language that vile regime understands best – electrodes and such. A man could die of thirst – I came for a drink, not culture.'

'A little family place, Petroc. The beer is Gosser or Murauer.'

'Let's hit it.' He slapped Sidney's back, almost with affection. The lights were ahead of them and he could see reflections off the water and a tug pulled a tail of barges. It was all so damned civilised. It was down to him. *Foxtrot on the run*. His baby. Most nights in Dubai he watched Iranian state TV's news bulletins: a medley of executions, in-camera trials where spies and saboteurs were condemned, military exercises and mullahs mouthing contempt for enemies or threats of retribution. A freshness came off the water. The village lights were behind them, and the cobbled streets still had flowers in pots. Litter and graffiti didn't exist. If the price of civilisation in this old Hapsburg corner was to turn a collective back on what happened when Foxtrot ran, with the boy from the School and the three contract men, *if*, he would have to cross to the other side of the street. But he needed the beer. 'I'm not fussy.'

They went inside, and the warmth bounced on him. A pretty girl behind the bar smiled in welcome. The beers came and Petroc Kenning felt a sort of peace. If it worked well, he was a made man. If it didn't . . . He drank.

It was not the job of the Signals technicians to interpret the messages that the great dishes high in the Troodos mountains sucked into the basement bunkers and projected onto the screens. They fed what was considered relevant, but did not anticipate the reactions it would trigger. From the Dhekelia base on Cyprus, details of transmissions were sent on to dishes that towered over Cornish moorland, then transferred to the analysts at GCHQ in Gloucestershire.

There was abnormal traffic on the secure nets employed by the Iranian police authorities and the security divisions of the Revolutionary Guards Corps. There had been a gradual but steady and measurable increase during the course of the evening, Tehran time. The volume indicated 'concern' and was not yet considered to show that 'crisis' had been reached. The details, with the preliminary opinion attached, reached Vauxhall Cross, where it was typed, below the synopsis of what had been learned:

'Manhunt. Setting up a dragnet. Attention of Tadeuz Fenton, Iran Desk.'

The speed of the van had changed suddenly three times, twice with sharp acceleration and once Ralph had jammed on the brakes. Each time it had swerved, and at the last, Zach had bounced across the floor, cannoning into her. She'd yelped.

Until then the drive had been smooth and unremarkable. No sense of danger had filtered into the back where they squatted or lay in semi-darkness. Not now.

Wally knelt in the hatch between the cab's seats, his bulk blocking any view of what was ahead.

Ralph stamped on the brakes again. Zach heard the tyres shriek and thought he smelled the burned rubber. He couldn't hear what they were saying above the roar of lorries alongside them. Then there was a noise he hadn't heard before: a sledgehammer beating on corrugated iron.

'What the fuck is it?'

The answer, dismissive, from Wally: 'What the fuck does it sound like?'

Wally shifted to give Zach a view into the cab. He saw the light, high above them. Its source was the origin of the noise. The helicopter nudged along above them, keeping pace. It was, Zach knew, locked on to them.

'How long?'

'What does it matter?' A snarl from Wally. 'It's fucking there.'

The jigsaw slotted into place.

Ralph had tried to ease the van's roof out of the light by using the big lorries as shields. The light wavered; it went between them and a lorry with a trailer, hauling timber, in front of them, then to a long-distance coach in the fast lane. The beam's focus switched across the coach and the lorry to rest on a truck weighed down with bricks, travelling slowly on the inside.

Had the helicopter crew been briefed to look for that make and colour of van on that road?

He craned to hear Mikey, Wally and Ralph.

'What they got?'

'Attack jobs, like the Apache, and they make one that's the Bell but with their own name on it.'

'What would the Bell type carry?'

'Might have a belt-fed, might not, or machine-gun-mounting capability.'

'Their Apache version?'

'They do a Hellfire. They have all the missiles.'

'What's an estimate?'

Mikey did the summary. 'If I'm right, a fair shout, they picked up intelligence this evening – where, don't know, how, not important – and they'll have scrambled the birds that were fuelled. They'll have done several roads out of the city and hope one of them strikes lucky. One has. If they were armed I reckon by now they'd have fired on us, done a bit of wasting.'

They were beyond Zanjan. Zach knew that because they had stopped there to buy fuel. She had been escorted to the kiosk and had paid with cash they'd given her. She'd also bought bread, cheese and water. He hadn't been asked to go with her. She had gone inside – he had seen through the windscreen – Wally hovering behind her. She had worn the scarf over her hair, and her veil, and had taken less than a minute and a half. Wally had stayed outside and kept her in view. Zach had heard him get out of the van, cocking his pistol. They didn't trust her, and there was no reason why they should. She might have asked for a phone, or spilled a story to the young guy at the cash desk, and she'd have been shot. Trust, Zach thought, came slow to these guys. He'd had some bread, and the cheese was creamy. They'd driven on towards Mianeh, stopping at a lay-by for a piss; the woman had been allowed a dark corner. He didn't know whether they were past Mianeh or not.

'What're they going to do?'

'Shepherd us.'

'And we just wait for the big bang?'

'They're hearing about us on the radios. There's a fix. Where we are, to the last metre, so they've scrambled.'

'Getting a block in place, sealing it tight.'

'Do we just wait for some ugly fucker to get his hands on us?'

'Who's going to do the business?'

'You Mikey. Get the zero right and hit it.'

'Your shout, Mikey.'

The helicopter was above them, the sound of the rotors bludgeoning the roof. Where would he rather be? A fool had said, 'Nowhere.' Her teeth were chattering.

He spoke: 'What can I do?'

'You can shut the fuck up.'

Wally was into the kit and scrabbled to undo a zip, then a Velcro restraint. He took out the rifle and fastened in a magazine. His movements let the light flood them. The pace stayed constant. He understood: for the people in the helicopter it was as if they already had them in handcuffs. They were boxed in, traffic on either side, in front and behind. The other drivers would have realised they were all under the control of the bird above. Zach thought it like a sparrow hawk, monitoring them. The rifle was passed to Mikey, who armed it. She was frightened – Zach reached out to her. She might or might not have seen his hand, but she didn't take it, even though earlier she'd touched his neck.

Wally was the biggest of the three guys. Ralph drove on. The roar around and above them burst inside the van. Wally had the door open and, with his other hand, held on to Mikey's belt. The guys didn't trust Zach or the woman, but they trusted each other. Trusted Ralph to hold the speed steady, trusted Wally to keep the door open against the thrust of the slipstream and hang onto the belt, and trusted Mikey with the rifle.

Mikey had the aim. Wally grunted at the weight in his hand. Mikey held the aim and Zach couldn't imagine how it was possible to be so still yet leaning half out of a van door. Two shots. There was the tinkle of cartridge cases hitting the metal floor. Zach didn't know how far above them the helicopter was. Mikey was back inside and the door slammed.

The light had been killed.

'Given the fucker something to think about.'

'He's away.'

'Hammer it, Ralph.'

'Great shot, Mikey.'

The helicopter had veered off. Wally said the pilot wouldn't hang around to hunt for medals.

They were into the fast lane. The lorry with the trailer of timber was behind them, and the long-distance coach. Ralph had killed his own headlights, used those of other vehicles, was driving fast and close to the central crash barrier. It had been going well – no longer. There had been a morning the previous summer when work on a site was progressing and a man had chucked down his spade – why not? Except that the spade's blade had carved into a buried wasps' nest, and they came out. Everything had been fine while the wasps were undisturbed, but now there was mayhem. Three men were stung and one collapsed because their territory had been invaded. He wished she had taken his hand.

Wally said, 'I'm thinking, Mikey, that they're in a shambles. They may not have crack guys at any block they've put together. At least, that's what I'm hoping.'

Zach shivered. He knew nothing of fighting men, but he was depending on them, now, as was she. They depended on a man who could – from a moving vehicle – hit a helicopter's searchlight. Mikey hadn't made any song and dance about it. It had been the guys' moment. His liberty, his life, rested in their hands.

He had been Lieutenant Ralph Cotton, then aged twenty-four, and was just back from running a platoon with a Rifles battalion in Helmand. The feeling in the mess, apparently, was that the major and his wife could patch up their marriage but not while he was so obviously the injured party. Not that it mattered, but she had bloody seduced Ralph and made the running. It would have passed off without notice, had not a packet of his cigarettes fallen out of his tunic pocket and been pushed half under the bed on the major's side. That might have been explained away, but a lance-corporal who had been paid to mow the grass in front of the major's quarters had snapped a picture on his mobile of Lieutenant Cotton beating his retreat.

The mess had ruled against him, and the padre had handed him the loaded pistol: Ralph's typed resignation from the unit, with immediate effect. He'd signed it. He was from mid-Wales, privately educated, good with people, and had had the wit not to set his sights at the summit but towards the foothills.

He had gone to Contego Security.

They liked former officers, were short of them. They had a full book of men out of the army – regulars, given the boot for indiscipline, or classified as steroid addicts. He wasn't a thug and was likely to charm a client. Open arms welcomed him at the offices off Ealing High Street. He'd had two years of good money on the British embassy detail, Afghanistan, and two years of rubbish money with an agricultural aid organisation, also in Afghanistan. The market there was contracting, restrictions on movement were more limited, immunity had been downgraded, and the Western governments' commitment was waning.

This time, he'd needed the work.

His address, on the Contego files, was a house set back from the Llangurig to Ponterwyd road: nine bedrooms and a bit more than two hundred acres, which were mostly woodland, hillside or bog. The roof needed repairing, which would cost. His mother was there, with his father and sister. Ralph was not a businessman or a farmer, and should have been a half-decent professional soldier. He had hoped private military contracting might bring in the cash for the roof. Life could be cruel. His age and lack of prospects caused conflict at home, so when the phone had rung, echoing in that bloody great draughty hallway, he had almost run to the car for the drive to Worcester railway station.

He was stockily built, with dark hair and a pale complexion. Since the major's wife, other women had considered him handsome, but none had had any money. Now there was Minnie. She ran a livery stable and they did hunt balls together and Christmas parties. She was cheerfully broke, and overdrawn from January to December. At the best thrashes she'd wear her mother's old evening gowns. Everyone said that, in her ancent finery, she looked fantastic. They'd fall into bed when they were drunk, and didn't talk about marriage when they were sober. He'd called her from the station to tell her he'd be away for a few days. She had advised, 'Don't get your arse shot off, darling. See you.' To their friends on the circuit, he was the Brat and she was the Bitch.

Each time he was far away, he worried about how to fund the roof and how to keep the place when his father and mother could no longer cope.

A natural hero? Not really.

A good man to have on the team? Probably.

Honourable? Possibly. Devious? No.

Reaction if the shit went up? Unknown. But he was a quality driver, and had toned down the accent that had been appropriate in the Rifles battalion but wasn't in Contego work. There was little else about him that anyone needed to know.

He drove fast, ignoring horn blasts when he overtook on the inside or made the chicken-run past on the outside, coming up like a shadow in a mirror. The Bitch didn't have a photograph of her Brat, had never asked for one. He didn't have one of her . . . Silly, but he'd have liked one – of her in boots, jodhpurs, a hunt jacket and astride a big horse. She would have laughed if he'd asked for it.

His wife was asleep. They were lucky in their apartment to have two bedrooms.

Kourosh sat on the floor of the second bedroom and wallowed in his misery. It was infatuation and he thought it destroyed him. His head was against the side of the bed in which his child slept. The boy's breathing was laboured – he had respiratory problems. The doctors said he'd be better off if they left the city, where the smog was so pervasive, and moved to the Gulf coast, anywhere from Bushehr to Bandar Abbas. He hadn't followed their advice. He had lied to his wife. He had told her that he was closely involved in investigations of the greatest sensitivity: it was impossible for him to move south, away from his team. Maybe in the future. He hadn't told his commander about the child's difficulties and requested a transfer. It would have meant leaving *her*.

He knew the contours of her body, dreamed of possessing her. He knew each wrinkle and flaw in the faces of the two men whose photographs stood in the room over the garage. It was as if she mocked him. Today had been bad for his child. It was always worse for him when it rained. Now his boy tossed and turned, and Kourosh's mind churned. If he denounced her anonymously from a call box or an Internet café, described the men with her, and the route they would take to the northern town of Khvoy, she would be taken.

And tortured.

Few could resist the torture. She would name him.

They would come then, men he had worked with, laughed with, and with whom he had done the long stake-outs when they hunted for the Zionist-paid spies. They would break down the door. His wife would hold his child tightly to her, and would hear that he was the lover of a traitor. Kourosh squirmed. She would be disgraced.

But he held open the wallet. The photograph was in a hidden pouch but it was close to him, with him.

The rain had stopped, but it was cold – the heating was off.

He weighed his options. He was entangled, knew the consequences, and was bereft of the optimism an ignorant man might have clutched. The mobile rang in his pocket. A text message lit the screen. He had to return to the barracks.

The technicians reported a spike in traffic. The analysts burrowed into the messages, in clear and coded. Work, for them, could be dull, but there were moments – rare – when the roof of the world seemed to have been lifted. To *Manhunt* and *dragnet*, a new pearl could be added.

Reported location is Route 2, 51 kilometres NW Mianeh – approx midway between Torkaman and Siah Chaman. Reported incident is relevant to earlier announced maximum alert for female fugitive. Vehicle believed involved in escape, and used by foreign hostile agencies, identified by helicopter and tracked until accurate shooting from vehicle destroyed searchlight. Action taken: road block in place. Other traffic is confused. High chaos among internal security organisations.

The analysts' views floated to screens.

Mehrak heard them. He was in his room. Anneliese had made him a mug of hot chocolate and he had brought it upstairs. He had been half dressed when he had heard PK and Sidney walking up the hill, along the lane, and into the back of the house. Mehrak thought that PK had set the pace, but the older man had not wished to be classified as slow. Loud voices. Mehrak, of course, was nominally without experience of men under the influence of alcohol. He didn't drink, but many did. The irony of central Tehran was that getting hold of alcohol was no harder than obtaining heroin. Did the brigadier drink? There had been mornings, in the Mercedes, when he had sucked peppermints continuously. He knew that when men drank, their voices became louder.

Mehrak was at his door, Auntie with him.

He heard PK – he might have been with Father William, or Nobby, say, 'Get the communications hotted up. The text said it was crisis time. Fuck-up on a grand scale, is what that means.'

Mehrak was put into his room. He heard the key turn. The lock clicked.

Footsteps came up the stairs. The door along the corridor opened.

Mehrak heard PK call, 'Coffee, someone be an angel – black.'

Then it was quiet. Then he heard voices, too indistinct for him to understand what was said. He sat on the end of the bed, bent and untied his shoe laces. He had been good that day and had tried to co-operate. His mood oscillated, but that afternoon he had been more buoyant: they had covered corruption, import and export of textiles, electrical goods, fuel, names, anything that had been talked about in the Mercedes while he, unnoticed, drove.

They were bringing her out. She would be alone, far from anything she knew. He believed in a new beginning. They would be together. It was *crisis time* and there had been a *fuck-up on a grand scale.* He knew how it was in north Tehran, in one of the favoured streets of regime officials, and where the academics who worked on the horizons of research lived, on those mornings when the pieces of a car littered the street, parts lodged in the trees, with legs, arms and clothing. He knew how it was in those same streets when a body lay half on the pavement and half in the gutter and, other than a bullet hole in the head, the face was unmarked, exceptional only for the shock, disbelief it expressed. The targets were men who should have been protected. Sometimes bodyguards were dead with their principals. His brigadier would have said, in the company of senior men, that this was *crisis time*, and when they had left the scene of an atrocity, his brigadier, in the car, would have spoken of a *fuck-up on a grand scale*.

He kicked off his shoes. One flew towards the window and the other came to rest in the corner by the pipes that carried the hot water for the heating system. He went to pick it up. His ear was beside the pipe.

Mehrak listened.

He heard PK explain *crisis time*, and fill in the detail of the *fuck-up on a grand scale*. He heard about a helicopter being fired on, a vehicle hammering along a road to the north and a road block being set in position. He knew that road, could almost have described the stretch that PK was talking about. It wound between low hills and was new, with a good surface. Hope died.

'Mixed feelings, Tad.'

'Yes, Director.'

'On the one hand, I like to be told, kept abreast.'

'I thought you might have wanted an updated briefing.'

'On the other, the joy of being ignorant.'

'Glad I caught you before bed.'

They were fighting cocks, dancing around each other. The pit was the director's grace-and-favour flat, a quality Westminster address. Tadeuz Fenton had caught him half dressed, on the way to bed, and the door was closed, which meant the wife was in residence. Whisky wasn't offered. Tadeuz Fenton, clever man and ladder-climber, had briefed the director on Petroc Kenning's brothel-trap concept, and they'd shared a chortle. The money had been authorised, and a vaguer message sent, via a handwritten memorandum, suggesting that the wretch caught in the trap would be an altogether better source should his wife find it possible to leave the Islamic Republic. Detail had been sparse. An approach by a language student, yes, a driver to be found, no problem . . . Less about firearms and the bare mention of the risk in a combat role for anyone at the sharp end. The director, a politician of the trade but perhaps not as honed in skills as his Iran Desk chief, would have preferred to hide behind 'Nobody told me,' but they were adults, and recrimination would follow failure.

'Not the end of the world, Tad.'

'Not yet, Director.'

'The boys you put in there, they're unlikely to throw in the towel?'

'Absolutely not.'

'You're expecting them to hit a block?'

'In their predicament, I anticipate they'll attempt to divert round it. Avoid the consequences of further confrontation. A few rounds at a helicopter will have proved chastening.'

'They're good men?'

'They're what I could get in the time I had available.'

He had his director at a disadvantage. Tadeuz Fenton had changed into a clean shirt before coming. His director's shirt was unbuttoned, showing his chest.

'Tell me – because we face difficult hours ahead – what's the reward?'

He had a winning smile. It exuded confidence. A glass was ever nearly full, never close to empty. It was an attribute that had served him well.

'We get to eat at the top table. You've had those days in Washington, Director, as have I, when you've been made to feel little more than a piece of cargo. On those days, with us, they go through the motions – and Jerusalem does it with even less courtesy. On this, I've them both eating out of the palm of my hand. A little good luck – neither of them has recruited a person of value in the last few months. Successful hits, but no one on the other side of a table answering specific questions. We have first-hand recent detail. He's an important defector. He's providing material that can be used for psywar black stuff, for the removal of talented scientists, chemists and engineers. If, Heaven forbid, a major assault had to be launched then this little man will have answered questions on security, defences and missile procedures. You see, Director, he's been everywhere, has seen everything. Give him his wife and I'm confident he'll go cheerfully into the very recesses of his memory. He's one of the best we've ever had.'

'Thank you. High praise indeed. Could be a long day tomorrow.'

'In my experience – not as great as yours, of course – things are seldom as dark as predicted. I'm grateful for your support.'

He pushed the chair back and eased himself upright. Time to allow his senior to go to bed. They were in the kitchen and the pans were in the sink. A wine bottle stood on the draining-board, only an inch left. He was probably only half awake, and tired, maybe a little tipsy, and he was without the young tyros who looked after him at Vauxhall Cross – they'd never have allowed a one-to-one at that hour of the night and would raise Cain in the morning. It was a good time to have found his man and kept him on board, and he thought his back was protected. It would be a long day, yes, and God alone knew what it would bring.

She broke the quiet in the back of the van. 'What do they think will happen?' Her hand brushed against his chin as she indicated whom she had meant: Wally, Ralph and Mikey.

'That further on there'll be a road block.'

'And we talk our way through it?'

'I don't think so.'

'They should hide. You talk as well as an Iranian, and with me beside you, we're man and wife.' It was obvious to her. 'We lie and we'll deceive them.'

'It won't be like that.'

'It has to be. A block is a block.'

He said quietly, trying to keep the quaver from his voice, 'I think it's their intention to go through the block.'

'That's impossible. Please?'

He tried to sound bold. 'Through it, or round it.'

'Why don't we talk to them?'

'The authorities have identified our vehicle. The helicopter followed us, had its light on us. That's why he killed the light. It bought a little time. Very soon we'll hit a block, and that's why we're driving without lights.'

No traffic came towards them. The guys understood: lorries, vans and cars were being held back behind the block. Zach realised it would be soon – but how soon? He didn't know and didn't ask. He doubted they knew. It was a lesson he'd learned from the site: faced with finding a solution to what appeared the impossible, questions helped no one. It was all right for her and him to talk, but *they* had the weapons ready and Ralph drove smoothly – Zach didn't know how he managed to see the road. They had armed two of the machine pistols and some of the grenades. The windows were down in the cab, and the three guys now wore dark glasses. Zach had nothing to contribute, and knew it.

'You do not have a job in this?'

'No. I was here to get them into the city, talk to you and get out of the city. I have no training with weapons.'

'You are not from the special services of Britain?'

'No.'

'You came to speak to me – and I told you I hated my husband. You persisted. I agreed to come. Why did you come?'

He hesitated. The darkness cloaked him and the only faint light came from the instrument panel in the cab. The quiet was broken only by the engine and the guys' breathing. He murmured, close to her ear, 'I was grateful to be asked.'

IO

No one Zach Becket knew could have told him that it was worth being on the Mianeh to Tabriz road with a girl who asked questions. That it was worth being with three men, carrying stated-the-art weapons and a trauma pack, a road block ahead.

It was past midnight, and the rain had stopped. A light cloud covered the moon and most of the stars were hidden. He thought, from what he'd seen through the back window of the van, that they had passed one isolated building, and further back there had been goats in the road. They were coming to the crest of a slow incline, and Ralph was changing down. The van shook as he went off the metalled surface and onto the hard shoulder.

She asked, 'Is it a comfort stop?'

A hand came back and made a gesture, unmistakable, for total quiet. They were all hunched forward in the cab, peering into the darkness.

Her lips were against his ear: 'Do I get to pee outside or do I just wait and . . . Or can I ask for a bucket?'

He felt she belonged to him, not to the three guys. He caught her upper arm and gripped it, trying to silence her. He failed.

'You're greatful you were asked. How grateful should I be? Would it have been better for me to stay?'

He was about to answer, but Mikey had turned. When he spoke, his voice was ice cold and hard. 'Tell the lady, Zach, that she's to shut up or she'll lose some teeth. Get out the back. No noise.'

Zach repeated it into her ear. He found another truth: she was a 'last-word woman'.

'Should I have stayed?'

Mikey's head was through the gap. 'I'll take half her face off.

But first, what sort of wild animals do they have here? The big ones, threat to farmers' stock. Ask her.'

He did. He shortened her answer, relayed its bones. There were wild boar, big cats, brown bears, wolves. She had a friend who had studied the cats – cheetah, lynx and panther — Mikey cut her off. There were wolves? She spat back: a homeless man living in a rough wood shelter in the north-east, a few years ago, had been mauled to death by a pack and the villagers had failed to drive them off. More recently, a woman had been attacked in her village, central Iran, had killed the starving beast and— He told her, again, to shut up.

Zach was out of the van. Inevitable that there'd be a road block in front of them, but he hadn't been told. He wasn't in the loop of shared information. He stretched. Mikey and Wally were with him.

Zach was told.

He couldn't turn on the man and say, 'Wait! Hold it there! I'm a civilian, not a part of a combat team. You're supposed to be protecting me.' He turned away. He was in the north-west, but not yet among the mountain people or in the Kurdish areas. It was a place of rural peasants and a torch would be shone in his face when he approached and while he talked.

It was ahead of them, Mikey said, about three hundred metres. They'd seen the glow of cigarettes, and the short flash of a torch.

Mikey said softly, 'There are ditches on either side, fields, with rough frozen ground, and grazing. There are some dried-out irrigation systems. We can't go off-road. So, what are you?'

'A herdsman.'

'What's your problem?'

'I've lost some goats. I've left the dog with the ones I've found, but I'm a few short.'

'What's the threat to your goats?'

'Wolves. They've been seen and—'

'Wally'll be behind you. You up for this?'

Well, he'd soon find out. And he'd soon learn whether Farideh would have done better to chuck the proposition back in his face and stayed where she was.

'I'll give it a stab,' Zach answered.

Mikey went to the side of the road and they heard the crack of a small branch breaking. He returned with a length of sapling and stripped off the secondary branches. He handed it to Zach – what a drover would carry. Zach was remembering accents and what little he knew of country dialect.

'Do you want me to talk it through with her, get her thoughts?'

'No. On your way.'

Zach started to walk. He heard the lever on the machine gun slide forward or back, and imagined the safety was off. He strode ahead and began to call, like there were goats to the right and left of him. He called loudly because he had to find them before the wolves did. He didn't know how far behind him Wally was.

A flashlight came on, wobbled, wavered, and found him. The beam blinded him.

'Have you seen some goats?' he yelled at the light. 'Have you heard any wolves?'

A young voice, tainted with nerves, answered. 'Are there wolves here?'

Zach answered, a countryman's vernacular. 'Yes.'

He didn't know how far behind him Wally was.

Wally was in a ditch on the left side of the road. No traffic came through. They were inside the bubble, vehicles held up behind them and ahead. He estimated he was two hundred yards away from the torch beam. Wally thought he was there to give the boy confidence. Could he intervene if it went badly for him at the block? He could see a police car parked sideways but that was all. They were relying on Zach. Could he intervene if a knot of them formed round him and a rifle butt smacked into his head? Could pigs fly? He might drop one, and the lad might break free. Might . . .

He would not be able to help. He saw the light on the boy. It threw a long shadow behind him. Zach had courage, and no choice but to show it.

He was Walter Davies, had always been Wally, was thirty-six.

There were days when he thought he had little to offer, and fewer when he reckoned a spark still burned. He was from the north-east, had joined a Fusilier regiment at nineteen, and had come back from the Province on the usual high. Natalie was his girlfriend, and they hadn't used anything, so he had a daughter. A son was conceived on his return from the first Gulf scrap, born in '92, and another after he'd returned from deployment to Basra in 2008. He was a platoon sergeant, reasonable at his job, but Natalie had said he had to come out, or she and the kids were on the move. Difficult to cope with that: one thing being a soldier and having all manner of shit to contend with, another to deal with a woman's ultimatum. He'd come out, the start of the slide down the slope. No jobs in the north-east, and he had no skills to offer other than killing or leading kids into the zones where they could kill. He was on the dole, feeling lost and failed. Natalie had left with the kids. She'd moved in with a printer-ink salesman.

What had Wally to give? He was a bayonet-pusher, and there were enough of them at the big firms with the offices in London's West End. He'd ended up at Contego. They had restored some of his self-respect, but not all. As a private military contractor, regarded as a low-life by the regulars, and with his sergeant's rank meaning nothing, he had done close protection and convoy escort in Kabul, then had six months of decent pay and utter boredom as armed watch on bulk tankers running the risk of being hit by Somali pirates. Best place he'd been was the Cape, South Africa, and it was possible there to sign on, three months at a time, and work with ambulance crews in the townships. Knifings, bullet wounds, head injuries, he'd done them all. It was the most useful contact Contego had, and that placement meant Wally was high quality at saving life in the golden minutes after the ambulance had pitched up. It was better than any simulation, better than being in the field because then the trained people stepped in and he'd be elbowed aside. He knew now how to save the life of a wounded client and, from what he'd been told by the crews in the Cape, he also knew when the chance of survival was lost. Contego had kept him busy, but less so recently. He was classified as a remote medical assistant, which helped, but the competition for placement was heavy.

He sent cards and money for his kids' birthdays but never heard back. He had no love life – except Leanne in Contego's accounts office. She was the unexceptional, none-too-choosy office bicycle, and she did a turn with him sometimes. His hair was thinning at the front and there were grey strands at the sides, and life wasn't a bed of roses. Where would he rather be? He hadn't yet persuaded the boys to play the game with him, but he loved it. It was the best laugh he knew.

An honourable man? Yes, why not, when there weren't alternatives available? He had little scope for fixing his expenses because Leanne and her pal went through them penny by penny, cent by cent, dinar by dinar, afghani by fucking afghani. And there wasn't much he could do with tax because he didn't earn enough. There was a bed-sit in south London that was the nearest thing to home. How honourable? He'd do his best for the client but wasn't a bullet-catcher. That was beyond the contract's terms.

The torch was full on the boy, and then the shouting started.

'Stop.'

'Who the fuck are you?'

'We're police and *basij*. Identify yourself.'

'I'm Mahmoud. Have you seen my goats?'

'Come forward – slowly. Put your hands on your head.'

'Why? I'm looking for my goats.'

'Don't argue. On your head.'

'I've lost some of my goats. Have you heard any wolves?'

'Come close. Put your hands on your head.'

'Is your road block to stop herdsmen finding their goats when wolves are about?'

'We're here to catch Zionist spies. They shot at a helicopter.'

'I'm looking for my goats. I'm not scared of Zionists, but I *am* scared of wolves.'

'We have to search you.'

'Do I look like a Zionist spy? Have you cigarettes?'

'Here.'

'God watch over you, keep you safe. Is this all you have to stop the Zionists?'

'There are twelve of us, and more coming from Tabriz, with two armoured cars. They'll be here in fifteen minutes. In an hour there'll be a helicopter which has the equipment to find men hiding at night. That's coming from Tabriz too.'

'I have more than a hundred Raeini goats. If you see them, send them back up the road. My dog's with the ones I have found – and if you see the wolves, shoot them.'

'Go on, then.'

'My wife's young and pretty and I want to get home – but I have to find my goats. I don't have time to talk to you about Zionist spies. Listen out for the wolves and shoot the fucking things.'

'Goodnight, Mahmoud. We hope you find your goats.'

'Thank you for the cigarettes. Hey – and the Zionists? Kill the bastards.'

Zach walked back. The torch was off and he had only natural light to guide him. He was in the centre of the road, and twice there was laughter behind from the police or the *basij*, whatever they were, then quiet and his own footsteps. A light wind blew on his face, and he was shivering, perhaps because he had no protection and had seen the weapons – or because he was scared. It was hard to walk – his legs felt weak. At the School, they hadn't studied the language of a semi-illiterate peasant who kept goats on a subsistence farm and grew a few hectares of maize and vegetables. The Farsi he had learned had been formal. He reckoned he'd given a masterly performance but he'd learned in the last cramped hours that his achievement would win no recognition.

His arm was grabbed.

He hadn't seen Wally, but now he was propelled at speed back up the road towards the crest, a dark line against the faint light in the sky. He was frightened that his legs would give way, and didn't think Wally would carry him. He fastened on to her face, its seriousness, and the defiant jut of her chin. It cleared his mind. Him:

grateful to be asked. Her: *should I have stayed?* He stumbled, tripped and would have fallen, but Wally held him.

They hit the crest.

His breath sobbed in his throat.

Mikey was in front of him. Wally held him up.

He talked, jabbered. Armoured cars were coming, and a helicopter. He was asked how many he'd seen, where the weapons were, the layout of the block and the uniforms. After a minute or two, he had blurted it all out. Each time his voice had risen, Wally had slapped a hand over his mouth. He wasn't a part of them, was just the news courier. But without these men, their intolerance and impatience, he was dead. Where would he rather be? Nowhere. 'Better to have stayed?' He couldn't have answered her.

He was taken to the back doors of the van, helped up and pushed in.

Zach sprawled forward. He heard her gasp as the air was pressed out of her lungs. His back was jarred by a paint pot, and he swore. His arms flailed, hitting her. She caught and held them.

They talked, Mikey, Ralph and Wally, short and staccato. Time was precious. A helicopter was up and might now be fifty minutes from the location. Two armoured cars were lumbering south from Tabriz and were some ten minutes from the block. Time was too precious for explanations. Zach understood that. Ralph would drive, Mikey in the passenger seat beside him, Wally squatting between the seats. The weapons were readied, the grenades parcelled out. Ignition in, dashboard lights on, and the quiet throb of the engine. They moved forward.

They topped the crest. Zach had told them where the weapons were and the layout of the chicane. Critical: at the block they had used a torch. They did not have an image-intensifier lens. They rolled. The van gathered speed. No lights, no engine sounds, going faster, speed increasing, with only the grinding of the wheels, the creaking of the bodywork, and the darkness. He was close to her, she to him. They lay on blankets, rugs and the tarpaulins builders used. He sensed that – very soon, seconds away – there would be an impact.

There was a whisper, side of mouth, from Wally. 'Keep down.'

He felt her cringe. She seemed, then, to wriggle a little under him, to insinuate herself below his chest and right hip. Her hands were over her ears.

They were careering down the last of the slope. Then came the jolt, the engine's cough and the lights blazed. Ralph would have had the traction and would have swerved right, then left, and accelerated towards the gap. He hit his horn. Noise and speed, light and disorientation – Zach supposed – was what he aimed for. Zach tried to get a view past Wally's hip, but the man must have felt the movement: a hand came off a weapon, caught his forehead, pushed it down, then went back to the weapon. Now his face was buried in her hair. The first grenade went.

Mikey threw it, reached through the window. Pin out, half a breath in, lever loose, heave. Ralph timed it, braked hard, then swung the wheel, clipped the front of the police car that made the first line of the block, and was past it. The lights showed the faces, and guys were heaving at the cocking rifles' levers. Had armed the weapons.

Wally threw the next, past Ralph's shoulder.

All of them knew the figures: 300,000 candlepower for the flash and 160 decibels for the bang. A third pin flew, the lever snapped free and the grenade was thrown. The first detonated. In front of them, men reeled away. Others held their ears and all had arms in front of their eyes. Ralph took them past the front car, then swung sharply and was clear of the second. The final grenade detonated as he took the van past the third. They heard her scream.

Zach couldn't stifle it. It was from deep in her throat, animal and primitive. He had his arms wrapped round her and her head buried in his chest. She cried out the name as the van swung left, right again, and they slithered on the flooring. 'Johnny!'

His hearing was wrecked and his eyes watering, but the name had been clear. She had a photograph of the man, Johnny. She was shaking, he didn't know whether with tears, fear or just reaction to the grenades. Not a shot had been fired at them.

A triumph.

The van seemed to accelerate and his hold on her loosened.

One hand off the wheel, Ralph did high fives with Mikey, then Wally.

'Fucking good, Ralph. Quality.'

'It was kids there – couldn't cope.'

'Just amateurs. Great driving, Ralph.'

'Let's burn it.'

Lights on, the way ahead shown up. Wally was giggling and Ralph chuckled. There was even a small smile on Mikey's face.

The shout – the change.

'For fuck's sake, what's the idiot—?'

Zach saw it. It would be played out in front of him – six or seven seconds of it, a life span. He had a good view through the gap between the seats now that Wally had eased to his left, and the headlights were on full beam.

He was a policeman or a *basij*. Difficult to tell because he wore a black anorak over his shoulders and chest. The giveaway would have been the trousers – blue for police, khaki for the paramilitary – but they were round his ankles. There was another behind him, but in shadow. The kid staggered onto the road but his trousers impeded him. He had a rifle. Zach didn't know much about weapons but recognised the shape. It was the Russian one, what the Palestinians had. It featured on all the 'resistance' posters against the imperialism of America and Britain. People called it an 'iconic' image. He had whitish legs in the headlights, spindly, fragile.

The headlights centred on his privates, and Zach heard Ralph gulp. A ditch to the right, and another to the left.

The kid couldn't see through the headlights. He was struggling to pull back the cocking lever – and had it. He lifted the thing – a Kalashnikov, so recognisable. He would shoot, Zach thought, into the heart of the light that was fifty metres from him, forty, thirty. A kid who wanted to be a hero, who had sloped off from the others to drop his trousers, hadn't kept his head down. He'd come out on the road and confronted them. Ralph couldn't spin the wheel, pass him.

The van hit him. It picked him up, threw him high, and the rifle spiralled out of his hand. It landed on the bonnet, fracturing the windscreen. The body hit the roof, bounced and made an echo inside, as if a rock had fallen on the metal. He didn't shout, scream or cry out – his eyes had been glazed from the moment of impact. There was a thud below – like a sandbag on a site had been dropped from scaffolding and hit concrete. Zach saw what was in front.

The kid had screwed them. He had probably never fired his weapon except on a range but he had wrecked them.

That was why the kid was there – he'd gone a hundred paces from the block to watch the Stinger. It was like a big-link chain with sharpened nails sticking up. They'd catch a tyre's treads every time. There was no escape from it. It was silvery chrome, shiny and bright in the lights, and was across the road. The kid would have been there to retrieve it when the two armoured cars came up: the cavalry on the rescue mission.

A chance, Zach reckoned, that Ralph might have been able to manoeuvre round it if he'd been able to go slowly and nudge the edge of the ditch, or stop for Mikey to get out and move it. But the kid hadn't been alone.

Maybe the sergeant had thought him too nervous to be isolated from the main group down the road. Beyond the strip the shadow was rising to its full height, and the shape of the rifle was thrown far back, with the body, by the headlights. Cocked, firing. Ralph drove through.

It would have been on automatic, not single shots, and they came in a spray behind the cab and across the back of the van.

Zach covered her.

Wally had to shoot behind Ralph's shoulder.

He couldn't have taken aim faster, and was pressed into Ralph's shoulder. Mikey couldn't intervene.

Wally's shooting – the clatter of the weapon and the cases

spilling out of the mechanism. Useful shooting because the second kid – in love with Paradise – had no chance to aim at the cab, couldn't get a bead on Ralph, himself or Mikey, and they went through. But there was the shaking.

A tyre had gone.

They went on through the darkness. No lights, no high fives.

Mikey said what was needed. Maybe he was right, and maybe he wasn't . . . but neither Wally nor Ralph could come up with a better idea. They limped on. There was a cluster of buildings ahead, with a lamp or security light over a barn entrance. No celebrations.

They had pulled up. When they stopped, she wriggled clear of him.

'What do we do?'

Zach said they'd stopped because they'd had to get off the road, beyond the angle of the headlights approaching them, and the armoured cars that were on their way.

'The shooting, and the explosions?'

Mikey was out of the van, and Wally had crawled after him. They were circling it.

'The guys used grenades at the block. They did the necessary. We were through and thought it had been successful. There were two more of them down the road and one came into the headlights and was going to fire. He was run down – I think he was killed from the impact. There was a second man – maybe *basij* – and he fired at us. His shots hit the van. The guys put him down. I think he was killed too.'

His voice was flat. They had crouched, were out of sight, checking the tyres that had clipped the edge of the stinger.

'If they had taken us, if we were to be hanged, those bastards would have been allowed to watch. They'd have been singing and dancing. That they were kids . . . is that important? Do you think I'm an idiot, Zach? If it's them or me, who would I choose?'

There was a rumble on the road, faint at first, but growing louder. Their own engine idled. Wally and Mikey were still by the tyres. Zach thought it was his fate to be like a crab caught under a stone as the tide pulled away. There was the stink of paint, resin and oil, and he could see the punctures on the right and left sides of the van, entry and exit.

The armoured vehicles had blazing lights. He heard Ralph call that they were Rakhash, a locally made personnel carrier. Zach saw them through the back, and the one that followed lit the one ahead. He thought their speed close to fifty miles an hour, at maximum, and their radios would have screamed that there was an emergency. Zach understood more. The guys had rifles, automatic pistols and grenades. They didn't have the kit to take on an armour protected beast. They were back in and the engine was gunned. A lamp had been lit in an upper room of the farmhouse beyond the barn.

The headlights disappeared, went round the bend. They'd gone south, would find chaos and casualties when they got there. It had been a snapshot of defining moments – as if they were on a slate and couldn't be erased – and there was no 'going back'. He had seen the kid without trousers run down, the kid with the rifle shot and killed. The world had changed. Zach might have screamed. The howl stayed in his throat. If he had screamed, he would not have been heard.

They bumped towards the north. How long would the tyres last? He had the right to ask, and the right to be told. And *she*, Farideh, had the right to be answered. *Should I have stayed?*

'Who was Johnny?'

'Why?'

'You called his name at the block.'

The van sagged and listed but Ralph kept the speed up. The headlights were off. The stars were up but the moon kissed clouds.

'They killed him.'

'He changed you?'

'I believed what I was told – everything. I believed in my place at work, in the apartment, in my husband's bed and in my duty. I had done nothing that gave offence, nor would have wanted to. I was beaten on the street. I was left with my clothing torn, modesty lost. He found me and saved me. He was their enemy. He fought them and I loved him. They would have tortured him before they killed him, but he didn't tell them my name. He died and I lived. I called out his name for protection when they shot at us. Do you understand?'

He remembered the photograph. The young man, the smile, the floppy hair, Zach wondered if, ever, he could earn that love – and the frame the picture was held in; there had been no fear in the face.

It was not in its place. The picture of the man who had been hanged was gone, as was the photograph, head and shoulders, of the officer who had died in Afghanistan. The rugs on the floor were removed, the soft chairs, and the bed on which he should have lain with her, but hadn't.

There were footsteps on the stairs behind him.

Nothing remained. Everything had been replaced. On one wall there was a life-size portrait of Imam Khomeini, on another a magnified photograph, in a plain frame, of the Supreme Leader.

The two old men were in the doorway. A light was switched on and his torch dulled. Engine parts littered a long bench that straddled the room, and the floor around it showed the stains of engine oil and lubricants. One of the old men carried a wrench, the other a lump hammer. They had dead eyes and showed him no recognition.

A question was put to him: 'Are you a thief?'

A second question: 'What have you come to steal?'

Kourosh was a junior official in a unit that worked on the surveillance of state enemies, a married man, father of a child with bronchial difficulties. He was not an adulterer because she had refused to allow him the final moments of the sin. What had he come to steal? A motor-scooter wheel, a spark plug, a wing-mirror, a chain? He had brought her a necklace that she never wore, chocolates that he had never seen her eat, and a silver pen. He had given her a photograph of himself but it had never been displayed alongside those of the dead men. He had come to search for the necklace, the unopened box of chocolates and the pen, which was likely still in its padded case. He was an investigator: he understood searches and the work of the scientists who did forensic examinations of crime scenes, the gathering of DNA samples and the weight they carried in the eyes of the regime's judges.

She would break before the will of the interrogators.

He had been to the barracks, had driven there in his old car, and attended a briefing: a team was to be put on stand-by and would be flown wherever it was required. A helicopter had been fired on. Reinforcements were on the move, with an armoured gunship helicopter. Road blocks hemmed in the fugitives. He had come to remove the items that might carry on them the traces of his sweat, skin and saliva. All gone. The room had been cleaned.

He thought they were laughing at him. They would deny knowledge of her and him.

He had left the barracks without permission. He was condemned, but in his own time and without the poison falling on his wife and son.

He knew of nothing to say. They stepped aside. He went out through the door and started down the steps. The light was switched off behind him and they followed. He had climbed the gate to enter the yard. Now it was pulled open for him. He thought the pen and the chocolates would have gone into a street rubbish bin, the necklace too – gold and turquoise, made by a merchant from Mashhad. It had cost him, second-hand – probably once round the throat of a young bitch from the Peacock's ranks – more than he earned in two weeks. It would lie in a bin and be there until the refuse collectors came in the morning. He had lied to his wife to explain the loss of money, had said he'd been robbed. Perhaps she'd believed him.

He went out through the gate into the alleyway. The night closed around him. He knew when it would be light, and where he had to be before dawn.

He put down the phone. It was a call that Brigadier Reza Joyberi, a man of influence and authority, who was regarded as exemplary in his piety, made on average every two months. That it was past midnight did not matter as the dealer he had spoken to, in the code familiar to them both, dealt with prime customers twenty-four hours a day, seven days a week. The delivery would come within an hour. He would walk down to the main street from the side road in which his home was, go to the fuel station and be at the back, in shadow, as there he would be given the package. He would pay in American dollars.

He dealt with an Armenian, and the man's customer base ensured that he operated without interference but never with impunity.

The wealth he had accumulated, which was banked abroad, he would have regarded as a fringe benefit of his position. There might come a day – if the bazaar mounted a co-ordinated campaign, if the Revolutionary Guard Corps was led in rebellion by the lower ranks, who did not enjoy similar advantages – when he wanted to provide new passports for his wife and children, with new names, then send them out from a provincial airport, probably Isfahan, to Dubai or Istanbul. He would follow.

There might come a day when his allies backed away and he was unprotected. It might happen. While he was protected, and his connections were strong, it was accepted that he didn't pay prohibitive taxes and Customs duties. But his wealth was across the Gulf, and his driver was in the hands of an enemy. He would have spilled the account details. He could not, now, lift his telephone, get the international code, quote the number of his account, speak to the Lebanese who managed it, and demand that it was kept safe from being sanctioned or wiped. There was sweat on his forehead.

His wife slept, and so did his children.

On the nights when he was at home early enough to eat with them, he didn't bring his work to the dinner table. He hadn't told her that his driver had gone, that an armed gang had snatched the traitor's wife from under the noses of security. He had not told her that his own position was threatened. He checked his watch. It was time to walk from the villas at Shahrak Shahid Mahallati, go past the security guards, who would be smoking in their cars and would recognise him. He had given enough time to the Armenian, whose family had been hairdressers, in great demand, expensive. They had looked after the women from prominent families when the Shah had ruled. They had served the women well, but since the Air France plane had landed from Paris, and the Imam, scowling, had come down the steps, headscarves had been required and the women could not show off their new hairstyles. Would his own wife have enjoyed the attention of an Armenian hairdresser? He didn't know. Did she talk about it with her friends in the villas around theirs? He didn't know.

Without hair to tend, the Armenians had made their mark as suppliers of alcohol, brought in from Turkey. He slipped on a coat. He checked the money. His choice was Scotch whisky rather than American bourbon. He wouldn't have touched the bootleg vodka, kept in plastic containers once filled with anti-freeze; it was drunk by those who were not of the élite.

He needed to drink to forget.

It was all the sounds, meshed together, that woke Dunc Whitcombe in the small hours. He heard voices calling, horses neighing and the clip of hoofs. He was cold and the bed was cold. He didn't know how long he had been asleep and groped for his glasses. At the window he saw torches near the field where the horses were. He slid from under the sheets and blankets, and slipped on his suit jacket. He went to the door, opened it.

A side light had been left on down the corridor and in a corner of the living area. He and Mandy hadn't been disciplined enough to clear the table. The plates were gone. The glasses had been taken to the kitchen, and everything they had used during the meal had been washed and stood on the draining-board. The maps were scattered across it, and they'd done one of those useless recap conversations – 'So, where are we as things stand?' – which they loved in London and added another fifteen minutes to the length of a meeting.

Simple enough. They were at the extreme edge of Doğubeyazıt

, a ten-minute drive from the road junction that was a designated pick-up point – they were within daylight sight of it, if there was no fog and no low rainclouds over the upper ridges of the hills along which the frontier ran. They had been told all of that by the young man who had met them off the feeder flight. It was a diabolical failure of tradecraft to leave the maps on the table.

She was by the plate-glass windows. Of course, a woman would have packed a dressing-gown. He had not. It was thin material, a functional blue, and dropped to the knees of her pyjama trousers. She held the poker from the fire irons on the hearth set.

He murmured, 'Is there a problem?'

It was unusual for Dunc Whitcombe to ask such questions. She gestured with a hand at her hip for quiet, then pointed beyond the patio. He stood beside her.

The horses were on the move. He thought they were roped together and the boy was there, close to the front. The animals skipped willingly to keep up with him.

Another torchbeam, solitary, away from the path of the horses, was aimed towards the house. It bounced on the rough ground between them and the churned field where the horses were kept. At some moments the torch showed the frosted path ahead, and at others the grip must have wobbled and they could see boots and muddy trousers advancing. He wondered if she had been on one of the courses recently. They ran them down at the Fort, a Napoleonic-wars artillery position on the Hampshire coast. They did small arms, unarmed-combat basic training and refreshers; the instructors liked to liven their lectures with talk of high physical threat and the dangers posed by hostile intelligence services. But the worlds of HPT and HIT seemed far removed from the bleak corridor in Ceauçescu Towers – as Dunc always referred to Vauxhall Cross and its eccentric architectural lines – and he had had his name removed from the list of staff taking the train to Portsmouth. Would Mandy offer up her life in his defence? He thought she would make a fair job of wielding the poker.

A man came onto the patio.

She stood her ground.

The torchbeam came full into her face.

The man waved. A confident gesture.

Self-defence, as a hobby, was an art-form Dunc Whitcombe despised, and he had never been required to consider its virtues for self-preservation. The man pointed to himself, then to Mandy, then to the door latch. It was past three in the morning. The horses had gone, with the boy, who should have been in bed, and a man now invited himself inside.

'Any ideas?' she asked him.

He had not been to Monkton Fort for the refresher course, but it was possible she had. Silly, but at that moment, Dunc Whitcombe thought Mandy Ross seemed unfazed. In recent years the only two women he had been close to were his mother – 'I never want to be a burden to you, darling' – and his former wife, who had said on the steps of the court, 'Good riddance, and goodbye. The big thrill in my life is that we will never meet again.' Mandy sat across a table from him at meetings. She didn't use scent, and wore minimal jewellery but she was defiant, magnificent. She opened the door.

He came in. He had a rolling gait. His trousers were old and torn, and sagged from a wide belt at a big belly. His woollen jersey had runs on the chest. His leather gilet was scratch and smeared with dung. The front fastenings were undone and it bulged at the left armpit. He had a rounded face, a week's beard, and a mole sprouted darkly on his nose. His eyes were close-set and bright. The light danced in them.

No hesitation, good English. 'Welcome to my home. The holiday home.'

'Your home?'

'Rented out for visitors, their "holidays".' He laughed loudly. Poor teeth.

'For holidays?'

She said briskly, 'Don't repeat everything he says, Dunc.'

'I am Khebat. In the Kurdish Turk tongue that is "Struggle". You have seen my son, Egid, which is Hero. I hope you have settled, that you find what you need in the house . . . that at night you are not cold.' He leered.

Only on London's Green Lanes, between Seven Sisters and Stoke Newington where the Turkish Mafia had their bunkers and businesses, had Dunc Whitcombe come across such a man. In the days before the al-Qaeda call to arms, parts of the Service had been hived off as policemen and were supposed to be the dog's bollocks in the hunt for organised-crime barons; the Green Lanes clans were big on heroin importation. He had been there to liaise with 'assets' supposedly capable of infiltrating the groups in Turkey: money had been spent, but little had returned in recompense. There had been men like this one in cafés.

'Fine, thank you. Everything's fine,' he said. Tiredness swept over him, as it always did when he woke too fast.

Khebat peered at her and asked the question, 'The people you wait for, when do they come?'

Dunc choked. Mandy chuckled – the first time Dunc had seen her amused. Abject failure.

'You come to meet people. Am I not permitted to ask when they come?'

'I'll put the kettle on,' Mandy said.

Dunc tried. A cover story should always, it was said, be given opportunity to breathe. 'We wanted to visit the mountain, see Ararat, hear at close hand the legend of Noah, and I'm an archaeologist. It was a chance so we took it and —'

'Those you are meeting, when do they come?'

'We'll have some tea,' Mandy said. 'Or, maybe, a drink.'

The dishes consumed more from the Signals bunkers, sorted and brought it to the screens. Boredom died among the analysts fielding a torrent of radio and telephone communications among agencies in Tehran, between the capital city and out-stations in Tabriz, in the north-west and the principal city close to the Turkish frontier. It was rare for the young men and women, with computer skills and knowledge of Farsi, to feel themselves caught up in a slipstream of events. There was fury in the messages and reprimands flew. Men on the ground, and in the close-pursuit units, gave assurance that a trap had closed and escape for the killers of two young policemen, martyrs, was impossible.

Several technicians, surfing the airwaves, sensed the panic of flight. They shivered at the thought of the fugitives, what was arrayed against them, and . . . It was another night on shift, but a welcome escape from the usual tedium.

The reports would be read, and men would drum their fingers in frustration because they had no power to help those who were running for their lives.

The dawn came up above the lake and the mountains, but hadn't yet spread under the trees. They had reached the clump of pines by a rough farm track, more recently used by scientists investigating the water's salinity, four thousand feet above sea level and fed by streams, with no outlet, making a hostile place to all but the flocks of migrating birds that paused there, pelicans and flamingos. The scientists had left for the winter and would return only if further government funding was made available. The farmers had gone, because every year the grazing was poorer as the deposits spread wider. Among the trees, at a lop-sided angle, there was a builders' van. Its occupants slept, exhausted by the longest day and night any had previously experienced.

11

Zach's left arm fell away from him and he rolled on to his back. He shouldn't have done that, he thought, because of where she was. He might have hit her. He hadn't. The back of his hand lay against a crumpled rug.

Some guys were good at dawn and others weren't. Some of the lads at work were efficient with bricks, electrics or saws at first light, and others needed a sandwich and half a flask of tea before they could get to it. He was usually good.

He sat up. She wasn't there. Zach heard the guys.

The van was tilted, as it had been when they had parked it under the trees. Memories came: the shooting, the grenades, two dead, the spikes across the road. Another was of his fear when he had joshed and lied with the men at the block – he'd been brilliant but no one had acknowledged it. Yesterday's complaint – a useful lesson his father had taught him: 'Yesterday's complaint should be left there. Move on, Zach.' He rubbed his eyes.

The guys were murmuring. Zach assumed that fighting people switched away from the immediate in favour of talking nonsense – apparently it was the same for ambulance crews, fire teams and police clearing up after fatal road accidents.

Wally: 'Boys, second time "Where I would rather be". Take it, Ralph.'

Ralph: 'Same as the first. Where would I rather be? At home, about this time, the little red van comes down the drive, bumping over all the bloody holes, and the postman delivers an armload of brown envelopes, all with red over-stamping, which means final demand. If I'm at home I can run down to the post office and pay them off with a cheque that'll bounce. Mikey.'

Mikey: 'In a surgery. Been there half an hour but they're running late. Same seat as last week when I was there and handed in the piss bottle because they'd asked for a sample. Reading the magazines about women with false boobs, and waiting to be called in because they've got the test results. I'd give plenty to be there.'

Wally: 'My turn. At home, so I can field the phone and row with my ex, and we'll argue over who's having the kids next weekend – she'll want to dump them so's she can shag her new bloke. We have great rows.'

There were chuckles. What might have been Zach's answer? He couldn't have matched the guys' ability to face away from catastrophe: the road block and the spikes that had done for the tyres. He hadn't been asked – because he was separate from them, and his work, in Farsi, was done. He crawled out of the back.

There was a portable jack out. The tilt seemed worse when he stepped back two paces and looked at the van's angle. They had their weapons beside them.

He walked now in a different world from anything he knew. Where would he rather be? A piece of bread was pulled off the loaf and thrown to him. He hadn't been ready for it and it landed in the mud beside the wheel tracks. He picked it up. They didn't jeer at his failure to catch it, and didn't apologise for not having passed it to him carefully. He thought they were playing a game, protecting themselves with banter. He wasn't asked to join in.

He said, 'Sorry I slept in. I'd crashed out. Where is she?'

Wally grimaced. 'The lovely Foxtrot? With you, in the back.'

'Catching up on her beauty sleep.' Ralph grinned, then frowned. 'Isn't she?'

'She's not inside.'

Silence fell.

Swearing broke it, then recriminations: who'd done stag in the night and at first light? And the inquest, but no one was blamed so there were no excuses.

Mikey took charge. 'I did five till seven, Wally was after me and was fine. Ralph did two till five, sharp as a pin when I relieved him. That woman did not go off for a piss, blunder into the darkness and bust her head open on a rock. Two of us at all times in the front cab. Him in there with her. She went quietly and did her damnedest not to be heard or seen. She was fully dressed, which doesn't indicate a comfort break. I did movement when I was on stag, so did Ralph and Wally. Anyone going for a nature call would have had a word on the way out and another on the way in. That adds up to a runner. My mind tells me it would be hard for us to ditch the van and start out on a trek without her. Why she's quit on us, I don't know.'

Mikey had a good voice, soft, and Zach had to lean towards him to be sure of understanding what he said. Ralph scratched his armpit. Wally was emptying cartridges from his pistol and letting them clatter in the palm of a hand.

'I don't like the idea of turning up at a town on the wrong side of the border, meeting up with the Six people, and telling them we got it wrong. "At one stage she did want to come with us. No, her feelings of camaraderie did not last and she went walk-about." Go down a bomb. It's a big effort, involves too many people, has a grand budget, and even some cash left over for us – the idiots in a bad place at a bad time. I don't think we'd be welcomed. We'd be failures, and failures don't get work. If you want to wait for brown envelopes, or negotiate about the kids with your ex, or sit in a waiting room with a sample bottle, we let her go.'

Zach said, 'If she ran it's because she didn't think we'd manage the business. If she's going to be taken, and killed, she'd want it on her own terms, not holed up with us. That's how I think she is.'

Mikey peered into his face. 'Speak when you're spoken to, answer when you're questioned. We're being paid to bring her out. I don't intend to go back empty-handed. How we move on from here, I don't know. We will, and she'll be with us. We'll find her.'

'That's crazy,' Zach snapped. 'She could have gone miles!'

'I doubt it.' Mikey couldn't suppress the note of triumph in his voice.

He walked two paces past Zach, then crouched. He picked up the heel of a boot, medium height, black.

'I doubt it. And I doubt she's reached as far as she might have wanted. In this world you get what you pay for, and likely those boots were pretty rather than functional, so it broke. She goes with us, like it or not, because that's what we're paid to do. Let's find her.'

The shores of Lake Urmia, vast, flat mud and crystal salt, were to the west, and all that moved in the low light were the flamingos, the shorter-legged pelicans and some ducks. Ralph went south and took a machine pistol. Wally went south-east and would be next in the arc to Ralph; he had a pistol. Mikey said he would work along the shore, then pointed to the north-east – that would be the area for Zach to search. They split, fanned out, were walking away from the van, when Zach heard Mikey arm a weapon. He stopped, turned. 'I don't have anything.'

'If you don't know how to handle it, you're better without. Might shoot your toe off.'

'What happens if . . . ?'

'Good question. What happens if you get bounced?'

'What do I do?'

'Call for your mum to come and get you.'

'Fuck off.'

'I met a padre in Kabul last time. A bit of a literary man. Had a good voice. There had been a bad story about some contractors, Canadians who were taken out of a convoy, three of them, and they were all in bits when the corpses were recovered. The padre did a Kipling poem for me, written a hundred years back and nothing changes:

When you're wounded and left on Afghanistan's plains,
And the women come out to cut up what remains,
Just roll to your rifle and blow out your brains,
An' go to your Gawd like a soldier.

'What was your question?'

'What do I do?'

'When the Soviets were there, if a unit was trapped on the ground and couldn't be reached or if a chopper was downed and couldn't be extracted, they'd shoot up their own people. Kinder that way.'

'And . . .'

'You run to me and I'll do the business. It's a shit world out there, and an innocent walks naked. Go and find her.'

His last birthday had been his forty-ninth. Most days, not that he showed it, age was a burden to Michael Wilson. A decade before, he had been a corporal in the 2nd Battalion of the Parachute Regiment. Might have made sergeant with full responsibility for a platoon, or gone on to the company job, but he had declined and walked away. Twenty years in the Regiment had ended a decade before. A lieutenant, seventeen months out of the Royal Military Academy, had told Mikey, in the hearing of the squaddies up the A6 highway north of Basra, that his patrol briefing lacked a 'clear mission statement'. He had put in his resignation, wouldn't be talked out of it, and become a civilian, a life he barely knew. He'd signed up, on the rebound, for Contego Security.

It was a staple of Mikey's life that, right or wrong, he never changed his mind or backtracked on a decision.

His wife was Megs, his home a modern semi in Aldershot, and he had two children. Soldiers with a settled domestic life, money in the bank and kids who put up 'Welcome Home' banners were short on the ground. Most of the contractor's men were drifters or guys with a love of the fantasy and glamour that were supposed to go arm in arm with being a hired gun.

His qualities were recognised and invariably he was the team leader. He bossed former officers and once-senior NCOs. It meant nothing to him that for this trip Contego had put him above both ranks. He had been given this job, and the command, because the top man in the Ealing High Street office had developed total trust in him and reckoned Mikey had the rare ability to make decisions on the hoof. But why had he accepted this mission, a dose of lunacy, when he had family and more than most to lose? One fear existed in the mind of Mikey Wilson. The boss would ring, offer an assignment in a bad place, escorting crap people, with the chance of difficult opposition, high risk, and one day he might say, 'Sorry and all that, and thanks for thinking of me, but there's the wife and the kids, and I'm not as young . . .' Might be told that his attitude was reasonable, that when something else turned up he'd be at the top of the queue. Might *not* have another call. Might be murmured in west London that he was 'past it', living off the old days, was history. There was something else.

Sometimes he winced. There were days when he hadn't eaten properly and the cramps came hard in his gut; a couple of times there'd been a trace of blood in his stools. He hadn't been to the doctor, which would be, likely, a visit of last resort. There had been a quiet word in the right ear in Ealing and a sort of promise extracted that Megs would be 'looked after': nothing on paper, but on trust.

Mikey didn't do panic. On the convoy runs with Contego in Iraq and Afghanistan, he'd been in some of the worse fire-fights, when they had looked to be on their own, abandoned, and he had created calm and brought people through. What hurt? More than that, what pissed him off? It was the attitude of the 'regulars', the regiments who had the big numbers and the big kit and looked on him and his type as dirt – jealousy, perhaps, over what went into a contractor's bank. His attitude, forged in the recent conflicts, was that when he was in trouble it was for him to work a way out of it.

Looked difficult that morning.

They hadn't bothered to draw the curtains at the sides, or try to cover the windscreen. The light had come from behind the hills and had extra strength from the snow on the top ridges. They woke together, close and entwined – any movement from either would have disturbed the other.

The camper van was a miracle. It was a VW model, had survived thirty-six years since it had rolled off a production line at the factory in Emden, west Germany. It was the T-2 type, had a 1.8-litre engine, had done at least a quarter of a million miles, but the engine had been kept alive with love and care. Only the mattress in the pull-down double bed had needed replacing. It was called 'Alex', had that name sign written on the driver's door. The current owners, who saw themselves as custodians of the old girl, were the fifteenth to take charge of her, and the name had changed pretty much with each new driver. They were Joey Farrow and Beth Skelton, and the camper was nine years older than them.

They slept naked, as they always did, and would probably continue to until their relationship was formalised at St Mungo's Union Church on Killarney Street, the best-known in Alexandra, which was in Central Otago and far down on South Island. They were coming to the end of what for them was their epic journey away from the claustrophobia of home and family. They had done this great voyage of discovery in the certain knowledge that soon they would be shackled by finance, kids and responsibilities. The opportunity wouldn't come again. They had picked up Alex in Baku, Azerbaijan, after a couple of months spent teaching in an English-language school. From there they had headed across the frontier into Iran, and had driven south a thousand kilometres to the Gulf of Oman, then turned north and crossed the Zagros mountains. They were now on the shores of Lake Urmia, and would take in views of the last migrating birds. Eventually they would drive Alex into Turkey and would hang around in Diyarbakir or Van till another couple pitched up and they sold her on. Joey and Beth were of farm stock. Their families owned land; they grew stone fruit, and grapes for the wine industry; when they went up the aisle at St Mungo's they would bring together two slabs of industry, a necessity of modern commerce. Before that day . . .

Near to home there was an albatross colony, and another of penguins. Here they could see, as the light cleaned the shoreline and the huge salted flats, pelican and flamingo. It was why they had turned off the beaten track, something New Zealand-born kids were practised at, and bumped over tussock grass until they had found the sheltered space in front of a small rock escarpment. The wall behind them was crusted with salt, and the early light caught the formations and made it flash, like jewels.

A hand came out of the bed and rubbed at the condensation on the window. They had been an item since their early days at Dunstan High School. They had sucked up the pleasures of a hard year of travel, had absorbed the Middle East, the cradle of the great religions, and had gorged on the history and monuments of Iran. They had been almost overwhelmed by the kindness shown them, such as when Beth's molar had cracked and a dentist had opened his surgery on a holiday to treat her. The sun would shine on them for another day.

It was a languid waking.

The binoculars and the camera with the big lens were within reach, the pelicans and flamingos in sight. They thought the flamingos were the more precious of the two. On their return home, they'd expect to be asked to offer the bird pictures to local museums and wildlife groups, and would treasure sharing their experiences. She was across him and peering through the window. He was laughing, then grappling her.

'You going to do the breakfast, girl, or am I?'

'I will.'

A kiss, and Beth Skelton crawled out of the bed. She was, her mother said it, as tough as an old boot. She opened the door, and the cold came in. She pulled a face and leaned further out, assimilating the emptiness and silence. She grabbed the toilet roll beside the door and bolted.

He stretched, yawned and followed. He was a big man, played rugby in the back row, could manage the days of farm work. Now he tidied the bed, stowed it and waited for her to come back.

It would be another good day – the skies were clear.

His mouth felt like a monkey's armpit. It didn't happen often to Dunc Whitcombe. He sat up suddenly and his toes hit the low table. The glasses on it rattled, and the bottles wobbled. He was still in the living area. It wasn't often that he missed a night's sleep, never made it to bed. It could only happen when there was a sharp-end night at the Desk and matters that seemed important were reaching a decision.

What had been said? He struggled to remember. His memory

was usually considered excellent: tonnage coming out of the refinery at Abadan, age and biographical history of any mechanical engineer labouring on warhead development at the Technical University, the lifestyle of Zach Becket. The maps were still on the table and he couldn't have said whether or not they had been disturbed. The man had sat in a deep leather chair and the empty bottles were thickest in front of it, with a full ashtray. They couldn't have evicted him because he was their landlord.

The man had lounged far back in the chair. 'You are doing business with the Jews? They drive a hard bargain, too hard for me. I am five thousand dollars per person, but they will not pay more than two thousand, and want bigger discount for more than two travellers. I was asked by your embassy man, from Ankara, only for the accommodation. Why does anyone come here without hiking clothes, if not to meet people from the other side?'

No answer given, other than a weak repetition of the archaeology story. A hand had waved it away.

'I am from Istanbul. I understand you to be people of discretion. I am a Kurd first and a Turk second, but my family was based in Istanbul. We traded across the Dardanelles – cigarettes, precious stones, narcotics, unemployed men, children and whores. It was a good life and a good trade, but too good. The world arrived in Istanbul. We had established "arrangements" with the local authority, expensive but manageable. Then came the Americans, the British and the Germans. Their law enforcement and their Special services came. I was targeted. It interfered with my business so I moved.'

The sofa stood alongside the chair where he had sat, heavy leather and noisy when an occupant shifted. Mandy Ross had been there, still was. Her head was back and her mouth open. Her pyjama top had ridden up and her midriff was exposed. Had the Turk seen her in that posture? Would she have cared if he had?

'I came here. All of my family came. It was a homecoming, my territory, my place. I live off the border with Islamic Republic. The border feeds me and I live well. The Americans are not here, nor the Germans, and I am not investigated because of my cousins who operate north of London, the Green Lanes of Haringey. It is tranquil for me here.'

Twice, Mandy had glided into the kitchen and come back with more beer. Now their supply was exhausted. Mandy hadn't drunk any, but Dunc had tried to match the visitor, who had had nine.

'My problem here is not with foreign agencies but with the local military. He is the major, Emre Terim. His unit is mechanised infantry, and he is the second in command of the garrison. The commander I could make an arrangement with, not with the bastard Terim. With the police also I can make an arrangement, but not with Terim. I am better on the far side of the frontier. With Iranian Customs I have arrangements, and with many of their border troops, but not with Terim. The military send men here from the other end of the country and they are taught to hate Kurds. That is my problem.'

When had he fallen asleep? Dunc didn't know. He didn't know when Mandy had drifted off either.

'I have a wife who looks after me. I do not go with whores . . . I have four daughters. Two live still in Istanbul and refuse to come here. They will go to Germany when they have finished education. Of the other two I need one to make a good marriage, into another clan, and then I have an alliance. I built this house for them to live in. I need an alliance because the future worries me . . . if a rival can be trusted. The future is difficult. My boy has a handicap. I do not believe he could survive as my successor. His condition is the pain of my life. He is wonderful with the horses, but I fear for him.'

They had crashed out with the maps on the table, the rendezvous point marked, the call sign for their communications and so much else. He didn't know whether Mandy and the organised-crime baron had talked after he had fallen asleep.

'I was reasonable with Major Terim and offered him "opportunities", but they were rejected. In Iran, *anyone* can be bought and sold. He said to me, "You are scum and I do not have a price." Offensive, yes? If my people are caught with fuel or heroin, or with those needing to leave Iran, or going the other way with alcohol, and the soldiers take them, they will be arrested, charged and put in the prison at Van. If they are intercepted but cannot be taken they will be shot. The boy has to be with the horses because of his understanding of them, and love for them, and their response, but the soldiers – I worry – will kill him on one night. It is a dangerous place, the border. You must hope the Jews have made a good alliance. I am the best but the people they will use, coming from Khvoy, are cheaper. Was it a good economy? Of course, without an arrangement – even for trained men – it is impossible to cross. I enjoy talking with you . . .'

The horses were back, grazing on freshly scattered fodder. Mandy would wake when he cleared away the bottles and the ashtray, but first he would make coffee.

His wife brought him the phone. She looked hard at him, puzzled. He was out of the shower, had scrubbed his teeth, had swallowed several glasses of cold water – and had no regrets. The bottle, what remained in it, was locked away.

Reza Joyberi had come to bed after her and risen before her. Her confusion would not have been caused by him joining her late or waking early, but by his strange aloofness. He didn't discuss his work with her. When he travelled to another city in the Republic, he would bring back gifts for her and their son, but he wouldn't tell her where he had been and what the business had involved. He never shared anxieties. Together, they did not socialise inside the upper ranks of the Revolutionary Guard Corps. He didn't tell her about the visits he had made, covertly, across the border with Iraq, or when he flew to Damascus and was infiltrated to the southern hills and valleys of Lebanon. Their conversation at meals was polite and attentive. He listened to progress reports from the school – always favourable for the child of a man of rank – but confidences were limited. She had not asked where his driver was. He had not talked about the clouds gathering over him. She didn't know that he had plans in mind, if not in place, to ship her out. He was dressed in civilian clothing, tying his shoelaces, and took the phone from her. His smile was brief, wintry.

He answered, was told who had called, then given further information.

He was not asked whether he had pressing appointments that day, whether the meeting was convenient. He was given a time and a location. In the early afternoon he was required to present himself at Block Six of the Kazemi Garrison's sector, inside what had once been the Nest of Spies. Had he told the caller to go fuck himself a squad of boot-faced functionaries would have been at his front door almost immediately to bundle him into the back seat of a car and take him to the building that had, in former times, housed the US embassy. He ended the call, and went into the kitchen.

His son had books spread on the table with his breakfast. He kissed his wife briefly, then the boy.

He wore the shoulder holster under his jacket, with the automatic pistol. Reza Joyberi could not then have said whether his enemies were gathering in front of him or closing on his back. He didn't say when he would be home or whether he expected to eat with them. He didn't know. He had seen others falter many times. They had been great men who stumbled, fell from grace, and became isolated. Enemies gathered. Those others would all have had plans in place to slip away at the signs of danger, to put their families on aircraft flying out and themselves to head for the border with Turkey, Armenia, Turkestan or Pakistan, or board a fast boat on the Gulf coast. When to make the move? It was always difficult.

He shrugged into his coat. He would fight. Of course. He was a respected servant of the regime. An *untouchable*? He called a farewell, and was gone.

It was a fine morning. He headed for the bus stop but might find a taxi before he reached it. Two of his neighbours, in chauffeur-driven cars, passed him but they avoided his eye. There were no offers of a ride down the hill towards the city centre. He didn't have to leave that early to keep the appointment at the Kazemi Garrison, but he had thought panic might overwhelm him if he stayed at home.

* * *

The packages of refined heroin resin reached the city limits of Tabriz. It was appropriate that the city, founded by Armenian migrant settlers more than two thousand years before, should retain a vibrant commercial sector dominated by that ethnic minority. An Azerbaijani trader purchased the twenty packages, and paid for them in cash at $7,500 per kilo. He would expect to make an additional 10 per cent on his outlay when he sold them on. It was an ancient city, lying close to the north-eastern end of Lake Urmia, on one of the inland sea's tributary rivers, and had been a centre of commercial dealing for more than a millennium, a principal junction for Mongol rulers, the Turkish Ottoman empire and Soviet forces. It had ancient mosques and a citadel that drew visitors, the Arg. Khayyam Avenue was beyond the historic district, out of the centre and past the bus station. Off it, to the right and beyond a filling station, a narrow street led to lock-up garages with unpainted concrete walls, corrugated-iron roofs and doors that had rotted at the corners. One was different from the rest. Behind the walls there was an additional lining of brickwork, under the roof there was the additional protection of compacted and reinforced chipboard; behind the doors there were steel sheets. Owned by the Azerbaijani, the garage was a fortress in the tradition of the Arg, a place where precious items could be stored in safety. The packages would remain there for thirty-six hours, then would be taken forward and – in accord with further deals done by Internet and satellite phone – moved into other hands.

Tabriz had been astride the great Silk Road; moving goods with discretion was fundamental to its existence and its economy. Before he had paid, the Azerbaijani had cut into the wrapping, through the waterproof paper, of a single package to satisfy himself that he had not been duped. In his world, alliances and enmities could be speedily exchanged. He would have said, if asked, 'We can shoot each other on one day and kiss each other on another.' He was a man of great wealth, but used this insignificant lock-up as his principal storage centre. He couldn't flaunt luxury in the city and sent his money abroad where it was administered by relatives in Germany, Great Britain and the United States. He allowed himself two week-long breaks each year, in Paris and Rome, for extravagance. One day he would slip away across the border, with the same discretion and with the same couriers who would carry the packages, but that day had not yet come.

The slanted sunlight fell on the doors, further flaking the paint. Behind them, he worked and worried as to how he would divide up the seventy-nine packages now stockpiled; which would go to which clans for transportation on the most difficult section of the journey, and who had the capacity. The value of what he held that morning was in excess of a million American dollars, and for the Azerbaijani that was not remarkable. There was a man he trusted, who was reliable, the best. That morning, the radio had reported an incident on the road, bandits at a police road block, but it had been far to the south and hadn't troubled him. It was important for him, and his colleagues across the border, that alerts and emergencies did not take place in the security zone at either side of the frontier, that the armed forces of both nations were bought or careless. Otherwise there was potential for disaster.

She was on a moonscape. He came over an incline and she was ahead of him, perhaps half a mile away.

She was going slowly. He had picked up the trail within a few hundred yards of the van when he had come out of the trees. He had seen the guys going their separate ways, and they were spokes on a wheel. At first he had seen places where the salt deposits had been kicked or were broken. Further from the water, heading inland from the shoreline, the salt was more evenly spread and thinner. There had been rain enough for the ground under the white crust to have soften, and she had left one clean shoe imprint, and another that dragged. There was no cover for her. The salt had killed grass shoots and the autumn flowers. It was an aberration that they had found trees under which to hide the van. Here, in the open, the wind had gained force.

She didn't look round, and wouldn't have known that he was closing on her.

She was in the wind's teeth and the *chador* made a tent that billowed behind her. When he was nearer, Zach could see that her right foot was bare and that she was carrying the boot that had lost its heel. He thought, when he caught up with her, that she would be dry-eyed: life would, already, have thrown too much at her for tears after a struggle against a cutting wind. Nothing lived here. No flowers, no bushes, no rabbits, no mice and no rats. No birds flew over them. The pelicans and flamingos were far behind. It was a place where hope had died. No farmers lived here, and there was no fodder for cattle, sheep or goats. No one witnessed her flight.

He cupped his mouth and shouted her name. The wind whipped coarse salt grains against his cheeks and dispersed his voice.

She didn't acknowledge him – might have heard him and might not. He saw blood on the ground where her bare foot had trodden.

He shouted her name. She didn't turn.

Zach closed the distance between them and was alongside her. He reached for her arm. She tried to pull away from him, slipped and fell. He wouldn't let go of her so he went down with her. He looked at her. He saw neither fear nor that she was glad he had found her. He was near enough to notice each pore in her skin, the tiny lines around her eyes and the fine hairs on her upper lip. Her eyes were dry. He knelt, easing away from her.

'We have to go together. It's why I came here. You have to be with us.'

'I hate him.'

'You can go to him or turn your back on him. It'll be your choice when you're there.'

'And I'm a burden to you.'

'No. Not at all.'

She pushed herself up and the wind tore at the scarf of the *chador*, dragging it off her hair.

'And what if you're a burden to me, all of you?'

'We're ordinary people, doing our best, hoping it'll be enough. With our best you're stronger. Without it you're weaker. I promise.'

'Do you understand, Zach, where you are, who you're with and what you're doing? Perhaps it's better if you don't.'

He stood, and she did.

He picked her up and put her over his shoulder, one arm around her legs, behind the knees. He braced himself for a struggle, but none came. The wind was behind him and he could follow his footprints to the top of the incline, then over it. The pocket of trees was faint in the distance, and beyond was the pure white of salt where once there had been water, then the blue of the lake and the dead landmasses that were islands. He had no idea how to keep the promise he had made.

'I have nothing to say.'

Petroc Kenning had thought himself good with alcohol. Wrong. He had rarely, as a student, nursed a substantial hangover. There had been beers with Sidney. Then, with Auntie, there had been coffee, and brandy from the emergencies cupboard. The night had been punctuated with calls from London. What the hell did they expect him to do? Never explained. His head ached. The drink was to blame, and the wrecked night.

'Ask questions. I don't answer.'

Either Tadeuz had called him on the secure link with a commentary on everyday life along the Qazvin to Tabriz road, Route 2 or Route 32, or Sara Rogers had taken over, allowing the boss to cat-nap.

'No answer, because it is lies I have been told.'

He sat opposite Mehrak and more coffee steamed in his mug. Father William and Nobby had recognised they were at the critical moment, and hovered close to the back of the corporal's chair. The man's chin jutted, and the eyes were no longer evasive.

He said again, loudly, 'No. I have nothing to talk of. No.'

Petroc knew that a helicopter had been fired on, that road blocks had intercepted an identified vehicle, that grenades had been used, that the local force had suffered two fatalities, that a

Stinger had been laid across the road, that the vehicle had broken through it, and that a larger force was now deployed. He knew also that the director had been briefed and would want more that morning, that Tadeuz Fenton was shivering at the implications of what faced him.

'You said you would bring her out. I do not believe you.'

He worked for a respected intelligence-gathering organisation. It walked – almost – in step with the great agencies of the United States, the new Russia and China. The crowd at Vauxhall Cross were at least the equal of the French and the Germans. They had a tradition of success and had accumulated bucket loads of hostility from opponents and yet . . . For want of a bloody tyre. Men and women in workshops, in the building's basements or elsewhere, turned out some of the most high-tech products used anywhere in the world: audio stuff with long-range pick-up, cameras with extraordinarily powerful zoom qualities, telephone intercept equipment backed by unique software, but 'little things' had the potential to screw all the pricey gear available. A 'little thing' was a shredded tyre. They would have one spare wheel but a Stinger would have taken out two tyres on one side, or the front two, or all four. They had the skills at Vauxhall Cross, and the kit, but none of it was relevant to the plight of three men, a language student and a woman who photographed like a dream.

'We've been entirely truthful to you.'

'I do not believe you. I will never see her. It was a lie.'

'We're doing what we can.'

'You talked but you cannot act. She will not be able to leave Iran. It cannot happen. It was your trick to deceive me. I say nothing.'

It took a moment of supreme control. Petroc could have leaned across the table and slapped the corporal's face. It had come through during the night, coded, a mass of questions to which the analysts wanted answers: the location of missile silos, IRGC contingent readiness plans, airfield security.

'I urge you not to take that sort of attitude, Mehrak. We're bending over backwards to reunite you with your wife and —'

'I think you lie.'

Father William caught Petroc's eye and gestured towards the door. They went out. Father William, eyes cold, made a suggestion. Petroc nodded and went to call his sage.

'Nice of you to ask, Petroc, but, sadly, no news. We were out at first light, Stephie and I, with plenty of volunteers, but there's no sign of him. The trouble is, you can ask the farmers, "Have you seen him?" and you won't get a straight answer.

'So, your defector . . . What you need, Petroc, is discipline for him and a completely predictable road along which he can walk. The discipline must be the rock. Remember, most of these creatures are utterly boring and totally limited: they are third-rate or fourth. We used to have the Irish coming through our hands, supposedly hard men from the Provisionals, but they were so easy to turn. Just had to stop them blubbing about their kids. All the old Soviets wanted was a bottle of ten-year-old malt by the bed each morning . . .

'Now, the wife. You've given your word that you'll bring her out. Until, on the other side of that border, she's in handcuffs, with the people you sent to fetch her, your promise is alive. The proposition of an excursion is acceptable but it's not a jolly in the countryside. He must be left in no doubt that he has to earn such privileged treatment. Then, when you have him back, you squeeze and squeeze until you have the final drop of useful information from him. After that, well . . . Call me tomorrow. We're both suffering. Petroc. I know the ways of that damn building you belong to. Praise and reward when success blooms, but a more vicious place when a coming man falls on his face I've never known. Brutal when confronted with failure. So, remember, discipline.'

There was a place, Kourosh knew, where the dawn light didn't reach. More than fifty kilometres south of Tehran, but north of Qom, there were two hills. The rail track ran between them and a cutting had been opened. He had been on the train that went from

Tehran to Isfahan and Yazd, and remembered the place. He didn't think that the early brightness of the sun, fierce after the rain, would penetrate there.

He had been to the briefing, had heard what was said. He had been to the repair yard and seen the workbenches, the scattered parts of scooters and motorbikes. He had climbed the steps and entered the upper room. Before, it had been a shrine. Some days, going there, he had thought she almost welcomed him. On others he had believed her expression was of resignation, as if she didn't know how to rid herself of him. He couldn't stay away. He was there mostly every third day, and certainly every fifth. She made tea, and he ate cake, and sometimes she let him fondle or kiss her. It was a drug.

There had been a time when the surveillance team was deployed to Ahvaz to search out a Jew who had come into Iran to build a team of spies, bomb-layers and assassins from among the Arab population. They had been in Ahvaz, billeted inside the IRGC garrison camp on the Chahar-Shir Circle, also a prison, and after a week there – seven nights away from her – he had told his commander that his wife was ill and requested leave to return to Tehran. He had seen the room, had seen all of her, except the small place that, for modesty, was denied him. There, he was now forgotten, and the photographs of his rivals had been removed.

He held her. The picture was small. She had given it to him. The light was sufficient, just, for him to see the dark cloth covering her face and hair, the slash in the veil and the brightness of her eyes. He listened.

He was crouched beside a cement-block shed, where workmen repairing the track might have stored tools. He was out of sight. The near rail was some three metres from where he crouched. Kourosh knew the train's schedule. The system had a reputation for punctuality. He could have drawn a pistol from the armoury and a magazine of ammunition, or he could have gone in the small hours to one of the city's parks, thrown a rope over an upper branch and made a noose at one end.

It was because he had seen men shot and had witnessed

hangings that Kourosh did not feel certain of his courage. He had never seen the aftermath of what he intended, couldn't picture the final moments, and trusted that his nerve would hold. It was not a picture of his wife that he held, or of his child, but of the woman who had played with him, dancing near but never close.

The sound was clear, unmistakable. A whistle blast penetrated the grey shaded walls of the cutting. He had to wait, couldn't move too quickly.

He glanced up once, held tighter to the photograph and imagined the face beneath the veil. He saw the lights at the front of the engine. He would take three steps forward, then duck down and his knees would settle on the sharp stones into which the sleepers were laid. An alternative? He couldn't think of one. She had destroyed him. He ground the photograph between his fingers, praying he wouldn't lose it.

The noise hammered in his ears. He went forward. The pain pinched in his knees, through his trousers, as he knelt on the sharp edged stones and he laid his head on the rail. It was cold against his throat and his eyes were closed. The scrap of paper, her picture, was locked in his fist.

He heard a low whistle from among the trees, and Zach looked back. He saw a shadow flit between the trunks, as light as a feral animal.

He had brought her back. Wally and Ralph were already by the van and they'd had it jacked up. The flooring at the back had been lifted aside and the spare was out – to no purpose: the Stinger had shredded the two nearside tyres. He had put her down. The other two had been sitting on their haunches, their weapons close to them, smoking. Their faces showed their feelings. Now, they cared less for the money than for their safety, their survival. They hadn't said anything as the smoke had played in front of their faces. She hadn't cowered but had stared at them. She was, Zach had reckoned, a cornered cat but wouldn't back off. He thought they could have said *something*.

He'd taken water from the van, torn off a piece of blanket and cleaned her foot. She hadn't flinched. The boot she had taken off had nails protruding through the heel.

Zach wouldn't try to start a conversation, either serious or humorous, that might lift his morale and help her. He was fucked if they'd beat him. He aped her, and kept his eyes on them. He realised he hadn't tried to evaluate their personalities, their skills, or to wonder what lay in the depths of their minds. He'd had no interest in the other students at the School, or in his fellow workers on the sites. He could survive alone.

It was different with her, though. He was fascinated by her.

The whistle came again.

Mikey materialised through the trees, soft tread, fast and hard to follow.

He wore a cheeky grin as he came over to them. He looked at her and nodded, then sat down. The grin widened.

'The news, guys, is that Christmas has come early. It's gift-wrapped, and it's what I've always wanted. Christmas with all the trimmings.'

12

They approached the camper van. There was no cover – a featureless landscape, the salt crystals crunching under their feet. Zach had watched Wally and Mikey, observed the way they moved and realised that the crunching was unavoidable. He observed also that a hierarchy existed between the two men, without the military style recognition of rank: Mikey wasn't 'sir', not even 'guv'nor' or 'boss'. Mikey set the pace and Wally followed; Mikey spoke briefly on the line of approach they'd take, and Wally grunted acceptance.

Mikey had a pistol. Wally had a pistol and grenades in his anorak pocket. Mikey said they would be tourists. Closer, Wally had identified the sticker on a back window as the flag of Australia or New Zealand. Ralph and the woman had been left behind, but Zach had been told to come. Why?

Mikey gestured for Zach to catch up, close the gap. Mikey said, 'We're all in this together.'

'Meaning what?

'All in this together – you and the lady, Wally, Ralph, and me. We're all in this together and we're all going out together. That means we have to have their vehicle. We can do it gently, or with whatever unpleasantness is required, but we'll have it. You, Zach, are educated and may be a little more fluent with an explanation than me. You may be able to smooth it. I don't want anyone hurt, but I must have the vehicle. You'll explain better than I can that argument isn't the way for them to go.'

'Do they come with us?'

'No.'

'What do they do?'

'They walk.'

'Is that reasonable, in the back of beyond?'

'I'm not asking you if it's reasonable. You do as I tell you.'

Zach buttoned it. In a former life, as a student, he would have argued the toss. In the days when he was at the School, and riots had disfigured the streets of Tehran, other kids had made excuses for the regime – foreign intelligence, international banks, Tel Aviv, Arab despots – but Zach had stood his ground. He'd argued that the Supreme Leader and his gang, the corruption of the élite, deserved trial and conviction. It had been different on the building sites. Sometimes he'd heard rubbish spouted, and opinions that made him cringe inwardly, but he'd kept quiet. Now he pressed his hands together and walked towards the camper.

He saw a black bin liner, partially filled, with a stone on it to stop the wind blowing it away. A string hung between the front windscreen and the back hatch; pegs held a row of socks and underpants, knickers, a bra and some T-shirts. Beside a blackened place there was an old grill pan and a water bucket. He had come into their lives – Zach almost despised himself. Their footprints were marked in the salt and went towards the shore.

Beyond where their feet had gone – two of them, a boy and a girl, from the clothing that dried and stiffened with the salt and the wind – there was a group of flamingos. The men's approach had spooked the birds, which edged away, beautiful, elegant, the pinkish feathers clear against the salt white, and headed towards a capsized boat, once a ferry across the lake but now abandoned as the water level dropped. He was surprised that no one came out to greet them, but music was playing, soft and indistinct, likely from a foreign station – Turkey or Armenia. Perhaps they had done their washing, had their breakfast and were snoozing . . . Mikey prodded him. 'Do the talk.'

Zach nodded.

'Tell them we want the vehicle, and they have five minutes to get their stuff out. Then I want their mobiles.'

'Yes.'

'I'm behind you, and if I have to show a weapon I will. Wally's a few paces further back and he won't tolerate anyone bolting. Bad idea for them to try. Go for it.'

They wrote their cards.

He had chosen a view of the lake with a crumbling column of stone that rose out of the saltscape. It was a duty but would be well received at home, although they'd be back long before the postman dropped it through the front door.

They had a list of names to whom they had to send cards. Hers was of the Blue Mosque in Tabriz, the interior of turquoise tiling. She ticked off a name and the Blue Mosque joined the pile.

There was a knock at the door, quiet but insistent.

He dragged back the blind: one man beside the door, another behind him and a third further away. Their bearing didn't fit the place. They were not peasants, farmers, or tribespeople like they had met in other wildernesses, and there was no vehicle. He was reaching for the catch that would lock the door, and was checking that the keys were in the ignition, when the door was pulled open. Joey Farrow saw discomfort on the man's face, as he filled the doorway, and hesitation.

'Just do it nice and easy.' A drip in Zach's ear. 'Best voice.'

'Excuse me . . .' No need for Farsi, just clear English.

'Who are you? What can I do for—?'

'It's hard to explain but—'

Behind him: 'Get to the point.'

In front of him: 'What's hard?'

'I'm really sorry, but—'

In front: 'What for?'

Behind: 'Shift it on.'

Zach saw a pleasant-faced young man, but a frown was knitting the guy's forehead, his chin was jutting, and his eyes had narrowed. It was an open face, and the cheeks had a rugged outdoor colour. It was the face of a man who looked after himself – and the young woman. She was behind him, boxed in by the table, and their postcards were scattered over it. She was pretty enough, in a scrubbed way, and wore neither cosmetics nor jewellery, not even ear studs. Zach reckoned, glancing from him to her, that she might prove as hard an adversary as him. A last look: a ring on her finger. They probably weren't married but it was easier in Iran to wear it and escape the attentions of the modesty police. He had rehearsed what he would say as they had walked towards the wagon, but had forgotten most of it.

'I'm British. I'm a fugitive in Iran and I need—'

'What's that to us?'

He ploughed on: 'I'm British, with British colleagues. We're fugitives and have no transport. To save ourselves we need to take your vehicle. You won't be compromised and—'

'Take our vehicle? Like fuck you will.'

'You have – and I apologise for the intrusion – five minutes to clear what you need from inside.'

'Yeah. And—'

'Don't, I urge you, make it harder. We're taking the vehicle.'

The man lunged, his hand snaking out. Zach lurched back and was half out of the door, but the hand went past him to the dash where the keys hung. There was a blur of movement. Zach was pushed aside, stumbled, slipped on the step and hit the ground, and Mikey was over him. The boy squealed and the girl had begun to scream. Zach pushed himself up. Mikey had hold of the boy's arm. Mikey pulled him out of the vehicle. The boy had sense. To have struggled more might have broken his arm or dislocated his shoulder. Zach thought of him as a boy: he was about the same age as himself, and had put together a gap-year trip that many dreamed of and few did. He was not traipsing along the 'kids' route' from the Australian Great Barrier Reef to the Northern Territories rainforest, but was in the Islamic Republic, cockpit of the world, place of historic literature and the earliest cultures. The girl came after him, cleared the step and jumped to get her hands on Mikey's throat or her fingers in his eyes. She hadn't catered for Zach's knee and went down, winded.

'You're just wasting time,' Zach said. 'I'm trying – God help me – to be sympathetic. We're taking the vehicle and you're losing the opportunity to get what you need – a bag, clothing, documentation. I'll want your phones. Sorry and all that.'

He thought of the road block, his lies about the lost goats and the risk of wolves, of how he had lulled the men's suspicious then the charge and the gunfire. He had seen two men killed.

The boy was supine and had made eye contact with the girl. They were both breathing hard. Zach had never been close enough to a girl for a glance between himself and her to tell a story.

She pushed herself up and used her hands to show that the fight was over. She forced a thin smile. 'I'll start to get our stuff.'

Wally had come to the boy, pistol drawn. The boy sat down.

Mikey eased Zach to one side and followed the girl inside the wagon. No trust. A rucksack was on the table and she was rooting in the cupboards filling the bag. Some food went in, and she heaved another bag onto the table, then dropped cameras and a radio inside it. He saw the passports and a wallet for airline tickets or money. She said nothing. Zach had not been involved in fights at school, or in a pub brawl – he had always made for the nearest door if matters got out of hand in the bar the builders used outside Coventry or on the way into Leamington Spa. The first bag was zipped and she threw it behind her. It was angular, bulky, and caught Zach's hip as it went through the door.

Mikey said nothing, just watched.

She didn't speak but continued to fill a second bag.

Zach said, 'We're not doing this for fun. You just happened to be in the wrong place at the wrong time. I can't tell you what it's about, only that it's important. We need the vehicle and . . .'

He tailed off. He realised that Mikey had made him their spokesman so that he and Wally were free to supervise the clear-out and watch the boy.

'You're talking horse-shit,' she said.

'I've tried to be polite.'

'And fucked up. Just so you know, people here have gone out of their way to treat Joey and me with kindness and courtesy. They've made us welcome. You're screwing us up. So, fuck you.'

He thought, in a fight, she would have killed him. He forced himself: 'We want your phones, so put them on the table.'

Zach saw it, and Mikey, too, would have noted the tightness of her jeans at the left pocket. She put one phone on the table, had taken it off a shelf. She seemed to shrug, as if that was the only one they had. 'That's it.'

It was not about a mission and not about getting a defector's wife over a border. It was not about saving humanity from a nuclear device, had nothing to do with supporting the democratic instincts of the Iranian people. It was about himself. First it was Zach Becket, then maybe the bed-fellows he hadn't chosen – Mikey, Wally, Ralph – and somewhere it was about taking a young woman across a frontier, but not because she was a defector's wife.

'And the one in your pocket,' he said.

He might – God willing – never again see a look of such loathing, directed at him, cross a woman's face.

She swivelled, tried to make greater space between Mikey and the pocket where her phone was. Predictable that its card would hold the contact number of everyone dear to her, and an archive of pictures. He didn't have a phone with him, had lodged it at the first departure lounge, and Zach had no idea whether here, on the salt flats by Lake Urmia and probably only twenty-five miles due west of Tabriz, there was a mobile signal. Her face said she would have called the police in a state of hysteria before the tail of salted dust had dispersed behind them.

Zach said again, 'The one in your pocket.'

She wriggled away. Mikey went after it. His hands were at her waist, groping for it. There was a yell.

Zach turned.

The boy had to get past Wally to reach the door, where Zach was. Behind Zach, Mikey was struggling with the girl. The boy swung a fist at Wally, which was countered by the forearm, then pushed down. The boy sprawled, but came back with a momentum that took him past Wally and within range of Zach. Pain exploded in his face, a short-arm punch, and Zach reeled, but in time to see the retaliation – the swing with the pistol barrel. The boy jolted. Zach saw blood and teeth. The boy went down on his knees. She put a hand into her pocket, took out the phone and slapped it on the table. Mikey let her go and grabbed it. As resistance it had been futile, delaying them for less than a minute. The violence had been done in his name, Zach thought, but had served a purpose. He swallowed hard.

Mikey said to him softly, 'We're not army, we're survivors. There are rules of engagement for the military, and doctrines of minimum force. And there's yellow-card rules about what you can do and when you can do it. We're outside that. If he plays stupid he gets whacked. If he plays sensible he doesn't. Most people understand it.'

Zach nodded. Wally eyed him. The boy and girl sat beside each other, near to where they'd had their fire, with their possessions around them.

Zach thought Wally reckoned him weak.

Mikey took the phones, opened them, took out the cards and pocketed the batteries. An afterthought: he dropped them. He smiled, pleasantly enough. The cards would be in the glove box, and he said, they'd look after the wagon as best they could.

She put up her hand, as if she were asking her teacher for permission to speak.

From Mikey: 'Yes?'

Beth Skelton did her smile. It was always a winner, and had been since she was a child. 'You'll look after our wagon?'

'We'll try to.'

'It's about all we have that's a home. We're fond of it, and it's way older than us.'

'We did what we have to do.'

She said, 'If you're telling me and Joey that you'll look after her, and I believe you, there's something you should know.'

'What?' The man in charge was at the front and had waved the boy to the driver's seat. The one who had hit Joey went to the side door but had the pistol and covered but didn't aim at them.

'We filled up with fuel in Tabriz. More than fifty litres. It cost us.'

Mikey pulled the wad from his hip pocket and peeled off two hundred dollars. He tossed it at her.

'Thanks. You didn't need to do that to Joey. You look after her. We expect the police to give her back to us. Only one thing wrong.'

'What?'

'The fuel gauge. It won't go further than halfway – it hasn't all the time we've had her. It says she's empty but doesn't mean it. Half on the dial means about full, empty on the dial means about half full.'

The engine gunned and the exhaust belched. Her Alex pulled away.

She held Joey's hand and pursed her lips. 'Do you think they believed that?'

'They might have.' Slurred words through the blood and the swelling.

'Then they're fucked,' she said. 'If they go cross-country and believed us.'

'Do you want to say it or not?'

Zach drove. It responded sluggishly to the gears and the steering, but the engine rhythm, even on the rough surface, seemed reasonable. Mikey was beside him and Wally crouched behind them: it had been his question. To ignore it, massage it or confront it? Zach saw in his mind's eye the face that had been pistol whipped and the blood and the tooth.

He answered: 'I thought the violence was unnecessary and, unforgivably, you looked like you enjoyed handing it out.'

Sarcasm. 'You can read me, right? That goes with intelligence?'

'It was heavy-handed, almost brutal. They were good kids.'

Wally said, 'Do it polite? Sit down, have a cup of tea and "ask" for a hitched ride? Give them the opportunity to say, "That's not convenient"? Go on to the next stop, and hope it's an X37 bus on that route, and going where we want? Or take what we need? Facts of life, kid. If, when we're having the cup, making the request, or waiting for a bus, we're lifted, what happens then? You reckon it'll be probation or a community-service order? Do you think the mullahs will put us to work decorating old people's homes? Kid, we'll hang.'

'I was trying to say—'

'Hang high, and hang slow. What were you trying to say?'

'Nothing.'

'Final word. Better to knock out a tooth than to hang high and slow.'

'I hear you,' Zach said.

He gazed at the ground ahead, looking for places where the salt had made ridges or there were deep holes. He didn't look at the old boats stranded in the salt flats. When they came to the cluster of trees, they stripped out all that was important from the builders' van and loaded the wagon. The woman helped.

When they were loaded, and all aboard except Mikey, Zach drove clear of the van and stopped at the furthest line of the trees. He saw the fuel dial was at a fraction less than halfway. Mikey ran towards him and scrambled in beside him. Zach saw the flames rising behind, and the smoke. He drove fast and hoped the maps they'd brought would cover side roads to bring them wide of Tabriz and Marand, then take them, from the west, into Khvoy. They bumped towards a track, leaving a trail behind them.

He felt chastened, small, and hadn't spoken to Farideh, who seemed alone.

A few days ago it had been important to play his part in opening a defector's memory, but that was a lifetime past. He could barely see the man's face now, the photograph, or what had been said of his importance.

'I do not believe anything I am told. I have been deceived and tricked.'

Father William watched.

Petroc said, 'I'm trying to be patient, Mehrak. Help me, please. I repeat, did you travel with Brigadier Joyberi to the Parchin military complex?'

'I have nothing to say.'

Father William saw Petroc Kenning's fists tighten. The knuckles glowed.

'I'll ignore this stubborn response. I've told you that we're in the process of extracting your wife from Iran. If you went to Parchin, did you hear discussion on "implosion explosives"?'

'You lie to me.'

A mirthless smile played on Father William's face: if the interrogator beat the daylights from a valued defector it would be a first. He intervened. 'Forgive me, Petroc, if this is out of court, but I feel the need of a break. A day out, or what's left of it. Change of place and a change of mood. A word, Petroc?'

He was through the door and Petroc Kenning followed him. There was whispering and the voices wouldn't have reached inside the room where Nobby and Auntie watched over the sullen little man. Later PK would go into Vienna to receive detailed questioning angles and the demands of 'customers'. Father William explained his idea, and its implications.

He said, 'It's the story an aged aunt, a matriarch in the family, told. I think it'll go down well.'

'I'd be depending on you – the back-stabbers will be queuing as they always do.'

'Let me tell it. You have her photo up in the communications area. Pixelled, but still special. His actions have put her at risk, and he knows it. I think he loves her.'

'Whatever that means.'

'Imagine the love – and the guilt. You brought the rose back. Try another of Burns's work.

'To see her is to love her,
And love but her, and love for ever;
For Nature made her what she is,
And never made anither!

'You read a picture, Petroc, and see a face, gaze at a distorted blown-up photograph. "*To see her is to love her, And love but her, and love, for ever.*" Powerful stuff.'

'I'll buy it.'

'It'll shake the wind out of him.'

Father William went back into the big room and said they were going for a drive, time away from the house above the village on a bend in the Danube. 'Very interesting, it will be, Mehrak. It'll put perspective on what we're doing and where our people are.'

His joints cracked. Petroc forced two fists together. They had reached a crucial moment. He thought of many brave words offered up, hostages tossed towards Fortune, and his knuckles whitened.

'Excuse me, it's Len, isn't it?'

'Yes, I'm Len Gibbons.'

'I'm Tadeuz.'

'Tadeuz who?'

'Tadeuz Fenton. I do the Iran Desk.'

'Do you?'

'Most people know that. You did a show out of Iraq and into Iran a few years back.'

'If you say so.'

He stared into the face of the man he had trapped in the fourth-floor corridor of the Vauxhall Cross building. Nothing handsome, but careworn features. A poor shave that morning had left a fleck of blood on a collar. Pale complexion, and eyes without warmth. The tweed suit was nowhere close to the style today's men and women would have chosen but he had the aloofness that came from success. There was no swagger in the man, who was over sixty and likely closing on retirement. As Tadeuz understood it, Len Gibbons had been given the bureaucratic role on a mission that had been executed with the active co-operation of Friends and Cousins. It had not seemed necessary, before that moment, to consult him. Why, then, had Tadeuz backed him against a corridor wall, and been close enough to smell the pipe tobacco on his breath? The loneliness of running a show explained much.

'Please don't piss me about.'

'Would I?'

'It seemed easy when we were setting it up on a gale of optimism, but it's harder to cope with as each hour passes, and original necessities become fogged.'

'I'd concur.'

'If you don't mind me asking, what kept you upright?'

'Lack of imagination or sentiment, immersion in detail. You have people inside?'

'I do, yes.'

The eyes had dulled and the breath came a little faster. He said quietly, 'You forget the mission and its aim, whether it went well or not. You think of recovering the boys inside. It's what saps the soul. I made a mistake, a bad one, and am not ashamed to admit it. There were two and one survived. I once saw the survivor across a street. I saw him, my mistake, because allowing that opportunity to arise merely accentuated my sense of personal responsiblity. He looked to have gone to hell and back. As I said, it saps the soul. If you get them out, your people, don't ever go afterwards to find them.'

'I was looking for guidance on what I could do, anything to smooth the way.'

'They're running. If they weren't running you wouldn't have corralled me. Fuck all you can do for them, except have transport on the safe side of the frontier, with a filled hip flask. Do excuse me. I'm meeting someone for lunch.'

The shoulder dropped, and Len Gibbons was off down the corridor.

They had climbed until they were wheezing. The snowline was still far above. They had driven through the village and had found a lay-by that looked like a parking point for expeditions that went all the way, sixteen thousand feet above sea level, to the peak. It had majesty. She had served in the Ankara embassy, in the Vauxhall Cross secure area, but Mandy Ross had hardly been out of the building in working hours, and only a couple of times as far as the Mediterranean beaches, never anywhere remotely close to Mount Ararat.

They were killing time, and it diverted their minds from the messages coming in on the secure mobiles about the dragnets – 'Always bloody tightening, aren't they?' Dunc had said – and security cordons. They expected no communication. To activate a call now would have been tantamount to hoisting a Union flag because the pride of Iranian geeks would be searching for messages on the airwaves that gave locations and . . . The team, the woman and young Zach were running, were out there and over the ridges of hills to the east. Mandy didn't know him. Dunc had met him on the site and had shared the ride to London with him.

It was not the tourist season, and the snow would come soon enough to coat the foothills. There were no other vehicles in the lay-by except one battered tractor attached to an antique trailer. She hadn't noticed it when they'd parked and started out on a worn path that climbed to the summit. A peasant was coming down. He wore wellington boots, baggy trousers, a wide belt, the moustache of a Mexican revolutionary, a long raincoat and a beanie hat with the logo of Queens Park Rangers from west London. He was bent under the weight of old timbers tied together with baling twine.

She had Turkish and Kurdish in the dialect of Doğubeyazıt . 'From the Ark?'

'Of course – genuine.' The laugh split his face.

'A lucky find for you.'

'Very lucky because very genuine.'

He went on, still laughing. Dunc Whitcombe had a useful grin: it reeked of scepticism. She said it would be a good conversation piece in the office if she could show off a bit of timber certified as having come from Noah's Ark. They talked a little as they walked about the myth of the Deluge, the supposed sunken cities of the Black Sea, the earthquake that had unblocked it at the Dardanelles, and *The Epic of Gilgamesh*, written around two thousand years before Christ, which spoke of a great flood. The talked also of an expedition made only thirty years ago, which had discovered 'a boat-shaped stone formation'. For a little while Dunc Whitcombe and Mandy Ross were the same as any other couple introduced after they'd paid a fee to a dating agency: they worked at making each other smile and finding common ground. She rather liked him. Once she had rather liked her husband. Time ebbed. He broke away from her and ran down the hill. When had Dunc Whitcombe last run? Might have been for a bus, if he was late for a brain-stormer called by Tadeuz Fenton at seven or a little after.

She gazed at the mountain, captivated. They shouldn't have been there because there had been warnings at the tourist centre in the town that the slopes were used as safe havens by Kurdish fighters and by the gangsters who smuggled contraband into and out of Iran. She hadn't rung her husband but he wouldn't have expected her to. They would have had little to talk about, and if the washing-machine had broken down it was of no interest to her – it wouldn't register against the mountain, the dawn of history, and her sense that she was but a feeble witness.

He came back, panting from the exertion of running down, then stumbling up, and gave her a piece of wood. It was nearly six inches long, two or three inches wide, and a couple of inches deep; it was rotten, and had suffered from exposure and age. 'I think it came from the rudder,' he said.

'Steered by Noah?' she asked.

'Not necessarily. Might have been one of the sons.'

'And the dove sat on it?'

'Absolutely. The old boy assured me that there was bird poo on it but it washed off yesterday. We were lucky to find him.'

'Very.'

She could do worse. Mandy Ross slipped her free hand under Dunc Whitcombe's elbow. He had made her laugh, which she liked, and seemed to enjoy her company, being close. He didn't pull away.

She could do worse . . . They had killed time, and the light was slipping. Tomorrow . . . She might not do a bit better. Tomorrow was another day.

Zach was told the schedule ahead. He had noted a big bird, an eagle maybe, about the size of the buzzard he knew from home, over the yellowed grass clear of the lake's shore. He had pointed it out to Mikey, but Mikey had kept his gaze, unwavering, to the right of the bird as it wheeled, hunted. Zach reckoned he had good eyesight but Mikey's was superior. Unless he had been shown, Zach wouldn't have seen the helicopter. It flew high, a speck in the skies. He had asked what to do if it veered towards them, and had been told to get out, stand in clear view and wave. It hadn't turned towards them.

The schedule was simple.

They would have skirted Tabriz, using the back roads, by dark. Away from the lake they were likely to find a river and trees. They would get into cover and sleep. They would make an early departure from the lie-up, so they had time to backtrack if they approached road blocks, but the goal was to get into Khvoy, the rendezvous town, an hour before the pick-up. There was enough slack in the schedule to cope with handicaps, delays and detours.

He would go forward alone, scout and make the contact, then bring the transport to wherever they had stopped. They'd be on the road and heading for the border by three in the afternoon. Simple. Zach imagined that the Israeli planning would be of high quality, likewise the guys they employed. Mikey had told him the make of the vehicle, a Nissan Pathfinder, and the location of the square in Khvoy.

Simple enough.

The guys talked among themselves – alert but calm – and ignored Foxtrot. In running away from them she had broken their trust. He saw her in the rear-view mirror, sitting beside Ralph at the extremity of the bench seat. She was the reason they were there, the cause of the danger around them, which she shared with them. Her head was down and most of the time her eyes were fastened on her knees. Her future? Too early to say. He drove along a rough road, passing men who drove tractors, men who herded goats, and small homes from which smoke belched and behind which washing hung. He had seen nothing threatening since the helicopter.

If the pieces of the jigsaw were in place, it was a good schedule.

* * *

'You have it all worked out?' Auntie had asked.

'Yes, and it'll shaft the bastard,' Father William had answered.

Nobby drove and had the front to himself. He'd heard the response. A brief explanation had been offered and Father William had seemed set in his mind. The others hadn't argued, and Nobby supposed PK had sanctioned it. Sidney had overheard the name of the destination but hadn't registered the significance; he had prattled on about the historic castles they'd see on the way.

The route was south from St Polten, across the Danube, then through valleys flanked by mountains already snow-capped. They crossed picture postcard scenery, and the last of the cattle were still grazing but most were in the barns for winter.

Nobby revelled in the chance to drive along a near-open road. He didn't know when Father William would start to do the business, or how it would be done, and had no clear idea of exactly what had happened in Judenburg, their destination. He might, if there was time, get a decent view of the place on his phone and send it to the girl in Kazakhstan. It might or might not prompt a reply. After Bruck an der Mur, a railway junction below steep hills, they'd joined the S36, and were nearing the end of the journey, 150 kilometres almost, and a ninety-minute run. He anticipated the event eagerly: watching over defectors was usually little more exciting than seeing the proverbial paint drying.

Father William was behind him with the Iranian, and Auntie was in the back row. He didn't know how it was to be handled but sensed that a tipping point had been reached – in fact, two of them. There was one point at which the mission was teetering, like a guy walking with a pole on a high wire: the people doing the run from Tehran with the woman. The increasingly fractious PK had handed over bulletins on their progress and Nobby understood the pressure on the boss; he hoped the woman deserved it. The second tipping point was the open disbelief the little bastard harboured for the effort that was being made on his behalf. His clamming up and the frequent call-backs from London had ratcheted the tensions in the safe house. Only so many bloody hours that any of them could stay sane, peering out at the vineyards and watching the gulls circle the church tower.

Sidney liked to talk about the castles on either side of the gorge, especially the Burg Aggstein – they'd seen it when they'd been coming down the road alongside the Danube from the safe house and Spitz, and before they'd reached St Polten. It was a high, stone-walled keep built on a rock crag, extraordinary. It had been the seat of the Kunringer family, a Capone-style gang of the fifteenth and sixteenth centuries. They had robbed merchants trading up the river and taken the more affluent ones hostage, demanding ransoms. The Kunringers' speciality, Sidney said, was the rose garden set above a vertical cliff. The victims were lowered onto the ledge by rope, then left. If a ransom came quickly, they might not starve to death or topple off with exhaustion and fall to the rocks below. It was a good place for the little bastard. Nobby had nearly come off the road when he'd looked up at the place and imagined the corporal perched on the ledge, his tongue loosening. It had been a good castle to see, but he was sorry he hadn't identified the rose garden. He drove, and was alone with his thoughts.

Nobby hadn't known Father William before now. He sensed that the man was the least likely of them to wash his hands of the problem the little bastard posed. There were lives on the line. Time was not on their side, and the man had to be drained of information over the next few hours. If he was given too much time he would realise he had made as bad a move as it was possible to make.

The sign announced Judenburg. There was a modern bridge across a wide river, and the valley sides yawed upwards. The town was on the far bank. It was Father William's cue.

A pleasant voice, a friend's: 'Mehrak, pretty countryside, isn't it? Don't answer – don't interrupt me. You don't trust us and think we're deceiving you. We've come here so that I can explain why you should believe us when we give our word. Remember Gaddafi? Remember "Mad Dog"? Remember he was a pariah and loathed? We made him a promise. He came in from the cold, ditched his nuclear programme and we delivered on the promise. He was vile, but we'd given our word. There was a man called Abdul Hakim Belhadj – now a fat cat in the new Libya – an enemy of Gaddafi. We helped the Americans to ship him back to Tripoli where he was tortured and abused by that despot regime. Why did we do that? Because we had given our word. We stuck by it. That's what we do. We give our word to the devil for the sake of policy. Now, and then.'

They were over the bridge. Father William reached across Nobby and pointed to a narrow slip road running off to the left. They followed it past a couple of small hotels and some bars, then holiday cottages. The view was of the river, the Mur, a hundred metres wide. The sun had come out. The water was flanked by willows, looked deep and flowed fast.

Father William told Nobby he could park. He asked Mehrak to step out. Auntie followed and stayed close. Nobby slipped the short-arm baton into his pocket and locked the vehicle. Father William was conversational, relaxed.

'My grandfather was here. He died a few years ago, and never told me the story, but when he was old he told it to my nan. He woke up in the middle of one night, and told her what he'd done sixty years before, as a young soldier in the British Army, what he'd done and been ordered to do here. He never spoke of it again. She said he was a Jack the Lad, a wild boy, when he went off in 1944, and they'd been married three weeks. He came back a year later and was moody, morose, miserable for the rest of his days, because of what he was ordered to do here. You following me, Mehrak? Just keep looking at the water.

'The way he told it to my nan, there was an iron bridge across the river then. It was June 1945, the Germans and Austrians had surrendered and Hitler was dead. The Russian Army was across the river, and there was unfinished business.'

The river ran fast. Nobby thought it would have been higher in the early summer than it was now, autumn; the winter snows would have thawed and it would have been in spate, dangerous. He could imagine a rusted bridge, the arcs of the supports rising above a narrow carriageway, but didn't know the story.

'There were Cossacks who had fought with the Germans against the Red Army, and had fallen back in defeat. There were eighteen thousand of them here, with their wives and children. The Soviets hated them as traitors, and our leader had done a deal with theirs. London with Moscow, Churchill with Stalin. Did we love the Russians? Did we fuck. Didn't trust them an inch, but there'd been a deal.'

Nobby watched a branch float under the arches towards a weir. He saw the power of the water, and its threat.

'We kept our word. Our soldiers put eighteen thousand Cossacks, men, women and children, across the bridge. They were pushed with bayonets. They were singing hymns, and were beaten with pickaxe handles and rifle butts. The Soviets took them on the other side, marched them round a corner and the machine-guns started up. Everyone knew what was happening. Plenty jumped into the water rather than be taken by the Soviets.'

Nobby stared ahead, dry-eyed, and Auntie seemed to watch a kingfisher flash across the far bank, no emotion. The water was mud-coloured and he couldn't see down into it. It surged either side of the new bridge supports and speeded as it approached the weir.

'It was reckoned that some sixty of the eighteen thousand went into the water and reached the British bank. They avoided the soldiers sent to shoot them or bring them up again to the bridge and get them over. Sixty survived. The water, my grandfather said, was filled with the bodies of the drowned, and the noise of the machine-guns behind the trees went on into the night, a long summer evening. We did it because we had given our word, and that was worth the shame of what we had to do. We were true to our word. Understand me?'

Nobby saw the corporal nod. He realised why they had driven so far, and felt the force of Father William's message. The man's lips moved, but Nobby had no Farsi and couldn't decipher the murmur. He stood back.

Auntie was beside him. 'You think it worked?'

'I . . . don't know. Sort of shock treatment. So peaceful and serene here, but the atrocity makes it like a crime scene. I think it worked.'

He heard the snap of Father William's fingers, and saw the gesture towards the vehicle. Going home. No pissing about, no late lunch. Strike while the poker was glowing. He phoned PK, said what had happened, that they were coming back.

What Mehrak had said to himself was, 'You kept your word to the Russians. You *lied* to the people who trusted you and whom you betrayed by giving them to an enemy. It was *lies* you told them.'

He sat in his seat and was given a bar of chocolate. He believed in nothing beyond an old loyalty to his brigadier, and thought it shared.

He went from his office.

The traffic had snarled and he had been caught in a jam. His driver had been unable to reverse out of it or swing into a side road. The car had been on time, and he couldn't fault that, but he could fault the mood in his office. Both of his regular aides had called in sick. His telephone hadn't rung. Most days it rang incessantly.

He was late. Brigadier Reza Joyberi had changed in the office into his fatigues. The uniform was a camouflage design favoured by combat volunteers in Afghanistan, Iraq and south Lebanon. He wore the badges of his rank on his shoulders, had clipped the medal strips on the left side of his chest and wore a side-arm in a holster. He thought he looked what he was: a senior and influential figure in the regime.

His pistol was taken. He was given a docket. He could have argued, stood his ground.

He was escorted to a waiting room. It was a section of the Kazemi Garrison camp that he had not been into before. He heard voices down a corridor, aggressive, then a woman crying. Once a prisoner was brought past the open doorway of the waiting room, the stamp of despair on his face. He checked his phone. No messages. He waited. He was late for the appointment. He couldn't remember how long it had been since a functionary had kept him waiting without a message of apology, or asking for him to be given tea, with biscuits or cake. He hadn't used the phone to call those whom he expected would offer him support. Expected.

There was a handful of other brigadiers, the hierarchy of the Revolutionary Guard Corps – of which al-Qods was an élite entity – and political figures close to the Supreme Leader, generals in the army and admirals in the navy. He was a figure of importance. At gatherings, men who knew him only by reputation were invited to shake his hand and he would see, every time, their nervousness. In that hand he had held matters of life and death. He had not rung them to enlist their support because he had a vague fear, already, that they might decline to take his call, stall, or promise and do nothing. How many would regret his fall? Some? Perhaps. A few? Possible. None? Probable.

A door opened down the corridor. A man was led out. He wore a suit and wasn't handcuffed but had an escort at either side of him. He was taken from the corridor. Then a clerk came from that room, stood in the entrance to the waiting area and beckoned for him to follow. He did.

The door was opened for him.

Two men sat behind a table, turbaned, robed and bearded. They had hangman's eyes that lit as he entered. The clerk showed him to a hard chair in front of the table. There were men against the wall to his left, who wore dull blue uniforms that Reza Joyberi did not recognise. The door rattled shut.

No smile, nothing of humanity. Why should there have been?

'Joyberi, we have questions to put to you.' The older one spoke, and the other took notes.

He sat erect. 'My name is Reza Joyberi, and my rank in the al-Qods unit of the Revolutionary Guard Corps is that of brigadier. I should be treated with respect and addressed by my full name and rank.'

'Joyberi, we have questions to put to you.'

'Under what authority?'

'Joyberi, the Ministry of Justice is charged with the responsibility of protecting the state from malfeasance wherever it appears. The trappings of rank do not protect those guilty of crimes against the state.'

'It is ridiculous that . . .'

He knew the futility of argument and that, here, bluster would gain him no territory. He regretted already that he had not beaten a track to the senior men who worked around him, who kissed his cheeks when greeting him each morning, who took tea with him, who wished him and his wife well, who laboured alongside him to preserve the security of Iran. Perhaps he also regretted – already – that his wife was at home and his child at school, not at the airport. He stared at the man and won no response. The other's pencil was poised.

'Joyberi, it is important that you answer truthfully and co-operate fully or there is the potential of grave consequences for you, because these are matters that involve treason, war against God. What has happened to your driver?'

'He is missing.'

'He is missing and is believed to be in the custody of a foreign intelligence agency. And, Joyberi, what has happened to the wife of your driver?'

'She also is missing.'

'And is thought to have been taken out of the capital by agents of the United Kingdom – the Old Fox or the Little Satan. My first question of importance. You sent your driver to Dubai, Joyberi. Why? What business could so lowly a figure, the driver of your car, perform for you in Dubai at the expense of the Iranian people? I advise you to consider your answer carefully.'

'It was a matter of state security. I refuse to share it with you.'

'Does the security of the state involve the maintenance of private bank accounts that are beyond the reach of the tax authorities in Iran? I require an answer.'

The brigadier looked up. He saw blue, a small cloud in the midst, through the window and over the rooftops. He thought power was a skin that a snake might shed and that, deprived of it, he could feel the cold settling on him. How should he reply?

* * *

Zach sat on a fallen log.

'Fuck where I'd rather be,' Wally muttered. 'What I'd like to be doing. We did a march through Warminster, up Station Road and the high street, to the Minster. All the town was out to see us. I felt, sort of, recognised.'

The guys talked of long-ago army days.

'We did one in Colchester.' Mikey's voice was little more than a whisper. 'Pouring with rain, us in best dress, five deep on the pavements. Best I ever felt.'

The water she used for washing the plates spilled out under the wagon. Zach and the guys should have helped her. They had eaten well from what had been left in the cupboards, tins of sausages and tomatoes, and a bag of small potatoes. There had been lemonade to drink. They were near to a viewing point in a parking area that was deserted but for themselves. The darkness had settled round them. The logs were for use in place of tables and benches. He could justify stealing the couple's food, and transport, and abandoning them on the salt flats with the flamingos. He didn't feel bad about it and knew he had changed. There was a small light above the sink, which she had used while she was doing the dishes. Now she switched it off.

'When I had the boot I missed by a week the march-past through Winchester. I was shot of Basra a week before the parade at the Presidential Palace. I missed the Basra one because I was sent on a repatriation job, escort for a box. Don't think I'll be doing a march-past now.' A chuckle from Ralph.

She sat beside him, not close.

'Might be best to be in a box.'

He didn't know how much she understood.

'Worse to be on your back on a stretcher, and fucked.'

Zach reached out his hand. She took it.

'A good funeral is what you want, and a piss-up after for your mates, except we're beyond that.'

It was like they were teenagers at the cinema, the first time they'd touched. Maybe they'd go for a polystyrene plate of chips afterwards.

'What you don't want is amputation or your face buggered so you're blind.'

'Or to lose a bollock – worse, lose two.'

The question Zach didn't dare to ask was whether all of them would make it out. Best not to ask because a cheerful, evasive answer was worse than silence.

'Don't even joke about it. A long old day tomorrow.'

Tomorrow Zach thought, would be different from any other day he had experienced. He shivered, and the cold seemed to grip all of him except the hand that held hers. He valued the comfort he gave and took.

13

He heard what was said, and kept quiet.

The guys had done more of 'where I would rather be' orchestrated by Wally, but without enthusiasm: red bills coming through the door, putting buckets in the hall because rain was forecast and the roof leaked, dealing with the ex who flaunted a new man, traipsing to school after hours because the head teacher had an issue with a kid's behaviour – all seemed like flat beer, and was too close, Zach reckoned, to experience. Depression was growing among them.

The darkness was heavy. Far in the distance there was a sodium-tinted glow, which would be the lights of Khvoy – where they had to be early tomorrow afternoon. Beyond those lights there was no horizon. There would have been hills at the border, or near to it, and there were dank skies, which merged together, with no clear line that might have given a sense of distance. His thoughts rambled. Easier if he could have seen the furthest point they would be heading for. The clouds had thickened and the first shower had started, not heavy but sufficient to dampen his hair.

There were pin pricks of light to the right of the viewing point – farmers' houses. Zach gave a morose chuckle, stifled it. The farmers would leave lights burning outside their barns to ward off the wolves that would edge forward to steal calves or young goats. Zach knew about wolves – wild, hungry and continually searching for food – because he had concocted a peasant's tale about them and had deluded young guys who had manned a road block. He had spied on them, gone back to his own crowd and reported the result of his deceit. He had told the guys the layout of the chicane across the road. He hadn't seen the men further down the road. It had been espionage, and the penalty for espionage was . . . He was as guilty of espionage as the Israeli who had driven the van from the border to the slip road behind the disused fuel station on the outskirts of the capital. He could no longer remember what he had volunteered for.

A light came on. The guys cursed.

The camper's side door was pushed shut. The light died.

She hissed at them from behind him that she needed to pee. Coffee did that. They had stolen coffee and milk from the built-in refrigerator, and the guys had found sugar. There had been enough gas to heat the milk. He heard, clear enough, what she'd said: 'Just so you know, people here have gone out of their way to treat Joey and me with kindness and courtesy. They've made us welcome. You're screwing us up. So, fuck you.' Better if it had been dark and he hadn't seen the loathing in her eyes, the hate in the boy's, and the courage. Now, Joey had an injured face and his holiday was wrecked. What other option had there been? Zach didn't know. Wise people, old people and the people who wanted to flatten you always said, 'What's done cannot be undone.' There can be no turning back of the clock. Two men killed at the road block, and a tourist, had been hurt. Zach tortured himself.

She came to the log.

'You all right?' he asked.

'I'm fine. I had to . . . you know.'

'You should go back inside, where it's warmer.'

'I think not.' She had brought a blanket with her, had wrapped herself tight in it. 'What's wrong, Zach?'

She had read him. 'Where to start.'

'Because you took me with you?'

'You, Farideh, are not my problem.'

'Do you wish you'd never heard of me?'

'I haven't said nor thought that.'

'Do you wish you'd never seen me?'

'I don't think so.'

'Because of what happened on the road?'

'I'm not a fighting man. I came because I was flattered – I was told my skill as a linguist had identified me. I didn't think about it – my life was empty and I wanted it filled.'

'You think you were tricked?'

'What I think isn't important.'

'You blame yourself for the deaths at the road block?'

'I'm not a fighting man. I don't have the mentality for it.'

'Which makes you superior or inferior?'

'Different.'

'In four years, Zach, I loved two men. Does that make me a whore?'

'Of course not.'

'One was a political activist who made war on the regime and sacrificed his life. The second was a soldier. He wanted a soldier's life and earned a soldier's death. Both were different.'

'Have you any love left in you?'

She faltered: 'I don't know . . .'

He said, 'It started as a mission in the interests of national security. A defector has come in. He demands his wife joins him. The defector is valuable enough to be listened to. We're sent. The wife will come out, but not for her husband. We're at the bottom of the food chain. She doesn't want to join her husband, says she detests him. Our job is to bring her out and for me that's psychological fulfilment. For the guys it's a big payday – so, fuck the fine point of whether we're fulfilling the end game. She comes, we get the rewards promised us. Is there any love left in you?'

A small voice, and he had to lean nearer to hear: 'I hope so.'

'We take you out. Will you make another life?'

'Of course.'

She was close to him. He put out his arm and she wriggled nearer. Because of the cold, Zach told himself. A long night faced him, and he couldn't hurry it. It seemed natural that he should protect and warm her.

The photographer was a freelance. He relied on sources in the police force, the ambulance service and fire teams, who provided him with the type of blood-lust images the customers appreciated.

He had been told where on the line to the south-east of the capital he should drive to, and had found the knot of investigators and the team about to recover the decapitated body. He had also been told the cadaver's identity, and had been shown an identity card taken from the dead man's wallet. On it, there was a head-and-shoulders picture of the dead man.

The photographer was familiar with the agencies beside the track and was helped by one – a particular friend – who moved the tarpaulin hiding the corpse so that he could take a picture of the waist, buttocks, legs and feet of the suicide. In the same shot, but between the rails, the 'shape' had thin dark hair.

His regular point of contact was the picture desk of the Islamic Republic News Agency. Any photographer needed luck in placing his material, and he was rewarded that afternoon. There had been no spectacular accident on any of Tehran's main arteries, no public hanging . . . IRNA took the pictures of the self-inflicted death on the Tehran to Isfahan railway line. The *Kayhan News* was a principal client of the agency.

In the late evening, before midnight, the presses rolled. Prominent on an inside page was a large picture of the body on the stones, the smaller image of the ID card and the name of the young man who had been a member of the surveillance team of the Ministry of Intelligence and Security. Beside the body, ignored – why should it not have been? – there was a scrap of crumpled paper, which might have fallen from the hand at the moment of impact. Suicides were increasing in Iran and a paper with a conservative leaning, the *Kayhan News*, regarded the 17 per cent spike as a sign of growing decadence in the effete liberal society pushing for greater power and the lack of God-fearing discipline in current society.

As head of security, Hossein always worked late into the evening. The embassy in Vienna was on Jauresgasse. The buildings used by the Iranian delegation were of a traditional style, nineteenth-century Hapsburg, gutted and partially flattened by Red Army artillery in the last weeks of the Second World War and rebuilt with meticulous standards of imitation. The embassy housed two teams: one dealt with affairs linked to Austrian matters, good trade and access to high technology through local commerce. Of primary interest to Hossein, though, was Western hostility towards the legitimacy of an Iranian nuclear programme, and the enmity it directed to his country. In the capital, across the Danube, were the offices of the International Atomic Energy Authority. There, the world ranged itself against Hossein's government. He accepted that experts from Iran would travel to brief the ambassador and that they would be holding in their heads, and their laptops, sensitive information concerning the programme and its possible uses. Such persons were vulnerable as targets of Zionist assassination plots and were also likely to be worth the efforts of the American, British, German and French agencies. Their minds could be addled with promises of wealth, and their vanity exploited. Hossein believed that his reputation would be compromised should any man – on his territory – be killed or persuaded to defect. He worked hard: failure would end his career.

His office was on the ground floor of the building. One window looked out onto Jauresgasse and the other gave him a view across a small garden and the railings blocking off the pavement and Reisnerstrasse. Perhaps only the role of security officer to the delegation at the UN headquarters in New York carried greater prestige and a greater chance of personal catastrophe. Hossein was tough mentally and prided himself on his ability to cope with pressure.

He was a lonely man, but by choice. His wife and their children were in Tehran. They would have been a responsibility and a diversion had they lived in Vienna. He wrote and phoned most weeks, and twice a year he flew back to Iran, arms filled with presents. At home he sensed the weight of the sanctions on his country's economy. He was briefed on the killing of experts by the Zionists and the state of siege in which his country existed. His commitment never wavered. His belief was constant that the place for traitors, saboteurs and enemies was, first, in the interrogation rooms at Evin, and, second, on the table or chair under the bar and the ropes in the execution yard. He was busy that night.

The situation regarding a defector crossed his desk.

There were, of course, no *actual* defectors from Iran. There were incidents in which men involved in work on the nuclear programme, in the armed forces or the Revolutionary Guard Corps were abroad, travelling on state business or to the *hajj*, and were kidnapped. All Iranian embassies in the capitals of influential nations were alerted to the 'disappearance' of a corporal of the al-Qods section of the IRGC, who drove for a high-ranking officer. His wife had fled and was believed to be in the hands of a foreign intelligence agency. Why? So often, the mother-fuckers were vomited out again when their use was exhausted. The likelihood of the British taking the wretch to their own country was considered slim: he would be held for debriefing, it was thought, in a friendly but myopic country.

A villa in Austria used as a safe house? Possible. The chance of locating it? Impossible. But he was alerted. The message was filed. There was a shadow near the tinted-glass window that overlooked Reisnerstrasse.

The shape paused, then lunged through the railing. The bush convulsed, then fell back. The shadow retreated.

He was imbued with suspicion.

Hossein hurried from his office to the control area where the cameras were monitored by a member of staff answerable to him. He demanded a replay of the one that covered the angle of the two streets fronting his office.

Extraordinary.

A man of around his own age, but taller and leaner, wearing a good suit and tie, dark glasses, a scarf high around his face, masking his mouth and nose, leaned through the railings and snipped off a cluster of the last red roses of the year. He laid it on the pavement then stood tall again, cut away more flowers, retrieved the first and was gone.

Confusing.

The Foreign and Commonwealth Office liked to remark that the British establishments were cheek by jowl with those of their Iranian fellow diplomats.

A sherry was taken.

The Briton in the Viennese capital did not seek to be privy to Petroc Kenning's mission, but it was an opportunity for him to meet the young man from London and to socialise with the station chief, who shared floor space with the more conventional first secretaries and chargés. The laughter flowed between them. His PA had gone in search, as requested, and had returned with the sherry and a glass vase. Into it had gone the rose clusters, and now it dignified his desk. This officer complained frequently that the younger breed coming into the Service were duller and less eccentric than those of his own generation. He liked the man: a rare creature who behaved like an undergraduate on his way to the Girton Spring Ball in nicking a rose from the garden of an illustrious vice-chancellor, getting a pretty girl to wear it low on her chest . . .

The Iranian embassy garden produced good roses, but he didn't imagine that Petroc Kenning, going to a secure-circuit conference, London and Vienna, would have pinched Iranian property without reason. He knew the Iranians well. He found them formidable opponents – not as contrary as the North Koreans, with whom negotiation was impossible, but a competitive second. He disliked most the parading of piety, humility and the demand for prayers before meetings. He remembered the shock-horror when a secretary he had taken with him had worn the briefest bloody skirt. The sanctimonious beggars had feasted. He had heard it said often enough that, during the frostiest days of the Cold War, it was still possible to meet KGB and foreign ministry Soviets at a May Day knees-up or a Queen's Birthday thrash, and down enough gin and vodka to float the proverbial aircraft carrier. Not with their neighbours down Jauresgasse. There was no compromise, a rigid denial of ambition for nuclear weapons, no worthwhile response to the offering of carrots, and only the shrug of the put-upon martyr if a stick was threatened. Hard work. So, it was amusing that roses had been stolen from their garden.

Two glasses drunk.

He was a little behind Petroc Kenning and the station chief as he escorted them to the front door, where the visitor's car waited, but he was blessed with good hearing.

'The babysitters shook him up. Don't know the whole of it but they gave him a verbal third-degree, took him into the mountains, exposed him to some history and jolted him. He's changed. Wants to co-operate now. God, I needed that. We're back on course on that front. It's the other end of the equation that concerns me. No names, no pack-drill. Tomorrow, listen to your radio. If the Iranians are bellowing, "Provocation!" I'm for the shit heap. If there's nothing tomorrow, or the day after, I might just have squeezed home. "The nearest-run thing you ever saw in your life," I think the great duke said, and that's what I'm looking for. Actually, the one I like best is from Churchill: "People sleep peacefully in their beds at night because rough men stand ready to do violence on their behalf." We'll be rooting for the "rough men". If they screw up, and you hear it on the radio, I'm off to the Tower and they'll say hanging, drawing and quartering are too good for me. It's all about a red, red rose – I'll tell you one day.'

He held it between his fingers, a fine strong bloom, handled it with care.

'God speed.'

'Thanks – it's God's help I'm needing, though.'

He was gone and the car pulled away.

The diplomat broke ranks. 'How bad is it?'

The station chief grimaced. 'On a scale of one to ten, try twelve. Thanks for doing the sherry.'

Zach couldn't move. Rain had become sleet and now fell as light snow. He couldn't move because she was asleep against his shoulder. The guys had their own places on their log benches and had brought out sleeping-bags from the camper.

The wagon was a dozen paces behind Zach. Inside, it would be warm and dry. There was a couch that could be pulled out to make a bed. None of them had used it. The snow had begun to settle on her head and on the part of the blanket over her shoulder.

She could have been inside the wagon and so could he. If they had squeezed up, the guys could have been in there too.

The lights on the barns were hidden from him by the driving snow flakes. What was her future? He hadn't asked her. Where did she want to go to? What work would she do? What was there for her in an unknown city among unknown people? He hadn't asked. Bridges burned? He assumed so, but she had run from them, and now slept against him. Contradictions. There would be a time for answers. There had been two photographs in the room above the repair workshop, different men but each possessing a powerful personality, each confident, each her lover, now dead. If she allowed a man into her life he would have to stand against those two. The snow made a wet scarf across her head, his nose and upper cheekbones.

Zach didn't understand the guys. Two sleeping-bags between the three. Low laughter, and murmured remarks he couldn't make out.

The noises, above the laughter, were of metal on metal. The older scrape of parts being detached, and the newer sounds of pieces going together. He didn't understand the mentality that made it acceptable to sit outside in the dark and snow to strip down the weapons on which their lives might depend and reassemble them. There was a clinical moment when each man finished the procedure, cocked the weapon, then pulled the trigger, a final sharp click. Laughter always followed.

To Zach, the three men had merged into a single shape. He had not taken the trouble to learn what motivated, excited and terrified them, or what they hoped for. He had assumed that each was gripped in a cycle of bills and failed relationships, and that each missed the companionship of the one family that had mattered to him. He had created for them stereotypical types. It had been laziness. Whether he came out of this place the next day and into the next night was in their hands. Fuck that.

She didn't move. He was ignored.

They had stripped and reassembled the rifles, emptied and refilled the magazines – all by touch. Now they started on the pistols.

How long could the bloody night last? He couldn't move and cramp twinged in his thigh. It would be cruel to wake her.

They were two camps, and only a contract held them.

Mehrak was in the day room. Maps lay in front of him, crudely drawn but bold lines, of the entrances to the sensitive rear areas of the Parchin complex and the Marivan testing range. They were not the routes that would have been used by officials of the International Atomic Energy Authority, but were for important Iranians. They led directly to the underground workshops where implosion and liquid fuel were studied. It was, Mehrak told them, where he had been with his brigadier, a pace behind, carrying the attaché case. The areas were considered too sensitive for admittance to be granted to any of the young officers who usually accompanied Reza Joyberi. No one bothered about the driver. On other sheets, A4 size, he had made similar plans showing the living quarters of the more highly rated scientists and engineers working on the projects. He knew of them, he said, because hospitality had been offered to the brigadier at both locations. He was complimented on his work. It was late in the evening and the house was quiet. A new rose had gone into the vase with the previous one. They laughed, but not with him. He had been told that his attitude was pleasing. It was a pretty flower, but it had no relevance. He made his request with a humility they would not have seen in him before.

'Sidney has told me of his love for the castles here. I have an interest. I have visited the place of the Assassins, at Qazvin, and in Lebanon I was at Jrebda, Tibnine and Beaufort, which were for the Crusader armies and for Hezbollah today. Sidney spoke of a castle here for your king, for Richard of the Lion's Heart. Tomorrow could I visit it with Sidney? After we have talked. I would appreciate it. Please?'

They thought him an idiot. He didn't disabuse them. It was agreed. After work.

He thanked them in turn for their kindness – for fuck-all of nothing – climbed the stairs, went to his room and heard the key turn in the lock. He would undress and switch out his light, then crouch in the corner of the room away from the bed. He would contort himself and press his head to the pipes. Then he would learn the news of that day, and where they had lied.

'Are you happy with this?' Beth Skelton asked.

'Of course I'm not,' Joey Farrow answered.

'And we're in deep. Should we have talked it through more?'

'Wasn't you and me who put us there. We had no call to.'

They spoke in hoarse whispers. Her voice was sharp and his was blurred from the swelling.

'They called them gangsters, but they're not – are they?'

'They smacked my face, Beth. My jaw might be broken, I've lost a tooth and the trip's fucked.'

'Wrong. What's fucked is them, if they swallowed the fuel story.'

'He said, "I'm British, with British colleagues. We're fugitives and have no transport." I don't care. He wrecked me. He can take his chance.'

'If they're spies, and they're British, aren't we supposed to be on their side?'

'No, we're not.'

He walked ahead of her. They were the first hostile, contradictory words they had ever spoken to each other. Both were exhausted. Both were traumatised by the event and its aftermath. They had seen the smoke, taken it as a first marker point and had lugged with them as much as the rucksacks would hold. They had found the van, a shell, and had seen sufficient crime-scene TV movies to know about eradicating fingerprints and DNA traces. They had followed tracks on the salt, buffeted by the wind, until they had reached a path. An old tractor and trailer had come up behind them and they had hitched a ride.

They had been dumped at a police station in Marand. The yard had been full of paramilitary trucks, and guys in uniforms who were not police, carried weapons and were smartly turned out. A junior had spoken to them. He had seemed preoccupied with weightier matters until they had told their story. Then, action.

They had told the story again to more senior men, who spoke good English, and the control room down a corridor had heaved. A big guy was brought in by military helicopter.

Then they had been driven to where Alex had been, and their gear picked up. They went next to the tree cluster where the van was. They had been asked several times the make of the van, its colour and registration plate. They had gone over their descriptions of the three men, and in particular the one who had done the talking. They had repeated his words: 'I'm British, with British colleagues. We're fugitives and have no transport. To save ourselves we need to take your vehicle.' They had been recorded.

A telephone connection had been made from the police station and the phone had been passed to them. They had been told they were connected to the New Zealand embassy in north Tehran. He was Perry something, the junior. The ambassador and principals were at a reception in town. He hadn't sounded sympathetic. Joey had heard a hiss of breath over the teeth when he'd talked of the British involvement – as if the man had said, 'Why didn't you just shut the fuck up? Why did you open your big mouth?'

Now they were going to a car that would run them to the hospital where his jaw would be seen to, and maybe there'd be some dentistry. After the medical stuff was finished, they'd go to a hotel.

They would stay in Marand, in comfort, until the fugitives were captured. They would identify them. Then— It was obvious even to country kids from Alexandra, Central Otago. To Beth Skelton, she might as well have hitched the rope herself.

She said, 'Better we'd given them the fucking phones, said "Have a nice day," let them go and not made an issue of it.'

'It's where we are. Nothing I can do, kid. They have to take their chance.'

Life in the bunkers on Cyprus occupied by the Signals technicians was usually the definition of tedium. Not that evening.

More men and women – from the services, and civilians drafted there from GCHQ – had gathered inside the basement than were needed for the monitoring exercise. The senior personnel did not dismiss them. High drama was being played out in front of them, on their screens and through the headphones. Enough had a knowledge of Farsi to provide a subdued commentary.

A young woman had asked her supervisor the basic question: 'They're ours, the ones who are stuck in there?'

It was not expected of a supervisor that he should interpret what the dishes on the higher crags of the Troodos mountains produced. The transmissions were for passing to the UK, where analysts and clients were waiting for them. This supervisor, with an archive of experience, shared the emotions expressed by the rookie. He wasn't sentimental, but every few minutes new transmissions came in, and the trap was closing. He had little knowledge of the type of men who might have been pitched onto Iranian territory, but could imagine their isolation and what faced them if they didn't elude the net. Many around him would have felt as he did so he didn't clear the area behind the technicians' chairs or snap at his questioner.

'I think we can assume that, Vicki. If it were Israelis, guys from one of the Iranian rebel factions or a team of our American friends, the instruction would not have been given to shift it on, unprocessed, to UK. They'll be our people.'

He knew about the young couple from New Zealand, their camper van and its registration. He knew also the physical descriptions given of three men who had car-jacked them. The detail had been relayed from a small police depot in a town outside Tabriz and was now circulated to every unit of police and the Republican Guard Corps that had been drafted in: local commanders spoke confidently by radio of a cordon covering routes from Tabriz towards the frontiers of Turkey and Azerbaijan.

'What chance would they have, boss?'

'Not for me to say. We'll do our job.'

Soon the shift would change, but he doubted that those who left the chairs facing the screens would drift to the bars and lose contact with the news filtering inside the bunker.

* * *

The Azerbaijani trader took meticulous care of detail. In the dark, with snow falling and settling, he was at the lock-up garage off Khayyam Street and would meet there, within the hour, the man who drove the Japanese-built four-wheel-drive. Together they would load a cargo of tea chests with seventy-nine two-kilo packages of heroin resin. His own car, a Paykan, was outside the garage and already had a layer of snow over the roof and windscreen. The brown envelopes were in the glove box.

They would be delivered to men of influence in the police and Customs who manned road blocks, and to the remote garrisons of the border patrols who were based some sixty kilometres to the north-west. Each envelope had been checked, and if they were delivered to the right men, in the right place and at the right time, he could be almost certain that the packages would have safe passage and free transit but . . .

It was a bad night. Not the weather. Any trader operating on the border with Turkey was comfortable with torrential rain, blizzards and gales across the high ground. He liked certainties. Trafficking demanded that schedules be met and material despatched on time, with due warning. The difficulty was in the town, on the main roads out of Khvoy that led to the frontier, and on the side roads. The men who created problems were strangers, from the Revolutionary Guard Corps. They had been deployed from Tabriz, with armoured cars and helicopters that flew high. He could predict with certainty that they would be flying again at dawn, however low the cloud base. Why? Terrorists were hunted. The difficulty was considerable for him, but could be managed.

There were, of course, other traders in Khvoy. Not all of them dealt with packages. There was a cousin by marriage, to whom he had spoken briefly that afternoon, who handled the more stressful ferrying of refugees out of Iran, had links with a foreign power and a contract for the next day. He was nervous. It was easier to buy co-operation for the transit of packages than for the movement of people, but the arrival of the Republican Guard Corps taxed both men. Whom to pay? No idea.

* * *

That night, Tadeuz Fenton would stay late. The next morning, he would arrive early. There had been the conference call, then a brief leg stretch in the street, with Sara Rogers left behind to guard phones and screens, and a gobbled curry at the new place in Tyers Street, alone. Then the new development had confronted him, sent up from the communications people. Back to the phone and the secure line.

'Bad, PK? I'd say worse than that. They stole the transport of a New Zealand couple, beat the lad up, and left them without wheels in the arse-end of nowhere. Trouble is, the couple trekked to a police post and a description of the vehicle is circulating far and wide. You thought it was bad before? Bloody hell, we're in a whole new league now. One mercy. This time tomorrow we'll know where we stand. Advice? Get yourself a drink and hope that the next we hear is from Dunc or Mandy at their pick-up place. I'll call you.'

Dunc stirred in the bed. He saw her in the doorway, back-lit by the last of the fire that had burned down in the living-room grate. She was wearing her dressing-gown. He pushed himself up on an elbow. She seemed to hesitate, as if uncertain whether to come on forward or turn her back on him.

'Is everything all right?'

'I think so.' He would have described her tone as laconic.

'The world not fallen in?'

'Nobody's told me if it has.'

Dunc eased himself higher. She was leaning against the door jamb. 'Can't you sleep?'

'I'm cold.'

Well, you will be cold, Mandy Ross, wandering about the place at two o'clock in the morning with the central heating off and the fire more or less out.

'Would you like me to put the heating back on?'

'Not really.'

Did she want him to make up the fire? It was his responsibility to do that, along with his kitchen duties, sweeping the floor in the living room and hoovering the rugs. She did not.

There were blankets on the top shelf in each bedroom. Could she not reach them? Could he do it for her? She had no need of another blanket.

It figured. He had been divorced long enough to forget the little he had known or *thought* he'd known of a woman's mind. Oh, God . . . He eased aside the bedclothes and made room. The curse of the Vauxhall Cross Social Club struck again. Always a disaster.

She shrugged off the robe and wriggled close to him. He was middle-aged and it was unlikely that any of the women in the outer office had stuck photographs of Dunc Whitcombe on the inside of their locker. Her hands were on his chest and pushed up his T-shirt. It would be about the fear. The Vauxhall Cross Social Club was built on a foundation of fear, stress and anxiety.

What sort of catch was Dunc Whitcombe? A pretty awful one.

'Are you OK?'

'I just thought, Why not?'

'Frightened?'

'Yes.'

The fear was for *them*, and the danger into which they had been thrown.

They drank water, ate bread, a cheese triangle each and half an apple. Farideh nibbled hers. Zach and she had gone out into the darkness briefly in opposite directions, and the guys had checked their weapons again. The snow had melted off her shoulders, the blanket had been shaken, and the two sleeping-bags the guys had used were stowed inside.

It was the last thing they did. They called it the trauma bag. The curtains were drawn inside the wagon and the light was on. They checked the contents. A belt pack went to Wally. It was done like a Saturday-morning supermarket shop, ticking off a list: tourniquet, burn dressings, steri-strip, bandages, syringes, needles, flexi-splint. Zach listened. He had first aid, plenty to do on a building site, and thought what he knew was pitiful. They had the rifles, the grenades were shared out and the ammunition was in the magazines, then slotted. Zach was offered a pistol – SIG Sauer P226. Shook his head.

Mikey said, 'We were in Iraq, Gulf One. An old hack was going to be embedded with us, couldn't carry all his gear, was past it, must have been a friend of the boss. He was offered, night before the push, a Browning pistol. He took it and slung it on his webbing. He said to us that he'd been a young star in Vietnam, early days there. He'd been flown up to a Yank outpost at the top of a hill close to the Cambodian border. They had crap local troops with them, and the North Vietnamese unit in the area was a crack outfit. He was given an M16, an automatic rifle, in case they were hit in the night. He declined it. The officer asked him what he'd do if they had gooks hitting the parapet – "Hold up your passport, shout that you're British so they don't shoot you, and don't chop your balls off and don't put your eyes out?" The hack told us he was shamed. He took a rifle and a sack of fragmentation grenades, and said he'd feed the belt for the corporal on the heavy machine-gun. No white flag is going up from us.'

Zach reached for the pistol. It had gone. She had it.

Ralph showed her the basic workings. Zach said he would take grenades, smoke and flash-bang. Did they want him to drive?

Later, not yet. Ralph would drive. Mikey would do shotgun and navigate, with a map across his lap, and Wally would be on the bench seat between them. The side windows were opened wide, and Wally would be able to use them to cover Ralph's side. Zach and the woman were like the kids, a fucking nuisance; they would be in the back and would not speak unless spoken to. They should be on the floor where there was protection from the cupboards and drawers and more blankets. He might have tapped Ralph's shoulder and tried to win him as a friend, the one who might most easily talk to him. But none of them had any interest in him; he would be rebuffed, his pride dented. He said nothing.

One pistol between him and her, some grenades and the trauma pack. She had taken the pistol and they had each looked into her face and nodded, like she was almost a part of them. The engine kicked into life. The lights of the town were ahead and the wipers took the snow off the windscreen. They bumped away down the track.

The lights of Khvoy beckoned them.

14

The first indication was when they came up a hill: the wagon tilted on the angle of the slope and the engine stalled. Zach heard it, felt it. But the wheels took them over the crest and the engine kicked in again.

Wally swore. Ralph rapped on the dial with his knuckle. Mikey hissed through his teeth.

They went on down. It was a track of ruts and potholes. The prints of tractor wheels were clear on it, and there were goats and sheep, two different groups. They went parallel to the main road. They had gone round the north end of the lake and it was behind them now, shielded by rolling hills. The snow hadn't settled and the rain was steady. Kids were minding the sheep and Zach had heard their shouts. They had waved a greeting and their dogs had raced after the wagon with a death wish, but none was hit. He had seen other children and youths with goats but they were further from the track. There had been a group of buildings, but no telephone line had led to it, or an electricity cable, but a low hut would have housed a generator. There was a well head and more dogs had chased them. An old man had sat on a chair at the front and smoked his cigarette. Zach didn't know whether the New Zealanders would have reached enough civilisation yet to denounce them. He thought it unlikely, here, that the buildings would have a mobile phone signal or that the farm families needed one.

They were on the reverse side of the slope and would drop another two hundred yards, then level off. There was a bridge ahead with rough planks over a small stream, then another rise in the track to be climbed. The last of the fuel would be dribbling into the bottom of the tank and they wouldn't clear the hill.

Going west from the lake and bypassing Marand was the easy option. Now they went north and were within sight of the road linking Shahpur, behind them, to Khvoy. No signs, but the estimate would be another ten or fifteen kilometres, no more . . . but time drifted. The tracks had been hard to identify, harder to stick with, and twice they had found themselves at a dead end, once in a quarry – exhausted – and once at a compound in front of a deserted farm building where the roof had collapsed. Then they had backtracked. They had rarely been faster than fifteen miles, twenty-five kilometres, an hour. Zach's mind jerked through the equations.

The weather was good for them, small mercy. They had heard helicopters, which had flitted into view over the main drag, then been lost in the cloud ceiling. The helicopters' problems with visibility were helpful, but the road near to them and away to their left was hard: they had seen road blocks on it, light armoured trucks, patrols of jeeps and open-top lorries. The rain was a friend: it would have dulled the fierce colour of the wagon and made its shape indistinct. The sodden track and water-filled holes ensured that they left no trail of dust. The hands on his watch moved relentlessly. Better to have taken it off, slapped it against a cupboard door and stopped it. They had calculated the time with care.

They came over the plank bridge, which rocked under them. A man was squatting low beside it, smoking and holding an umbrella over him with his free hand. He was old and wizened, the skin loose over his face. All of it was about enemies. A defection achieved through a honey trap was about gaining an advantage over an enemy; the smuggling of the defector's wife was to achieve a more complete advantage. Zach – and the guys who would 'rather be' anywhere but here – was on that track to advance the cause of besting 'the enemy'. Was the enemy squatting under that umbrella beside the track now reeling back because he was drenched in the rainwater that had collected in the trough at the extremity of the planks? He raised his head and saw the old man try to wipe the water off his face and out of his beard. He saw not an enemy but an old man soaked by the water their tyres had chucked over him. Had Ralph noticed him? Maybe not. Would Ralph have slowed if he had seen him? Probably not.

The schedule was the key.

At that moment, with the rain sluicing on the windscreen and side windows, they held to it.

They couldn't reach the square in Khvoy, designated for their pick-up, too early – it was dangerous to loiter. Suicide to be conspicuous.

They couldn't get to the square after the time given them. The Israeli had smacked his fist into the palm of his hand to emphasise it. The transport would not wait for them. A one-off opportunity – it wasn't a bus stop with another coming soon.

So, they had drawn up the schedule, their Bible, and . . . Ralph began the climb.

They had enough time. Ralph changed gear and the camper went on up and did about half of the slope. More coughs, more shakes – and silence.

There was no swearing, no belting of the dial and no hissing. Farideh, beside him, took second place. First place was for a girl from New Zealand. Zach knew her name from the postcards she'd left with her love scrawled on them. She was Beth Skelton and took prime position on the rostrum. Her boyfriend, Joey, had a bloody face, might need his chin wiring and to visit a dentist. He had thought the girl had thrown in the towel.

You'll look after our wagon? He would try to.

. . . and I believe you, there's something you should know. What should he know?

We filled up with fuel in Tabriz . . . Only one thing wrong. What was wrong?

The fuel gauge . . .

He'd nodded, he'd switched on the engine. Like a fish going after a fly. He'd thought he'd been all sweet reason, and won her honesty. What else would a country girl, from South Island, tough and resourceful, do as payback? In her head she would have seen the boy's face and the violence of the blow.

Farideh took her cue from the guys and stared at him. His shit was on their boots: what solution could he offer? It was too far for them to walk into the centre of the town for the pick-up. They had to have fuel. Mikey picked up the binoculars from between his feet, scanned with them then passed them to Zach.

He saw the logo on the sign, the blurred shape of the pumps and the outline of the military vehicles – armoured cars or lorries – parked on the forecourt.

Only he could do it. He checked each cupboard, but there was no big container. He climbed out. No one spoke to wish him luck. There was nothing from her, except a look into his eyes, which might have been trust. Or not. The wind slapped at his face and he took a line from where they were to what he thought was the fuel station, with the military there. He stepped out, the clock ticked, a hammer in his mind, some goats scattered from his path and a kid waved to him. Zach walked fast towards the distant road.

He had not replied. Asked by the investigator to explain why his driver had been in Dubai, and how the journey could be considered the state's business, he had stood up, indicated that, as far as he was concerned, the meeting was closed, pushed back the chair and walked towards the door. For the brigadier it was a moment of bluff, which was not called.

He was addressed neither as 'Brigadier Joyberi', nor as 'Joyberi'. He was told that he would be recalled for further questioning and should continue to be available. He had walked out on them because he hadn't known how to answer. Everyone did it: everyone of importance, stature, influence had an account on the far side of the Gulf, in Istanbul, Beirut or Bucharest. They had the 'right' to deal in import and export, the 'right' to avoid punitive taxation, the 'right' to buy development land at a reasonable price, and then to have an interest in the company bidding for the development. He had done what everyone did. He was to be 'available'.

He took the bus.

Reza Joyberi wore his uniform, with a double strip of medal ribbons on his chest. Some on the bus would have assumed that a man of such rank travelled with them to demonstrate his credentials as a 'man of the people'. Most, he realised, were made uncomfortable by his presence. An old man had a seat and rose to offer it. Joyberi saw that he steadied himself on a stick and had lost his right leg – a veteran of the war with Iraq. He declined it. No one talked near him. No one met his eye.

He went to his office. He was saluted at the gate. He walked down the corridor and saw friends, colleagues, rivals in their rooms. None caught his glance. He came to his door and went past it because his name wasn't there. It should have been on a plastic strip at eye-level on the door. It had gone. He backtracked. The new name was that of a lieutenant colonel.

He didn't knock, but pushed open the door. 'You're sitting in my chair.'

'I don't think so.' The officer stayed put and dropped his head to study some papers.

'That's my fucking chair and this is my fucking office.'

The man appeared annoyed at the interruption. 'I was told you had vacated the space and were about to be transferred.'

'Untrue. Get out.'

'I heard either to anti-smuggling operations in the Baluchi desert, or as military attaché in Tajik, Kazakh- or Uzbekistan.' Raza Joyberi was being laughed at.

'Get out.'

'I was told the posting to the wilderness or "nowhere" was the best facing you, but there could be worse. I heard the word "treason" used, and others spoke of "scandal".'

He came at the man fast, his arms outstretched. He focused on his adversary's throat, groped and was dragged back. His raised voice had alerted security, the section of the IRGC responsible for the barracks. He was held respectfully but firmly. He was walked out. The door was closed behind him. He was taken down corridors and into an area to which civilians were brought if they had to be questioned but were not in detention. He was shown to a chair and sat on it. A guard stood inside and the other was outside the door.

He couldn't answer the question put to him: why had his corporal travelled?

His mind was made up, a decision taken. At that moment, confronted by his corporal, he would have put the man on the floor and kicked his head to a pulp. He saw the wife of the corporal in her night clothes, with the blanket fallen from her shoulders. She watched, he kicked – and knew himself destroyed.

Rollo said, 'It's become a mess, Petroc, and you want comfort from me but I'm hard put to offer it. My difficulty matters more to me than yours. A herdsman has reported that there's a bear in the forest, injured or already dead. It's heartbreaking for Stephie and me, the thought of that fine animal alone and suffering. It will have been butchered by some cruel man who imagines he can protect something as mundane as a few bee hives. That's for tomorrow. The defector. Your nerves are at breaking point because you've invested so much of your credit on getting the woman out. You must make up your own mind. I can nudge you but I can't tell you.'

Petroc regretted making the call – but he had no one else to turn to for reassurance.

'Please, Rollo, keep going.'

'He'll be trying to read you. You tell me that the mission faces catastrophe. Keep the mood bright, show confidence and bleed him. Work the hours that God gives you, and get everything out of him that you can. If, then, you need to dump him, there's no harm done. What I always say of these people – they're vain, unpleasant and deceitful. More advice: believe nothing he tells you unless you can verify at least some of it. Petroc, can we finish this? I'm anxious to keep the line free.'

'Of course, Rollo. Difficult hours ahead for all of us.'

She called him. As Dunc Whitcombe had predicted, it had never happened. She was in the kitchen and he was making his bed. It had never happened in his bed. She was at the sink, clearing up their breakfast, and when he had done the hoovering he would lay the fire. She whistled for his attention and pointed through the window. She hadn't asked if he'd slept well. Neither had he asked her. Their eyes had met frequently over the meal but neither had shown that a differing relationship existed between them. Would it last? He didn't know.

He switched off the Hoover, went into the kitchen and stood beside her. She pointed to the track that led off the road and down to the house. Two open jeeps were splashing fast through the puddles. The first carried an officer of rank and his driver; the second bristled with weapons and would have been the big man's escort. She wiped her hands on the towel and he had spun on his heel.

They were together in the living room. The maps were swept off the low table, and the file that had the photographs and biographies was snatched up. He took them into his bedroom, reached for his bag and tripped the padlock. She was beside him with another file, the Contego material, from her room. Everything went into the bag; the padlock was fastened. She gazed into his face – a good-looking woman, too good for him. Then she was up and searched fast around his bed, pulling open the drawers and slamming them shut. The cover story was sacrosanct. Her finger jabbed at him. He would propagate the legend. Gravel scattered close to the house.

They were in the living area, facing the front door. They were kept waiting.

Through the window beside the door they saw him roll on his feet, in polished boots, slap his hands together behind his back and strut a little. He took in their view. He would have seen the main road leading away, the lorry traffic on it and the bend that took it out of sight as it climbed. The hills in the distance were faint in the wet mist. There had been a dusting of snow during the night. It would come on again in the late afternoon, and then – Mandy had predicted – they would be unlikely to see anything of the border and the higher ground from a vantage-point at the rendezvous. The officer moved.

They saw him from Mandy's room and she had left her pyjamas on the bed – they would be a distraction. He admired her for it and wondered if it had been an instructor's suggestion at the Fort one weekend. The officer came around the house and paused by Dunc's window, kept going, did the full circuit and ended up back on the patio again.

There, with the rain falling on his uniform, he paused again. He looked across the scrub. The boy struggled to move a bale of fodder and the horses jostled, trying to hurry him. Ararat was truncated by the clouds, but the officer stared long and hard at the boy – then spun.

He faced them. He had a pistol at his belt, fastened to a lanyard that was looped at his neck and held in a holster of well-buffed leather. Two sergeants or corporals stood behind him: same age, middle forties, experienced. None had smiled or gestured a greeting.

He murmured, 'Best foot forward, Mandy.'

'Just stick with being an idiot and hold the legend.'

Dunc smiled through the windows, as did Mandy. It was not returned, and there was mud on the uppers of those cared-for boots. She opened the doors, letting in the cold and the officer. The others stayed outside.

There had been holidays when Dunc and his wife had stayed in converted barns in farmyards in south Devon or west Wales. They had gone for walks along byways, read the books they had brought with them, and there would have been a pub within easy reach. The farmer would call on them out of courtesy and curiosity. The trick was, Dunc remembered, to stop him sitting down and thinking himself their new best friend or they'd have him for an hour. Not now, not this officer. Their smiles were not reciprocated. They'd proffered hands but the officer's stayed behind his back.

His boots shed mud on the carpet. He spoke quality English. He was, he volunteered, Major Emre Terim.

Dunc held the smile, forced it, and nodded to show interest.

The major had attended the joint-services training command in Oxfordshire, had had experience of the British military from war-games. He commanded a mechanised infantry unit in the town. He had two problems.

'I'm sorry to hear that, Major. What would they be?' Dunc asked.

'The problems are from the murderous fucking bastards, the Kurdish terrorists, who operate in this area.'

Dunc thought the obscenity was designed to shock. He didn't react. 'Very difficult, I'm sure.'

'My second problem is with those fucking scum the smugglers. They move back and forth across the Iran frontier with class-A drugs, people, and kids from Asia for sex perverts in Europe. I detest and despise them.'

'Another extremely difficult problem, I'm sure.'

Would he like tea or coffee? Mandy asked. It was an interruption, might have been from an overzealous housekeeper. He flashed a glance at her, then beaded on Dunc.

'I would not wish to have a third problem added to my professional life.'

'Of course not.'

'It would irritate me to learn that foreign intelligence officers were using my territory for their affairs, pissing on me, shitting on me, as it would annoy you, should I be found pissing or shitting in Oxford. You understand me, sir?'

'I'm Dunc Whitcombe and my friend is Mandy Ross. We seem to be, Major, at cross-purposes. I am, of course, interested in your problems, but we are here to study the environs of Ararat and to see—'

'For intelligence officers to be in this location, staying on these premises and allowing themselves to be linked closely with what I call *fucking scum* is offensive to me.'

He persisted, saw no other route: 'I'm an archaeologist, Major. That is my academic discipline. The chance arose of seeing where the Ark might have been, where Alexander marched, to be on a route travelled by Marco Polo and—'

'You are staying on a criminal's property. You and your *friend* are agents of the British services. Don't treat me as a fool. There is an unpleasant gaol in Diyarbakir and a worse one in Van, but the worst would be the cell block in my garrison camp. Do you wish to experience them? You should be gone tomorrow.'

'I think, with respect, you're in error. Already we're finding fascinating sites to visit—'

'Don't waste my time. Be gone by tomorrow. I don't understand you people, the arrogance. At the college they talked much of "punching above our weight", not of interfering where they were not wanted. It is extraordinary, the conceit. What did you do in Iraq, except fail? What was your success in Afghanistan? Too small to measure. And now you are involved in the affairs of my neighbour, Iran, not your neighbour. Who gives you the right? You stay in the house of a criminal, a smuggler, and at my convenience I will deal with him. Your talk about the mountain is the poorest cover I have heard. Learn some humility, but first you should fuck off by tomorrow. Good day.'

He was gone.

She closed the doors. She saw him walk away and thought the rain might be heavier by the evening.

Two cars came down the main road heading north and towards Khvoy. The rain had eased. He didn't have the luxury of time to slow down as he came closer. A fine drizzle settled on his face.

He had no training and his experience of stress was minimal. Three pumps. A small fast-food outlet at the side of a mini-mart where the cash desk was. A sign pointing to the toilets. A workshop at the back where a car was jacked up. Half a dozen Guard Corps men that he could see, dark olive uniforms. Some had rifles and others had snub-barrelled machine-guns, and were lounging near their transport. Zach felt they were used to being astride their world. Two wandered towards the road and one went into the centre, where the white line was painted; the other stayed close to the drive-in for the fuel station. They paraded their superiority, waved for the drivers to slow, then stop. They were bawled at. A sergeant, a small barrel-shaped man with a straggling beard, a pistol holster flapping against his thigh and a rifle in his hand, came from behind a truck and yelled abuse at the two men.

They were 'shit'. They were 'idiots'. They were a 'disgrace' to their uniforms. Did they not know that down the road two men from the *basij* had been martyred by the foreign bandits? Were their weapons cocked? Did they stop vehicles as they'd been instructed? No one sauntered into the road again. The two cars were checked. Zach came out of the field, his shoes squelching from the bog he had been through. He reckoned he had a few seconds before attention fell on him. He heard two grumble.

They were looking for several men, all British, and one Iranian woman.

The men and the woman would be inside a big orange Volkswagen van, of the sort used for mobile camping.

The two cars they stopped and checked had no common point: an old man and an old woman in the first; a young man, intelligent, well dressed, in the second. They were allowed to go forward after their papers had been examined, the boot of each car lifted and the bonnets. The grumble continued and a motorcycle came close. The rider was yelled at. One motorcycle, one rider, no passenger. Zach crossed the road. A lorry came fast, going south, and the driver ignored the half-hearted gesture for him to slow. It was a big lorry, pulling a trailer, and threw up spray. Zach was surprised that he had, still, evaded attention. He was remembering why so many motorcycles in Iran were underpowered. The tutor at the School had told them that high-performance bikes were used for assassinations in the early days after the revolution by the Communist resistance to the Ayatollah: leading clerics were targets, the judges who passed down the most death sentences and the torturers of the new VEVAK agency. Big bikes came up behind them and they were shot from the pillion by a marksman or had bombs with magnets clamped onto their car roofs, and the bike was away at speed. Nobody in modern Iran was allowed a motorcycle beyond the limited power of 125cc. Gunfire crashed in his ears.

The sergeant stood, legs braced, in the centre of the parking area beyond the pumps and had his weapon jammed at his shoulder. The spent cases tinkled on the concrete. The lorry's brakes and tyres screamed. Zach saw it lurch across the road. The cab swerved and the trailer went ahead. There was the smell of burning rubber. The moment came when the cab might have toppled and the trailer have gone over on its side. Other soldiers crouched in the firing position. The young man in the Audi was out of his seat, left his door open and his engine turning. He lay on his stomach in the road. So did the two old people, the woman covering her husband. There was the stink of the cordite.

A man came down from the cab, about a hundred yards up the road from where the sergeant stood. He came forward, blood running from his forehead. Zach thought it would have smacked the side window. More blood dripped from his nose. He was not intimidated and yelled abuse.

Zach moved. A God-given opportunity . . .

He came past the old couple – the woman in her black *chador* was wriggling off the man and her veil had slipped, which meant modesty was on a back burner. The old man's denture plate had come loose and was half out of his mouth. Zach slipped past the young man. It was a God-given opportunity, and would hardly be repeated. Every man in uniform was watching the lorry driver with one eye and the sergeant with the other.

The shouting was at fever pitch. A lorry driver with his face dented and a sergeant in the Guards Corps, who believed that insufficient respect had been shown him. Zach had little time to play with because his watch showed an hour had been used up.

He went past the café. The customers were cowering on the floor and the owner was by a back wall. There was the door for the toilets and a man huddled there, but Zach shrugged at him and gave no explanation of the gunfire. He went into the repair shed where he found two men. They had a radio turned up loud and there was the throb of a generator, the whine of an acetylene cutter and a welder. Zach – on the hoof – gave his explanation.

'There's a complete fool out there, a sergeant who thinks he's a general. They have a road block for foreign terrorists, and a lorry goes by with a load of furniture or pistachios or luxuries for those bastards in Tehran and it doesn't slow down. The driver has a schedule so he doesn't stop. The sergeant believes that was disrespectful to his high rank – a sergeant! – and starts shooting. Now the lorry's blocking the road and the driver's hurt. Soon they'll be fighting. I have a problem.'

The radio was turned off, the cutter unplugged, the welder shut down. They could hear the abuse yelled from the road. They were starting to shift and wanted a front-row view.

Zach had his wallet out. 'I can do it with dollars. My wife's in the car. She's pregnant, very heavy – maybe a week, two weeks to go. I could burn in Hell for this – I didn't fill the tank and we're out. We're going to the hospital in Khvoy for a check-up, I hope routine. She lost one – six months, born dead. Please, a can for the fuel. And will you fill it? I don't want to be at the front with those idiots. Please, it's for my wife. Just ten litres. We're not from these parts but from the south. Heaven bless your kindness.'

Two ten-dollar bills were taken from his hand. He did the shrug, helpless, of a man who had cried for help and expressed sincere gratitude. The price of an old jerry-can and ten litres would be half of what he had given them. He palmed another ten-dollar bill, which was taken.

Zach said to their backs, 'The man's a lunatic. I'll be here for an hour if he sees me at the pumps and my wife's appointment is . . .'

He waited. He came out of the workshop, rounded the corner of the building and stood by the toilet door. The sergeant and the lorry driver were toe to toe. They were screaming into each other's faces. The audience grew. A mechanic was at the nearest pump and had the nozzle in the can. The lorry driver shuffled, heavy-footed, readied himself and swung. The rifle was coming up, and two men, one uniformed, one in the kit of the garage company, inserted themselves. There was a scrum.

Zach ran. The mechanic still had the nozzle in the can, but Zach snatched the handle, slapped down the clasp and was gone. A last look at the fight: every eye on it, none on him. A last glance at the watch on his wrist – taunting before, now mocking – and he went over the road and started across the sodden grass. Murphy's law – fucking Murphy. He was well into the first field and the nearest goats were watching him. He thought he could see the wagon in the mist, far away, and the shout echoed.

Who was he? He should stop. He *must* stop.

Zach imagined a rifle raised to a shoulder and thought he heard the rasp of it being armed. He seemed to feel the mark on his back where the view through the sight latched. He did what a lorry driver might have done, one doing heavy haulage in north-west Iran or in the south-west Midlands of his own country. He kept his back to the garage and wondered if the fight had finished. He raised his free hand and did the one-finger salute. He kept going, neither faster nor slower.

No shot was fired.

He carried the fuel and the herd parted for him. The kids' dogs came close, yapping, but stayed clear of his ankles. He went as fast as he was able.

A boy brought their coffee. It was always late in the morning when he came and they had worked enough hours to need the break. Their throats would be dry with the stink of old engine oil and from the fumes when they ran the engines they had repaired. With the rain, the pollution pressed down and was trapped in the yard.

The two old friends revelled in the names they had acquired – Highness and Excellency – and would take the opportunity to sit and glance at the newspaper. The boy always brought the paper too. The rule of the mullahs was conservative and the paper reflected their views, but both men thought it sensible to read those opinions, be able to repeat them verbatim and survive. The order book was nearly full and they worked every hour they could because it was a diversion and their nagging worries could be pushed back if they toiled on the benches. They put in long hours . . . and missed her already. She had been like a candle that illuminated their lives. Now only a dim bulb was left.

They had their coffee. They shared the paper. Highness had the news section and Excellency had the supplement with the teasers and puzzles.

The breath whistled in Highness's mouth. He reached a hand behind his head and scratched hard at the skin where he had long before gone bald. He passed the page. So clear. A big photograph of a body, its upper torso and shoulders covered, a small photo of an ID card and a name. A good likeness. Johnny had been theirs. To them Johnny had been a god, and the day he had died had been one when age had seemed to catch them and make a mockery of any serenity they had felt in recent years. Johnny had brought her here and – from afar and with correctness – they had loved her. The captain had invited himself, had swept aside her reserve, had made them both laugh and smile, and had treated her with a tender love that might have been temporary but might have lasted. It had hurt when his death in combat was reported. The intelligence officer, infatuated, had tracked her to the yard, had insinuated himself into her life. How was it possible to send such a man away? Gone now. Never liked, never wanted.

The paper the boy had brought the day before had carried a story of a shooting at a road block on the main trunk road to the north-west, the borders; two men had died there. They knew how far she had gone, and thought they would have heard if she had been taken. Both men had prayed the quiet words used by random believers. Excellency held the paper closer to his face, then unhooked his spectacles and used them to magnify a whitish speck on the stones, near to the rail, between two sleepers and close to the hand that protruded from the covering.

'Even he had it.'

'Even him.'

'You remember their laughter when she gave the picture to Johnny, no face shown.'

'Her eyes were clear – wonderful eyes.'

'And the soldier had the picture. You remember he told her – and us – that the picture of her, all black but for the eyes, would be with him, against his chest, all the time he was at war.'

'A sniper shot him. This man had her picture too.'

'And is dead. Three pictures, three men. To take a picture from her is to be dead.'

'The guards, they were cowboys, but the boy with the Farsi was outstanding – you said from the south and I said from the south-east. Anyway, as good as a native. He persuaded her. Will he be rewarded?'

'She is so beautiful.'

'The most beautiful.'

'Will he be rewarded as they were, given a photograph? Will it kill him? Is he condemned if she gives him the photograph?'

Excellency crumpled the page of the paper and threw it accurately into the bin near the door. He swigged the rest of his coffee and tossed the cardboard beaker after the newspaper. He went back to his bench, then snarled. 'It was too easy to love her.'

'You've not done this before.' Not a question, an accusation, intended to belittle.

'No,' Sidney answered.

'It's what I do. I'm a babysitter,' Father William pressed.

'Don't mind me,' Sidney said, 'but I'd call that an empty life.'

'And I share that opinion with Auntie and Nobby. We're as one.'

'Lives without purpose. I weep for you. And don't forget I'm on this team because Petroc wanted me. He was given you, with all your skills and expertise, but he wanted me – needed me.'

'So, where do you feel your understanding comes from?' Father William held a mug of coffee and his hand shook, stopping it. It was in the nature of the work that confrontations were used only to serve a purpose: without meaning, they were valueless. He had been pushed forward. Auntie wasn't a fighter and always backed away from verbal confrontation, and Nobby was a coaster. Petroc Kenning had done the questioning; there had been a light reference between him and the corporal about a castle visit. Auntie did not think a loosening of the leash appropriate, and Nobby rated it premature; Father William had claimed insight and called the Iranian 'as slippery as a bloody frog'.

Sidney had won Petroc's support. It wasn't for them to argue. Father William couldn't have put his finger on the reason for his concern, but it nagged. He had lost, and out in the corridor he had snapped at Sidney – insufferable, a chancer, and one of those who, as his dad would have said, 'sails too close to the wind'. He repeated: 'What's the spring from which your God-given insight flows?'

'Just life's rich tapestry. Having a nose for people, finding out how they tick. It's an art form. Try it.'

The previous afternoon had been an emotional journey for all of them. The long drive to Judenburg, the story he had told, the new bridge in place where the old iron one had been, the tumbling weir water and the swirl in the big pool below it. They would all have had little difficulty in summoning the images of young soldiers with fixed bayonets or wooden clubs as they forced the men, women and children across the bridge into the arms of the Red Army. They could picture the men who had held their children to their chests, clutched a wife's hand, sprawled over the side of the bridge and plummeted down. They could watch the soldiers, in khaki, working the banks of the river and shooting those trying to escape. *His* reaction had been strange: he had listened, said little on the drive home, had sat down in the evening, worked with them, done what had been asked of him, and again that morning had seemed to co-operate, as if his commitment was resurrected. Father William's wife might have read it better than he did, because she had more education and claimed better nous. He shrugged. 'So be it.'

'He recognises what we're doing for him, for his wife. He's grateful and sings.'

'Right, forget it.'

'Nothing to forget. Come with us. Amazing place, where Richard the Lionheart was a prisoner. A bit of a climb. You up for that?'

He heard the chuckle but turned his back and went inside again. They had broken and were smoking.

Mehrak dragged on the cigarette. The talk that morning had been about the diary of the brigadier: whom he met, whom he considered most talented, who had the ear of the Supreme Leader. Who would the fighters follow if an attack came? Now it was conversation, not truths.

He could have said, 'She hates me. We go for days without speaking except about housekeeping money and the utility bills, whether I am at home for dinner and what time she should serve my meal. We don't talk – we have nothing to talk about. We have not had even the pretence of love for years.' He didn't.

He could also have said, 'We had no sex. It is my right to have sex with my wife. She would not so I hit her. I lost my temper. One blow, to the face. She was bruised. She could have said to my mother and her own mother when she saw them that the bruise was from an accident. But she gave no explanation – so they knew the truth. She took her bruise to work. I was made to look like a violent fool. Since then nothing. To have sex with her would have been to rape her. I think she would have fought with her life.' He said nothing.

He might have leaned forward, demanded confidentiality, and said, 'The brigadier arranged our marriage with my father. Everyone I work with knows that Farideh, my wife, is a beautiful woman. Many, I know, are jealous of me . . . I could divorce her. In legal terms, in Iran, it is easy. In reality, I'm the poor fool who has not found love with a beautiful woman. "Perhaps he cannot satisfy her", they would say, "is incapable, inadequate. Maybe he wants to fuck a boy." I would be humiliated.' He didn't.

He might have confessed, 'It is four years and some months since she allowed me. I go across the Gulf. Do I want a woman? I am on my knees for a woman. I burn for it. They took me to that place. She was an old whore with a slack stomach and I could see the veins in her legs. I couldn't do it – I love my wife.'

He could have let the tears flow, taken a handkerchief offered him and said, 'I thought that if she was brought out of Iran she would be far from everything she knew and would come back to me, that I would be her rock. It was to win her that I asked you to bring her. The hope that she would learn here to love me.' He held back the tears.

Last, he could have told Petroc Kenning, the enemy, of two evenings spent crouched with an ear to the pipes and of what he had heard. 'You had neither the skills nor the resources to bring her out so now she is hunted, and the men with her. She will be caught. She will be arrested, tried and sentenced. She will be . . . I love her.' He did not, and reached for another cigarette.

'I want to help. I want you to be pleased with what I can offer you. I want to be trusted. We have fine castles in Iran, and I have seen some in Syria and Lebanon. I look forward to seeing the one where your king, Richard of the Lion's Heart, was kept a prisoner. It will be a privilege for me – and you know, Mr PK, that I am sincerely grateful for what you do for me – and for my wife.'

He came across the field. Exhaustion slowed him. On the way out, towards the petrol station, Zach had taken a fast but meandering line from the camper van across the open ground. He had hopped from one tussock to another when there was bog. Now he had ten litres in the plastic fuel container. It grew steadily heavier. His tiredness and increasing desperation about the time led him to blunder erratically forward.

There were places where he went in up to his knees, then had to drag out his feet as the mud clung to them. Once, a shoe had come off and he had gone down on all fours, had reached into the water and groped until he found it.

His sight of the wagon was blurred. There was mud on his face.

Two of them carried weapons. One, Ralph, was by the bonnet and Wally was at the tail. She stood by the open side door. He wondered where she had hidden the pistol that had been offered to him and she had taken. Only when he was close did Wally start to unscrew the cap for the fuel tank. None of them could have done it. None of them could have helped him. He wouldn't be thanked. Zach thought she was now a part of their team because she had taken the gun. Getting the fuel would not have given him entry to their club. He was swaying as he took the last few steps. Ralph reached down from the track, grasped his hand and pulled him up, then took the container from him.

Mikey called, through the open door, 'We heard the gunfire.'

'Difficult not to.'

'Thought you might have started a war.'

He listened as the stuff gurgled down the pipe and leaned against the door. He was wrecked. She was close to him but didn't touch him. He wasn't thanked, might have been, should have been, but wasn't. They couldn't have achieved what he had. Zach wondered if each of them, in their own way, was jealous of his skill with the language. He might have expected, on those last exhausted strides, that the praise would be fulsome, his back slapped, and that he would be permitted to enter their tight circle. Her eyes held him, challenged him. He glanced at his watch. They no longer had hours: the time remaining to them was measured in minutes. Wally threw the can into the field. They were running late. He flopped on to the bench seat, making it filthy with mud. The girl from South Island would have laughed. Quite late.

15

They parked.

Mikey had the map. He had made Ralph drive round a block twice, then decided where they would stop. To the front there was an arcade of shops, and at the back there were loading bays. Zach reckoned it the same architectural non-event he'd seen in a hundred English towns or cities; the concrete was stained, the paint was flaking and there were puddles. Mikey said that was where they would wait, except Zach.

Zach thought they were already late. He'd assumed they would drive into the square where they were to do the transfer, pile out of the camper, dump it, get on board the new wheels. Mikey would have seen his confusion because he said, 'We're the customer, they'll wait for us. They're likely in a side street, watching for us, and they'll come running when we pitch up. But there's a hunt on and I'm not having the five of us stuck on a pavement with the gear. You meet them and bring the transport to us.' That was what he had been told.

The bloody rain had started again, heavy now. His legs ached from crossing the fields. He had no headgear, no umbrella, would be drenched by the time he'd done the walk and met the wheels.

Only Mikey spoke. Not Ralph or Wally. The hands slid on his watch. Late . . .

Zach hated that he was one of life's punctual people. Ralph had driven into the town cautiously, hadn't overtaken or used his horn, had given room to jay-walkers. Big dilemma: to keep, as near as possible, to the schedule or stay unnoticed and unremarkable, except that the colour of the wagon and its unique lines were a give-away if the description had been broadcast.

'Good if she came with me.'

'I don't think so.'

Farideh would have heard Zach's words, but might not have caught Mikey's answer. She was already slipping off the bench seat towards the wide-open side door.

'She'd have a feel for the place. I'd never heard of it, know nothing about it, and she'll read it better than—'

'She stays.'

'I was trying to say—'

A hand was on his arm. He was shoved away. No ceremony. 'Get moving.'

She watched him, gave the slightest shrug and a small grimace, then eased back onto the bench seat. With her fingers she adjusted the scarf round her hair and dropped the veil over her face.

He was gone. Another look at his watch. On the schedule, they should have been aboard the people-carrier three minutes ago, and he thought – from Mikey's map – it was a ten-minute walk to where it would be waiting, six minutes' jogging or four running. But he couldn't: his legs were leaden from the bogs. He looked like a tramp. There were derelicts who lived in the woods off the A445, outside Leamington and beyond Cubbington. They did gardening in the summer and lived like animals in the winter. Some said they should be ignored, others that they should be moved on . . . He could hardly have had Wally or Ralph do close escort for him, with their goatee beards, their shades, the waistcoats with every pocket filled, grenades, spare magazines, radios, phones and a machine pistol held at the ready. He would have liked to have her beside him. Wrong. He was in Iran, the Islamic Republic: she would have been a half-pace behind.

He had rounded the side of the arcade and was heading past the shops. A tailor, a fast-food outlet, a barber, second-hand furniture. He went to the lights. The traffic came, filled two lanes going to his left and was solid in two lanes going to his right. He couldn't stampede across. The derelicts in those woods . . . He couldn't clean himself up.

There was no trust. There were two groups and no melding:

himself and her; Mikey, Wally and Ralph. They would have thought, because she had once bugged out on them, that he and she might get aboard the wheels and drive away. Maybe easier for two than for five. That possibility wouldn't have crossed Zach's mind. He reversed it: he seemed to see the three of them inside the camper, slamming the door, giving the driver a thwack on the shoulder, then leaving him and her. But tension and trust were rarely in the same bed together. They wouldn't have let her go for fear of being abandoned. He needed to slap his own face. There was a good guy, a site manager, back home – he'd been a long time on his father's payroll – who would have done it for him, or clipped his shin with the steel cap of a safety boot.

The traffic halted. He hurried to cross the road. A police car was stopped at the lights. He felt so vulnerable. There was a truck behind it with uniforms and guns. He imagined eyes stripping him. To run or walk . . . the compromise. The hands were slipping on the face of the watch. More time lost. He didn't dare, then, to run, but he walked briskly. There was an avenue of trees, a small park and at the end of it the square that led into the pedestrian approach to the Shams Tabrizi Tower – and he'd studied the poet's work composed nine hundred years before, and . . . He missed the kerb.

Zach fell forward and groped with his hands to break the impact. His shoulder caught a woman's knees. She staggered. He rolled as he fell and the woman was pushed aside, her two plastic bags scattering. His hip hit the thigh of a man carrying a craftsman's toolbox. The pavement was slippery with a sheen of rain: Zach saw a wild face staring at him, the fear in it. Some people stopped to help the woman and retrieve her shopping, others were concerned for the man with the toolbox. Someone helped Zach to his feet. The lights changed. The police car went on but all the eyes behind the windows watched him, and all the heads in the military truck were turned to the pavement.

He said he was all right. He said it, God be blessed, in Farsi. Instinctive. He shrugged off the hands. The kindness of people almost suffocated him. Etiquette would have demanded he praised them and showed gratitude, but he did not. He was gone. Two faces, many times life-size, glowered at his back, but he barely noticed them. It was late. He was a stranger in a town he didn't know and had only the directions dinned into him by Mikey to guide him.

The town of Khvoy, in west Azerbaijan province, was known as the sunflower centre of Iran.

It was a little more than eight hundred kilometres from the country's capital, Tehran, but there were police barracks, an army camp and the necessary communication towers to guarantee that the exhortations from responsible officials for the apprehension of criminals and terrorists had reached it. The sunflower trade produced cooking oils that were sold and processed through middle men across Europe. With efficient labelling, many who lived in countries boycotting Iranian goods were in ignorance of its source.

Trading had always been good for the community. It was astride the Silk Road, and reeked of history and old conflicts. Tamar of Georgia had been there as a conqueror in the thirteenth century, then Mongols, Ottoman Turks, and the forces of Imperial Russia and the Soviet Union. The town had more than its fair share of tourists, who spent a few hours photographing and drinking coffee, then wandered away to the bus station for the crossing to Van or Doğubeyazıt. Few would have looked like a wretch who slept rough. They would all have possessed the necessary paperwork to leave Iran without difficulty. Many would have nurtured the image of a Turkish café that evening, a beer or several, and women would dump their shrouds. As it had always been for a community on the Silk Road, the trade through Khvoy was in commodities of value – not merely sunflower oil.

That afternoon the Azerbaijani who traded in packages – not his cousin who ferried passengers – used his phone to make many calls. All were coded, brief and from an upstairs room at the kebab shop on Shahid Samazzade Street.

He spoke to a colleague; as a Kurd from Doğubeyazıt, a man he trusted. They were business partners and enjoyed mutual respect. The seventy-nine packages were on the way. There were, however, matters beyond his control on the road going west from Khvoy: road blocks, reinforcements of Revolutionary Guard Corps units and patrols in armoured vehicles. The only mercy God had shown them that day was the low cloud ceiling that had grounded the helicopters.

His driver, he said, expected to take longer on the journey and would not be at the transfer point on the frontier that evening. He would spend a night edging close, then lie up at a remote farmstead for the daylight hours and move forward again at dusk. The packages would be delayed by some twenty-four hours.

It was not a small matter. He knew that his associate, a man with a reputation to uphold, would have to pass messages along a tenuous chain that ran the breadth of Turkey, then to the haulage contractors crossing to mainland Europe, who would receive and conceal the two-kilo packages. The delay would have to be factored into a timetable drawn up by men living between Rotterdam in the Netherlands and the Kurdish heartland of Turkey, some 4,600 kilometres. The continuity of supply was uppermost in the Azerbaijani's mind.

That day an additional matter nagged. He had never been close to his cousin but they met every few days to discuss the tactics of working the border and exchange information on new officials who had moved into those sectors. They talked about the major who now had charge of Doğubeyazıt but he was not their prime concern: they were focused on the Iranian side of the border. There was chaos. Some said a full battalion of Revolutionary Guard Corps troops was in the town and working through the villages to the east, west, north and south of Khvoy. They had come from as far away as Tabriz, and no one knew their officers or senior NCOs. Bribes could not be paid. Difficulties faced him and his cousin. They had talked, and disagreed. He would delay by twenty-four hours with the packages; his cousin would go for the border that night. The Azerbaijani had wished his cousin well, and assumed the money was good. What else mattered? Money ruled on the border. It always had.

He could picture the make of the vehicle and its colour. He was late for the rendezvous. In his mind's eye he saw the Jew and heard the man's emphasis on punctuality. The vehicle would not wait for them. Zach ran.

He was past the avenue where the bare trees dripped rain, had crossed another main road and was in the small park. Men and women hurried past him, desperate to be out of the weather, but some kids were still playing football and splashing in puddles. Ahead of him was the square, then the pedestrian area and the tomb of Shams Tabrizi.

He thought he saw it.

The vehicle would be blue. How many shades of blue were there? Bright blue, dark or light? There was a people-carrier on the far side of the square and traffic streamed past it. He tried to stretch his stride. A glance at his watch, as the rain trickled off his forehead into his eyes. His view of the hands was blurred. He thought he was twelve minutes late, and still had half of the park to cross, a road, then the centre of the square where there was a bust on a plinth, more traffic and a blue people-carrier on the far side.

He hobbled forward, lurching. He was stared at. He kept on, didn't make eye contact. He was late, and the Israeli had said that the transport wouldn't wait. It had.

He ran through the rain.

Exhaust fumes came from the back of the vehicle. The driver was impatient to be gone. More military trucks were entangled in the traffic passing the people-carrier. There were police in the square, two pairs of them, and they carried automatic weapons. Zach didn't think it was safe to run, to make an exhibition of himself: few people, an old law of life, had good reason to run.

There was a driver alone in the front, two passengers behind him. Zach saw that clearly. Then a lorry came with a long load. One of the pairs of police was near but they talked and smoked, didn't seem interested in him. The military trucks, open to the elements at the back, cruised by. The lorry with the long load went slowly. Only the pavement and two lanes remained, and then he would reach the vehicle. Hope surged.

He was panting, about to step off the pavement, when he heard the scream of a horn. A whistle blew. A stream of cars came past him and his foot wavered on the kerb, inching towards the gutter. The whistle came again. Zach looked for the source, had to turn, and one of the policemen, in the nearest pair, had the whistle to his mouth. Their eyes met. The policeman gestured to him – he should step back, the traffic had right of way on the road. He did so meekly and waited on the pavement. The lorry with the long load had moved on in the clogged mass of cars, vans and pick-ups, and was gone.

The gap yawned. The space was empty. Another car, a black Paykan with a dented bumper, jockeyed with a delivery van. Horns were hit. More whistles from the police, and whether Zach crossed the traffic, took his life or did not, was off the policemen's agenda. He ran forward.

His legs were weak, and he needed to dance round the backs of vehicles and skip past the front bumpers. He felt one car in the outer lane touch his knee. He tried to follow the people-carrier. It and the lorry with the long load went faster. The road, going away from the pedestrian area in front of the tomb, was straight and the lights ahead were green. The gap opened.

Zach tried to suck air into his lungs. He remembered, long ago, a teacher for year ten had demanded cross-country running from the kids. They'd all start together, then the fit ones would pull away. Zach Becket was always in the second group. He would see the gap between the front of the field and the also-rans widening but could never close it.

He couldn't shout – he wouldn't have been heard and, in any case, he hadn't the breath. Far down the road, past many bare trees, there was another set of lights. As best he could, Zach sprinted. He saw the back of the people-carrier. A glimpse of hope: the traffic had spurted and now slowed. Brakelights flashed at the rear of the people-carrier.

Two jeeps, close together, went in the other direction on the far side of the road. Zach lost his balance and thought he was going to fall: he had trodden on wet leaves and skidded. He didn't go down.

He kept running. There were moments when he thought he was closing on the people-carrier, when he believed he would reel in the gap. Far up the street, the lights were his last chance.

Men gazed at him and stood aside, women gave him room, kids backed away from him.

A feeder road came into the main route. He hadn't seen it so he was in full stride and halfway over it, vehicles going both sides of him, horns blaring, and he saw where he was. He heard another whistle, and a policeman yelled at him, but he kept running. He could barely see. Nothing ahead was clear.

The fumes from the exhaust of the people-carrier merged with those of two lorries in a different lane and with what other cars pumped out. The gap didn't lessen.

When to give up? He could no longer see the people-carrier.

Zach didn't do surrender. He hadn't at home in family arguments, or the School, or on the building sites when, as the son of the boss, he was ripe for being smacked down. He kept running – which was pointless because he had lost sight of the blue people-carrier, and he no longer knew how great the gap was. The lights were in front of him. If he had given up, he would have had to turn, retrace his route, head for the pedestrian area in front of the tomb and the shopping arcade, where there would be the smell of kebabs and music belting from the barber's. He would have to go round the back and do the honesty bit with the guys and her. The guys would swear, and he thought she would challenge him. Not verbally, but with her eyes. She would tell him with them that he was inadequate.

Zach ran on. He went slower. Then he realised he had started to keep level with the vehicles and was passing them. A queue had built.

The traffic lights were in front of him. He reeled forward on the pavement, was either a drunk or at the end of a long-distance race.

He staggered towards the bright traffic lights that were slung on a cable across the road, showing red.

Zach saw the blue. Saw the shape. Could have said a prayer.

He willed the lights not to change. He lurched the last steps and came closer to the back of the blue people-carrier. He passed two cars, and the strength left his legs. Tears welled. He banged on the front passenger window, then snatched at the door handle. The lights were changing. The door opened. He heard screams.

A woman cowered away from him. It was the children behind her who were screaming. The man who drove, bearded, turbaned, aged, thrust out a gnarled hand, caught the handle on the inside of the door and heaved it shut. Zach's hand was caught in it outside. His arm was wrenched, the pain came and he let go. The people-carrier pulled away.

He stood on the pavement. Now his view was clear.

It was black, barely similar, except in outline, to the one he had seen parked and waiting before the lorry had obscured it. He couldn't have said how long he'd been chasing the wrong vehicle.

He started on the journey back and went slowly. He had to force himself forward at each step, the rain in his eyes and the wind beating into his face.

They had no vehicle to drive them to the route out, and no guide to lead them.

There was a clear answer, a plausible one, to the business of the horses and their work.

The boy, Egid, had come for them two hours before and now led them back. They had found the sight emotional because of the extraordinary backdrop against which it was played. Mandy had asked Dunc how she could go back to her suburban home now. He had said he had no idea.

Then he said, 'They had the call. The cargo's not coming.'

She said, 'But plenty already through and plenty in the pipeline, so a hitch over a delivery won't break the bank.'

'Had the call and turned round.'

'Not an option we're looking at.'

She imagined that her team, on the far side, would be pressing on. Straightforward for a cache of class-A narcotics to be delayed, but not for people to be held back. Their phones had flickered often enough with the updates that spoke of the net that was tightening.

'I want to go.'

The murk of early evening would soon close in. She supposed the tension of the business in hand had bitten into her. Her stomach was knotted and she felt sick. She looked at her watch every three or four minutes. She was concerned that the toad-like major, who spoke such fluent English, might show.

'I'm not disagreeing, Mandy.'

'This place is like a bloody gaol. They should be on their way.'

'Should be.'

'Give me five minutes. I'd prefer to be out there – snow, sleet, whatever – waiting in the right place rather than pacing around here. Five minutes.'

She left him. He was looking out across the patio beyond the rough ground. The horses and the boy would have been dwarfed by Ararat. Mandy Ross, experienced counter-intelligence officer, supreme analyst of information coming into Vauxhall Cross, had never felt so feeble. They would go up the road and follow it to a junction, then turn onto a track, as they had been told, and wait. She would be there for as long as it took.

'No bag, no suitcase of your own,' Reza Joyberi had told his wife.

Another bus ride home, and more veterans of the war with Iraq wanting to stand and give their seats to him in recognition of his rank. His mind was in turmoil and he'd waved them away.

'The child's sports bags are what you take, the Nike ones I brought from Beirut. Fill one for yourself.'

She had been surprised to see him home again at that hour. She was trained as a doctor but no longer practised because her mother had died young and she had remained at home to look after her child. She had no financial need to work, and her husband was more of a visitor than a resident. A car stood at the bottom of the road, four men in it. He had seen a mobile lifted as he had passed it.

'Fill one bag for him. Nothing else. He should wear tennis clothes, and have his racquets.'

He had been to the safe and taken out cash in bank notes: several million rials, and several thousand American dollars. His wife, of course, had jewellery. What else was there to buy at Damascus International, and at Beirut's airport? The pieces of real value, rings and necklaces, earrings and brooches, were wrapped in a handkerchief at the bottom of her handbag. She would wear modest *hijab*. Also in her handbag there were two passports, hers and the boy's, with altered names. She didn't question him, never had and wouldn't start now. She was Noor, meaning 'Light', and their marriage was based on respect for each other. Her father was retired, in good health, and had commanded a unit of the *basij*. He could not, with any honesty, tell her she would see her parents again, or return to Tehran.

'When we go out of the door we will all be laughing – we don't have a care in the world – and we're a family. You don't look back because you have no reason to. This is hard but necessary. When you get there, you'll text me. Ring no one else till I'm with you, perhaps in two days or a week. Ring *nobody* and don't use the mobile after the text. Lose it.'

She was an intelligent woman: she would understand that the security of the Iranian élite was as precarious as it had been for the Shah's people, and for those who had led the revolution in the early days after the return of the Imam. She had not asked why, and had not asked what had destroyed them. She had not asked him when the world she knew would collapse. She would have noted that his driver, a man of limited importance, was no longer outside the door at dawn or late in the evening. She didn't need to ask questions and would understand that they faced personal catastrophe, the likelihood of arrest and conviction, the possibility of execution. It would hurt her to leave her parents. Many had, many more would have to.

What loyalty did he feel now towards the revolution? None. In the hall, where no one could see them, he kissed her and clung to his son, then prised them off him. He told them to smile and laugh on the doorstep. She checked her bag for the passports and airline tickets. She would explain to the child either on the aircraft or when it had landed. He had not known how to.

'Have a good game. Play well. Make sure you win. God go with you.'

The dusk was falling and it was a foul night. With luck, the car at the end of the road would have steamed windows and a fug of cigarette smoke, which would give them a poor view of his wife taking the boy to play tennis. He waved, stood under the light in front of the door so that he couldn't be missed, then went back inside. They were booked on the direct flight, mid-evening, from Imam Khomeini International to Istanbul. They waved back. His wife drove past the watchers to the end of their road and was gone. He went back inside the house, moving from room to room, noting everything that was familiar – their bedroom, her wardrobes, the one with his uniforms, the boy's room, everything that was precious to them. It was because she was intelligent that she hadn't questioned him, had known they lived on shifting sands. He saw everything, then pulled down the blinds. He started to fill a rucksack, took a weapon from the back of the safe and food from the refrigerator. He played music loudly in the kitchen, and switched the TV on too. He was destroyed – not only by the corporal, but by the corporal's wife.

'She'll be over tonight, PK, won't she?'

'That's what I'm hoping, Sidney.'

'I think he's making an effort now.'

'Seems to be.'

'Not that anyone shares my opinion.'

'We all have the same aim, Sidney – to suck the little beggar dry.'

'You're talking like your uncle would have – they were some scrapes we had. Did I tell you about the party at the Russian embassy when Mr Hector supposedly went off for a leak and managed to get into the naval attaché's office? He had his Minox in his pocket, but was caught and thrown out. All he had was a snap of their annual-leave chart. God, we laughed, and there was the time—'

'Thank you, Sidney.'

'I always say, and so did Mr Hector, that if you can't laugh . . '

He betrayed himself: 'Sidney, I'm not that bothered by what you and my uncle achieved here. What's going on there exercises me. It's not easy, and it's unpredictable. It'll be a waiting game here, so I'm happy for you, him and the boys to be clambering over the rocks. Don't hurry back.'

Sidney said it would be light for another hour, and the weather had eased. Quite pleasant out there. By now they would have done the pick-up in Khvoy – wherever that was. They had, of course, all the communications gear they needed for a link, but each time the machines were switched on they left footprints, as clear as those on a wet beach, and signatures. They always said in Ceauçescu Towers, that bad news beat good news by a mile. He imagined that, up there on the fourth floor, Tadeuz Fenton was by now in a well-practised mode of damage limitation and the buck would have been passed. Where would it end up? He flexed his hands, cracked the joints of his fingers. It would be in his palms, if bad news beat good to the tape. And the corporal wanted to go and look at a castle. So be it.

He went up the stairs. Down the corridor, the door of Mehrak's room was closed and he heard low music playing inside. He had been in the room set aside as the 'command post' for most of the afternoon: he had spoken four times to Tadeuz and Sara Rogers, and had had the intercepts force-fed to him. Petroc Kenning was frustrated: he couldn't picture Khvoy, or visualise where the pick-up would have been done. He couldn't imagine the hills, mountains, roads over which the first part of the flight would be made . . . but the silence from there was golden.

Only when he was clear of the outskirts of Khvoy did the driver rummage in a pocket for his mobile phone. He called a nephew who lived in Tabriz.

The Azerbaijani driver who dealt with people was surprised that an arrangement made under the umbrella of the Jews had not worked out. His nephew would call a business colleague who operated from Shahpur.

The Israelis were always reliable and organised so he did much business with them. They paid poorly but were regular and provided him with a good income overall, most of which could be paid into the Bank Respublika on Baku's Jafar Jabbali Street. They demanded complete discretion and total punctuality to set schedules. He delivered.

His nephew's colleague would call a travel agent across the border in Van, and the message would have travelled nearly to its destination.

He couldn't have waited any longer. He owed it to himself – his ultimate health and his neck – to be gone, and to the two clients who were already inside the people-carrier. One was a student activist, plainly frightened – he never stopped smoking; the other was a middle-aged man of the Baha' faith. The Azerbaijani didn't involve himself in politics or religion, and didn't understand why those of the Baha' faith were persecuted. His concern was money-making. Activists and heretics were a good source, but the Jews were the best. There should have been five more passengers to fill the people-carrier, but he could have waited no longer – there were police and military patrols in Khvoy.

The travel agent in Van would call the trader in Doğubeyazıt to tell him how many mules were needed that night, and why the number was reduced. There were many traders in the Kurdish town, but this was cheapest: he used mules, which were uncomfortable, slow and stubborn, not horses. He gave his message: 'They did not come, I could not wait longer, they were not here. There should be no blame for me.'

It was done. He drove to the north-west on a side road towards Maku. Ahead there would be a four-wheel-drive Daihatsu, then a scramble across the open hillside in the snow. There would be times when patrols came close and the fugitives would lie in terror in the darkness, barely daring to breathe. Then there would be the mules to ride, and last there would be the Turkish Army, which had units out each night, hunting smugglers. Its men could not be bought and would hand back to the Iranian authorities anyone they caught in flight. One day, he dreamed, he would return to Baku and live without the stresses of working the border. He drove on.

What would they do, those he had left behind, if they were not already in custody, not already dead? He would have said, based on many years' experience, that it was impossible to go into the hills and the mountains and cross the frontier without guides.

They did not come . . .

He saw her. Zach was past the arcade, then around the corner and walking fast towards the loading bays.

She gazed at him. He knew her from the trainers that protruded beneath the hem of the *chador*. They would have belonged to the girl from New Zealand and were white with three red stripes on the sides and the Adidas mark. He knew her, she knew him, seemed to take half a pace forward, then backed away.

Just before she tracked behind the building, she looked beyond him. Zach turned. A crunch under his feet. He had stood on a syringe. There was another at his feet and more against a wall. He saw used condoms abandoned among rubbish. Everywhere else had been so tidy and clean, but now he was in a junkies' corner. Maybe it was a place where boys brought girls or other boys. There was a door, closed, and three heads peered at him. A policeman appeared. She had seen the man follow him. He was young and wore a well-laundered uniform, what Zach could see of it under the wet-weather anorak. He was called.

He would have appeared to a policeman as a dealer who lived rough, was likely an addict himself, and sold to kids who could pay for what went into a syringe. The policeman followed him, had not yet reached for his pistol.

Zach didn't know whether to go forward or back. He could see now into the bay where the wagon had been and it was empty. There was a scurry of movement at the edge of his eyeline, and three boys, teenagers, running. The policeman didn't bother to chase or try to block. Bigger fish: a dealer, an adult addict.

This was where it ended.

The policeman called Zach forward. He was a good-sized man and looked fit. Zach doubted he would have trekked across boggy, sodden ground to a petrol station, then lugged fuel in a can back the way he'd come. The policeman told him to come forward and put his hands on top of his head. He had his back to her.

The policeman was tasked to patrol, with his partner, that part of Khvoy, with particular attention to the loading bays where druggies came. Mikey and the other guys had found themselves too close to attention and driven away, but had sent her back to lead the pick-up car to the camper.

He was called again. His hands were on top of his head now, clenched. He had no weapon and could not outrun the policeman. He didn't know where she was, assumed she had edged back, unnoticed, would get to a corner, hitch up the hem of the *chador* and run. What would happen? The policeman called louder, sharper, for him to advance. He would be patted down, then told to produce his ID. He wouldn't be able to. He had no ID, and his cover story would flake in less than an hour.

The policeman's impatience was growing – annoyance in his voice, the first realisation that all was not straightforward. He would do the noble thing. What she needed most, and the guys, was time. He would buy time for them. Years ago he hadn't crossed a road to help a poor bastard against his muggers. He hadn't even gone to a police station to make a statement. But he had changed. The guys needed time. He couldn't see her.

The policeman's impatience grew, and his suspicion.

He should produce his ID. Play helpless and act the idiot. A fist was on the truncheon, and the other fingers flicked to the radio on his upper chest. Where was his ID? He did an idiot smile. The truncheon was up and smacked his shoulder. It hurt – and the weapon was raised again. Zach was on his knees. He could think only of time and the price he paid for it.

She came from the edge of his vision.

The policeman seemed unaware of her approach, fast, catlike in the stolen trainers.

She had the pistol, huge in a small hand. The policeman was about to hit him again, the truncheon raised, demanding the ID.

She brought the barrel of the pistol down hard on the bridge of the policeman's nose. He squealed, an animal sound, shrill. His truncheon fell and his hands went to his eyes. She was between him and Zach, reached forward, with the pistol in her fist, and toppled him. He had crumpled, now moaned, and was sprawled on the ground, his thighs apart. She kicked. Zach winced – and she did it again. Then she grabbed Zach, dragged him upright.

They ran together.

He gasped, 'I thought you were going to kill him.'

'I couldn't.'

They crossed a small park and then were by a river, heading towards a tower block of apartments.

'Because to kill him I would have had to shoot him.' There was no emotion in her voice. 'There's no silencer on the gun. If I had killed him, the shot would have been heard.'

They ran, her leading, him trailing. The dusk was closing and the rain fell on them.

16

An inquest of sorts. What else?

From Mikey: 'Where is it?' An answer about the delays with the fuel, the hike across the fields, the traffic coming into Khvoy. Their faces fell.

From Wally: 'How much did you miss them by? Did you see them?' Zach said he had seen a people-carrier, right colour, right place, a driver in it, the engine going and two other passengers. He had started across the street but it had pulled away and he'd lost it.

From Ralph: 'Didn't you leg it after him? Didn't you get up alongside?' He tried to explain that he had run himself into the ground, lost it and latched onto the wrong one.

The brutal response: 'God, what a wanker . . .'

Zach said, 'It gets worse.'

A ribald and overplayed snort from Wally. Zach said he had been bounced by a policeman and Farideh had intervened. They had a few minutes' grace, no longer.

Mikey told Ralph to drive.

They were in the van, and the engine kicked into life. Mikey was crouched in his seat, peering at the maps. He called back to Farideh that he wanted her to read signs that would take them towards Maku, or north of that town, by back roads. Zach felt like a schoolkid. Should he have shouted back at them? He reckoned fear fuelled the abuse.

She intervened, soft voice: 'I expect he did what he could, what was possible.'

They went fast. As Zach saw it, if they hit a road block they would shoot their way through it. They were away from the centre of Khvoy in straggling suburbs where the houses were built of breeze blocks and mud bricks, with vegetable patches and tethered goats grazing on the autumn grass. Black-tented women walked along the roads with heavy plastic bags and the children braved the rain for games, football and chasing. They waved at the camper van and were splattered with water from the puddles. She made the calls at junctions. The anger was on a back-burner now. Sometimes they were off the tarmac road, on chippings or tracks with potholes, and Zach realised that Ralph drove supremely well. The light failed.

The needle on the dial showed the tank at low.

Their lights were full on and there were lonely farm buildings. Soon the kids would be in, the goats would be led to the sheds and the chickens rounded up. There might not be wolves here to massacre the chickens if they were left out overnight but jackals were everywhere. He started to shiver.

He was on the carpet, and she was on the bench seat beside him; the guys were in the front. Ralph drove, Wally had the Heckler in both hands, and Mikey had the map wedged on his lap. The cold ripped in through the side windows, with the rain.

When Mikey wanted her help he asked for it, and she would lean forward to point. A small torch would light the map, then she would ease back. Zach was ignored. When they wanted her, they called for her. They were two groups, distinct and apart.

The guys talked about money. Zach didn't doubt that they were trying to stay alert: that silence would have dimmed their concentration on the road, the map and the threat that swam around them. Ralph needed the money because the roof of his home leaked. Wally wanted the money because his ex-wife's new partner had lost his job and, although none of his former family had any time for Wally, it was his duty to provide for them. And Mikey? He wanted out of Aldershot: he talked of hills, a dog, a village pub, and maybe a converted truck that could be parked in lay-bys to do bacon baps, teas and breakfasts for lorry drivers.

Zach couldn't control the shiver. To fix a roof, buy kids' shoes and a catering truck needed survival. Zach doubted the guys had forgotten that. What did she want? He didn't know. And himself, what did he want?

The wind through the window cut into him. In places the rain turned to sleet, and sometimes snow flakes. He took off his anorak, then his sweater, shirt, T-shirt and vest. She stood up, crouched over the seat, lifted it and rummaged. She took out blankets, dropping one onto the carpet. The vehicle shook, but Ralph didn't slow down. Zach was scrabbling at the laces of his trainers but his fingers were too clumsy to grip. He must have cried out in frustration.

She pushed him back gently, reached down, and he felt her fingers working at his ankles. She took off both shoes, then peeled away his socks. Could eyes laugh? They might have done.

Mikey had the torch on. Its beam identified a junction where there were two valleys and the lights had lit a sign. She leaned forward to read it. The light was on her face – no veil – and he thought her eyes were laughing.

He had started so he would finish. He wriggled. His jeans clung to his legs. He had the waist undone and the belt. Then her hands grasped them at the thighs and pulled them off. She let him do the job on his pants. He used the towel hung below the basin under the work surface, then cocooned himself in a blanket.

She asked, 'There's no going back?'

'No.'

She stood up, rocking with the movement of the wagon. He laid his hand on her hip to steady her. She dragged the *chador* over her head, exposing a blouse, sweater and jeans, then tore off her head-scarf, and shook her hair free. She leaned forward and threw the garment out of the open window, with the scarf. Zach understood the enormity. It was gesture of rejection. Many would curse her for it and few would applaud her.

Mikey took the cue: 'There was never a chance of turning back.'

He took a slug of whisky: defiance. He drank it from the bottle, then tipped the rest down the sink and sluiced it away. He didn't hide the bottle: he left it on the draining-board above the dishwasher that was loaded with dirty plates from the meal his wife had given the boy after school. Next to the dishwasher, the washing-machine held the shirts, underwear and towels she had done that morning, and beyond it was the drier that still contained the sheets and pillowcases that would have been ironed the next morning by the woman who came in, a widow who was almost part of the family. Beyond the drier was the fridge-freezer. It would be looted.

It was dark outside. From the living room, with no light on, he could see into the cul-de-sac to the parked car, with the glow of cigarettes. His kitchen lights were bright, and the radio was on.

Brigadier Reza Joyberi would never come back to the house. Neither would his wife, Noor, nor his son. He had already shredded his personal papers, those dealing with his holdings in the world of import and export. It was said that the East German regime, toppling under the weight of protest and abandoned by the USSR, had used its last hours to shred thousands of files detailing agents, and millions of pages of surveillance reports. The shredders had overheated and caught fire. Still, to this day, some three dozen Germans laboured to reassemble the shredded pages; they hadn't even dented the mountain of sacks holding the paper. It wouldn't happen in Iran: what he had shredded was destroyed and beyond their reach.

He had been a good servant of the revolution.

Until his driver had visited a brothel in Dubai, people had spoken well of him. A climb to authority such as his inevitably provoked enmity. No one now would speak of the merits of Brigadier Reza Joyberi. It was over. Those who lived around him, an élite of the regime, would denounce him for fear of contagion by association. A week before he had had no known enemies. Now he was without a friend. His wife's aircraft should have taken off.

There was a small garden at the back, with a fence that was not covered by lights. There was a side road beyond it. He knew where he would go: he had chaired a meeting eight months before to discuss the flow of refugees from justice through this particular needle's eye. It was also where the more expensive smugglers took their clients. He might see her there one last time. God would decide. Lights blazed in much of the house and the radio was loud. He would lock the back door behind him.

Sidney drove, with Mehrak beside him. He talked about castles and was glad to have found a fellow enthusiast. Nobby and Auntie were in the seats behind, but Father William had refused to come. Sidney didn't do as much walking now as he'd have liked – a hip problem – but he would enjoy this expedition with another man who loved historic fortifications.

He talked. 'What you have to understand, my friend, is that the Danube was a highway into Europe more than a thousand years ago. You had the Silk Road in Iran, and Europe had the river. Goods of all sorts came up and down it. If you were a gangster, and had the right connections, this was the place to be and the pickings were fantastic.'

He thought Mehrak was quiet, but his eyes roved from the windscreen to the side windows. Nobby and Auntie were on about the TV satellite news, Afghanistan, the stock market, floods in China. Mehrak might have been distracted but nodded firmly.

'There was the Kuenringer family. They thieved off the merchant classes using the Danube but would have provided funding for the aristocracy, who were the real godfathers. It went from the twelfth century right through to the seventeenth. Even then the Kuenringers were trying to hold the line against Turkish invasions and the Swedes. The river had to be fortified wherever there was a vantage-point. Strategic positions were made into strong points.'

Another nod. He'd hoped that, for this expedition, Mehrak would be a soul-mate. His Iranian castles and fortresses and what he knew of Lebanon and Syria should be the bonding agent between them. They drove through the middle of Spitz, passing tractors delivering the last grapes, and saw more pumpkins in doorways for the festival at the weekend. The man deserved a break after the concentrated scalping of information from him.

'The people who held the river, Mehrak, were those with the

power. No expense had been spared in the building of their castles. And this was a fault line here, as far as the Turks reached. Don't think it's all ancient history, Mehrak. See that tower – the one on the left – and the monument just short of it? Napoleon was defeated at this point two hundred years ago, pretty much to the day.'

Again a nod, but no comment – and a yawn from behind, which Sidney thought rude. The river was on their right and a long line of barges was brought downstream by a tug boat, headed for Vienna, then Bratislava and Budapest. Amazing and fascinating. He was warming to it. There would be word before the evening ended that the wife was across the frontier. She might be with them by the next evening. Sidney had seen the picture of her, lovely woman. Mr Hector would have said, 'Get that woman to him, drop her knickers, strip her off and give them thirty minutes to hammer at it. Then get him out and answering until he drops.' It would be a hell of a show for the Service, like Mr Hector's time, and Sidney would be proud for the rest of his days to have been a part of it.

'Here we go, Mehrak. This is Dürnstein. Above the house with the cross on the wall – it was the hangman's house – that's the castle. The English king, Richard the Lionheart, was on his way back from a Crusade in what's now Lebanon and Israel, or occupied Palestine, travelling incognito – know what I mean? He was recognised and arrested by men of a local noble, a margrave, then handed to the Kuenringer family for safe-keeping while the ransom was raised and brought here. It's like the Kuenringers had the franchise then, or al-Quaeda in Iraq today. It was going to be payday. They wanted a hundred and fifty thousand marks in silver. That's a fortune. Actually, the story has it that a troubadour, a guy who goes round singing, who was devoted to Richard, worked his way round all the castles in the Babenberg country and sang under the walls. Richard sang back from his cell. That was how the English knew where he was. I don't know if that story's true, but it's a nice one.'

There was a car park, almost empty now. The day for visitors was nearly over.

Mehrak laughed. 'In Iran, Sidney, we say "A falsehood mixed with good intentions is preferable to a truth that excites strife." It is permitted to lie if it gives happiness. I want you to escort me and tell me everything you know of the Dürnstein castle.'

If would be Sidney's pleasure. It was three years since he had last been up the lane and into the woods, where the lane became a track, steeper and cut out of the hillside.

He led, Mehrak at his shoulder. He heard Auntie's curse, and Nobby's wheezing. They climbed in the interest of progressing the debrief, and to show trust.

They were leaving one of the co-operative stores in the main street of Doğubeyazıt, and were close to the biggest of the backpackers' hostels. When Dunc and Mandy had gone inside – staples to feed the team when they arrived – there had been chanting down the street from Kurdish youngsters, and the military had been in stand-off. There were light armoured vehicles and the troops had riot shields, clubs and rifles. She'd been about to pay when the dusk outside was lit by petrol bombs. Then the gas came.

They'd paid and scampered. The gas mixed with the smoke rising off the broken bottles. He had one plastic bag, she had another, and they ran for the car.

More gas came and the canisters bounced near to them. A loudspeaker warned that the next response would be live rounds. The kids were chanting Kurdish freedom slogans. The schedule would go to hell if they were trapped between the two forces.

She had the key in the ignition and was stamping on the pedals when the lights arrowed through the gas and the smoke and they saw Major Emre Terim standing in his jeep with a loudhailer.

Dunc said, as she pulled away, 'Molotov cocktails were not a Russian invention – not many know that. They were down to the Finns in their war against the Soviets in 1939. Molotov was one of Stalin's henchmen and the cocktails were an insult to him. Used properly, they could take out a battle tank. A Finnish drink manufacturer switched from booze to the cocktails for mass production. Interesting, yes? Actually, neat petrol needs thickening, which is why this lot aren't too effective. They should pop into the mini-mart and requisition baking-soda as a mixer and raw eggs. Shall I tell them?'

'Don't be a total idiot.'

More Molotovs was thrown and more gas fired. It was inside the car . . . It would be a crush in the car but only as far as the airport, and there was a flight out at sparrow-fart in the morning. Then they would go back, him and her, to the house and sanitise it. There might be time for— The gas was in his eyes.

He said, 'CS gas – don't ask me the full name – was invented by Americans but the serious tests were done in Britain. We used to make the bloody stuff. Same old story: most of what's chucked around in Tehran, Damascus, Cairo, Berlin and Rome is made in China. Hold on a minute.'

Water from a bottle on to his handkerchief and he leaned across. She kept the car moving as he wiped her eyes gently. They were going slowly and had turned right into a side-street when a woman pushed a cart in front of them. Mandy braked. Someone rapped on the window, insistent.

It was Khebat. The gas swam in the car. The old Kurd grinned. 'I cannot do this but my friend pays big money and achieves it.'

'I don't understand,' Mandy snapped at him. Riddles – when she'd been gassed and her eyes were burning – annoyed her.

'My friend has a riot, but it's expensive.'

'Why would your "friend" pay for a riot?'

'To keep the fat pig in the town.'

'Because?'

'Because he brings over clients tonight and doesn't want interference. For me it is not so necessary. For him, interference with people is a big problem. The pig is here and occupied. But to make a riot is expensive, and you may have the cost of a funeral also. What time do your people come?'

Dunc said they were hoping the night clouds would lift and the moon would be full – when last seen it was a sickle – so they'd see Ararat in its glory. He was laughed at. Mandy said they'd needed to stock up in case heavy snow blocked them into the house. He said there was a security alert across the border, inside Iran, and wished them well. She drove away. Dunc thought, a nightmare, of men and women brought across the frontier, at heavy cost, enduring the terror, lying in ditches while patrols crossed close, being taken by the Turkish military and handed to the Iranian guards. Worse than a nightmare – a vision of hell. They left the town, the chanting, the sirens and the explosions. The snow had settled, but the road was slush-covered and lorries were on it. They turned off where they had been told to, and bumped along. She hadn't thanked him for treating her eyes, but when he had finished, she had touched his arm lightly. They came round a bend and saw parked vehicles beside a low stone shelter, such as a shepherd might use in summer. A man came towards them, a chain of beads flicking in his hands. He spoke.

Mandy translated. The man finished, shrugged, then left them.

She said, 'They aren't coming. They were late at the pick-up point. The driver waited, then had to leave. There's big military activity across there. I don't think there's a fall-back. Another pick-up in twenty-four hours? No.'

The motion of the camper was violent. He broke the quiet: 'What's the dream?'

The shivering had stopped, and the rug had warmed him.

A question answered with a question: 'Must there be one?'

'I think so. If you break from a culture, from family, from what you know, then, yes, there must be a dream.'

Another question, faintly asked. He had to crane to hear. 'Is it conceit to dream?'

'What do you want me to say?'

'Is it selfish to dream, to say how past life was intolerable? Is that arrogant?'

He whispered, 'No. I had everything. I was fed, housed, had work and a mind of sorts. I wanted to be challenged. That was my dream. I could have done it at home, but didn't know how to find something that would stretch me. My dream was to find myself. I suppose I have, at a cost.'

'What am I allowed to dream of?'

'Anything.'

'There was a boy and he loved me. They hanged him. He dreamed of a free country, elections, speech, opportunities. He dreamed of loving me. While he waited for them to hang him, I think he would have thought it was good to dream.'

'I dream of living with someone worthwhile and of finding that person.'

'There was an army captain who dreamed of fast bikes and fast cars. He dreamed of the excitement of fighting and combat. He dreamed of me.'

There was quiet in the front, except for Ralph's grunts of frustration when he failed to swerve round a deeper hole or wider rut. The rain had stopped and the wipers now shifted the mix of sleet and snow. They climbed, and it was cold in the wagon. Mikey didn't call on her because there were no turnings off the route to confuse him, and no signs. They were blind but they had to hope.

She said, 'I dream of swimming in the sea, feeling water on my skin, sunshine touching my arms and face. I dream of being my own person. To dream is free.'

'They can't stop you.'

'I dream of living, not of death.'

The vehicle coughed.

A moment later the wheels locked and skidded. Zach leaned forward and tapped Mikey's shoulder. The small torch came on and a finger jabbed at the map. They were north of the town of Maku and must have crossed the main road from Tabriz, Marand and Khvoy to the border, but he hadn't registered it.

There was another splutter from the engine. Zach thought a lesser driver than Ralph would have lost it and they'd have slipped into a ditch. The guys had gone silent, concentrating, and he had been prattling about a dream. He wondered whether to say, 'Sorry, guys, that was so pompous.' He said nothing. He had believed in all of the dreams, and in hers, and owed no one an apology.

The headlights showed only the snowstorm as it gathered strength.

* * *

It was bald and bare, but bad messages always were. Tadeuz Fenton gazed at the screen as if added scrutiny might scramble the original text and replace it with something more palatable.

'TF. They missed the pick-up – have a good evening. SR.'

It would be a grand dinner. He was halfway up the steps into the main entrance of the Royal College of Surgeons, black tie – sadly dry – hosted by Foreign and Commonwealth for an emir up from the Gulf. Nothing altered on his screen.

A line of hosts were at the top of the steps, and the guests for whom the thrash had been arranged were arriving in a Roller behind him. He could either go up the steps, hand in his visitor's card, be filtered to the coat kiosk, then the museum to wander around cases of preserved anatomical samples, or he could back away and head for the open, dark spaces of Lincoln's Inn Fields to circle the floodlit netball courts.

He did that, hugged shadows, and called Sara Rogers back. 'There's no mistake?'

'It's the good old "two sources", Tad. The Jerusalem Friends had it about three minutes before Dunc. He and Mandy are up some bloody mountain at the drop-off point. It was early, but they were there, and the locals had already learned it from the driver. They didn't show at the pick-up. Not good.'

'What can I usefully do?' He relied on Sara Rogers. She was the best thing to have come into his professional orbit. She was, in all senses, his gate-keeper.

'Try a couple of glasses of *citron pressé*. Offer a couple of Hail Marys and, between chatting up your neighbour, consider some strategies.'

He told her when he would be back at Vauxhall Cross and did two circuits of the courts at the extreme edge of the light pools. Tadeuz Fenton's reputation was as a 'safe pair of hands', but its maintenance, as he recognised, depended on an absence of controversy, embarrassment, cock-up and fuck-up. Poor bastards – and that pretty girl. It happened often enough. So-called 'incidents' on the way out of Iran were frequent. It was not an easy place. Truth was, and he didn't need Sara Rogers to do him a memo, it was bloody near impossible to get out without reliable guides. The necessary people had been arranged, but they had missed the pick-up.

He pondered. Total denial.

Their loathsome TV stations would be doing full coverage of the men; they'd be in jumpsuits and chains as they parroted their confessions. There would be total denial and covert briefings to chosen sources, murmuring about men from a fourth-rate private contractor, the Israelis' desperation for information. Stories of a brigadier's driver, and a brothel in Dubai, would be dismissed as an Iranian fantasy: Her Majesty's Government 'simply is not engaged in such fanciful games'. That would be about the best he could do – and was probably adequate. Back in the office he would call Petroc, urge him to put a rod across the wretch's back and extract what they could – fast.

He retraced his steps. After dinner, he would go back to his office – he was a lucky man. He had the best war in the building, and it was a privilege to be a part of it. Events like tonight's – and casualties – were what made the intelligence-gathering combat so exceptional. He skipped up the steps into the college and headed for the museum. He felt good.

He and Mehrak had climbed. Near to where the outer gate would have been, they'd had to come off the track as a party of schoolchildren, mostly American and likely from the international school in Vienna, came rampaging down. That was when he had looked behind him and seen Auntie and Nobby settled on a bench at the side of the track, swilling water. At that point the trees pressed close to them, giving shade, and it was a warm evening, exceptional for late October. In his opinion, a man allowing himself to be called 'Auntie', was pathetic – his main source of conversation was a dog left behind in Northern Ireland with his sister. No love there. In Northern Ireland, Sidney had abandoned bits of his sanity in a Lisnaskea hotel when a bomb had ticked, and a client had been left behind after general evacuation, with a bit of Sidney's muscle, and bone splinters from a high-velocity round in his leg.

He reckoned he did a better job than Auntie. The kids passed, raucous. He thought Nobby pleasant enough, all right to meet on a train, but without the ability to take the initiative with the defector or the world of discounts, favours and debts-called-in – which Sidney lived off. When they loaded up the cars to quit the safe house, with Mehrak and Mehrak's wife, he might just tell the three of them what they were worth – fuck all of nothing – for all their superiority. Anyway . . . They walked on up.

He talked of the techniques of the craftsmen and the defensive needs of the day. Why the walls at the gatehouse had been state-of-the-art for that century, and the arrow slits in the walls, used by cross-bow mercenaries before the arrival of gunpowder and cannon. They were approaching the keep, ruined but recognisable, and Sidney could show off the remnant of the tower where the English king had been held. They were alone and other visitors had gone.

He said, 'A tragedy that the castle was destroyed, such a wealth of history here. If it had survived it would be a wonder of the world. It was 1645 when the Swedes came. Their commander was Field Marshal Lennart Torstenson. Took the place from the successors to the Kuenringer family, killed them, sacked it and blew it up. It's never been reconstructed. Then, of course, they came on towards Spitz, our village, and attacked by the Red Gate. He was the most scientifically minded artillery officer of his day, and these wonderful walls were simply toppled over. He would have gone all the way to Vienna but he suffered terrible gout and had to go home. You remember, Mehrak, I told you about the Red of the Gate when the Swedes came?'

He wasn't answered.

'Oh, and the English paid up. Well, not all of it. They said after a third had been handed over, fifty thousand marks' worth of silver coinage, that the rest was on the way. The locals believed them and let the king go back to England – which would have been flat on its back after raising that sort of wealth. They never did get paid the rest. You could say that today the folk here are still owed a hundred thousand marks by my lot. Their fault for believing what they were told. Fabulous, isn't it?'

Still no answer.

He turned. He gazed around him.

Three different areas had become viewing platforms. He had to check them all. There was an angle that looked towards Spitz, the great abbey at Melk and the bend in the river; another had the view of Dürnstein, the church by the water and the great nineteenth-century villa; a third looked towards the next line of hills, the dense trees and their golden foliage. He peered up the river – no sign.

He strode quickly into the ruined room – for entertaining or torture – with view of the village, the villa and the river's bend. It was deserted. He licked his lower lip. His arthritis twinged in his hip, but the old wound in his thigh hurt move.

There was the third area. It had a room where the outer wall had collapsed and gaped out on the trees that grew up from the crag on which the foundations were set. Nothing.

He went down the main steps from the keep to a wide area where the kids had left rubbish. It was abandoned. He was panting. It was reasonable that Mehrak might have wandered a few feet, even yards, from him while he was rabbiting on about the history. It was not reasonable that he would have gone past where Sidney now stood. His world caved in.

The defector had been there, was not now.

Gone for a pee?

At the start he kept his voice down. 'Mehrak? – Where are you?'

He listened. He heard nothing but a radio played far below in Dürnstein, a train going down the track alongside the river, and traffic murmuring on the main road.

'Mehrak! Over here, Mehrak!'

His voice echoed off the stones but silence lapped him. The enormity grew, and his understanding.

He yelled, 'Mehrak! Where the fuck are you?'

The last group of the day was approaching steadily, like infantry up the track. They were elderly and many of the half-dozen men and women wore shorts. They all had walking boots, poles and rucksacks on their backs. They advanced, had heard his shout and some understood.

'Bloody hell, Mehrak! Don't piss me about! What the fuck have you done? Mehrak, get your arse back to me – now.'

The anger bounced back at him. What had frightened Sidney was that so many paths led off the main track. Two dropped in a scrambled descent to the village, steeper than the slog up which he had come, and many more wound off into the trees where the foliage was dense.

They had gaunt faces, wide hips and ugly knees. They looked at him as if he were demented.

A last time. 'Fuck you, you bastard. Come back.'

Face flushed, heart pounding, he went down through the walkers, who parted, did a Red Sea job, staring at him in astonishment – that a man should come to such an interesting relic and bawl as if a wasp had stung his arse. He careered down the slope.

They were round the bend. How many? There had to be three. His eyes were blurred. Only two. They looked up at him – they must have seen his panic, and heard it. Auntie was standing, Nobby beside him: the question was frozen on their lips. They didn't have to ask.

He blurted, 'Have you seen Mehrak?'

An idiot response: 'He's with you.'

'Open your bloody eyes! Look at me! I can't fucking see him, can you?'

Auntie said, 'He's not been past here.'

Nobby asked, 'When did you last see him?'

'I don't know – five or ten minutes?'

Auntie turned a knife. 'Sorry, weren't you supposed to be minding him?'

Nobby looked Sidney in the eyes, and twisted it: 'Minding him, not giving him a history lesson.'

Sidney said, 'The little bastard's done a runner on me.'

Mehrak didn't know where the path would lead him, except down. He stampeded along it. His feet slipped and he clung to the bushes at either side. He had money in his pocket, but not much. There had been some small-denomination notes and coins on the kitchen table.

It would have been left by the woman, Anneliese, or by Sidney, PK or any of the others, perhaps for cigarettes or an English-language newspaper. It would have been assumed, when it went into his pocket, that one of the others had picked it up. He thought that.

Several times he was off his feet and on his back. His trousers were ripped in the seat and his elbows were scraped. He went towards the road and behind the house where the cretin – who thought he was so clever and kind – had said a hangman once lived. He found there that the path branched and took the right fork, which would lead him away from the village. That was what he wanted, and he thought it gave him time. He had been in flight before: twice in south Lebanon and once in southern Iraq, with the brigadier. They had been targeted and helicopters had searched for them. He had been inducted into Special Forces training, had not competed with the élite but had learned.

He wanted a bus and a telephone. He didn't know what the number would be but reckoned on finding it. He was confident. She would love him, of course. He would have saved her. With his ear against the pipe in his room, he had heard the conversations that PK, his tormentor, had with London, and PK had the habit of half repeating each item told him. His wife was in Khvoy. Khvoy was filled with military units and the Revolutionary Guard Corps. She might already have been arrested. He would save her, and she would love him.

In his mind it was so simple.

He believed he controlled his and her destiny. She would recognise what he had done, and he would be believed.

There was a small stream and water bucketed down. He used it to wash his face and hands, tried to straighten his hair and checked the money in his pocket. He spilled out onto the road and began to jog.

He saw a bus stop ahead.

They drove back up the road towards Krems, then turned and drove the other way, past Dürnstein, where the castle lowered on the hill, and on towards Spitz.

They repeated it.

From Sidney, at the wheel, keeping to less than thirty miles an hour, not giving a toss about the traffic building up behind him, there came a series of moans.

Their body language did their talking. He drove, but Auntie and Nobby let the criticism drip off them onto him – as it always did when a man of supreme confidence in his own judgement was tripped. They went as far upstream as the fields of cultivated vines, and downstream to the Burg Aggstein. The last time they did the run was as good a time as any to accept failure and do the hard job.

None of them volunteered.

Auntie, the Ulsterman, had been in disciplined Protestant-biased schools on the Ards peninsula where a succession of teachers would have told pupils that 'owning up' always brought a reward. He didn't suggest himself as the best man to call Petroc Kenning. Neither did Nobby. Nobby spent his life deflecting guilt and responsibility. It was down to Sidney, and he knew it. He took out his mobile and dialled.

He was connected to the landline and his wife picked it up. 'Me. Don't ask anything, just get me PK . . . A crisis? Some would say so. Now, please, get him.'

He turned to face Nobby, but his shoulders were towards Auntie. He said quietly, 'You're fucking gutless, both of you.' He felt better for that, but neither answered him and he had hoped to provoke a reaction.

'Petroc, it's one of those things that doesn't get said easy. Can't sugar it. We've lost him . . . Probably down to me, but I haven't any idea where he is. Not much more I can say.'

He rang off, then used the next junction to turn and head back for Spitz, where the grapes were in and where the safe house was, and where the catastrophe was monumental. It would not be Petroc's way to bawl him out. Petroc, right now, would be considering how to pass the parcel on and keep the Teflon touch. He was glad he'd coughed it.

* * *

'Sorry, Petroc, no can do. He's at a dinner.'

'Sara, I have – I'm sorry to say – indigestible news.'

'Kick it my way then.'

He had never known Sara Rogers to be flustered.

So he told her – carefully. He had been inducted into the Service fourteen years earlier, courtesy of strings pulled by his uncle Hector. Nothing in his time had ever approached this level of disaster. He believed his reaction to it would be noted. Was he steady under fire or not? Did his nerve hold in adversity?

He told it as it was.

Petroc tried to recall what had been expected when the funding of the Dubai brothel had been nodded through. What had been their mission statement? What had they expected to achieve? A business man, a foreign-ministry official, a junior mullah from a scholastic background in Qoms travelling on pilgrimage, a bank official: they would have been heaved out of the whorehouse into a car and then to an interview room. Petroc would have rubbed the sleep out of his eyes and threatened dire exposure, then put the man on his flight in the morning. They had been looking for an agent in place. Long-term access and the requirement that the fly in the web infiltrated himself where he could be useful – might take a year, or five years. But Petroc had not been there. Katie had – and he didn't fault what she'd done. Actually, she'd done a brilliant job on the hoof. And they'd done well with Mehrak. Actually, looked at calmly, it was one to shout about. He wouldn't apologise.

'That's about it, Sara. I think, from a standing start, we've done quite well.'

'Missing something, yes?'

'What am I missing, Sara?'

'We have four men on the wrong side of the border in Iran. And they've missed their pick-up. And where they are is alive with security-force presence. And they have that woman. "Done quite well", Petroc? I'll tell Tadeuz when he's back that you've lost your asset. Goodnight.'

His shin had been kicked. He heard the car pull up outside,

scattering gravel. Guilty as charged. Four of them across the frontier, and it hadn't seemed a priority. Shame caught him.

The exchange found the number. He pushed more coins into the slots, and she put the call through. It rang, and was answered.

'The embassy of the Islamic Republic of Iran.'

He spoke in Farsi and asked to be connected to the officer in charge of security.

'I cannot say whether such a person is still in the embassy at this time of night. Can you leave a message—'

He said he was IRGC, of the al-Qods, and demanded to be connected.

'It may not be possible, but I will try and—'

He told the operator he was a motherfucker, that he must be connected.

'Please wait, the number is ringing.'

A gravelly voice answered. A security officer at an embassy would be from al-Qods. He gave his name, took a gulp of air and spewed out the story he would stay with. He was the driver and personal protection of Brigadier Reza Joyberi. He had been in Dubai on the service of the state and had been kidnapped by agents of the British. He had been flown as a prisoner to Austria and had escaped. He needed help. He was believed, and his confidence soared. No questions were asked and Mehrak was told to stay close to where he was, but not in the light. A car would come, a Volvo estate, and it would not have diplomatic plates. It would drive in circles close to the location of the phone kiosk, then flash the headlights three times. He should run to it. Just that. The call was terminated.

He left the kiosk and found a bench in a small garden. Two others had teenagers on them, groping each other, not noticing him. Of course he would be believed. And belief in his story would save Farideh. He waited.

They were on an incline, a track, and the engine was straining. Then there was a judder, a cough, and it was gone. Ralph rammed on the brake.

It sleeted steadily. Zach snuggled into the blanket and felt his clothing. It was still wet so he rifled through the drawers. He put on underwear, a pair of baggy jeans, two T-shirts, with logos from a sheep-nuts manufacturer, a sweater, a thin windcheater, which would be almost useless, and trainers with holes in the soles. The last item was a baseball cap from the Lincoln University College of Agricultural Sciences.

Farideh took two sweaters, socks, knickers and the toilet roll. The guys had their own agenda. They were arguing about what they could carry and its weight. The communications gear was for taking, the trauma bag and the firepower – the machine-guns, ammunition magazines, and the pistols that Mikey and Ralph would have. Wally had held out his hand for his but Farideh had turned away from him and would not have given it up. The grenades were divided among them so that each had a flash and bang, and gas. The cold scythed at them.

Mikey did the calculations with the map and the compass, which was now hooked on his chest. They would take hand torches but only the one used by the trail-blazer would be lit. The rest would take their chances amid stones, boulders, ruts and holes – and it was hard to look ahead because the sleet was coming from the north-west.

The postcards were still on the work surface. Zach had a silly moment. In the light from a cupboard, he memorised the address of an obvious parent, took an unused card and scrawled, 'Sorry you just happened to meet us on a Black Dog Day when we had a heap of aggravation. Wrong place at the wrong time, Best, Foxtrot, Zulu, and the guys'. They were loaded and slung on the rucksacks.

They went on climbing and the wind hunted them down. Mikey was in front and set a good pace, then Wally, who cursed each time a gust slapped him. Zach was with Farideh. He would have called himself 'virtually fit' from working on the sites, but keeping a brickie or a sparks in supplies through a day was different from heaving himself up a hillside in the teeth of a gale, with the cold and wet insinuating themselves under the layers of his clothing. He knew he would struggle. He thought Farideh would have had no significant exercise in Tehran and could hear her wheezing. Ralph came last. The torchlight was increasingly hard to focus on, the track less well formed and narrower. Mikey had said they were around forty kilometres to the frontier. They would walk through the night, then make a bivouac and try for the border the next evening.

Her breathing became more laboured. Zach had to check his stride to stay with her, Ralph pushing them forward.

They went on without rest stops.

She took his hand, which was frozen, like hers. She murmured about 'turning back', the chance of it being over, and he felt a hard shape pressed into the palm of his hand. It was the size of a credit card, smooth, laminated.

She said, 'With no turning back, I don't need it. Perhaps you might want it.'

Zach pocketed it, didn't know what it was, and they struggled on. The sleet had turned into a fine wet snow, and their trainers slipped, but Mikey set a hard pace.

There was a warbling sound, like a bird's song on a spring morning. Zach identified it as coming from Mikey's rucksack. Wally closed on him, rummaged and dragged out a cable. There would have been a microphone attached and an earpiece. Contact from outside their world. Mikey's pace did not ease off, and his voice came back, lifted on the wind but indistinct. Mostly he listened, and they climbed.

17

Zach closed on Mikey and Wally. Mikey had stopped and was crouched. The guys had said that contact on the satphone was not made lightly and they'd been scrupulous in not using it. Mikey was huddled, and Wally tried to shelter him, but there was only the small torch to help him find the earpiece in the rucksack, the little microphone and the transmit switch.

'Yes, it's Mikey . . . Hearing you? Not bad considering . . . How far? Reckon it's thirty klicks . . . Yes, "secure" is on. . . . Who am I speaking to? . . . Please yourself . . . Conditions? They're good but foul. It's snowing and we're hitting a plateau, but we're making reasonable time. The ceiling's too low for helicopters.'

Wally swore at the cold. Ralph tried to stamp his feet. None of them had thermal lining in their boots, or quilted anoraks. They hadn't eaten properly, had no hot drinks and their flight had gone from confused to chaotic. Zach listened. His body gave Farideh some shelter.

'Would you, sir, repeat that?' Mikey wedged the earpiece further into his ear.

Zach's hand was in his pocket and he could feel the hard shape of what she had given him.

'We need to confirm and close because my battery's running down. You said, quote, "Our man, her husband, has run. We no longer have control of him", unquote. Agreed . . . Thank you.'

Wally murmured that it was a pretty bloody stupid place for a phone conference. Where would he rather be? At the front door, welcoming his bloody kids and waving off the ex-wife with her new shag to Travelodge. Where would Ralph rather be?

Mikey said, remembering he had once been a soldier, 'I confirm your instruction. Quote, "cut and run", unquote. I'm repeating your observation, quote, "Your lives and your freedom are the only matter of importance. You should dump everything surplus and make best speed." Unquote. Am I hearing this right?'

Ralph would rather be in a house in mid-Wales that needed a new roof.

Zach thought they were close to an edge. He thought Farideh was crying quietly beside him, that the cold was brutal and— He was jolted.

Mikey's voice: 'You don't want Foxtrot? You don't need her? Quote, "surplus to requirements" unquote. Yes, she's slowing us. Yes, we expect it to be difficult, closer to the border. Yes, I can drop her. Might leave her at a bus stop. I'm sure Foxtrot'll think of something. Quote, "Not, any longer, our problem", unquote. I reckon the buses round here are pretty regular . . . Been a pleasure speaking to you, and a pleasure working for you.'

Mikey contorted himself to insert a hand into his pack. He stood up. 'It doesn't matter whether I like the order given me or not. It's clear-cut and there's no room for misunderstanding. They don't have a defector – either they booted him out or he ran away from them. Without him, they have no need for Foxtrot. It's an order. We leave her. She's also a handicap to us as we approach the border and it's spelled out that our priority is to make the safe haven of Turkish territory. Sorry, but that's how it's going to be.'

She understood.

'Thanks, Wally, for the distraction,' Mikey said. 'If you'd asked me, I would have said that I'd rather be anywhere other than here, *anywhere*. Two-minute break, then we go. That's all. It's not negotiable and it's from the head honcho.'

More rummaging, cigarettes produced, hands cupped over a lighter flame. Zach realised that the discussion was over. The guys reckoned it right that Farideh – once worth their freedom and likely their lives, now without the value of a can of beans – could turn around, go down the hill, might be allocated a torch and allowed to keep the pistol. Hands washed. He was not offered a cigarette. Neither was she. The guys were on their haunches and the wind deflected off them. The snow had turned back to sleet and dripped from Zach's nose and chin. He was a passenger they tolerated. She was not.

He weighed the worth of an order.

The cigarettes glowed in the dark and the wind made them burn fast. Zach understood the phrase 'cut and run'. It was of naval origin. For quick movement, the rigging teams would slash the yarn that held the sails furled, and the sails, released, would catch the wind and the ship would move. But 'cut and run' today implied cowardice, and also that a decent cause should be abandoned. To the guys, it wasn't a big deal. To him? His mind churned.

The cigarettes were thrown down.

Ralph coughed, convulsing. Zach supposed it to be the first law of holes: if you're in one, stop digging. It was close to 'cut and run'. Ralph coughed again, spat, then hoisted his rucksack.

They had given Ralph Cotton a fair education at that school, sufficient for him to earn entry to a good, if not prestigious, regiment. He had learned at school that points of principle tended to be sharp and generally achieved little. He had learned in the regiment that most officers were keen to appear conventional and enthusiastic; he had found that tiresome. The job, in the shit-heaps of Iraq and Afghanistan, was acceptable, but the bullshit days in the garrison town at home had bored the hell out of him: he had become used to the concept of men looking after each other, watching backs and protecting. To him, the regiment's battle history was interesting in the sense that conflict had raged for it in some equally stinking shit-heaps as those he had experienced.

Sacrifice, and walking into the firing line for the benefit of the rest of the section, platoon, company, had not seemed sensible. A sergeant had been zapped, charging a machine-gunner in Helmand when his frightened teenage squaddies were pinned down. At the send-off from Bastion, the padre had intoned, '*Greater love hath no man than this, that a man lay down his life for his friends.*' Ralph had not bought in. It would have been simpler to call in a fast jet strike and dump half a ton of explosive on the bastard, and the sergeant would still have been holding down a corner of the Red Lion or any British Legion bar. The best 'love' Ralph had experienced during his years with the regiment had been in the arms of the woman in the company commander's married quarters.

He regarded himself as a survivor, as did his father and mother. Their tax returns were minor works of art, and his sister . . . Ralph Cotton saw himself, again, riding in Minnie's car, the beaten-up Morris Minor that somehow kept going, up the avenue of old beech trees that flanked the drive. There was no chance that his 'love' would stretch to dragging this woman along in the slip-stream of their flight. He didn't feel good about his acceptance of that situation; neither did he feel bad about it. He didn't look at her and was careful not to nudge her as he came past her, but the snow was impacted where she had stood and he slipped, barging against her. They had a hell of a barrier ahead of them and to burden himself, and the guys, further – a handicap enough to have the language guy with them – wasn't on. Actually, a good call from London to ditch her.

'How did I do?'

'Quite well.' Her fingers, working at the taut muscles of his neck, calmed him, a talent of Sara Rogers.

'Won't win me any plaudits,' Tadeuz Fenton observed. The sofa in his office pulled out to make a bed, but she would use the one she had set up in the outer office. She had found blankets and pillows in the store by the lift.

'They're better, of course, without her. Stands to reason. Hideous ground to cross, but they're fit, able and resourceful. With her it would have been like driving a car with the handbrake engaged. And men under pressure will always do something stupid when a woman lags behind and needs carrying. To their credit, they put up no argument.'

'I think you were right, Tadeuz.'

He almost laughed. 'You know I was right. It had to be right because that was the approach you suggested. No complaint.'

'There are still chestnuts in the fire, ripe for pulling out. I have a good feeling.'

'Dunc will sort them out when they come over, smooth over any pangs of conscience. Bit tired, sorry and all that. I feel very confident.'

She kissed his forehead and smoothed his hair, dimmed a light, switched off his phone and tucked the blanket around him. She wondered what the morning would bring. Around her the building slept. The river was quiet: cargo barges had stopped running till dawn and the pleasure craft were back at their moorings. She could see the top of the London Eye, and thin lines of traffic coming to the bridges. She would have walked away from anyone who wanted her to bet that the men would leave the corporal's wife. She closed the door.

They fed off stress and the anxiety that whitened knuckles. It was so good. She kicked off her shoes, unzipped her skirt, hung her blouse on a hanger from the wardrobe. Her alarm would wake her at five. She lay on the bed. Sensible of the guys not to bring sentiment into the argument. The woman was nothing to them. A positive spin was required, and she'd do it.

She took a step back and seemed to stagger, then limped another half-dozen paces.

Zach stood his ground.

Ralph called him.

He hadn't seen her limp before the satphone link had been made. He hadn't noticed either the change in the weather but it must have get warmer – the wind had slackened, the snow had gone, and the sleet had been replaced by a fine rain that lashed his cheeks. She had turned away. Small mercy, they hadn't asked her for the pistol.

Wally called him. His voice was less clear than Ralph's had been: another indication that the force of the storm had moved on – the words didn't hang on the wind.

Wally called: 'Do the goodbye, like it's a railway station, and get to us. She's tough. You're not part of it. She'll win through. Now, get the hell on.'

He could see, from their torch, that each of them had faced him. Now they swung away, hesitated. Mikey snapped his fingers and they began to walk. Zach watched the torch move away.

He assumed they believed he would touch her hand, mutter something, then run. Forget the cold, the wind and the wet, and up the hill into their arms. He'd get a cuff on the shoulder, a bit of man-talk, or just a grunt. They'd have told him they were going home and taking him with them. He expected they were going slowly to let him catch up. He'd have looked back once, they'd have reckoned, and seen the small back and the floating hair.

There had been that short, stifled conversation.

There's no going back?

His answer. *No going back.*

There was never a chance of turning back, Mikey had said, before the call and the changed direction.

When they had started to walk after the death of the old wagon, she'd said, *With no turning back, I have no more need of it. Perhaps you might want to have it.* He still didn't know what she had given him.

Who had the torch? Her or him? Where was it? In his rucksack or her pocket? He searched, found it, pencil thin with a beam sufficient for reading a map in a darkened car. He brought it out of his chest pocket, switched it on and took the shape from his pocket. He had her identification card. He read her name, her date of birth, her place of residence, her marital status, and saw the passport-sized photograph of her, a scarf covering her forehead, her cheeks, nose, lips and chin. She was dead without her card, and she had given it him. She had no clothing left that was 'good *hijab*'. A van had been hijacked, tourists beaten and robbed, a policeman assaulted, and it was likely that two of the *basij* were dead. There was no turning back. When he looked up the hill and saw their footprints, Zach understood that the link between them was broken. They would not come back for him.

They were fighting men. They'd taken casualties, seen blood. They would have learned not to 'make drama from crisis'.

She limped, trailing her right leg. He thought that if she'd had a stick she would have leaned on it. He went after her.

Her arm was gripped. She tried to pull away, and failed. Zach spun her round. Her face was below his, but she confronted him. She said, 'Go and catch up with your friends. Leave me.'

He slapped her face. It was the first time she had been hit since Mehrak had blacked her eye. Zach hadn't hurt her but her skin stung and her eyes watered. She hit him back.

Farideh had not fought Mehrak. Then, her husband had dragged her out of their bed and had clutched at her thick night-dress, which she had refused to let him lift. She had tumbled onto the rug, and he had lifted her by her hair, then punched her. As the blows had rained on her, she had wondered if Mehrak would kill her. It wouldn't have been a big thing if he had because he was a 'wronged' husband and she was a 'stubborn' wife; he was a member of the al-Qods and connected by work to an all-powerful member of the élite, while she sat at the reception desk of an insurance company. He might have killed her, but did not. He had crumpled and wept. He was pathetic. If she had killed him, she would have hanged. If he had known of her men – Johnny and the Captain – and denounced her, she would have hanged.

Probably the swing in her arm would have warned that she would retaliate, but he didn't lift his hands to protect himself. She caught him on the nose, then punched his stomach. He turned. Anger burned in her. He backed away and she followed.

No words were said, but their shadows merged. He rode her next blow. She came close and lashed out. He caught her shoulders and Farideh caught at his clothing. He dropped the torch. For a moment the beam was on his face and she saw real anger. She fell and dragged him down. His weight was across and against her.

'You hit me!' she spat at him.

'You were faking.'

'You hit my face, without provocation.'

'You were faking and that was reason enough.'

'Faking?' she echoed, confused.

His breath was on her face. 'You faked being hurt.'

'Why would I—'

'You faked being hurt, starting to limp.'

'I did that?'

A little of his warmth seeped into her clothing. She reached up and held his head, her fingers in his hair. The anger leaked away.

He said, 'You faked being hurt to give me the excuse to leave you. You pretended you couldn't keep up, that you were the burden that would slow us. You did it to make it easier for me.'

'How easier?'

'I was supposed to turn away from you and jog to them. I would have carried it for the rest of my days.'

'Carried what?'

She had hurt him – but not by punching; with the limp. He said, 'I would have seen your face, Farideh, every hour of every day of every week. I would have remembered my last sight of you and hated myself. You didn't have to fake an injury. I would never have left you.'

'What am I to you?'

He said, easing himself off her, 'Nothing. How could you be anything to me? Let's move, together.'

She took the torch, wedged it into her mouth, undid the ice-coated lace and pushed off her right trainer. Then she peeled off the sock and aimed the beam at her heel. The blister had broken and bled. It covered the back of her heel. The cold air relieved the pain a little. She had been behind him as they had come up the long, gradual slope, slipping, slithering, and he hadn't seen the anguish on her face or her awkward gait. The soldier behind her, Ralph, hadn't had a torch. He knelt beside her and pulled a handkerchief from his pocket. It was crumpled and muddy. He took water from his rucksack and doused the handkerchief.

He said, 'I was angry because I thought you'd faked the injury and therefore made it easier for me to leave you. I wouldn't have done that.'

He cleaned the blister, tried to be gentle, but the pain was sharp. They did civil-defence drill twice a year at the insurance company, and had lectures each month in first aid. There would have been horror in the training sessions if an open wound had been treated with a filthy cloth. She struggled, but he held her foot firmly. Then he folded the handkerchief into a strip and smoothed it so that it would act as a membrane. He started to undress – the same as in the wagon: successive layers came off, and last his vest. He was shivering as he flicked it off his shoulders and over his head, then dressed again, everything except the vest. He ripped it and made a bandage. The handkerchief would be the cushion, and the vest would hold it secure. He took the trainer, the light of the torch ebbing, and eased it onto her foot, over the protection he had made for her heel, then tied the lace.

She stood and let her weight settle on that foot.

He said, 'I'm still angry. You should have told me.'

'They don't want me.'

'I want you,' he said. 'And I'm taking you.'

They set off, following the prints into the wind and darkness.

The light, high and bouncing, alerted them. The doors of the two vehicles close to them opened quietly and cigarettes were thrown down.

For most of the wait, Dunc had stayed in the car but Mandy had paced, smoked and talked, but she had been with him when the light had appeared. A wobbling, waving star was likely to be a hurricane lamp. While she was smoking she had learned much. On returning to the car she had been pensive and had shared little. Dunc thought that most of what she had picked up would have flattened her morale. But he would hear it at first hand. They had agreed on that.

There should have been a line of mules, but there were just two. There should also have been half a dozen handlers, and perhaps another half-dozen with weapons.

The big team had been stood down when the warning had come of the failed pick-up. Had a caravan of foreigners arrived, there would have been a throng to meet them, but word had spread and the crowd had thinned.

Two men leading the mules, two more walking with them, two as an escort, with assault rifles angled on their shoulders. When they came to the junction in front of the old cattle building, the mule men and the guards were greeted, with brushed-cheek kisses, fierce handshakes and back-slapping. A vehicle's headlights came on.

Dunc didn't need to show Mandy what he saw. He was invariably short of emotion, the legacy of the divorce and of having been, for most of his career, categorised as an 'eternal flame' – *never goes out*. The sight of them rocked him. He was not one of those service officers who patrolled hostile borders and welcomed home the agents, men and women, from the far side, then took them for a drink, bled them, then sent them back and lost no sleep. Mandy had learned what these two were. The older man, of the Baha' faith, would perhaps have faced execution if he had been taken. The activist would probably have hanged if he'd been caught in the escape bid. In the glare of the headlights they looked gaunt and terrorised.

They came off the mules and winced. The headlights were off but the lamp gave enough. Each fumbled at his waist, unbuckled his belt and dropped his trousers. He saw a pair of spindly thighs and a pair of stocky, hairy ones. Two vests were pulled clear, rolled up and made into padding. Dunc witnessed the sores from the makeshift saddles. The men waddled, legs apart, towards the vehicles.

The younger man stopped in front of Dunc. Was he American? he asked. Dunc said he was British, from London. Why was he there? Dunc said he was a *rapporteur* with Amnesty International – good enough, reasonable. He asked how it had been, coming over.

He was told: 'It was hell. The weather was impossible. We had snow and high wind, then sleet and rain. We went a long way on foot, with no lights. You walk on tracks, among rocks, without lights, and you fall, but you cannot cry out. There are patrols across the whole of the plain on the far side of the border. It is a big security alert. The guides said it was worse than they had known in the whole of this year. There was a chance we were to go with other people but they did not come to Khvoy. We waited for them, too long, but they never came. The security is for them. Because we were small, and they were not with us, we were able to get through. It is very dangerous. Three times we had to lie in the snow, and if one had coughed we would have been finished – they were so close. The guides are good. They risk their lives for us, and for the rewards they get. I think we were very lucky with our guides.'

If they had not had guides?

He snorted, as if the question was posed by a fool. 'Impossible. I was at the university, a student of mathematics. I do numbers. Without guides, to cross, the chance of success is one in one thousand. The troops hunt, it is said, for gangsters and terrorists and want a kill. Does your work, sir, in Amnesty, give you an interest in gangsters, terrorists?'

'I have a general interest in the border. Good luck.'

Dunc walked back to Mandy.

The young man called to him, 'It is very difficult up there. I would not be confident you will see your friends, the gangsters and terrorists, come through. Good luck to you.'

The boy, Egid, talked late with his horses and into the small hours. Packages coming through that night were delayed. They would be brought onto the plateau and towards the border the following evening. Vehicles waited for them, their schedules disrupted, in Doğubeyazıt. There would be more vehicles, privately owned cars, and the massive lorries that hauled twenty-tonne loads and trailers. They were backed up on the far west coast of Turkey and waited for the ferries to mainland Europe. At the distribution hubs in Sarajevo, Bucharest, Munich and Rotterdam, more vehicles would be inconvenienced. Packages from faraway Afghanistan that contained the new bullion of the age would be late on delivery.

He couldn't hear his own voice, or the horses, or his father's words. Instead, they were written on paper. They would go the next evening. Often he stayed late with the horses and would be there in the summer when the mosquitoes floated on the wind, and in the winter when the snow bruised the ground and the animals needed rough coats to survive. They would always come from the shelter of the lean-to when they saw him or when he clapped his hands.

He didn't use heroin. Few of the men who brought the resin from Afghanistan, forceing their way across the frontier into Iran, used narcotics. Had he wished to, Egid's father, Khebat, would have beaten him. The men who controlled the trade, at the centre of the trafficking, despised addiction, the same in Asia as in Europe. Egid's longing was for the horses that went high on remote ground where the trucks of the Iranian and Turkish military couldn't reach. But his father had communicated to him that there was excessive activity on the far side of the frontier. Units combed the plateau on foot and were at a high state of vigilance. He knew his father trusted his ability to evade enemies, with his allies, the horses. They could hear and scent danger.

The trade was brisk, the customers' appetite undimmed. The next evening he would be high on the bare hills in the darkness: for one night the trade could be interrupted and the delays absorbed, but not for two. His bond with his animals was unique. He knew it, and treasured the relationship he had with them. He had no other friends, and his family couldn't match the love he had for them. It would be a slow night but he didn't feel the cold and the animals kept close around him.

He drove hard. The night hours slipped by. The road was empty, and when he closed on slow-moving lorries he flashed his headlights and they pulled over for him to overtake. A brigadier who had worked in south Lebanon, Syria and during difficult days inside Iraq could get into a car with a screw-driver, wire it and drive it away. It took a couple of minutes, and he could have dealt with an immobiliser inside five. He hadn't wanted a high-range

BMW or Mercedes because either would have belonged to a man of status who could demand a faster, more efficient reaction. A few hundred metres from his home, he had taken the car. Behind him, the radio would be playing and the lights on. The idiots would sit in their surveillance car with their ashtray overflowing.

They had arrived safely, her text had told him.

He knew where men might try to cross, and at their last meeting to discuss the flights there had been accurate maps for them to understand the area. They had talked about that part of the border and its vulnerability.

He thought that was where she would be taken. Just to see her as a speck in the distance or close up and beside him – as she had been when the blanket had slipped off – was the best he could hope for. It was a diversion. He was broken. In the present harsh economic times, the regime would look for traitors, for the corrupt, as a diversion from the miseries of daily life. Where better to search? The car, a Peugeot, had been well maintained, and he drove it fast.

'Brigadier Joyberi will speak for me.'

The security officer drove and they were alone in the car. They would take the A4 toll road, then the E58, and be over the border using the A6 toll. Hossein wanted to be clear of Austrian territory.

The man blathered: 'I am very close to Brigadier Joyberi. I have been with him for many years.'

As a security officer responsible for a large delegation of his own nationals working at the International Atomic Energy Authority in Vienna, Hossein was primed to deal with traitors.

'It was very frightening to be kidnapped in that way. I can't say exactly when I was drugged, whether it was when I ate something or if it was put in my coffee or mixed with the juice. When the drug wore off, I was handcuffed and put on a military aircraft. Most of the time I was hooded.'

The only anxiety Hossein entertained was that, one day, he might be careless: an act of treachery might be displayed in front of him and he would miss the obvious. A man might smell of alcohol; he might be exhausted at work after frequent late nights; he might have a wife who complained to another that she and the children hardly saw him in the evenings; he might take leave and fly to an expensive resort on the Black Sea or the Mediterranean. A man might come into his embassy office earlier in the morning than colleagues and have access to files. There were always signs. And the greatest anxiety came from the certain knowledge that, for missing signs of treachery, he would fall under the spotlight of investigation, his own loyalty scrutinised. With this man, on a matter of innocence or guilt, he had no doubts.

'First Cyprus. Then a small aircraft took me to a military base in Austria, up the river. I was their prisoner, but strong. It was a torture of exhaustion, lights, and always questions as to where I had been with Brigadier Joyberi. I told them nothing. I resisted.'

But on the matter of innocence or guilt, regardless of an opinion he had formed, he gave no indication. His task now was to deliver the man to those who would make the ultimate decisions on how to use him. He allowed him to talk and permitted himself little hisses of apparent sympathy.

'At the first opportunity I evaded them. They took me to see a ruined fortress, with history connected to Great Britain, and I ran. You know what followed. It was my first opportunity and I had deceived them . . . I fear for my wife.'

They crossed the border without checks. He took a route over the river to the south of Bratislava, capital of Slovakia, where he came for discreet meetings involving senior figures of the VEVAK who would not wish their presence in Europe to be noticed. He headed for Stefanik airport, where a plane waited. Hossein could always make arrangements speedily.

'The British said they would bring my wife out of Tehran. She is a fine woman, well known to Brigadier Joyberi. He was at our wedding. She is devoted to our revolution. She, too, has been kidnapped, and I will stand up for her. She is loyal, as I am.'

Hossein would not be flying with the traitor, condemned from his own mouth by his own blatant deceit. Two more junior officers, from the Iranian delegation to the Slovakian tourist fair, would accompany him and they would, no doubt, during a long journey, hear the same dirge of lies. The aircraft would not be of the executive standard provided by the agents of the Little Satan but a two-engine, propeller-powered light aircraft.

'I love Iran. I am the devoted servant of the revolution and was kidnapped . . .'

Petroc led the cleaning of the safe house and had allocated areas for each of the others to work through. He would do the living room, where the debriefs had taken place; Sidney and Anneliese had responsibility for the kitchen and the toilets. The babysitters were given bedrooms and the vehicle. They worked late, the lights blazed and the village below them slept.

He had used the vacuum cleaner, and now Auntie had taken it upstairs. Every washing-up bowl and plastic bucket was in use and Sidney's wife kept the kettle on so that near boiling water was constantly available. Each surface was cleaned, the fingerprints erased, DNA traces eradicated. Any sign that they had been there was conscientiously removed. Cheerful music spilled from the kitchen, a late-night station that seemed appropriate. Later he'd get Rollo Hawkins out of bed, regardless of the hour and whether the bloody bear had been found. The music dwarfed the drone of the vacuum-cleaner but couldn't lift the gloom. Trust had failed.

Because the trust hadn't bound them, they were cleaning the safe house. He couldn't have said whether there had been much more to be extracted from the corporal or whether they had squeezed him dry. He had been looking forward to meeting the wife, gazing into those captivating eyes and evaluating whether she was worth the sweat of the extraction. He had heard that Tadeuz Fenton, breaking radio silence, had told the boys behind the lines not to entertain delay by bringing her. He had swallowed and continued cleaning. Upset? Hardly. Troubled? Not really. If he dusted, dried and wiped, his mind was diverted from the situation of the men and the linguist – it didn't bear close examination.

The table where he had sat with Mehrak. The view through an open curtain was of the lights of the village, a couple of communications towers with red lights and the sheen of the river. The roses were still there. He stopped, let the cloth drop, gazed at them: still perfect. It was such a 'nice' place, the village, with the house and the view of the river but it was flawed. Hard to make the connection between men running for their lives up some mountainside, hunted like a fox with hounds in full cry. Another connection, as difficult, with a young woman set loose: people who had done the Balkans had said thc hardest thing was when villagers fled before the arrival of a paramilitary murder squad leaving their family dogs behind. They had driven off in their cars and the dogs had run after them till they dropped. He was trapped by the roses.

Sidney was by the door. He recited, '"My love is like a red red rose, That's newly sprung in June . . ."'

Petroc murmured, '"So fair art thou, my bonnie lass, So deep in love am I; And I will love thee still, my dear, Till a' the seas gang dry."'

And, beside Sidney, Father William held the picture. 'If there wasn't an objection, PK, I'd like to have this. Just to put in a drawer somewhere for when I'm old and my memory needs a jolt. "To see her is to love her, and love but her for ever". All right?'

Petroc said, 'No problem. "For Nature made her what she is, And never made anither!" Absolutely.'

Nobby hovered. Petroc took the roses from the vase. He slid one into the button hole of his jacket and gave the other to Sidney.

A small, bright moment.

Nobby spoke. 'He went because we told him it was fouling up. All the stuff we said to his face meant nothing because he could hear you, Petroc, and your end of the communications with London. He knew it was bad, and the cordon was closing on them. He knew they'd missed the pick-up. The carpet in his room's all scuffed in the corner where the pipes come in for the radiator. There's no dust on them and I reckon his ear wiped it clean. Heard everything. Sorry to be the bearer of that news and don't shoot me. A lesson for the future, I'd say.'

Petroc nodded briskly. Work to be done and then they'd be gone.

'I'd call that a very serious mistake,' Rollo Hawkins said. 'He'll maintain he was drugged and coerced into going with our people, but the first problem will be the blood and toxicology tests. No incapacitating chemicals in the system. He won't have thought of that but it'll blow him out of the water. There may be a warm welcome waiting for him wherever his flight lands, but then he'll be taken somewhere quiet and the chances of him being seen again are virtually nil. Many have done this . . . Russians, Koreans, Iraqis and Iranians. They believe they can talk their way out of a sack with the neck tied, but they can't. From the moment his foot touches the apron, he'll be the walking dead. They'll believe nothing he says – neither would you, Petroc. If he prevaricates they'll torture him. I hope, Petroc, you didn't get to like him.

'Anyway, good news at our end. What was identified as a bear's carcass is now known to be a cow's, fallen off a cliff. The vultures had messed it about, hence the error. Better than good news, we think there's been a sighting of our old boy. Great excitement. As we like to say, all's well that ends well . . . if not for your defector, who – by going back – has made a terminal error. Goodnight, Petroc, sleep well, and move on.'

Tadeuz Fenton slept. Another day would dawn and new horizons beckon: a morning meeting with the Germans, and he was hosting a lunch for the senior trio of French officials – same trade – in London; in the afternoon he had a session pencilled in with the Service's man in Oman, and they'd talk about running assets across the Strait of Hormuz – there was an exciting prospect of getting a bright young fellow, Iranian, into a position on an uncle's fishing boat. Always useful, fishing boats. They could go anywhere, weave among naval formations. Their skippers the world over had a reputation for single-minded obstinacy when told, in any language, to bugger off. The Revolutionary Guard Corps had fast missile-patrol boats, Kaman class and home-built or the

Chinese-made Houdong class, and kept them in creeks off the islands where the Strait funnelled international oil transport. He sounded a useful boy.

There was always another day and his thoughts before sleeping had been that the fresh horizons promised well. Sara watched over him. They'd talked a little of the spin that would be appropriate for the following day and had options open whatever the outcome. The old Cousin and the old Friend had seemed pleased enough with the last load of material sent on to them from Vienna. Sara would fix a lunch for a digest of the mission. He slept well – and why not?

His hand was over her mouth.

She had said, 'Across there, what are we going to do? What's next?'

He hadn't been sure of what he'd heard. 'Don't talk, just imagine.'

'Imagine?'

'Don't talk.'

'Why?'

He didn't know if he had heard the voices. 'It's a waste of breath.'

The clouds scudded over the moon. The rain had gone, and the sleet: the snow had turned to a slush and he knew she was struggling with the blister. He heard voices. Zach didn't have the torch on but they could sometimes make out in the light of the moon the tracks the three guys had left. At others the snow cover had been whipped away by the wind and he'd lose the trail, but the general direction of their route was clear. He had not known at first whether he heard voices or the wind on the bare branches of the few trees as they climbed. When he had identified the sounds as voices, he had assumed that the guys had sat down to rest – maybe not as fit as they'd thought, or they'd felt they'd made their a point and bivouacked, expecting him to catch them up alone. He thought she was talking either to keep herself awake or because the blister hurt too much for her to struggle on in silence.

Now the voices were clear.

His hand was over her mouth and she tried to bite his fingers, then must have heard them. Talk in Farsi with the Tehran accent. She stiffened against him. He crouched and eased her down beside him.

Zach heard what was said.

One of them wanted to shit, but if he dropped his trousers he'd lose his bits to frostbite – and he'd be dead if the sergeant found him with his trousers down. He had no paper. He would have all the paper in the world if he shot the terrorists who had already killed two good boys. But shooting was too good for them. He had heard from the sergeant that a whore was with them. Maybe they'd fuck her before they shot her. The sergeant had said that the man who shot the terrorists would be well rewarded – not rials but dollars.

Zach thought they were like the men on the building site.

There were stone outcrops between where he hid with Farideh and where the soldiers were. The boy who needed privacy would come to the far side of the heap of rock, and when he did, he would be beside them.

They went on their hands and knees.

The snow was between their fingers, under their nails and in their sleeves. He imagined a shout, a torchbeam, the arming of a rifle and another shout. No shot yet because the reward for a prisoner would be greater than that for a corpse. Maybe, afterwards, a trophy photograph of themselves standing close to the wretched Zachariah Becket, twenty-six, and . . . She would shoot, and then all hell would break loose. A half-dozen automatic rifles. Now they were on their stomachs. He tried to force his backside lower and bury his belly in the snow, then the rough grass, and make no noise. She moved like a cat.

He heard the boy call that he might lose his dick but had to shit.

Zach considered what sort of trail they were leaving, slithering about on the snow. It was colder without the rain, and at dawn their track would be better preserved. They had barely begun. They stood up when they came to a riverbed. There were stones of all shapes and sizes, smooth, and just a trickle of water. She let him slot her arm into the bend of his elbow and he took part of her weight. If the blister beat her, they were dead. He wouldn't leave her. Never would. *Across there, what are we going to do?* An answer, but not spoken.

18

Zach couldn't know how the day would end. Where might he be?

He took as much of her weight as he could over the rough ground. Put one foot in front of another and didn't linger.

A weak light grew round him. He could see some twenty feet ahead, and then the mist made a curtain in front of him, opaque, defying his efforts to see where he was going.

The day might end with him lying on a bed in a hostel, or sitting in an economy-class seat on a feeder flight, heading for a hub with a beer in his hand. He'd have her beside him. It was possible. As it was also possible that a rope would be tied to his ankle and he would be dragged down the hill to where the military had their vehicles. His head would be battered to a pulp on the stones. She would be beside him on another rope. The clothing she had taken from the New Zealanders' cupboards would be mud-smeared and blood-drenched. They would have been slaughtered. It was also possible, probable, that by the end of the day they would be huddled beside each other, their hands tied and their ankles manacled. They would be blindfolded and lying on a concrete floor, waiting to be interrogated, tortured and sentenced to death.

She had little spare flesh on her, but she weighed more than he'd have dreamed. It was one thing to have a woman draped over him in his bed, but with each yard they went she seemed heavier.

He had no footsteps to follow in the snow. They were long gone.

The mist had thickened. In the dawn he had been able to register features of the ground. They were in a shallow valley, perhaps half a mile across. Then the sides rose in a gentle gradient. The ground they crossed was ragged, and some of the stones were glacier-smoothed, but others were sharp and hurt him when he stumbled on them. He had been able to absorb an impression of the valley before the mist had closed again. He could have said to her, with confidence, that it would lift and that they needed to press on hard while they had it to cloak them. Would it lift? He had no idea.

He thought it important to be decisive.

He paused and the wall was close around him. A track that might have been from goats or sheep went right and left. Ahead – at the limit of his vision – there was more difficult ground: the stones were larger, the rocks sharper. He had no light to tell him that they were heading west and that the sun would rise behind him. To cross the larger stones would have further slowed them. He reckoned the blister had opened again – he had heard several gasps of pain and knew she was trying to hide them. He hesitated.

But he must be decisive. 'We go to the left.'

'Are we lost?'

'Of course not. We go to the left.'

'You're sure?'

'I hope – no, I'm sure.'

He looked into her face, searching for reassurance. He couldn't read in her eyes whether she believed him or not. She tapped his arm with her hand: they must move. She had one arm looped over his back, and was clutching his anorak; he had an arm across her back, his fingers gripping the clothing above her hip. He could feel her bones and her softness.

Who were they sharing this place with? The guys who had walked out on them, border guards, professional military, and men from the Revolutionary Guard Corps. He thought they had blundered through an armed camp, their only protection the pistol she had and the grenades he was carrying. To the soldiers in the camp, the one magazine in the pistol, the grenades, two of flash and bang and two of gas and smoke, would amount to a mosquito swarm.

He was slower and she was heavier.

They hadn't rested in more than five hours. He didn't know how far it was to the frontier or what the frontier was. It might be a ditch, or a strand of wire or a collapsed watch tower whose stilt legs had crumpled. It might be nothing. They might have to walk for four more hours, six, or to the end of the daylight. He tried to follow the path and didn't know what direction they were heading in. It would have been good to talk. The kids at the School used to gather to chat about optimism, the disasters in their lives or the hopes that carried them forward.

Voices . . .

From behind and in front, muffled in the thickness of the mist.

The moment of panic.

Zach dragged her off the path and they stumbled among rocks. He had her arm. The voices closed on them. He remembered how the day might end: freedom, death, caught and waiting. She hopped after him. Maybe a dozen yards and they were at the edge of the mist. The voices grew in clarity. He dragged her down and lay across her. He didn't know whether his buttocks showed between the rocks or his shoulders.

The voices melded. Two foot patrols. They cursed the weather. They swore that the frontier was sealed, that the net mesh was tight enough. They talked about the woman who was with those they hunted – laughter cackled. What would they do to her if they caught her? They made bets as to who would go first, if there was no officer. Cigarettes were lit, backs slapped. They cursed the mist again and went on their way.

Zach raised his head and had a fading view of uniforms and weapons. Then the curtain closed on them. He couldn't go either way on the path for fear of bumping into them. He pulled her up, hitched her arms high and caught her waist. 'Stay strong, Foxtrot.'

'You'd be better off without me.'

She was giving him the opportunity to lose her. He clung to her.

Wally hadn't argued.

Each had a theatre of responsibility: Ralph talked well, was a quality driver, the best shot among them. Wally was the medical wizard and he could shoot nearly as well as Ralph. Mikey was their main man and took the decisions.

They had talked it through.

Mikey's insistence.

They were nestled among big rocks on a tump near to the centre of the valley, which made a natural fortress. If it hadn't been for the cloaking mist they'd have had fields of fire all around them. It had been Mikey's demand that they stop there and debate the decision. Press on, hit the dirt, regard the mist as a gift from God, use the compass and keep going towards the border. Or lie up, find a vantage-point and wait. With each step they had taken, they had expected to hear the pursuit behind them. Not from the 'ragheads' or 'camel jocks', but from the young man who had the education, the language, and should never have been sent. They were certain that the girl would have dropped out and he'd have come on. Good enough that he had salved his conscience by hesitating, but he'd have seen sense, waved her off and legged it.

No dissent.

They were there, watched, waited and stayed quiet. They itched to smoke, but didn't, and expected to see him.

They saw patrols. Troops came close enough to smell them. They had good kit, machine-guns, light mortars and snipers' rifles. They moved easily and were formidable. Once they could have sniffed the fumes from a trooper's cigarette. Another time they could have reached out and shaken a hand.

Wally would not have made the decision, but he had gone with the flow. Who would know? He doubted anyone would. It would not have been Mikey's style, or Ralph's, to stand on the high street in Ealing, up from the Broadway, rant about waiting for a guy to catch up five miles or so on the wrong side of the Iran border. Natalie had never known what he did in Afghan or Iraq, and Contego distributed no medals. He was bloody cold and wet, his stomach was growling from lack of food and his throat was raw because he'd drunk all his water. Mikey hadn't said how long they would wait, and what chance there was of the mist lifting.

He would have kept walking but it was easier to move with the tide. It was a shit place to be. He leaned forward, across a rock, eased aside Ralph's H&K, the G36, slid the trauma bag back across his shoulder and whispered, 'Right now, where would I rather be?'

He won nothing back. They all endured the wait.

They came forward and used the path. It was the same as others they'd been on – the same stones, the same rocks, the same slimy mud.

He supported her, which was difficult because the path that the goats or sheep had made was so narrow.

The blow fell like that of a sledgehammer. Everything was the same: the path, the stones, the wall of mist. She had sniffed all the time he'd taken her forward and had said she'd lost her handkerchief. Now he'd found it. It lay at his feet. They had walked in a circle and ended up where they had started out from before first light. Zach could have cried.

He felt himself shake. He wanted to sink to his knees, and lift his face and howl. Through the mist he heard a voice, likely that of a warrant officer or a senior sergeant. He berated a trooper who had dozed and should have been alert.

Easier to give up. Chuck in the bloody towel and let it fall against the referee's ankles. Her eyes quizzed him. He could have made a speech: 'I'm really sorry, Foxtrot, my fault. Because of me, we've squandered precious energy, put you far over the pain threshold, achieved a near perfect circle and have come back to where we started.'

He mouthed it. Then he turned her round. He lifted her so that her foot didn't catch the loose stones on the track. He set a pace. They scuffed stones and kicked into mud.

He went faster than he had through the first hours because he had looked up. The light was brighter. The mist hung close on them, but not over them. Above, it had thinned. There was no sky yet, and no clouds, but they would come. He had wasted precious hours in doing the great circle to end where they had begun. He had not owned up to his doubts or shared them. The mist above his head would clear first, then what hung over the ground. They would be exposed. He hurried. She didn't criticise him. Zach felt the hand on his shoulder and his own hand above her hip.

They went on, and the light grew around him.

They came back to the house.

Mandy Ross thought she had been pushed further, that night, towards an abyss than ever before, that now she was scrabbling at its edge. Anger caught at her.

The mist was on the ridge they had looked up to from the rendezvous point, but down at the house there was a clear view towards the majesty of Ararat. On any other day, she'd have joshed Dunc with talk of artefacts from the Ark, and the need to buy some more well-rotted timber. Far below the pyramid peak, covered with snow, were the foothills, then the closer ones and the meadow where the horses were. The boy was still with them. He lay on the ground, wrapped in a blanket, but his face was clear and his breath made clouds. The horses' hoofs were around him but they wouldn't trample him.

The calls had come. She and Dunc had kept vigil. Neither had known where else to be. She climbed out of the car, slammed the door after her.

The first call had come from that hideous bloody building on the Thames. Sara Rogers had reported, 'We've parted company with the corporal. He's done a runner.' Half a dozen questions had risen to her lips, and Dunc had barked his into the receiver, although Sara had hung up. The second call had been from the big man: 'We've told them to cut and run, drop the woman off, excess baggage, and get to the border. They'll be with you later in the day. Get them out of that theatre and onto an aircraft. Talk more later.' Not for discussion, and she'd thought it done with a ruthlessness that was hard to stomach.

He unlocked the door. She went through to the kitchen, switched on the kettle and the oven, then raided the fridge: sausages, eggs, mushrooms, tomatoes, potatoes.

She said, 'Don't they know it's fucking people they're talking about?'

He said, from the living room where he was heaping kindling and small logs into the grate, 'If you're not a human being, would you know how to treat one?'

The ring heated and fat bubbled in the pan. 'It was all for nothing. We're on our bums here, there's guys hiking in that place with a half of a bloody army out searching for them. Those guys were put across for *nothing*. Lives on the line. Say something!'

He was calm, almost icy. 'Sorry, Mandy, but you're wrong. It wasn't for nothing. It's about top table, having a seat there and being "inside the loop". We were walking with the big guys. We were alongside the creeps from the Agency and the humourless automatons from Tel Aviv. We thought being at the top table about justified anything. Isn't that what we should be thinking?'

'For fuck's sake!'

'The wife was probably never worth the effort because the corporal was about dry.'

'You never said so.'

'I never said, "She isn't worth the effort", true, and neither did you.'

He came to the door. Mandy flicked the food in the pan. Hot oil splashed the front of her fleece. 'I might take it to my grave that I never spoke up.'

'Why did we ever think our world could be mysterious and exciting, stressed out, and *clean*? Foxtrot put her life in our hands.'

'More fool her. How's that? It's as dirty, Dunc, as shit on your shoe. Do you want this food?'

'I think what I want is . . .'

'Why not?'

She turned off the ring, and wiped her hands on the tea-towel. She glanced at the cooker to confirm that she had switched it off. She looked at Dunc – a decent enough man, and as troubled by the morality of it as she was. To have gone to bed with him once was, perhaps, careless, but to go past the door of her own bedroom and into his marked a different stage. There would be consequences and life would move on, change. She had a husband and a child. He looked at her, steady-eyed.

She shrugged. She said it again, 'Why not?'

Mandy Ross thought it was the only way she knew of evading responsibility for never having said, of the extraction, 'She isn't worth the effort.' They went through the living room, past the big window that gave a view of Noah's mountain, the horses and the sleeping boy, and went into his room. She kicked the door shut after them.

They had worked through most of the night and into the early morning. Sidney had proved a stickler for thoroughness.

The babysitters had gone. Petroc Kenning had marvelled at their resilience. No concern shown over a job well screwed, and actually a degree of bonhomie that had previously been under wraps. A final communal coffee on the patio and a smoke, then Sidney had gathered up the butts and bagged them. They would leave nothing behind – neither print nor trace.

He was with Sidney now, and Anneliese waited in the big car.

The others would be at the airport and would take the same flight to London. Then Auntie would be on the link to Aldergrove and was already talking of a walk with his spaniel in the fields around Cloghy. The red rose was in the button-hole of Father William's jacket, contrasting sharply with his shock of white hair. He'd kissed Sidney's wife's cheeks, and had complimented her cooking, then shaken Sidney's hand as if they were old friends. A bus from Heathrow would take him home. Nobby had seemed reluctant to leave: his route to his occasional girlfriend's flat was by Underground. There had been no recriminations. The little beggar wasn't mentioned over the coffee. The last word had been from Father William, who had thanked Petroc for the chance to take that trip to Judenburg, where old family had been, and how a part of their history now had an image to it. The 'little beggar' was gone, and the memory of him consigned to a grave. They had waved as the car drove away. He didn't find fault with them.

'Are you about ready?'

Petroc nodded.

A mission finished, his own rose was pressed flat inside a Filofax in his bag. On the scales, the outcome would be rated good, not exceptional, and certainly worthwhile. The brothel outlay had been recouped. The only discomfort he felt involved the security of four men on the wrong side of that border . . . but they were not Petroc Kenning's responsibility. He had not recruited them. They had taken a sort of gamble that they might or might not win. Did any of them feel bad? No.

Yes, he was ready.

A key turned. He noted that Sidney and Anneliese had worn latex gloves for the final run through the safe house. Sidney took the key. They walked away, Petroc leading. He paused. His eyes raked across the vineyards. The harvest was in, the tractors in the barns, and he could look down on the village, the church, the narrow streets, the station, and on the winding, eternal river. He might not say it – the man already possessed an inflated ego – but he believed Sidney had chosen the location well. With a bit of luck the SPAR might already be open and he'd get Sidney to buy two or three bottles of the local wine, a souvenir. He'd be in London long enough to down a couple and might leave one on Tadeuz's desk. It was the sort of thing the demi-Pole liked – made him feel wanted.

They edged onto the winding downhill lane and Sidney drove with a chauffeur's care. Petroc thought the festival decorations looked well on the doorsteps. They came towards the square in front of the church. He saw the number plate. Saw the *Corps Diplomatique* logo. Saw the two men who sat in the front seats, their faces blurred by smoke. Quietly he asked Sidney to pull over and stop. When Petroc Kenning intended to throw a fragmentation grenade, he was always quiet and polite. He'd be a moment.

In the car the windows were up. Both men were smart, well turned out – better than Petroc, who'd had no clean shirt to wear. They watched him. He walked easily towards their car and stopped beside the driver's door. An older man sat closest to him – Petroc thought he might be the security officer for the delegation: he wasn't a junior. There was no movement from either and the engine ticked over. It was confirmation of sorts that they had their man and had shipped him on. Now a senior figure had come to the village and retraced the coporal's steps – as told by Mehrak. They had put themselves where they could see all the traffic coming down the Rote-Tor-Gasse. He stood by their car and smiled affably. Those who knew Petroc Kenning often commented on the quality of his smile – an ice-melter. He smacked his hand on the bodywork immediately in front of the windscreen, hard enough to shake the vehicle and make the wipers bounce off the glass. He was about to do it again when the window came down. He thought it was as his uncle might have played the situation. The window was opened to its limit. He held the smile and spoke Farsi.

'Lovely day. My name is John Thomas. My apologies for having disturbed your evening at home. Anyway, in the UK we have tits and chaffinches, sparrows and robins, and we call them songbirds. I believe that, in the Islamic Republic, yours would include the bulbul, the bar-tailed lark, the tawny pipit and the rock bunting. Don't know about you, but we've found that the best singer of all is the canary, which originates from islands in the Atlantic.'

They gazed back at him, impassive, and Petroc held his smile.

'I'd call your boy a canary. He sang long and he sang loud. He sang till he was hoarse and had no voice left. We didn't have any more use for him then. For men like me, and I'm a right John Thomas, it's a grand thing to have a man walk through the door and sing – a lovely voice before he lost it. We call him a "canary", which is our way of saying that he sang well and did us proud. Gentlemen, it's been a pleasure meeting you. Oh, yes, he sang in harmony to every tune we played him. Safe back into town . . .'

He went to the car.

Sidney drove away.

He thought Sidney had been offended by his betrayal of Mehrak, who had been deluded enough to reckon repatriation was possible. Sidney had believed in him, had thought friendship existed between them. He said, 'I thnk that's how Hector – mean old bastard – would have played it. Never abide by the Queensberry Rules, not if you want to win.'

They drove at funeral pace towards Vienna. It was cruel to have made the canary speech, but he felt good about it.

Sara had made the links for the conference call to the offices of the Friend and the Cousin and had patched in the scrambler. Tadeuz Fenton – 'bright-eyed and bushy-tailed', as he liked to say – was effortless with charm and appropriate calm.

'Don't get the wrong idea, Gunther, nor you, Ja'acov. We're not talking about an "escape", far from it. I had expert people on the ground with him and the impression fed me was that the little man had pretty much exhausted his usefulness. We'd sucked him dry. We left the door open. He may have been under the impression that he had outwitted us, tricked his way back into the arms of Iranian security people, but it was as we intended. He was kicking at an open door.'

Did they believe him? Could an elephant fly? Were they merely polite, and not wishing to exacerbate his discomfort? That would be a first. A few moments of silence, then the beginning of an interrogation.

The American, with what Tadeuz believed to be the pomposity of Agency people, asked, 'After the co-operation you received from us in logistics, did you consider enquiring of us as to whether we had loose ends to tie, a few outstanding questions, before you opened the door?'

He deflected it.

The Israeli's query was harder to handle. They usually landed meaningful punches. 'We helped you to go in, helped you to come out, because you said it was important to get the woman. What is the situation with her, and the men we ferried, and why is this a matter of principal concern one day but not the next?'

He spoke boldly. 'We evaluate risk constantly and take very seriously the safety of our people. They've dropped the woman and she's free to go home. Unencumbered by a passenger, our people are now striking for the border and should be across it late this afternoon, maybe at dusk. I'm very confident of a successful conclusion. As I'm sure you realise, we've supplied our allies with first-class original material, which should be cause for gratitude, not carping. We made an assessment and stand by it. You have been accorded information not previously available to you, and that is where, I suggest, we leave the matter. The Service is a big player and intends to remain one. We're all busy men, so let us go back to work. But, worth saying, it's been good to do business with you both.'

He drew a finger across his throat. Sara cut the call.

He murmured, 'Bastards. Ingrates.'

She told him when his first appointment was and gave him the file. He went to the window, massaged his face with the razor and flicked through the pages of the brief. It was a dreary start to the day and he should have felt elation, but it had been snatched away.

He turned to her as she tidied away the folding bed. 'If it doesn't work out, Sara, it won't be our fault. It'll be down to failures on the ground.'

'Yes, Tad. Of course.'

The boy brought the coffee and the paper. Neither wanted the coffee, both wanted the paper. From the time he had woken on the thin mattress under the workbench, Excellency had heard each bulletin on Radio Tehran, and Highness had fiddled with the small set that carried a short-wave channel, trying to connect with the BBC's Persian Service.

'Nothing?'

Excellency turned the pages fast. 'It would be a big story, but it isn't here.'

'It would lead the radio bulletin.'

'It says they're hunting for terrorists near Khvoy. It would be on the front page if they had her.'

'And on the radio. Highness, I think she's still running.'

'Does he have her photograph?'

A chuckle. 'Poor boy. I pray not, or he's condemned.'

They readied themselves for work. They had no picture of her but she was in their minds and always would be.

* * *

He had been shown the woman's abandoned clothing. More junior men had been disgusted that the fugitive running with the foreigners should have abandoned all pretence at modesty. His features had remained impassive. He had been led to see the stolen camper van and had heard where it had been left. He had been told the criminal gang were on foot, had left tracks, were heading towards a cordon. What were the weather conditions? Poor at the moment, but an improvement was imminent.

At the forward command post, the uniform of Brigadier Reza Joyberi carried weight. A major had gathered his staff under a brown tented roof, and there was the clatter of radios' squelch, the howl of atmospherics, and the softer patter of fingers on laptop keyboards. Instructions were mouthed into chest microphones. A map was pinned to a plywood board and the plastic covering rippled in the wind. He had been fully briefed. He said his role was that of an observer, he would not interfere. He had decided that the operation under way was a fine opportunity for him to study the terrain and topography of this most sensitive border region in the event that . . . The major, young, enthusiastic and perhaps ambitious to be drafted to the al-Qods division, didn't need warning of the danger of a foreign military incursion. How could the brigadier be helped? As always, with transport. The brigadier said, in confidence to the major, that more was learned from studying a panorama than from maps, computerised simulations and second-hand reports.

He would see little, he was told, before the mist lifted. The major, more confident, expanded: 'The mist is a robe that a woman wears. The mist lifts and it is as if the robe falls, revealing all.' He remembered the blanket slipping from her shoulders, the nightgown and the shape of her body. He wanted transport, needed only a driver. He would see for himself, from close to the frontier with Turkish territory, the flight of the fugitives and the blocks set up to intercept them. He felt a chill because deceit didn't sit easily with him. In recent years he had had little call for it. He might see her, perhaps see her taken, then would walk on towards the horizon and the highest part of the ridge where, on the maps, a line was drawn.

A driver was allocated him, and a jeep. He was saluted by a fresh-faced boy who showed his appreciation to be so honoured. The brigadier thanked the major for his courtesy and assured him that his co-operation would be reflected in a confidential report. He was driven away on a savage track that climbed in the mist to the plateau.

An investigator owned great powers, but limits existed. He faced them. Could he name a suspected fugitive when that individual had rank and status in an organisation with the prestige of the al-Qods division, then issue a general warrant for arrest-on-sight, or should he pass responsibility for such an edict to a higher level of authority? He pondered. A general warrant would mean that every member of the IRGC, the gendarmerie and the *basij* had the right to make Brigadier Reza Joyberi his prisoner. It was a daunting decision that faced the investigator.

Predictably, in his office where suspects usually sat stone-faced or jabbering, he dithered. Already many hours had passed.

There had been surveillance men at the end of the road where the brigadier and his family lived. They had watched, at a distance, a house where lights burned and a radio played. They had seen the wife and children leave with sports kit. A new detail had taken over and the lights had burned through the night, the radio had continued to play, dawn had come and suspicion had grown. But it was hard, so early in the day, for the team to gain permission to approach the house. It had been achieved, but only when the morning had worn on. More time lost. Then further permission was granted. The door was broken down. The house was empty.

Perhaps a dozen hours had been lost.

The interrogator's superior reported only to the Supreme Leader, and was in Qom on spiritual retreat. His aides suggested that matters outstanding should be settled without disturbing the director of intelligence.

He hesitated. No order had been issued. He would be at the extreme limits of his power, where it was dangerous to stand in the Islamic Republic. He teetered when confronted with that limit.

A telephone was on his desk, and his juniors pressed him to use it, but he smoked, drank coffee and weighed the implications. Always, in the Islamic Republic, it was a risk – which could be of life and of death – for a man to climb too high, walk too far, from his power base.

The mist thinned. Zach saw continents of cloud and lakes of blue. When he dropped his eyes he was in the midst of the mist, but with each minute the area of sky above him grew and the distance to the edge of his vision extended. The advantage of the mist clearing was that he could see milky sunshine. He trudged on towards where he believed the border would be, confident of being on the correct line now.

There were no trees. They passed outcrops of rock with deep clefts and bushes growing in them – and heard more voices.

Matches were asked for and given. Gruff thanks were expressed and silence fell. Zach couldn't have said whether the voices were twenty feet from him, at the limit of the mist wall or behind it. He thought the troops were spread out in a line of small groups.

Zach had become used to her weight, as though she was a rucksack on his back, filled with stones. They had not talked for half an hour. Their last conversation had been premature and dangerous.

'What is there?'

For Zach or for her?

'What is there for you and what is there for me?'

For him there would be the search for a job, no idea where – he might be labouring again on a site, but not his father's, or perhaps doing something else. For her, he didn't know.

'When we cross the border?'

When.

'When we cross the border, I suppose you are met, but what of me?'

What to say? The rucksack on his back had a sort of damp warmth, precious. He knew old people said, 'be careful what you wish for'. Perhaps to 'wish' was to tempt fate. He didn't tell her. Instead he was distant: it would be sorted. A pitiful answer, but he hadn't dared to offer a better one.

'You don't want to tell me?'

Zach didn't tell her that he wouldn't let her out of his sight in daylight or beyond the reach of his fingers through a night. That he treasured the warmth. She mustn't speak.

More voices.

A man in authority cursed the speed of his men and demanded they move faster. They were behind and closing. Zach dragged her to the side, made calculations of the route they took. Her weight, always, was on one foot. He hadn't looked down.

They were on rough ground. Stones were embedded in tufts of dead grass, and they had a sheen on them. He hadn't looked but she had snagged. Impatience from Zach, a flush of panic. He had tugged harder. She squealed, a tiny sound in his ear but buried in the mist. He looked. She was caught. The foot that took her weight was wedged between two stones that in turn were held fast in the ground. Her ankle was angled oddly. He did not know whether, in hurrying her, she had broken, had torn, had twisted her ankle. She did not cry out.

The voices passed.

She shook clear of him.

She was Foxtrot, baggage – no longer wanted. She should have been abandoned. He had brought her on and wrecked her. The mist was lifting, and the pace had to be kept.

He could have lifted his head and screamed up into 'that little tent of blue/Which prisoners call the sky.' A teacher had read *The Ballad of Reading Gaol* aloud to them, tried to introduce a class of Philistines to the poetry of Wilde. He had read well and his eyes were damp as the verses told of a condemned man taking exercise each day before his execution, peering up from the gaol's yard. He had destroyed her.

He felt her courage. Foxtrot convulsed against him. He hitched her up.

She scratched his face. He understood. She wanted to be put down. If he laid her on the grass, she would turn her back to him and wave him away. She would babble about burdens, and about him going on. She would invent nonsense about having seen the guys' footprints. He could feel the blood her nails had drawn on his cold skin. He hung on to her. Now her small fists battered at his face. Zach stumbled, almost lost his balance, regained it. One arm held her thigh and the other gripped her upper arm on his chest.

What of me?

They would be together if the home they shared was a cardboard box. He would live with her in a shop doorway, on a pavement.

She must have realised she couldn't win. She was draped over him, and they went on, as the mist edged back.

Zach didn't know whether, any more, he dared to hope.

They had landed. Mehrak had not been told how long they would be on the ground or where they had come down. They had not taxied to a main terminal and seemed to have gone towards cargo sheds.

It was Baku. There was a moment when the angle of the blind at the porthole in front of his seat allowed him to see out briefly. The hoarding was for import-export, into and out of the Azerbaijani capital.

The engines were off. Mehrak knew little of light aircraft, nothing about an American-built Cessna 380. There was a brochure, with the edges creased, in the pouch in front of him. He had turned the few pages on the flight. He had read the speed, the altitude it would reach, and its range. He had needed the diversion. Mehrak had never before been on an aircraft that had been so comprehensively thrown around by a storm. He had not wanted to seem fearful. There had been moments when it had heaved up, and others when it had dropped, as a hawk did, and the engines had screamed.

But they were down. He stretched in his seat, then flicked open the belt clasp. He stood up. He wasn't hungry but his throat was dry. He hadn't been offered anything to eat or drink. The co-pilot had come into the cabin after the worst of the storm and had talked to his escorts but said nothing to him. The door was opened and gusts of wind blasted into the cabin. A ladder was against the hatch and the same crewman went down it. Mehrak gave it no thought.

He went towards the door. The way was blocked.

A reflex statement, 'I want to walk.'

A shaken head.

'Then I want to stand and take the air.'

Again the refusal.

Mehrak pushed. A hand clamped on his arm from behind. First one hand, then the other: they were brought together, the feel of metal and the click of the cuffs.

He began to speak, voice rising: 'I am the driver and assistant to Brigadier Reza Joyberi. I was kidnapped by British agents and escaped. I demand that—'

He was pushed down. No respect. He sprawled in his seat. A nightmare broke in his mind. They towered over him. He was helpless, and certainties were lost.

They moved discreetly and well. For Wally it was the best stuff he'd done since leaving the regular crowd. He'd experienced nothing like it since he'd gone into the contractor industry. It was the way they would have progressed if they'd been in a Red force on the Brecons or on the Plain, and were fleeing from the cordon of a Blue crowd. They jogged, they did forced march, and four times they had dropped down on their elbows and knees for crawl drills when they were near their enemy – an enemy with live rounds and instructions to kill. Twice the safeties had been off on the weapons.

Wally reckoned they needed the drive of an officer, who would have done good 'talk'. Wally wanted an officer – any who had been in his old regiment in Iraq or Helmand.

Each step they took brought them closer to the border, a table of cold beers, a shuttle flight and a welcome for him from Leanne, good girl. It brought him nearer to the flat in Tyneside above the shops – there'd be a wedge of post behind the door, half of it in brown envelopes with red type – and nearer to her demanding he take the kids for the coming weekend. Near the border: each step was taking him further from the guy behind them, who hadn't caught up with them, and now would not.

An officer – a proper one, not like Mikey – would have squared it. He would have told him that their charge for freedom was justified: people 'made their own beds'. An officer would have dressed it prettily. There was no officer, though, and no way did it feel right to have left them behind.

Mikey called the halt. He took them onto a hump where the rock formation was clumsily strewn and there was cover. Were they going to lie up? Mikey said they were. Did Mikey realise the mist was clearing? He had fucking eyes in his head. How long did Mikey think they'd lie up? No answer.

He'd only get one night with Leanne because guys on the Contego books were always coming back from shit places. He thought he read Mikey, who likely felt as uncomfortable as he did that they'd left the guy and the girl. He strained to see deeper into the mist until his eyes ached. He prayed he'd spot them, but he didn't.

A crow flew from behind him. Zach saw it against the sky's blue. The shadow brushed past his feet and was lost in the mist. Her weight buckled him. He was following a track and didn't know whether it had been flattened by troops of the Revolutionary Guard Corps, by herdsmen or the guys. He remembered when he had first seen her, in the room over the repair shop, and she had worn the tent-like 'good *hijab*'. Even so, he had known immediately that she was slight-built, light-muscled, tight-waisted.

Her head was on his shoulder and her face was turned away. He trudged on, his sole aim to beat the steadily thinning mist. The flight of the crow and the distance its shadow had travelled had shown him that time was against him, maybe laughed in his face.

For strength . . .

. . . he could use the hand of the arm that supported her on his back to worm into a pocket.

To cling to what strength remained . . .

. . . he could put those fingers further into his pocket. He felt the edge of the card and the laminated surface. He took it out, jolting her. She moaned softly. He lifted his hand. His eyes were glazed with tiredness. Her face, tiny on the card, was blurred . . . He didn't know how much further he had to travel, or how much longer he could support her. The card went back into his pocket. Her ankle hung useless beside his thigh, but she didn't cry out.

He could see the sides of the valley. The mist was shallower and had no ceiling. The valley walls were tumbled rocks. Great boulders had careered down from the upper slopes, and far to the front there was a great mass of grey stone, a pyramid, with a white dunce's cap. He thought it was Ararat.

They came towards him. Zach hadn't the energy to step aside or to cower in any cover he could find.

First he saw the heads. The ears were up – they were alert to him – and eyed him. They were good strong beasts and had panniers strapped to their backs. They were roped so that they came in single file, and the leading horse had a coat against the cold of thick black hair. He counted six. The bags were empty and the animals fresh. They were sure-footed and didn't slip. A boy was at the head of the second horse. The horses' heads were higher than the mist, but the boy's was lower and he came out of the wall, a hand on the harness.

What to say? Zach said, in Farsi, quietly, that he wished him well and that God should go with him. The boy looked hard into his face, and at the woman he carried. His lips moved but Zach didn't hear the response. Then they were gone. Four men followed, each with an automatic rifle. They ignored Zach.

He went on. He thought of survival, and was deep in the reservoirs of his strength, draining them. The mist was clearing. Then they would be seen.

19

Zach had his head down. He feared he would trip and looked for each step. She was so heavy now.

Two moments.

The first: half a dozen crows were above him and shrieked.

The second: a scrap of warmth on his cheeks. It went into the scratches and played on his forehead.

The birds, ebony black, with wide wing spans, spun, dived and soared over him and he realised they had a view of the ground, and that they could begin to hunt because the mist roof had now blown away. They were fine birds. Zach had never paused when he was on a ladder or on scaffolding to watch crows, kestrels, buzzards or magpies. Birds gave him no pleasure and animals were outside his orbit. Now they hunted high above him, looking for carrion.

The sun made a clearer shadow of his body and hers. He couldn't have said when he had last felt the sun on his face. He didn't sit on beaches: the guys on the sites yearned from Christmas onwards to be in Greece or on a Costa shore. The sunlight tickled him.

He lifted his head and tried not to break his stride. He could have wept.

The sides of the valley were clear to him. From the angle at which the plateau began its climb he saw the tumbled rocks, the clefts in the crags and the few scrub bushes that had a hold there. He looked ahead.

He could have sworn at the unfairness of it. He was on the path that the horses would have made. It stretched in front of him, the gradient shallow. The ground was a mix of scree, on which rainwater glistened, yellowed grass and the bigger boulders. He could see each patch of scree, grass – where the last flowers of summer still showed faint pink or violet petals – and where the rocks were. Clear and precise. He knew now that he would be watched.

He sucked air into his lungs, heaved her higher and took the next step and the step after that.

There was a target. The path that the horses had made, the indents of their shoes, went to the west past the scree and skirted the humps of boulders where the crevices threw big shadows. It went on until he lost sight of it at a ridge. Beyond it there were no more horizons until Ararat. The ridge, Zach thought, was the border. He couldn't evaluate whether it was one mile, two or five, but there were pinpricks of colour at the limit of his vision. There would be flags at the border . . .

As he saw it, he was a third of the way to the horizon. There were other boulders that were nearer, and more that were further and higher. One had his attention: the sunlight caught a surface and the reflection was crystal bright. It might have been from the shaft of a bottle thrown aside by one of the men on firearms escort for the horses with the panniers – or the lens on the telescopic sight of a sniper's rifle.

He felt bare. He assumed that many had a good view of him.

Zach went on. The sun's line would have changed, and the reflection was gone. In its place were the rocks, the grass and the scree, and far in the distance the colours of what he thought were flags at the ridge that would be the border.

He didn't know if she had seen the reflection. He didn't tell her. He didn't dare to stop for rest in the shadow of a boulder. He went on, the sun warming him and the crows keeping him company.

He stirred. Mandy's head was in the crook of his arm. The sunlight came through the window and its force slapped cruelly on her face. She wore no makeup to mask the lines at her eyes and those starting at her throat. He believed she made a virtue of eschewing glamour. The light swamped the room, rested on the lower part of the bed where the covering had slid away and was on one of her legs and one of his feet, the rugs and clothing scattered on the floor. He saw his bag near the wardrobe, but never unpacked.

He tilted the arm on which her head rested. Her only jewellery – put on the previous evening for the first time . . . why? No explanations – was a pair of stud ear-rings and a fine chain, with a small crucifix. It was permitted at work, too discreet to offend the Islamic brothers and sisters who'd joined the Service. More than the sunlight, the jewellery disturbed him. Who had given the items to her – or had she slipped down to the high street and bought them for herself? He almost hoped she had. It cut at him that her husband might have handed to her two little gift-wrapped boxes. He swallowed it, looked at his watch and jerked up.

Her head bounced and her eyes opened.

She wore nothing. Neither did he. Mandy caught Dunc's eye, had that moment of confusion – 'Who the hell are you?' – might have quizzed him but didn't. Then her eyes squeezed shut.

She said, 'Oh, my God. I don't believe it.'

He didn't hold her. Dunc Whitcombe didn't tell Mandy Ross – fellow struggler in the middle ranks of personnel assigned to the Iran Desk – that she had been the best he had known in pretty much all of his adult life. She was good news, and he was *fond* of her.

She kicked off the rest of the bedding and was on her way to the bathroom. He heard the toilet flush, then the shower start up, and imagined she'd be lathering herself in the hope of getting rid of the traces. He lay on his back.

When she came back in she had a towel round her. She bent over him, the towel fell, her breasts sagged down and she kissed him lightly on the mouth – as if it was the office party and someone had tracked down some mistletoe.

Dunc said limply, 'I didn't know what time it was.'

Mandy said, matter-of-fact, 'I'm blaming you. I reckon this marks the most unprofessional behaviour of my working life. I'm ashamed. But I'm not bothered that we shagged, Dunc, or that I cheated on my husband. I'm ashamed because I've been in bed on my watch.'

'I think I hear you.' He was off the bed, passing her.

'I'll never forgive myself. God . . .'

He was at the window. A brilliant light bathed Ararat, and the myth of the Ark was in his mind. He shared her shame at having treated the trip as if they were on vacation. It was the biggest mission of their lives, and they had pushed it into second place, giving priority to personal gratification. He could hardly believe it of himself, let alone her. He was at the window.

The horses were gone, and so was the boy.

Far away, light nuzzled the ridge that was the border over which, *perhaps*, that day they would come. There was a faint flick of colour high up there, and he strained to recognise the red of the Turkish flag against the sky's blue. If the horses were gone and the boy, there was a chance that the border was porous, that smugglers at least believed they could avoid the patrols – but only a chance. He should have been there, and was not. He threw on his clothes, didn't wash or shave, and didn't need her to echo, as he scurried to the car, that it was 'unprofessional behaviour' on her watch and his. Mandy was still zipping her jeans when he drove away, and the house door was wide open behind him. His shirt was unbuttoned to the waist.

He had forgotten about the four men, and shame curled in him.

'Are you sure, Brigadier?'

'Yes.'

He stared out from the place he had chosen, a low eyrie. He was on a rock slab. Millennia before, it had fallen from a higher cliff, come to rest and now made a flat, level surface. He sat cross-legged in the sun, the wind blustering around him. He could see her.

'Do you not need me, Brigadier, to stay and guide you back?'

'I do not.'

He was on the north side of the valley. If he looked to the right, to the west, he could see the twin, separated, flags and the ridge. Beyond it was an abyss, then a vague view of open ground, finally blocked by the bulk of the mountain. If his gaze switched to the east, the expanse of the valley floor stretched away. Beyond it there were more mountains, and far beyond what he could see, the towns of Khvoy, Maku and the city of Tabriz, all inside the country of his birth. He carried a small monocular, convenient enough to fit into a tunic pocket. Up here, exposed, the cold raked him, and the young man deputed as his driver and guide flung his arms around himself. When Reza Joyberi held up the lens and focused it, he had a good sight of her.

The young soldier persisted: 'Shall I sit further away, not disturb you but be here?'

'Go back to the transport.'

The boy, pleasant enough, no more than twenty-one, would fear a verbal attack from his commanding officer if he returned to the jeep – three miles back, left where the track they'd used had petered out – and abandoned the senior man, then couldn't answer a barrage of questions: what happened to him? Where did he go? What did he say? The brigadier felt composed as he watched her. He could see her face, and most of her hair brushed like a veil on the man's chest. He gorged on what he saw.

The boy was standing, still unwilling to leave, confused. 'Should I go to the vehicle, then come back for you? I don't think it will be long.'

'It won't be long.'

'Those two are walking into the block . . . But, Brigadier, we were told that there were three others with them, foreign terrorists. I haven't seen them.'

'You should go back to the jeep and wait for me there. Young man.'

'Yes, Brigadier.'

'Consider. Did I reach such a senior rank in our armed forces, in the al-Qods division, by fearing – in daylight – my own shadow? Must I explain my intentions to a private, second class, then act only if he approves? Go back to the jeep, and wait for me as long as is necessary.'

He hadn't raised his voice. He believed he had spoken kindly to his guide.

'Yes, Brigadier, if you're certain.'

'I am.'

He smiled. He heard the kid scramble away, dislodging a few pebbles, and he was alone. His faithful Mehrak had destroyed him. His own man's wife had killed him. He didn't doubt that if he had stayed in Tehran and attempted to face out an investigation by that cold-faced bastard, the interrogator, he would have ended on his knees in a garrison camp yard, waiting for the cocking of a pistol behind him and the firing of a bullet into his neck. Or they would have hanged him in the Evin. Who would have spoken up for him? No one. In his mind he saw the many faces of officers and officials he had worked with. None would have risked their own necks and their families' futures by standing with him.

He could have taken his pleasure with any number of girls. They would have been available easily and cheaply at the bazaar and brought to any hotel room he had chosen. He had not used his position for that purpose. He had sex only with his wife: he was fond of her, and of his son. He had had to see the corporal's wife. He couldn't escape from her and watched her. Would she have slept with him? Would Mehrak have driven his wife to the Laleh International, five stars, or the back entrance of the Firouzeh?

His eyes were on her and he saw the pain in her face each time the boy stumbled. Her ankle hung loosely and he thought it was broken.

He might have done – his corporal might have driven her to a hotel in the centre of the capital. As for himself, he might have sat in a chair, fully dressed, and made her sit on the bed, also clothed. He *might* simply have gazed at her, not spoken, let silence drift around them. Jealousy burned in him. He saw how the man carried her, with an arm under her thigh. He looked ahead of them . . . A fantasy ran its course, and his life jolted forward. She was behind him. It had been a powerful fantasy, but it was past.

On the route to the distant twin flags there were two clusters of stones, dumped there in some massive earthquake, and the private had said that men from a commando force of the Islamic Revolutionary Guard Corps were hidden in the shadows and gullies of the one nearest to the fugitives. His face had glowed with pride when he had spoken of them. Then there was a second mass of stones and flat ground, empty, to the flags. He had watched the boy and his driver's wife long enough to estimate that they would blunder close to the rocks where men waited for them in twenty-five to thirty minutes. Why did they not go faster? Why did they not lie up, now that the mist had lifted, and wait for the cover of darkness? Why did they go up the centre of the valley and not take a route at the side where there were rocks and scrub they might have flitted between? He saw her . . .

. . . and saw her in the small, cramped room of the apartment when men had stripped open her drawers and cupboards, had rifled through her clothing and the blanket had fallen from her shoulders. She had gazed back at him, challenging him. He pushed himself up. The brigadier would not be seen. He was skilled in making broken ground. His friend had done it in Iraq and Lebanon, and had survived. He slipped away. He wouldn't look back, search for her: his eyes would lock on the flags, distant Ararat and his future.

Mikey watched them, Zach and her. He was high in the rocks of their vantage-point and could see over the top of the jagged formation ahead. They were beyond it. He thought it was like watching a death. He'd done that. He'd seen men, colleagues in arms, slip from life in the sand of Iraq, and others go when a leg was taken off by a bomb in an irrigation ditch of Helmand. He had seen his mother go down slowly in the hospice near Worcester. There was a weakening, an acceptance of inevitability, then a leaking of fear. There had been a young squaddie in Helmand, who hadn't lasted long enough for the casevac helicopter to arrive – he'd bubbled a request for the photograph of his girl to be taken from the breast pocket of his tunic. Mikey's mother had asked – a last smile – for a final cigarette. He thought they faced it, and understood it.

Wally covered the side approach to their covert lie-up and Ralph had responsibility for the rear. The distance from Ralph to the flags was around two thousand yards and they hadn't seen troops manoeuvre into position where they would be cut off from the last dash to the border. Truth was, Mikey was uncertain about the implications of them being where they were, without food or water, other than what they could scoop into their hands from the rain deposits. No bloody cigarettes either.

If they hadn't hunkered down among those stones, they could have been over whatever the border was and scampering down the reverse slope. They could have been banging into the airwaves and demanding transport. They could have been starting on the drive to the airport. There would have been no high-fives. They would have been unresponsive and evasive.

So instead they had stopped, and taken positions among the stones. They had their firepower and . . . They had seen the short convoy of horses going through, led by a boy, followed by guys with Kalashnikovs. Mikey had also seen a man edging through rocks and bushes on the north side; he had rank because Mikey's binoculars had picked up the brightness of his medal ribbons.

He watched them. They came so slowly. He didn't feel good – neither did the others. His imagined outcome had not materialised.

They came at a pitiful speed, as if death faced them. He heard a drone far above, saw the silver flash in the sky and ignored it. He watched them come closer to the ambush point. Ralph and Wally wouldn't help him because he had command.

He sat in the seat. The handcuffs were fastened tightly enough to gouge into the skin at his wrists. The co-pilot pushed open the cockpit door, beaming. Current airspeed was 245 knots, and current altitude was fifteen thousand feet above sea level. The border was six thousand feet up so there was a decent view of the ground. They were in contact now with the tower at Tabriz and would land there in twenty-seven minutes. A minute earlier, they had crossed the international frontier.

The two men sat behind him, clapping enthusiastically. He remembered now when he had last been in a small aircraft. The British woman had been correct, civil, and had offered him drinks

– coffee, tea, juice. He had not been a criminal. He looked from the porthole. They were over a long, shallow valley, high hills flanking it, and behind him was the huge expanse of a great mountain, snow-covered at the peak. Below he glimpsed bright colours. They flew steadily, the aircraft rocking a little in the winds but not as it had on the previous leg. He was manacled for love of his wife. His safety rested on the word of the brigadier, and he was confident his officer would speak for him. He clung to that. He had nothing else to hold to.

He knew where the door was. He had seen the catch. He had worked out how many paces it would take him to get from his seat to the door, and how long before they reacted. He had thought he could kick them when they grappled with him but they would back away if he had successfully opened the door. Either he would fall alone or with one of them hanging onto him. He had not done it because he had believed the brigadier would defend him. Now they were alert behind him and the chance, small, had gone. He trusted.

Petroc Kenning recognised Tadeuz Fenton's ability to put a gloss on things. His juniors came away from an audience feeling better, reckoning their efforts were appreciated. He was greeted as he had expected: 'First class, Petroc. Your efforts have been outstanding.'

He had been sandwiched between the desk head's session with some Germans and – as Sara Rogers had explained, a lunch with a trio of Frenchmen, who might be fed a little of the operation just completed, enough to stir some admiration. 'But he wanted to see you, Petroc, because he's pleased. He has a meeting straight after lunch, then he's with the DG, but he'll want to catch up with you this evening. Sixish?' Sara Rogers might do an inquest report but it was unlikely that Tadeuz Fenton would allow the stain of failure to touch him.

'Never more serious . . . We've left our Friends and Cousins wanting more, which is good. What's better is that we've given them material they were short of. We can seldom say that, but in this case it was true. We've created a little hillock of debt, which is always healthy, and there has been collateral.'

She was in the doorway and poised to intervene. It was another little game that Tadeuz Fenton liked to play: she would indicate to him that he was already late for his next appointment when in fact his schedule was intact. Everyone liked to do that – it made their importance bloom.

'Stands to reason that the corporal's master is holed below the waterline. We've generated in the highest echelons of their military formations a very real sense of chaos and distrust. All down to you, Petroc. I'll catch you later.'

He was gone.

Half a dozen questions were skipping in Petroc Kenning's mind: five dealt with the team put in there; one involved the woman.

He said to Sara, 'Do you know the Burns line, "*To see her is to love her, And love but her for ever*"?'

'I don't think so. Should I?'

'Perhaps.'

'Is that why you're wearing the rose, Petroc? Very fetching, even though it's rather squashed from the journey.'

He smiled, he hoped graciously, then slipped out. The trouble with wearing a rose, already damaged in transit and flattened, was that it cut short its life. The scent was uplifting, but it wouldn't last beyond the day.

He was at the outer door, then turned. 'Sara, where are they?'

'On the last leg, if they can ride their luck.'

They were far from the beginning of their journey and far from its end.

The wrapping on the packages had stood up to the ferrying over the border and into Iran, to the hand-over supervised by officers of the Revolutionary Guards Corps, then into and out of a lock-up garage in Khvoy. They had been brought on by vehicle, over a cross-country route, with more money paid to border police. Then the seventy two-kilo parcels had been transferred to mules. The caravan had now to go half the length of the valley before it met the men who accompanied the horses that always did the last stretch before slipping across the border.

The descent into Turkish territory, using the tracks left by shepherds, led to the lorries waiting in an industrial estate outside Doğubeyazıt. This was the most dangerous port. In other circumstances, the transfer would have been postponed until the security alert along the frontier had been stood down. But timetables existed for feeding the habit of addicts in Western Europe.

Those who came with the mules and met them with the horses were in contact by mobile phone and talked in code to each other. The exchange was fast. The two groups did not take tea, and both would hurry to be off the plateau while the military was there.

The packages were loaded into the panniers across the backs of the horses. Gossip had been exchanged: the hanging of a dealer in Tabriz, a gun battle further down the Tehran road in which Guard Corps had been killed . . . a barrel protruding from a mass of stones and madness in the fog – a man carrying a woman in the middle of the valley. They had in common, the hard men who smuggled across this frontier, a love of the boy who couldn't speak and couldn't hear. He was revered. It was rare for them to harbour sentiment.

Another stage of that journey had begun. The boy led the horses, which moved with care.

Zach held the ID card tightly. The plane had long gone and the quiet was total. The crows had left them – would have gone to search and feed beyond the hills. He thought that if he shifted his grip, she would fall to the ground, and he didn't rate his chances of lifting her again.

Zach sleep-walked. Rocks scraped his shins and his trouser legs were blood-stained. She had begun to wriggle in his arms and he struggled to control her, but knew he would fail. He wondered if she would scratch his face again.

She said, 'Do you believe, Zach?'

'Do I believe we can reach the border where the flags are? I must.'

'I've always believed.'

'If we don't believe, we should sit down and wait for them to come. You have to think of "sunlit uplands".'

'What's that?'

'For you and me, it would be our finest hour.'

'I don't understand. I know about believing.'

'There was a speech by a leader, the "finest hour" speech. It was when defeat seemed certain and people had to be kicked into believing. The leader said, "If we can stand up to him, all Europe may be freed and the life of the world may move forward into bright, sunlit uplands." It was about our freedom as a people. I steal it.'

'Is this a "sunlit upland", where we are?'

'It's where the sun shines on that ridge. We go past there, that rock outcrop, or we fall—'

'Never raise our hands.'

'Fight them. He said, "We will fight in the hills; we shall never surrender." A teacher read that to us. The words didn't mean anything then. They do now.'

'We go to the end, Zach.'

'To the sunlit upland. We have the grenades, Foxtrot, and the pistol.'

'And we believe.'

He said, 'We believe.'

But Zach didn't. The sunshine bathed the upper limits of the valley and the ridge. It made bright patterns on the stones and diamonds sparkled among the scree. There were rocks ahead, with deep shadows. That was where he had seen, once, a flash of light – as from a broken bottle or the lens on the scope of a sight . . . They went on. He thought people didn't look for their God until they faced the end of life. They didn't hark back to speeches until their fingernails were scraping the bottom of an empty bucket. He had a strong grip on her leg and she hung on him. Her warmth thawed his body, and the card with her picture was tight in his hand. He didn't know how they would get past the heap of stone and rock.

* * *

Only once did he break into a run. The brigadier had come to the flagpole, a pine trunk from which the bark had been stripped. Above him there had been the tricolour of green, white and red with the symbol of the revolution and the woven words, overlapping and in a tulips shape, 'There is no God but Allah'. The flag had been outstretched in the wind. It had been designed thirty-three years ago, and he had faced it on many parade grounds at rigid attention. He didn't look up at it, but by the pole he stood at his full height, no cover and ran.

He was a military man. He wove. He didn't know if, at that moment, a rifle barrel traversed and a fore sight locked onto the small of his back, or whether a finger eased from a guard and onto a trigger. He ran at his greatest speed and in a zigzag without pattern. The shot never came. His anxiety had been unfounded. He found a rough track, stamped down by horses' hoofs, and passed an old wall of broken sandbags. Many had rotted and the sand spilled out. There were cigarette ends and he supposed it a place where smugglers paused, smoked and studied the ground ahead.

A decade or two before, the ditch had been excavated by men with pickaxes but the sun had crumbled the sides, and the ice beneath the snow had done more damage. He leaped across it.

There was a strand of barbed wire. It might have tripped him if he hadn't seen it. It was rusty and the posts that had once held it up were flattened. He skipped over it. All that he knew was behind him, as was the wife of his driver from whose shoulders a blanket had slipped. Purged. A lifetime finished with. His leading boot stamped on a rock. The jolt went up through his ankle and into his knee. He was free of their vengeance. The past lost, the future beckoned. The local authorities would pass him respectfully into the hands of the Milli Istihbarat Teskilati, the Turkish intelligence organisation, who would be rid of him as soon as possible, and the Agency in America would take delivery of him. He would be flown to the United States, his wife would join him, his boy would be schooled there and, after many months of debriefing, he would go to a university. Perhaps in California he would teach international relations . . . but that was far in the future.

He reached the second flagpole, made of prepared and treated wood. The red flag of Turkey fluttered there. He was at the peak of a ridge. The sun beat down on him. Stretched below him was a great plain, dun brown, with curls of smoke from small homes. He saw the mighty Ararat.

The brigadier slowed, straightened his tunic, flicked dirt from his trousers and straightened his forage cap. He began to walk down the hill, using a trail made by hoofs. Soldiers appeared. If he had looked for them he might have seen them, but had not. They wore the uniforms of a NATO country and carried American weapons. Nothing was said. Some closed around him; others sank back to their concealed positions. He set the pace, not them. He was no one's prisoner and the future gaped open for him. He was only surprised that he hadn't heard gunfire behind him, but maybe the woman and the man had surrendered and were taken. He was safe from her denunciation.

Vehicles were parked in an old quarry below, some civilian and some military. A knot of men and a woman waited for him.

'He wears the insignia of a full brigadier general and has medal ribbons for combat service. The flash on his arm is that of the al-Qods.' Imre Terim, major of mechanised infantry, had his binoculars raised. His brow was knitted in concentration. Then he gave a sudden smile. 'Tell me, do tourists who come here to search for archaeological treasures from the time of Noah know about the al-Qods and its position inside the Islamic Republic?'

Gazing at the mud on his shoes, Dunc Whitcombe declined to respond. He leaned against the bonnet of their vehicle and was a few feet behind the soldier. There were three jeeps and a lorry, and men had gone up the hillside, scrambling like rock monkeys, and disappeared from view near the summit of the ridge. The major hadn't spoken to them and hadn't shared his flask of coffee, or the bread and cheese his driver had given him.

'A man of that rank and position, travelling alone, has not made a mistake in his map reading. You understand me? There are reports, only reports, not confirmed, that troops and border patrols are searching for terrorist fugitives attempting to leave that country, a paradise on earth. Do experts in archaeology know about 'terrorist fugitives', madam? Do they also fit into your study of prehistoric myth?'

The buttons on her blouse front were not fastened correctly, which she hadn't realised till the major had driven into the quarry. Her hair was a shambles and her stomach growled. She had her mobile in her bag and wouldn't use it until the news was confirmed. She remembered the men on the long flight out of Germany and into the USAF base, that they had been taciturn and uncommunicative. She had thought then that had she scalpelled into the motivation of each she would have found no sense of noble heroics but of necessity: a sort of modern press-gang recruitment, regular-army drop-outs who had gone to a private contractor. She remembered too, the boy Dunc had brought south from the building site. She and Dunc might be consigned to hell-fire for what they had done. Now she didn't answer. Better to stay silent than to extend the irrelevance of the lie. She was a changed woman, had done her Rubicon thing – 'Why not?' – and regretted nothing. Should she? Not the time to indulge in a conscience-scouring exercise. Later . . . Not now.

It was a sudden movement, but the major took the binoculars from his neck and handed them to her. She fiddled with the focus, then murmured to Dunc, 'It has to be him. Only five of that rank in that formation. Can't see all of his face, but it looks right from the pictures. That has to be Reza Joyberi. In flight.'

Mandy passed him the binoculars. Dunc beaded on the face and features. The brigadier came down easily and, by his bearing, with authority. From his screen, high in Vauxhall Cross, Dunc had thought himself close-up to – the jargon phrase – high-value targets: they were brigadiers of the IRGC, generals of the navy and air force, mullahs, intelligence officers and negotiators at the United Nations in New York and Vienna. He had never seen an HVT in the flesh before. He gaped.

He'd talked about them, had never seen one. The man, assumed to be the defector's boss, didn't seem to notice the soldiers who escorted him, and came without effort the last few feet of the slope below the ridge. 'Yes, done a runner, Mandy. He'll have the dogs of Hades after him.'

A salute to the major, crisp.

Flawless English, a correct accent. 'I am Brigadier Joyberi, al-Qods. I seek political asylum. I wish to be passed to your own agencies and then to the Americans. I think they will welcome me. Please, make the contacts.'

The major reached out his hand. The brigadier pushed his own forward so that they might seal the greeting with a handshake, but the major twisted his to the side, then pointed to the holster on the brigadier's belt. A pistol was removed, given to the major, who passed it to a sergeant. It was cleared, the round in the breech ejected and the magazine taken out. With a gesture of his head, the major indicated his jeep. The sergeant handed the pistol and its ammunition to a corporal, then led the brigadier to the passenger seat.

Dunc Whitcombe thought a ranking Iranian officer had made an error of judgement in assuming his authority would rule the responses of a Turkish major. He stared up the hill, Mandy Ross beside him.

He heard a shot. Far away. Muffled, but a shot. She stiffened. Their hands touched, clenched, loosed. A long way off, a shot, from another world.

Zach walked forward, like a robot. In front of them was the confusion of rocks and stones, cracks, gullies, places where the sun beat down, and the shadowed areas. A soldier, festooned in webbing and gear, had stood up and seemed to be laughing in contempt of them. Another had poked up his head, and there had been movement, indistinct in the dark.

The first soldier had called to him to put her down. There was a platoon here who had not had the pleasuring of a woman for weeks. If he put her down – they wanted to get on with it – they could line up and—

She fired. The weapon was beside his ear, she had barely aimed, and he was deafened.

A first shot, which missed.

The laughter had stopped.

Zach doubted she had ever fired a live round before. He hadn't. It was different from when he and the guys had been in the builders' van, driving past the roadblock chicane, and the soldiers had come out of the dark and Wally had fired on them. *Different*. All the faces were gone. Rifle barrels jutted out. He saw each one.

Zach let his knees fold and went down. They might have taken cover from the slight rut of the path that the horses had made – eighteen inches, or less. Might have been twelve. She was fighting him. He tried to cover her, but her knees and elbows jabbed him and then she used the pistol barrel to smack his face aside.

Automatic fire spattered around them.

Earth was thrown up, fragments of rock splintered, and he heard the whine of ricochets. He couldn't get lower. Zach realised he was lying on soil, stones and dampness. He was no longer protecting her. Like a rejection.

She fired twice more. Free of him, her elbows taking the strain, the pistol held in two small fists, she aimed. The range? Twenty or thirty yards. She had fired three times. He screamed in her ear: 'How many shots left?' She showed him four fingers, a thumb and one finger. The bullets fired at them pecked close. A few were short, others long, cracking above them. Law of fucking averages. Not long. She had six shots left.

How could he throw when he was lying down? The new dilemma. How to chuck one of the fucking cans? He had talked of 'shall never surrender' and about 'sunlit uplands', but she had six shots left and there was continuous fire around them. The law of averages said that their luck would run out, and he didn't know how to throw when he was prone on his gut. So he had to bloody well learn. He didn't know whether it was smoke or flash-bang, but did the pin, heaved his arm back and threw.

Zach had white light in his eyes and a dull thud in his ears. The sunshine and the deafness minimised, for him, the flash-bang. He tried another, made a greater effort. It landed short of the stones and smoke burst from the canister. The wind blew it away.

He was an amateur. He knew how to translate the poetry of Mosleh al-Din Saadi Shirazi from old Farsi to modern English, he knew what mix of mortar was best for brickies and how much water to add, and he knew how to quote tracts of speeches. He didn't know that it was best to read the fucking instructions on the side of a grenade, that it helped with smoke or gas if the thing was detonated upwind. And two were gone. The smoke went fast and made a small cloud, which had no time to settle on the rocks where the guns were.

Grenades were thrown back at them – fragmentation: killers. She fired at the man lobbing them . . . four left, five fired and all missed. He heard the shouts: they were impatient now, and the laughter had returned. They wanted her.

Zach saw her face. All the beauty had gone. A hard face, defiant. He saw the snarl at her mouth, and the ugliness it gave her. He couldn't place her alongside the young woman who had been with him in the van, then in the street as the policeman had advanced, or at the start of the valley when they were alone and he had carried her. Then the face had been soft. Veins bulged in her neck and her eyes blazed. She fired again. He had a grenade in his hand, and he didn't know whether it was flash-bang or smoke. He didn't check the wind. It was a small gesture.

He saw another grenade arc towards them and screamed to her to duck. He didn't see his own burst, or where it fell, or if it had had the remotest value. There was a smooth-sided rock close to him, no more than a yard away, and the grenade bounced close to it. If it had landed, black and squat on the rock, it would have fallen into the cavity where he and she were taking cover, but it didn't. It rolled away from them.

He didn't know what to do. The sun was fierce on his face, and he thought it lit him. She had the pistol up, used two hands.

And she was hit. Then Zach felt a heavy blow to his chest, up near the right shoulder, and she sprawled over him. The firing kicked earth and the grenades bounced closer.

Mikey said, 'I reckon it's that sort of time.'

Wally said, 'I wouldn't argue with that.'

Ralph said, 'Be going the wrong way, might be the worst decision ever. But.'

He'd seen her hit. Mikey slapped on the satphone, rapped the pre-set key that held the open number where they'd be picked up – like a universal distress call, no security. Wally hitched the strap of the trauma bag over his shoulder. They had a few grenades and the Hecklers. They'd watched the grenades thrown and seen the volume of fire put down.

Mikey didn't say it, just thought: they didn't do medals for private contractors, or welcome-homes, with the British Legion turned out in Brize Norton or at the Final Turn, the roundabout on the way to the mortuary at the Oxford hospital; it was likely that both Contego and Six would wriggle at compensation payments for injuries. He had a small light, bright green, on the outer case of the phone. He'd seen Zach – decent enough, but a bloody passenger and an innocent – rocked by a bullet strike. They wouldn't have cried out. People didn't, not with gunshot wounds because the shock numbed the pain at first.

He said quietly, mouth close to the microphone, but for his guys, 'Do it like we used to and shove it up them. If we had bayonets we'd fix them. Frontal charge. It's what we have to do.'

A moment of clasped hands.

They broke cover. They ran towards the arse side of the rocks where the firing and the grenades had come from, aiming to take them from the back. They put down fire as they ran. They went back up the valley and away from the flags that marked the border. Fire came at them from the sides and the front. The surprise had barely lasted. They ran and the breath sobbed in their throats.

The voice boomed, the volume high. The technicians and their managers spoke only when it was seriously necessary, keeping their words minimal and hushed.

Vicki had been in the bunker communications area, burrowed far down into the rock below the sovereign base area of Dhekelia an hour before her shift was supposed to begin. That shift was now over by an hour and a half. She wasn't alone.

If we had bayonets we'd fix them. Frontal charge. It's what we have to do.

Until a few moments before they had been monitoring military traffic, the Iranian messages from a command post back from the frontier, the forward units placed in blocking positions. There had been a spillage of communications from the command post to more senior officers in Khvoy, and further traffic that informed headquarters complexes of developments. They had known, in the bunker, from dawn, that the day would bring closure to the mission that had been conducted in Farsi, which they followed at fourth or fifth hand. Abruptly, on a frequency they tuned into full time, a voice had shouted, over a mess of static and confusion. She – with many – had gasped.

Go for it, guys. Give it to them.

The sound then was of hammered breathing, a panting cough to clear a throat, the rattle of kit and the drumming of feet on rock. Then more noise. She had flinched, and others had tried to suppress a choke of emotion. They were voyeurs, the raincoat crowd that watched from the darkness and couldn't have played a Samaritan's part.

Incoming, guys, left at three o'clock, two hundred yards, automatic. Keep the fucking line, guys, keep the speed.

She, all of them, heard him clearly, because it was good kit.

Wally? Where are you, you bloody meathead? Keep in line, Wally. Wally, where the fuck are you?

The voice was pitched high and angry, the atmospherics had got worse, and a man murmured behind her that what she heard was gunfire. It was loud, constant, and battered out of the speakers. A fainter voice, from further off the microphone: she had to strain but heard it over the shooting.

Wally's down, Mikey . . . Wally's down.

Is he bad?

Lost half his head – that bad.

Keep going, Ralph.

Her supervisor was behind her. In a different age, she thought, he would have had his hands on her shoulders, his fingers massaging the knotted muscle. It would have been a comfort. He stood close to her, perhaps closer than was correct, and kept his breathing steady. She didn't know what any of them looked like, but supposed they were a composite of men who had been neighbours in her street – terraced and in a Yorkshire one-time mill town – and the brothers, fathers and cousins of the girls she'd known . . . She thought the woman would have been a beauty and—

Can you see them, Ralph? I can't, can you?

No answer came, and tears welled.

I know they're both hit . . . Fire from the right, automatic, one o'clock, or two . . . We have to get there, Ralph. Should never have left them. Shouldn't . . .

Her shoulders had started to shake. Her supervisor wouldn't have it, not from his team and not on his watch. A hissed command: 'Steady up, girl. Not a time for incontinence.'

Where the hell, Ralph . . .?

Fainter, and a whistle with it, as if air had been in a sealed cavity but now escaped.

Gone, Mikey. Down. I'm buggered, Mikey. They got me. They . . .

She realised that now there was one. She heard metal rasping and the supervisor spoke, matter-of-fact, of a magazine being discarded and another slotted. Two were down and one ran, air sagging in his throat, towards the guns that separated him from the young man and the young woman they had been tasked to bring out across the border. There would be no more commentary. Why should there? Who would he want to communicate with? His friends – muckers, mates – were down . . . She was wrong.

They're both hit. She's uppermost. She fired again with her pistol. Can see the blood on her. I've wasted some, and Ralph did. The guy, Zach, he's on his side. Must be her last. She's thrown the fucking weapon at them . . . Some kid, that one . . . Hey, tell them we did what we could.

The noise from the firing, his gun loudest and their guns as background, engulfed her. Vicki didn't understand how the man, Mikey, was still upright, going forward. She had blinked away the tears and stood erect. Her supervisor murmured that that was how she should be: 'Have some bloody dignity.'

Grenade – fuck. A grenade, she's bloody on it, crawled on it, and—

What she heard: shots that were closer, more distinct than before, a final volley that seemed to come from beside a microphone, and a shout, curtailed. Then, a moment after, there was a rumbled thudding and scrape, as if the microphone was grinding against a hard surface, He might have been kicking, writhing, in pain – and then the link was cut. Her supervisor said, soft in her ear, 'He's gone, he's on the ground. That's about it. Time, Vicki, to shift out.'

She thought it the worst silence she had heard. If a fly had flown across the bunker from her she would have heard its wingbeat, then the shuffling of feet, then the emptying of the space, except for those doing the screens.

It had bounced twice, then jagged sideways and come towards his head. He couldn't have moved. It was black-painted and had worm writing on it, but he didn't read it. He had seen the bare metal where the end of the pin had been before it was ripped off. Its momentum had gone and it had come to rest. Zach was almost close enough to smell it, and—

She had moved with speed, blood spilling from her onto him. She had made a final lunge and was past him. Her knees jostled his face.

She was lifted.

A fist might have caught her at the back of the waist, taken a grip on the belt where the pistol had been, and flicked her up. It tossed her, and he was spattered. Wet and mucous, mess and blood spilled over him. He saw, now, beyond her. He watched Mikey.

Mikey came up off the ground, used the shoulder part of his weapon to push himself up and got to his knees. It was as if he were punched. His body shook at the blows and blood was leaking from a shredded anorak. There must have been a last one and it took his neck. His head was wrenched round, and he fell . . . A great tiredness lapped at Zach, and he thought his sense of fight had expired with her, and with Mikey. He saw men coming closer. There were distorted views of boots, knees, and rifles aimed at him. His eyes closed . . . Too tired and too weak any more to care. He thought the sleep, now, would take him.

Zach sank, ebbed. He slipped and reckoned a last journey had begun. The bare skin of her leg, below the knee where the trouser hem had been rucked up, was against his face, and the cold was coming to it. It was in his hand, an identification card, held firm, and the grip would tighten as the hand chilled. He didn't care, and the darkness gathered round him.

20

The crows circled but were wary of the advancing cordon of troops. They made wide loops, poised to take advantage of opportunity. They lived, high on the plateau between the valley walls, on a diet of rotting carcasses: a fox that had starved or a goat that age had caught. If a mule or horse, bringing the trade along the valley, broke a leg in a rabbit's hole, it would be shot. The birds had enough food for their survival through the winter, but the going would be harder when the snowfalls were heaviest. They took opportunities. Languidly, deceptively casual, they wheeled over the carnage of the action. Had it not been for the troops scurrying forward, the crows would have been down, strutting among the rocks, pecking in eye-sockets and delighting in open wounds.

The day had gone on. The sun dipped towards the west and the valley's southern wall was thrown already into shadow.

They seemed nervous, the victors, of the fallen. The young men of the Guard Corps units had not before been a part of a close-quarters gun battle of such ferocity. They were shaken by the experience. There was no question, the NCOs forbade it, of treating the bodies with disrespect. At all ranks, they had realised that the charge from the hidden lie-up had represented an act of communal suicide. The bodies were not kicked. Neither was that of the young man who had carried the woman towards them. She was not a 'foreign terrorist' to any of them; neither was she an 'agitator' nor an 'enemy of God' nor a 'saboteur' nor an 'agent of the Zionist state'. She might have been if they had not, all of them, witnessed her final moment of life when she had lifted herself to the full height of elbows and knees and had covered the live grenade two or three seconds before its detonation. The same young men might have cheered, or jeered, as a condemned man or woman was brought to the rope hanging from a crane's arm, and snapped, with a mobile-phone camera, the moment he or she was lifted high off the ground. Here they showed respect . . . and caution.

The determination of the three men's charge had been obvious to them because it had taken so many bullets to drop them. The evidence was sprawled on the stones, the grass and across the narrow track. So many rips in their clothing, so much blood. Weapons were not touched and pockets were not rifled. That those men were dead was apparent from the spread of pallor on their unshaven faces, the backs of their hands, and the blood in their mouths, which contained no bubbles from final breaths. The woman had lost her stomach, and the man below her was still, but his face was hidden by her leg. Other than the clatter of weapons and kit on webbing, and the crows' cries, the valley was quiet. Some wept.

The tears on their faces were not from emotion. There were odd pockets in which smoke from the grenades had been trapped or held in narrow spirals by the wind. It was still strong enough to get into the eyes and do its job. The explosives, the bullets and the bodies left a sickly smell among the stones.

The crows could be patient. Their time would come.

Many of those young troops would have wondered why it had been considered so important to lead the woman towards the frontier, on foot and in danger, why other men had gone ahead, then come back and given their lives. Their NCOs could give them no answers. They smoked. They cursed the crows, always above them, watching. An eagle came but was high and would also have noted the probability of carrion. They waited.

They needed orders from superiors: what should be done, what would happen. A fire was lit. Coarse coffee was heated.

None seemed triumphant in the time of victory. They did not go close to the dead.

It was a habit that military men enjoyed when facing each other across disputed, volatile frontiers, and the habit went far beyond the strip of land on the border where the nearest centres of habitation were Doğubeyazıt and Maku. Officers talked. It was behaviour from eras long before the hot lines and 'red telephones' of the Cold War and times of 'mutually assured destruction'. In other theatres and different times, the officers might have enjoyed a slug of brandy, a bowl of rice or a pair of well-hung game birds, or they might have looked at snapshots of family while ironing out potential creases in their professional relationships. They would attempt to avoid the unexpected. There was a major of mechanised infantry in an old granite quarry below a Turkish flag and an officer of similar rank, another major, in a forward field-command post back from his own flag, Iran's. They talked.

There was urgency. The call had been initiated on the Iranian side. That major knew that a helicopter, back at the garrison camp at Khvoy, was being refuelled, would soon lift off and fly into the valley. At the back of the command tent there was a young driver who had acted as a guide to a brigadier in the al-Qods and the kid's teeth chattered nervously because his man had dismissed him, and the reason now was clear to see.

A radio frequency linked the two majors. If business were to be done it should be completed before the helicopter came and before the combat area bristled with officers of higher rank.

His name meant 'Struggle', but Khebat's success was based also on cunning.

He was in touch with his small caravan by text messages. He knew of the gun fight on the plateau and of the casualties, and also that his own people had taken delivery of some seventy packages. Now, they hugged the southern wall of the valley and were deep in shadow, winding along a trail that would have been unseen by any who had not grown up in that place. Great stones had fallen over centuries from the upper reaches of the walls and landed in the valley. They hid the horses, the escort and his son, Egid, as they made their way back to Turkish territory.

Khebat could not bribe Major Terim, and his fall-back position was a determination not to tease or belittle him. The caravan carrying heroin resin worth close to a million American dollars would enter Turkey on a route well to the south of where the major had positioned himself.

He hung back in the quarry and watched, but was barely noticed. He thought the presence of the brigadier, in the passenger seat of the jeep, was interesting.

Away from eavesdroppers, at the extremity of the quarry, Major Emre Terim paced. A small radio was slung from his shoulder and he talked into a handset, listened, shrugged and nodded vigorously.

He cut the call. His lips pursed.

His eyes alighted briefly on the Iranian brigadier, shorn now of confidence and watched closely. He saw, too, the pair of Britons, who affected to be archaeologists but played their parts poorly. He walked towards them.

Because he had been at Staff College and had attended lectures given by their intelligence officers, Major Terim believed he understood British people: he evaluated them as 'company creatures', aloof, wedded to a cold, pragmatic answer to all situations. He thought he knew the answer he would receive. Why, in fact, would he even ask the question? Why not simply act and field any difficulties if, when, they arose? He declined the obvious. *I tell you, they were lions*. Why? He had witnessed the admiration of his opposite. *The bravest men I have heard of – yes, lions*. A compromise was suggested but he felt the decision must be made by the couple, the purveyors of blatant, ill-disguised deceits.

His finger flicked. He had their attention and beckoned them. He lit a small cheroot. He faced his jeep. The brigadier sat motionless.

It was a liberty and his behaviour was no longer that of a major of mechanised infantry. He looped one arm around the woman's shoulders and another around the man's. The smoke from his cheroot was in their faces when he put the proposition.

'It comes at a price,' the major said.

'Whatever,' Mandy answered.

'You would pay a great price?'

'Whatever.'

She took comfort from Dunc's response, no hesitation.

'You are certain?'

'Yes,' Mandy said.

'Certain,' Dunc said.

'It is nothing to me . . .' The major allowed the smoke to waft at them again. His arms came off their shoulders. He was no longer their friend but again a professional soldier. He left them and strode to his sergeant. He waved imperiously to a group of soldiers: they jack-knifed straight and hurried towards him. He spoke to his sergeant. An eyebrow was raised, sufficient to indicate surprise. Mandy Ross knew enough of small units – she'd seen them on exercise on Salisbury Plain or up on the Brecon Beacons – to realise that a middle-ranking army officer operating far from his seniors had the autonomy and authority of a feudal baron in a castle on the Welsh Marches. The major called the order and it would be obeyed.

Mandy thought the brigadier didn't need to be told. The body language of the major and his summons for muscle would have confirmed what the man already knew. He should, otherwise, have been transferred to a chauffeur-driven car, taken to an airport, and would have waited in a secluded suite for an executive jet to fly him into the hands of the Agency. He sat on the passenger seat of a jeep. There were no handcuffs.

He would have been watching them through all the time he had sat in the jeep, would have known their trade and would have realised they were there to meet the fugitives, to welcome her and the boy who carried her. Mandy had barely glanced in a mirror that day. She was not at her best – pretty haggard, somewhat gaunt, no colour in her cheeks. He would have seen that they were waiting for a delayed arrival – probably had input to radio traffic. They could have ambled over to him, talked about the weather, offered the deal, which would have been a million in sterling up front and more to follow from the Agency. They hadn't.

He was walked from the jeep and the soldiers ringed him. He

went past them, and Mandy would have sworn that a slow, lost smile crossed his face. He ducked his head to her in acknowledgement, then was gone. He walked away briskly and the soldiers in front of him had to skip to keep up. He went out of the old quarry, never glanced at the major, and began to climb the slope leading to the ridge.

Mandy Ross watched him go. He went up the slope easily.

Her chin trembled and her voice was faint. 'They'd kill us, everyone we know.'

Dunc said, clipped, his feelings guarded, 'They weren't here, those who would kill us. They're in offices, wearing fucking white shirts, a world away.'

'It's about as off message as anyone in Six could get.'

'Their problem, not ours. I wouldn't want it different.'

'To have had him in our camp, down at the Fort, spilling to us . . . I mean, he knows every secret that exists in that country. He would have been gold.'

'Irrelevant because it won't happen.'

Mandy said, 'I've never played God before, and I hope I never will again. It's a death sentence.'

Dunc said, 'We owed it to our people. It's the way it is.'

The brigadier climbed steadily and at an even pace, with correct poise.

She felt the spit of rain, and the cloud had come lower. There were many at Vauxhall Cross who would have shaken their heads in disbelief at the deal she had made, and Dunc had said: *They weren't here, those who would kill us*. The flag was against the cloud. The brigadier never looked back. He might, she thought, turn at the ridge and face her a last time, look down and maybe wave as a gesture of contempt. He would have no doubt as to what faced him. He went into the cloud, was blurred and lost.

Half of a deal was done; half was outstanding.

The major was called on the radio link.

Then he waved Khebat forward, not a request but an instruction.

The old smuggler sent the text, and thought of it as another element in trading, as there had always been on the frontier.

A cairn of stones was built. It was placed a metre, no more than two, on the Turkish side of the collapsed barbed wire. Men from each side of the wire struggled with the heaviest stones they could shift. Three bodies lay beneath them. They used the biggest stones they could manoeuvre so that the wild predators of the valley – when winter came and they were famished – couldn't shift them. Too heavy for a fox, even a healthy dog. They wrapped them individually in canvas so that the rats would not be able to infiltrate and feast. The biggest stones were at the bottom of the cairn and those above were smaller and balanced better. If the cairn was not vandalised by humans it would remain intact for many years, decades, a century. Rumour of the place would spread and a myth would be born.

The men moving the stones paused briefly to watch the hand-over of a prisoner. He passed the flag of his country and the rain beat hard on him. The helicopter came in low and wouldn't linger: the pilot would have feared that the visibility he needed was fast disappearing. They paused again, and watched as the helicopter feathered, hands reached down from the hatch, grabbed a prisoner's arms and heaved him up. The hatch slid shut. They heard the lessening pitch of the engine, and went back to their work.

It would be a safe haven, and the men had the respect of those who built the cairn high over them. The rain stung the soldiers' faces and dripped off them. Two laden horses came towards the cairn, led by a child.

When Dunc Whitcombe first saw him, the boy was a blurred shape. He had not been anywhere before where weather changes were so rapid, so extreme. With the cloud had come driven snow.

It was the second part of the deal, and had been honoured.

The boy sat hunched on the back of a light-coated horse. Behind his saddle there were flapping pannier bags and beyond them – over the horse's haunches – a body. Dunc recognised the shape as that of a woman: her hair trailed stringily in the snow wet below her head and the legs flapped loosely on the other side. The boy and the body were not part of the deal Dunc had struck, and held little interest for him.

The second horse was stocky, squat and black. Dunc's view if it was obscured because the boy shielded part of the head and body of the second horse from the weather. The snow came thicker, more persistent. The boy held a rope that looped from his hands to the harness of the second horse. Both animals, coming down the slope, were sure-footed and neither showed any sign of slipping, but Dunc reckoned the ground beneath them was mud and wet stones, and soon ice would form. On the second horse, there was an awkward, bulging shape. He must have tutted, uncertain as to what he was looking at, because the major passed him his binoculars. Snow flaked onto the lenses but through them he saw the burden that the second horse had brought down the hillside. A body was wedged onto the saddle and twine was knotted to each ankle to pass under the animal's belly. He knew what he saw. The trunk lay forward, so the head hung against the mane, the chest was balanced at the top of the horse's neck and the arms hung down, secured, like the ankles, with a length of twine.

The deal was met. He hadn't doubted it would be. An understanding had been reached and honour was intact.

They came lower. The snow now made a white layer on the head lolling against the mane and settled on the body's back. It settled but didn't yet cover the clean white dressings. He jabbed Mandy's ribs, pointed and said it. She took the glasses, gazed into them, changed the focus and latched on to what he had seen, then passed them back.

They negotiated the steepest part of the track. The rest was more gradual. Dunc reflected. The deal could not have been brokered between London and Tehran. If politicians and assistant secretaries had been involved, or generals and mullahs, it would immediately have been bogged down in quicksand and the moment lost. He thought it was what happened in the field, where men and women worked out what was best for them and kept their word. There would have been a man in an office in Tehran who had equivalent rank to the head of Iran Desk, in London: neither would have dared, without going higher, to agree to it. He thought that enmities – which he would now have regarded as posturing and artificial – meant little at the level of men who faced each other and had the power of a satrap over small parcels of remote land. They looked after each other, had mutual respect. He would not be able to offer thanks to an unseen man who exercised his power from a command post, beyond a ridge and beyond the playthings that were national flags. It was almost treasonous to harbour such thoughts.

He gave the binoculars to the major, and hugged him. That was how Dunc Whitcombe showed his gratitude. The major broke the hold. Mandy Ross did not imitate him.

A military ambulance wound up the hill, turned off the road and into the quarry.

'What do we do with her?' he asked.

'Dead as mutton by the look of it,' she answered him.

'She was what we're here for. They brought her in spite of a contrary order.'

He reckoned it more what men did when they were on the ground, amid the realities, not standing back. He supposed he knew what had to be done. He turned on his heel and went to the back of the quarry. He walked to where Khebat hovered, and waited a moment while a whispered call was concluded. He had his wallet out, and his near-frozen fingers flicked through several hundred-dollar bills. He took out ten. He passed them into a grimy fist and said what he wanted. It would be done, he was assured. He thanked the man for the help his son, Egid, had given. He asked for an email address. He took another note, a ten-dollar bill, from his wallet and the man wrote it across it in pencil. He put the bill back in his wallet. It would be good for a smuggler of class-A narcotics to have an officer of the Secret Intelligence Service of Great Britain in his debt, a worthwhile bonus for a day's trading.

The arrangements were not his and the major did not try to involve him. Orderlies from the ambulance cut the twine holding the young man, Zach Becket, in place, massaged his ankles and wrists, lifted him from the horse onto a wheeled gurney and hurried him to the ambulance. One of his hands was on his chest and clasped tight in it was a small plastic shape but Dunc couldn't see what it was. Mandy was beside Zach and held his other hand; his breathing was laboured. His wounds and wet bandaging were exposed before a rug was thrown over his chest and stomach. He didn't speak. He looked into their faces. Dunc didn't know whether Zach recognised him or Mandy. Zach's face spoke of overriding pain and shock, and perhaps a shot of morphine with which the Iranians might have dosed him, or perhaps the numbness that came from an experience that was impossible to share.

Dunc realised that Zach Becket's eyes were not on him or Mandy, but struggling to hang onto a view of the other horse, where Egid sat, and the figure draped behind the saddle.

The doors closed. The ambulance manoeuvred to clear the haphazardly parked vehicles. Mandy told him it would drive to the airfield north of Van where a medevac bird, a Black Hawk, would meet it and fly the boy to İncirlik. There, he'd get the care he needed. The Americans usually tied up loose ends for them, and their dependence annoyed him.

Khebat's pick-up had gone, while the child and the two horses were distant, wreathed in the snowfall. Dunc had paid for a decent, respectful funeral – cheap at the price. Soldiers were loading their lorry and the major was a passenger in his open jeep, where a brigadier, who would have been the most prized intelligence catch of the year – for Six, Friends and Cousins – had sat briefly before he was thrown back to his death. A convoy pulled away.

When he was in the car he'd get on his phone, call up a junior staffer from the embassy and have him fly up, first plane, the next morning. The man would go to the town cemetery, witness the funeral and ascertain that Dunc's money had been well spent.

He took Mandy's arm. 'Come on. Time to go home.'

Rollo said, 'I wouldn't feel down, Petroc. Defectors are seldom the gold dust we think they'll be. Look on it as a glass half full. When did it start? A week ago? Not much more. You reacted fast and with due diligence. You extracted material that was otherwise unavailable, drained the beggar dry, and you've embarrassed his people. You've gained greater credence with our esteemed principal ally. I rate it good, clean-cut at the end. I'm not saying that defectors seldom deliver the goods we yearn for, but too many end up short of that line. Your man, Petroc, has given more than could sensibly have been anticipated, and you'll have created a storm of epic chaos back where he came from. Scapegoats will be sought, blood will flow and suspicion will spill out. It would all be such fun to watch from across the Gulf – and the silly man went home. A desperate error for anyone wanting to enjoy the sunshine next spring.

'Anyway, Petroc, here we've had wonderful news. Actually, Stephie and I are rather squiffy. Between us we've put back a bottle of Freixenet on rather empty stomachs. He's been located, our bear. He was spotted at first light this morning. Our old boy, who'd given us such heartache, was seen going across a field and one of our younger enthusiasts has been up to the farm, on the east side of Somiedo, and managed to take a photograph of the pad print in a patch of overnight snow. Massive, and the identification can't be disputed. He's the absolute prize specimen in our neck of the woods and mountains. He's magnificent and we've been through hell. Anyway, his being seen puts our priorities into perspective. Small things can matter so much. Am I rambling? Probably. My regards to your uncle, please. Do tell him our good news.'

The clocks would change that weekend. Lighter mornings and darker evenings but – at just a few minutes to six – there was still enough light in the skies over London for Tadeuz Fenton to gaze out over the river and enjoy . . . There was much to enjoy. A good session with the Germans, a fair session with the French, an excellent session with the director general, one-to-one and without an aide scribbling shorthand: he had been congratulated on a job well done. He had finished with his colleague who ran the desk in Oman, and they'd talked of a young man soon to be put across the

Gulf to crew a relative's fishing boat with a camera to mark out the coves and inlets where the fast patrol boats, with missiles, were hidden. A fine session.

Sara Rogers was at his door. 'Go well?'

'I thought so. He's going in a couple of weeks. We have high hopes.'

Unusually for her, she queried him: 'Is it considered a long-term business?'

He watched a tug boat and a police launch passing it. 'Wouldn't have thought so.'

'How long?'

'Say, four or five weeks before the alarm bells ring. Might be two months. They're usually rather headstrong, that type of youngster, and don't calculate risk. Not to worry, we'll get plenty before he's in the net.'

'I suppose so.'

'Please, get the sherry out – don't want you scratching for it when he's already here.'

She said, 'Petroc's gone home.'

'Can't have – we're talking over sherry . . . You all right, Sara?'

He hadn't looked at her before now, had breezed in. She was as white as a sheet, holding her fingers to stop them shaking. She told him. He'd been with the DG. Petroc had come in and told her the channel on the communications console to use. They had stood together, not speaking, and listened. The office had been filled with it. There had been the shouts. *Wally, where are you, you bloody meathead? Wally, where the fuck are you? . . . Wally's down, Mikey. Wally's down . . . We have to get there, Ralph. Should never have left them. Shouldn't . . . Gone, Mikey. Down. I'm buggered, Mikey. They got me. They . . .*

There had been the shooting, which beat back off the walls of the fourth-floor office on which there was a print of the Annigoni portrait of the Queen, a watercolour of the Cotswolds, and a photograph of Tadeuz Fenton bobbing his head to a cardinal, fully robed. She heard each grenade, and the screams. She said that Petroc had taken a squashed red rose from his buttonhole, held it tightly, shredded its petals and chucked it, a rather expert aim, into the rubbish bin by her desk. She told Tadeuz Fenton what Petroc had said: 'Sara, if I'd contemplated this scale of casualties, this carnage, I would never have launched it. Fuck the sherry. I'll be in Dubai tomorrow. If I'd known . . .' She repeated it, word for word.

Tadeuz Fenton came to her. His hands rested lightly on her shoulders. So calm. 'We're rather pleased with how it panned out . . . I didn't expect Petroc Kenning to show a trace of squeamishness. It's a war, for Christ's sake. There are casualties in war. We may have – or our allies may have – servicemen flying over that bloody place, even putting boots on the ground, and what this business raked up will save lives. Isn't that clear? Enough.'

'If you say so.'

'I do. We move on. It went well and is behind us. Please, Sara, would you fix a map of the strait, the Hormuz bit and the islands, on a wall where I can see it from my desk? It happened. Another chapter. No one ever said this was work for the faint-hearted or the limp-wristed.'

'Of course, Tadeuz. I expect you'll take a sherry after such an "excellent session" with the DG.'

Dunc saw him. The site was beside a main road, flanked by mesh fencing so it was easy to see. He was pushing a wheelbarrow loaded with slopping cement.

It was a rare summer's day, the temperature would have been nudging thirty, was certainly high twenties, with a clear blue sky. He was a fine-looking young man . . . It was eight months since Dunc had seen Zach Becket carried on a stretcher to an ambulance. It was eight months and not much more than a week since he had pulled the lad off a wintry, sodden site, brought him south and captured him with fine words about the 'national interest', having the 'privilege to make a real contribution' and— He was bronzed and, like all the other men, wore a uniform of heavy boots, soiled jeans and an orange safety helmet.

The two bullet holes were easily seen.

There was a conference at the University of Warwick, a 'brains trust' of military, intelligence and academics. They'd come together for a couple of days during the students' vacation. He'd driven up from London the previous evening, she'd taken the train, and the first session was due to launch at noon. They'd reckoned they had time to get across from the campus and find him.

Mandy had done the work – not difficult. It had been in no one's interests to proclaim an operation inside Iranian territory with casualties. The contractors' families, with a cut-off using Contego Security, had been generously rewarded but the details were kept sparse and the impression had been given that the deaths had occurred inside Afghanistan. The Becket parents had been proud to hear that their wayward son had shown exemplary courage for the good of his country. Their reward was a sudden flush of government-funded contracts: a chapel of rest as a new annexe at a local hospital, an extension to a public library, a state-of-the-art sports hall at a comprehensive school. The father would take back the son. It would be whispered that a wrong-place-at-the-wrong-time situation had seen Zach caught in a firestorm in an eastern suburb of Naples and hit twice in a rival gangs' shoot-out. His recovery had been good. Sara Rogers, with her considerable skills, had made the financial arrangements and charmed the family.

Where the holes had healed, indentations remained. One was on the chest, near to the heart, and the other lower down, below the lungs and ribcage. A longer scar was at the small of the back and would have come from a grenade fragment: Dunc wondered how that had been explained away – did the Neapolitans use hand grenades?

They would be there for a few minutes only, and would be back in time to greet guests, have the fruit juice and fizzy water on the tables, with biscuits and sharpened pencils, before Tadeuz Fenton gave the opening address. It had been Mandy Ross's idea that they divert here, to where a library extension would house IT equipment. He'd thought she seemed well.

Life, as Dunc Whitcombe had learned, was full of surprises. Her husband had met her at Heathrow, with their son, and Dunc hadn't known she'd sent them a message of her arrival time.

Probably for the best, but still dispiriting. She hadn't looked back, just slipped an arm through the man's and the other round the child's shoulders. The next day – at Vauxhall Cross – he'd found she'd been transferred to a desk more directly linked to the Gulf states. In corridors they nodded, at meetings they bobbed their heads in recognition. He made sure, and she did, that they didn't find themselves alone together, where memories might intrude . . . For the best.

The rule had been broken that morning when he had driven and she had navigated. The past, and Ararat, had been off limits – but Dunc Whitcombe had possession of the rotted log: it was on the floor under his desk and he was bloody well keeping it. The cleaners who ran the machines round the carpet were under orders, pain of death, not to touch it. He and Mandy had not covered anything personal but had talked about the weather, the government and television programmes. The operation to bring the woman from Tehran was not much referred to and the circle of need-to-know' had held tight.

The sunlight caught the man's waist, reflected off plastic and flashed at them. He dropped the window and could see him better. A barrowload of concrete was delivered, the empty barrow taken away.

Petroc was back in the Gulf. The flight of the corporal was not a matter for debate or inquest. Dunc had met one of the babysitters when an Afghan warlord had been offered an asylum package with his brood. He'd had a shock of white hair, and the talk had been anodyne, covering holidays: the man had said there was a superb wine-growing hillside on the west side of the Danube – he had been there in the autumn. Dunc had made the connection. Good wines, ruined castles and views to die for: the man had said it was somewhere worth returning to . . . But it was all put to bed and Dunc didn't know what had happened in the safe house: it was kept behind a 'firewall'.

Those who had been in Austria would not have known, afterwards, what had been done on the road from Tehran to Tabriz. Neither would they have heard about a deaf-mute boy who had led horses with drugs in their panniers, or the corpse of a woman who had fallen on a grenade, or the badly wounded young man volunteered by the Service. He knew about it, and Mandy Ross did. A minimum had been shared with Tadeuz Fenton and Sara Rogers – enough to justify the spilling of a thousand dollars as funeral expenses. He'd thought it best, on consideration, that the anecdotes were not chewed over, and the business kept local.

The satellite equipment the guys had taken in, their firearms and the trauma bag were across the border and would not be returned. He assumed that they were now the property of a nameless major in the Revolutionary Guards Corps, and had not been passed up the chain to intelligence for a propaganda airing. Neither would he hear more of the major on the Turkish side, Emre Terim, who commanded the garrison in the town of Doğubeyazıt, and had a fractious relationship with an elderly, expert smuggler . . . Christ, life inside Ceauçescu Towers teetered on the brink of boredom, the edge of futility. He did his work, knew no other way of earning a living.

The young man had refilled the barrow and pushed it back into view. The sun caught again at something on his waist. It was clipped to his belt.

'What is it? His site-entrance pass?'

She took a monocular from her handbag. He didn't think it was standard gear for a two-day seminar at the University of Warwick, and she was unlikely to be heading on an evening plane to the foothills of Ararat or monitoring a caravan of well-loaded horses. More likely, she and her husband had found an interest in bird watching – perhaps thrushes and larks made them more of an item. She looked through it, squinted, adjusted the focus. She was, he thought, unable to admit the need for spectacles.

'Well, it's an ID, and it's in one of the pouches. The lanyard that usually hangs round the neck is wrapped round the belt.'

'That all?'

'Have a look for yourself.'

They might have been strangers, trying to pretend that a casual impulse had brought them to this point, parked against a kerb, with a view of a building site, and had never made love on a wide bed with hail beating on the windows, perhaps close to where Noah had grounded his Ark. He took the spyglass, pressed it to his eye and fiddled for focus.

Dunc Whitcombe had good vision. The quality of the lens dragged him forward. A length of the lanyard dangled. He read: *Military Care Facility, USAF*. He looked at the card in the pouch. A foreman or the site manager was talking to Zach Becket. The pouch rested against his thigh. He saw a face shrouded in a black hood that hid the hair, mouth and cheeks. The Farsi writing, at that distance, was beyond him. A window opened: he looked through it and saw again the face that had been upside-down, blood-wreathed, frozen. The window was slammed shut.

The older man moved and Zach Becket pushed his wheelbarrow, spilled a little of the load and was gone.

He said, 'We shouldn't have come. We intruded on his life, changed it, and went to the limit of what was justifiable.'

'Beyond.'

'At the time it seemed important.'

He pulled away, and drove fast. He reckoned he would carry for a long time the image of a young man with healed holes in his body, the scars of grenade fragments, and the face of a woman, precious, strapped to his belt. Her hand slipped from her lap to rest on the hand that held the wheel. He thought the responsibility was shared, and wondered if he were shamed, whether he deserved to know of them.

'Why not?' She kissed his cheek.

They would be back in time to check that the small auditorium had been bug-swept, that the drinks, biscuits and pencils were in place. At the hotel breakfast Tadeuz Fenton had been on good form. He had been wearing a coral-pink shirt with an MCC tie and a limp linen jacket.

Dunc, driving easily, let the assumed lines of the speech play in his mind. There would be stuff about 'war': 'We don't fight to lose, we fight to win.' There would be grunts of support from the men and women in his audience. 'We don't play around with niceties, and we let those who cross us understand the meaning of real combat.' That would gain a sprinkling of claps.

No mention, of course, of a young man humping cement with ugly wounds on his body, or the corpse of a young woman, disembowelled, coming down a hillside on a horse's back, or a cairn of stones that rats, eventually, would tunnel into . . . or of a noose in the yard at Evin, high over the northern sector of the city, or of the death – detail unknown – of an army officer, a high-value target . . . never had heard anything of a corporal, a driver, who had been taken to a whorehouse. 'We play tough and we punch above our weight. We're loyal to our allies and hard on those who stand against us. People in many countries will sleep better at night for our, and your, efforts and dedication.' That would be rewarded with enthusiastic applause.

'Thanks. It's a shit job, and I know no other,' Dunc said.